Anita Faulkner writes warm and fuzzy romcoms from her upcycled bureau in the south-west of England. She grew up sniffing books and devouring stories. And she insists it was perfectly normal to squirrel boxes of pretty stationery that felt far too magical to actually use. She's also accumulated a brave and patient husband and a strong-willed little boy who brighten up her world.

A *Colourful Country Escape* is her first novel.

A Colourful Country Escape

Anita Faulkner

SPHERE

SPHERE

First published in Great Britain in 2022 by Sphere

1 3 5 7 9 10 8 6 4 2

A CIP catalogue record for this book is available
from the British Library.

ISBN 978-0-7515-8436-3

Typeset in Caslon by M Rules
Printed and bound in Great Britain by
Clays Ltd, Elcograf S.p.A.

Papers used by Sphere are from well-managed forests
and other responsible sources.

Sphere
An imprint of
Little, Brown Book Group
Carmelite House
50 Victoria Embankment
London EC4Y 0DZ

An Hachette UK Company
www.hachette.co.uk

www.littlebrown.co.uk

To the gorgeous souls who love books.
You're my people.

Chapter 1

If Lexie Summers was going to dress like a duck, it may as well be raining.

Anyway, what was so bad about a full-scale downpour? She wasn't going to fuss. As rain hammered down on her cheeks and sent shoppers scurrying into the gleaming stores along Manchester's King Street, she decided to push towards home. After what she'd just done, she needed a calming cuppa.

Of course, it would have been handy if her yellow-duckling rain mac had had a hood, but it had been such a bargain. Her rain-drenched pixie hair, which was sticking to her forehead like an unfortunate bowl cut, did not seem grateful for the scrimping. In hindsight, venturing out in April without her brolly had been a tad optimistic (even if two of the spindly arm bits were dangerously droopy).

Yet, somehow, the cold water against her skin seemed fitting; like she deserved this deluge. Because Lexie believed in karma. And guilt was a wriggly thing.

A clap of thunder from above made her jump, and, as the sky became white, a memory cut in: a dark, mothy shop with bars on the windows, and a carpet that smelt like soggy socks. Cash in a Flash.

She shook her head and hunched forwards, trying to move through the sea of dripping umbrellas. This was silly; she would get her stuff back from the pawnbrokers. It was all just temporary. A sort of swap, to get her out of bother. She'd handed over the jewellery, they'd lent her the rent money that was getting desperate, then, when she'd sorted herself out, she would switch everything back, and no one would be any the wiser.

'No one' being her boyfriend, Drew.

As an expensive, black tour bus rumbled past and sprayed her with puddle mud, an image of his floppy-haired face popped up. She swatted it away, along with the sludge from her mac. Feeling terrible wouldn't change anything, and Drew probably wouldn't notice. She'd never really felt worthy of wearing the funny Downton Abbey pearls he'd bought for her, as sweet as the gesture was. She'd have been happier with something cut-price and quirky.

Anyway, Drew would surely prefer her to keep her scary landlord off her back. And now she had some cash she'd make it up to him.

As her heavy shopping bag bashed against her knee, she tried on a smile. They'd have a cosy night in watching *Dinner Date*. She would touch up her chipped polka-dot nails; he'd play his guitar. All his favourite snacks were right there in the bag. Looking after him made her feel fuzzy.

Plus, she'd just put extra coins in the collection box at Tesco. Who didn't love a donkey sanctuary? So there. The angels weren't crying tears of punishment on her head. Perhaps the rain was just a coincidence.

'Oi!'

Lexie whipped around. There was some sort of commotion across the other side of the street, outside the new jewellery shop. A shop owner dressed like a bouncer was shoving a homeless girl out of his doorway. It looked like she'd been sheltering from the rain.

'Hey!' Lexie heard herself shout. How could he treat someone like that? Before Lexie knew it, she was darting out into the road towards the fracas.

Screeeeech.

Lexie heard the car before she saw it – all two tonnes of it as it careered towards her like a ginormous black cloud. The rain seemed to swallow her scream, her bag dropping to the floor like a dying wet fish. Her heart leapt into her mouth but, by the miracle of lucky angel tears, it didn't hit the SUV's windscreen. The car stopped just short of her quaking legs.

She caught her breath. *She was alive!* Although the driver didn't seem that chuffed about it.

The angry beep of his horn filled her ears. *Mooooove. You don't belong.*

Lexie held up an apologetic hand, sorry that she'd chosen to cut through this designer part of town. She backed away from the car and rescued her bag from a puddle. Drew's wontons would be considerably less crispy – maybe she'd get him some consolatory beers.

3

This time checking for traffic, Lexie waved another *sorry* at the angry driver and continued across the road until she reached the homeless girl. The gaunt youngster was trying to save her cardboard bedding from the downpour as Shop Man manhandled her onto the pavement. When he was finished, he swept his hands together with a flourish and retreated into the luxurious glow of Le Grand Bijou.

Lexie let out a huff. 'Here, lovely, take this.' She dropped her bag and tugged off her favourite ducky raincoat. The young girl with the threadbare jersey needed it more than she did.

As the stranger gave a grateful nod and shivered into it, they heard a loud honking of horns. SUV Man, clearly not satisfied with Lexie's meek apology, had done a U-turn to yell abuse through his window. As he veered towards the pavement to treat them to his full obscenity back catalogue, his oversized wheels hit a lake of gutter water and sent a monsoon towards Lexie and her companion. They yelped and turned away from the wave, wobbling face first like jellied eels towards the window of the jewellery shop.

And that was when Lexie saw it.

An 'it' that was about five foot nine with floppy 'I'm in a band' hair and a mouth shocked into an 'O'.

All of which were meant to be practising for a gig, not pondering platinum solitaires in a jewellery-shop window with Tabby Sidebottom.

Lexie froze, arms and legs suspended in motion like a puppet on strings. Something gripped her throat, yet there was nothing there. Why couldn't she breathe? And what was he doing here? Drew Chadwick. Picking out rings with the girl he'd sworn was just a fan.

Holy matrimony? Holy bloody crap.

'That's my b-boyfriend,' Lexie heard herself stutter, as the moment stretched out before her like a lazy cat.

As Lexie and the street girl stared into the glass, the awkward couple inside ogled right back. It was the most unlikely of mirrors: a rags-reflecting-riches not-so-funhouse. At least Drew had the decency to emulate Lexie's astonishment. Tabby's thoroughbred face was beginning to look overly pleased with itself beneath its luxury blow-dry. And what was that glinting around her neck? Lexie's stomach gave a lurch. The sapphire Tiffany necklace worth more than Lexie's entire world, which Lexie had picked out herself. Drew had said it was for his mother.

The mother whose face then appeared above the other two, pouting as though rain had just stopped play at Wimbledon. Lexie might have known Drew couldn't shop for diamonds without the Bank of Mum and Dad. Lexie had barely been allowed to say three words to Drew's rich parents in the eighteen months they'd been together. She guessed there was no need to bother now.

Yet as Lexie began to turn on her Boohoo-sale heel, a hand gripped her bare arm.

'Where the heck are you going?'

Lexie shrugged at her duckling-clad companion. 'I only came out to pawn some stuff. I need to pay my . . .'

The last word was 'rent', but she didn't dare say it to the unfortunate girl with the drenched cardboard boxes.

'I wasn't looking for your life story, lady. I just meant anyone wearing tie-dye shorts and a kid's duck coat in the middle of an April piss-storm has obviously got *some* balls. So if that prick in the suit that doesn't match his grunge hair was meant to be your bloke, you'd better go and brain him before I do.'

'I ... but ... I'm a drowned rat.' Lexie looked up at the sky, which was still leaking down on them, albeit more pathetic snivels of sympathy than full cats and dogs. Should she just pack up her humiliation and get the hell out of there? She never had belonged. The one time Drew's parents had turned up at his flat while she'd been there, he'd practically confined her to the kitchen, polishing glassware. The sad thing was, she'd felt relieved to have an excuse to hide. Lead crystal had never been more fascinating.

Lexie turned away from the window, pushing wet tendrils of hair back off her forehead, and began to retreat. 'Not sure his mum even remembers me.'

Glancing back towards the window, Lexie saw the three disembodied heads staring back at her across the sea of diamonds.

'Just imagine her with the craps. Always works for me when some twat treads on my sleeping bag on his way to the cashpoint.' The young girl grabbed her again and began tugging her towards the shop entrance.

'But I'll ruin their carpet,' Lexie tried to reason, looking down at her sodden pumps.

'Do you always put everyone else before yourself?'

The words hung in the air for a moment and Lexie blinked. 'No.' She didn't think so, but ...

'Quick, before Evil Shop Guy comes back.'

Lexie took a deep breath. She hated flashy places, where the staff stared snootily like she couldn't even afford their shopping bag. The painful thing was, they were probably right.

'Go on, do it for me. Kick off in that posh-arsed shop and make my day.'

Lexie looked down at those hopeful green eyes, beaming like a pair of traffic lights on go. Maybe this stranger had been right: she never could resist doing things for others. If only she was as good at sorting out her own mess.

Lexie took the girl's hand and hastily tipped her wallet into it.

Oh. Well, perhaps she hadn't meant for all of those pawn-broker notes to fall out too, but the girl gave a small sob of gratitude. And asking for a refund from a homeless person did not seem like the done thing. Lexie would have to worry about how she'd replace her last hope at rent money later; it was time for this ridiculously awkward show.

Chapter 2

As a loud bell announced Lexie's entrance into Le Grande Bijou, the three heads turned towards her, trying out a selection of expressions.

The theme on Drew's caught-in-the-act mug seemed to be 'oops'. At least he had the good grace to seem bothered. Tabby of Sidebottom fame seemed put out at being disturbed from her diamonds, and Drew's mother appeared mildly confused.

'Look, Lex, I can explain.' Drew was the first of this odd love quadrangle to speak, even if it was an infuriating cliché.

'I think I've kind of worked it out,' said Lexie, hoping she sounded braver than she felt as she stood under the garish spotlights, dripping like a wet umbrella. 'When were you going to bother mentioning you were getting engaged? Am I that unimportant?'

Tabby scoffed and Lexie felt it like a sarcastic prod in the ribs.

'And you knew we were together,' Lexie said to her. What she wanted to say was that, for all Tabby's upbringing, she didn't even have the manners to keep her manicured paws to herself. But Lexie couldn't bear to draw any more attention to the gaping divide.

'Oh, come on. As if he was ever going to marry you. You're from a totally different class.'

Ouch. Well, it seemed Tabby was on hand to do that for her. The prim-bunned fiancée looked down her beak at Lexie, making clear she didn't mean a better one. 'You're basically *poor.*'

Lexie sucked in her breath. Even Drew was wincing.

'Hang on a second, I don't understand.' It seemed Drew's mother was ready to stick her powdered nose in. 'Why on earth would this girl think you would marry her? I thought she was your cleaner?'

Lexie took a step backwards, the words physically winding her. 'Jeez, Drew, *what*? Your bloody cleaner?' She fought with her voice, which was wobbling high and low. 'Eighteen months and you're still pretending I just hang around to dust? *Urgh.*'

Lexie turned to leave and Drew pulled away from the pack, taking hold of her arm and steering her to the side of the room.

He lowered his voice. 'Look, you know it was so much more than that. I loved the way you looked after me, with all your fussing. But there comes a time when a guy has to grow up and think of his future. *Financially.* Can't we talk about this another time?' His eyes flicked to his toe-tapping fiancée and his mother. 'My tongue's tied here.'

'Well, untie it,' Lexie replied. As much as her wet pumps wanted to squeak their way out of there, she was keen never to see these faces again. At least if Drew said his piece, she could slink away for good. She shrugged his hand off her.

Tabby and Mrs Chadwick pushed their way back into the fray.

'Just talk, Drew.' Lexie hoped she wouldn't regret it.

He mouthed a 'sorry' at her before clearing his throat. 'Well . . . Tabby's right. It's not as though I was going to, you know . . . *marry* you. You must know we're not the same.'

Wow. So he was giving her the no-frills version in front of his wing-women. Lexie was regretting it already. She looked at Drew, in a suit she'd never seen before. She'd known his parents were loaded, of course. And she'd never felt at home in his penthouse apartment with all those pointless gadgets, but he usually wore faded band T-shirts and hung around in her crummy flat. She'd thought he wanted to be the same. They were both so creative. They had fun. Didn't they? But all along, she was the odd one out.

'Not the same,' she repeated, crossing her arms over her smarting chest and trying to ignore the others. 'Go on.'

'I don't think this is the place.' Drew lowered his voice again as the shop owner approached – another impolite man in a suit.

Lexie looked back to the window like a desperate duck out of water. Her homeless friend gave her a double thumbs up, her enthusiasm almost vibrating through the glass. Yes. She could do this.

'There won't be any other places, Drew, so you may as

well tell me here. What was this?' Lexie waved her arms between the two of them. 'Were you just sleeping with the common people until someone worthy came along?'

'No, of course not! It's not just the money thing.' He shot a nervous glance at his mother. Clearly that was some of it. 'It's the other stuff as well. You know. *You*.'

'*Me?*' What did that mean?

The shop owner had joined the crowd, along with his meerkat of a shop assistant. Everyone was hooked.

'What's wrong with me?' Lexie could hear the deflation in her own voice. Why had she even asked?

Drew reached for Lexie's hand, but Tabby slapped it away.

'Are you feeling sorry for her now? I'll tell her if you don't,' said Tabby, her face scrunched up like an angry plum.

'So is she the cleaner, or not?' Drew's haughty mother still looked befuddled.

Tabby put her hands on her hips and eyeballed her supposed fiancé. 'Do you still fancy her? Shall I cancel the venue?'

The venue? Could this get any worse?

'No, Tabby, darling ... '

Lexie shook her head. Who was this strange man? No wonder he'd kept her away from his 'other life'. Money really did make him ugly.

'I'll tell her, Tabby, of course I will.'

What. The. Hell.

'Look, Lexie, my point is, you're not exactly ... *suitable*. You're a fun girl, but as a wife? It would never work. You're too impractical, sweetheart. Look at you – out in the rain with no coat …' He tried to lighten his words with a jokey laugh.

'And your clothes don't match,' Tabby added.

'They're thrift shop.' Lexie tried to defend herself. 'It's a look.'

'You've never got any money,' Drew continued. 'And when you do, you donate it to the turtles or donkeys or whatever your latest world worry is. Did I just see you give a purseful of notes to that homeless person? Because I thought you couldn't afford your rent again. And no doubt you still haven't sorted the MOT for that camper van.'

'I …' Lexie floundered. 'I do work for a living. I've never asked you for a penny.' In fact, she was the one always feeding him. She was glad his stupid wontons were ruined. 'You never seemed to mind when you were the useless cause I was fussing over.'

Had that been part of his attraction, she wondered with a shudder. Had he brought out her 'save-the-pandas' instinct, with his big dopey eyes and ineptitude to cook a beansprout?

'What is your job, anyway? Backpacking blogger? Person who faffs about on Instagram all day?' Tabby interrupted Lexie's train crash of thoughts.

'Hey! I'm a social media manager.'

'You're working part time in a shop,' said Drew. 'And I mean this constructively. But you can be so flaky, Lex. You never stick to anything. I used to think it was because you were artistic and entrepreneurial like me. But, actually, you're just too scared to let yourself be good at anything. You're happy to canter along as someone else's workhorse.'

Lexie tried to ignore the trembling of her chin, which was just the tip of her internal iceberg. She turned to Tabby, who was all but pulling out the popcorn. 'Can I ask what you do?'

But Tabby just looked perplexed, like having a job had never actually occurred to her.

'Ladies like us do not need to work,' Drew's mother over-enunciated, as though explaining something to a silly child. 'So you gave up the cleaning? Because I could really do with another ...'

'That was never my job,' Lexie said firmly. Not that she would be embarrassed if it were – her mum had been a very good cleaner. 'It was one of your son's lies. A bit like "Tabby's just a fan – I think she's stalking me." I should have known she wasn't a groupie, in a twinset and pearls.'

The meerkat-ish shop girl began sniggering, and Tabby shot her a look.

'This is *caashmere*.' Tabby stretched out the word, such a fine material clearly deserving extra vowels. 'And I don't even like rock music. It's dreadful.'

'I do a delightful range of South Sea pearls,' the shop owner butted in. 'Extremely rare. *Frightfully* expensive.'

'Oh good! We'll take the tray,' said Mrs Chadwick, before she'd even set eyes on them. 'Do bring it over.'

The shop owner sang a spiel about pearls symbolising wealth and wisdom as he scurried away, rubbing his hands.

'My music is dreadful?' Drew's tiny brain had finally caught up.

'Everyone should have a hobby, sweetie.' Tabby patted

Drew's back as if encouraging a spaniel. 'You'll be working with Daddy in the business when we marry.'

Now it was Lexie's turn to laugh. She knew full well Drew's band was everything to him. They would never be huge, but he didn't do it for the money. Like Tabby, he didn't need to.

'What is your job, Drew? Faffing about with a plectrum all day?' And with that surprisingly brave quip, Lexie was ready to flee.

She could never win the war against these people and their money. She was unworthy, or unsuitable, or whatever the hell Drew had said. She probably always would be. But at least she'd thrown a cat among their well-coiffed pigeons; that was the best she could hope for.

She rushed to the door, her head bursting with tears which were desperate to escape. But what was that shape moving towards her?

'And of course, pearls signify new beginnings,' it was saying, as it held out a tray.

Argggggghhh.

The tray hit Lexie in the gut and flew upwards, releasing its contents to the heavens. Exquisite pearls hailed down everywhere, and as the party moved to avoid them they began slipping and tumbling like a room full of skittles.

Oh God, oh God, oh God . . .

Lexie hopped to the door, sensing the enraged shop owner hot on her tail. If he didn't skid on his precious gemstones, she prayed the trail of her rain sludge would at least slow him down.

She burst through into the damp outside air, straight into a pair of outstretched arms. Her homeless friend. Thank God.

'You did it – I'm so proud of you. Now run! And thanks for everything.'

Lexie choked out a sob as she felt the warmth of the stranger. She gave her a quick squeeze, but it was time to run. The shop owner was probably gunning for both of them. They tore away in opposite directions, hoping the art of confusion would see them safe.

Not that Lexie had to feign bewilderment. As she caught a last glimpse of her favourite duckling raincoat disappearing into the distance, she wondered when she'd started kidding herself. How long had she been floating serenely above the water's surface, when her feet had been paddling like a frantic duck?

And where on earth was she going to run to now?

Chapter 3

Lexie ran and ran along King Street, past the elegant buildings that towered above her and threw her into shade, through streets full of designer handbags and expensive watches she could never afford. She ran until her lungs burned, until she almost felt sick. But she couldn't face stopping. What was she even running from? She hadn't done anything wrong, had she? Other than encroach into a world where she'd never belonged.

Was it the words she was fleeing from? She hated Drew for what he'd done, and yet his words still stung. As her feet pounded the pavement, they became a chant in her head. Flaky, impractical, rubbish with money. No proper job.

Crap. At. Life.

And words couldn't hurt unless they were true. Maybe they were the pearls of bloody wisdom after all.

Urrrrrggggghhhhhhh. Lexie shuddered to a stop, the

feeling of suffocation reaching its peak. She couldn't do this any more.

Perhaps she'd been out of her depth for far too long. In that high-end shopping street, in her life with the privileged Drew. Who had she been kidding that he'd throw off his fancy future to settle down with a girl from a council estate? People like her didn't marry guys like him. Guys with money. From a *different class*. People like her cleaned their toilets.

Lexie looked around as she caught her breath. The adrenaline was draining from her and she wondered if her legs would give way. Instinctively, she had made it back to her tram stop, away from that pretentious mess. She'd done them a favour and buzzed off, no longer the unfortunate fly in their ointment. They could carry on with buying solitaire diamonds and arranging lavish venues, and she would ... she would ...

She flopped backwards onto the nearest bench before her limbs collapsed. What would she do?

The rain had stopped now, but her hair was still dripping. Washing away all traces of that rotten fraud of a man. If only the rain could have taken his hurtful words with it, but it wasn't possible to scrub away the truth. She was just doing a few hours in her friend Jake's shop, rather than working on her career. Before that, she'd managed social media and content for a firm that went bust, and had been putting off the fear of CVs and interviews. She never felt like she had anything good to say about herself.

Paying her rent *was* always a struggle; she forgot to

prioritise. But saving the turtles was important too, wasn't it? And that MOT ... what a faff. Sorting out other people's lives was always so much easier. Why was that? She'd never had any problems running multiple social media accounts and writing heaps of sparkly blog posts for other people's businesses. Maybe that's what she needed to do – get back to something she wasn't rubbish at.

As the teatime commuters bustled around her and tired clouds yawned in the smoggy sky, Lexie wondered if she was getting bored of this place. Manchester wasn't her home; she'd grown up in Lancaster. Although she'd felt restless there too. After the years of backpacking with yet another dodgy ex that had ended in disaster, she'd never felt settled anywhere.

Her parents and younger sister Sky were still in Lancaster, squashed into their crumbling terrace. And of course she kept in touch. But those rented walls had felt too small somehow, after she'd seen the world. When she'd landed back in the UK, she'd bounced from city to city. After finding Drew she'd thought she might stay here – but no. Perhaps it was time to rebound again.

'Jobs, jobs, jobs. Read all about 'em.'

Lexie searched around for the voice. Of course, it was job day in the paper she usually grabbed on her way to the tram.

Save your money, Drew used to say. You can read it online for free.

But Ron the newspaper seller had to make a living, and she always passed the paper on to the elderly lady in her block when she was finished. It was never wasted.

How had newspaper Ron's voice travelled all this way? It had to be a sign. Lexie hauled herself to her feet and fought through busy commuters to reach the stand. Her drained, willowy frame was jostled like a bulrush in the breeze, but suddenly she had extra determination.

'Exciting opportunities! Your new life could be waiting.'

Lexie was getting closer to Ron's sales chatter. She couldn't fault his marketing efforts, even if his message seemed unlikely.

'Fancy yourself as an astronaut, Madam? Butler to the Queen?'

Lexie couldn't help a small smile as she heard him drumming up trade. His magic was hypnotic – she wasn't the only one queueing up for their new life already. As she waited in line, she searched her bag for coins. There was her wallet. But ... oh. It was empty. She'd tipped it into her homeless friend's hands.

She exhaled a long sigh as she felt the last sliver of hope wriggle away into the evening air. It seriously wasn't her day. Her old life had been snatched from her and she couldn't even afford the tiniest hope of a new one. And what about her rent? Scary Landlord was going to have a field day.

Lexie snapped back to life and inhaled sharply. She'd reached the front of the queue. No, she couldn't face a fuss. Being reminded she was a penniless loser was not high on her list of priorities. Shoving her wallet back into her bag, she tried to back away discreetly.

'Lexie!'

But it was too late. Ron had seen her.

'Where are you off to, my old mucker? Can't I interest you in a paper full of fresh beginnings? I could see you as a tightrope walker.' He gave her a wavy-armed impression and a smile that would ordinarily have been infectious.

She tried to smile back. 'I think I've been balancing precariously for too long, Ron.'

He nodded towards her bag. 'Didn't have enough coins today, kid?'

Nor a single note, she thought miserably.

'Don't worry,' he continued. 'This one's on me. You overpay me every day as it is, what with never accepting your change. I probably owe you half the stack.'

He shoved a paper into her reluctant hands. 'No arguments. This little bundle of new dreams is all yours.' He looked her up and down as she stood on the wet pavement, dripping and shivering like one of those skinny, hairless dogs. 'It looks like you need one.'

He had no idea how much.

Chapter 4

It had been three long days since Lexie had stood shivering outside Le Grande Bijou, watching her so-called boyfriend choose engagement rings with Tabby Sidebottom. And she was absolutely done with snivelling and moping over a relationship that had apparently been built on a pack of juggling jokers. She'd thought Drew had enjoyed their cosy nights and crispy wontons. It turned out she was as disposable as their greasy wrappings. If he could see her now, he'd probably call her impractical. Well, *good*.

Ron's magical newspaper fluttered on the dashboard as a spring breeze blew through Lexie's beloved orange camper van, Penny. She really should fix that draughty window. But with her whole life crammed inside like a pocketful of promises, she was trying not to look back.

The van was chugging down the motorway more than Lexie would have liked, under the sheer weight of it all. The dashboard clock ticked loudly at her and she tried to ignore its advancing hands. Her trip south wasn't meant to take this long; she couldn't afford to be late. The poor old banger shuddered and let out another dubious cloud of smoke, and Lexie winced. She made a mental note to donate some money to somewhere or other, to make up for her ugly carbon footprint. Just as soon as she had any cash.

But Lexie had just maxed out her credit card to pay off Scary Landlord, and she'd never see her deposit again. Maybe Ron's paper full of new beginnings would be just the ticket, if she could only get to this interview on time.

The job advert had looked intriguing. Social media manager for a company with pretty much zero online presence. What was all that about? It would certainly be a challenge.

'Come on, Pen,' she willed the vintage VW. 'You're not trying to tell me something, are you?'

Lexie looked in the rear-view mirror, trying hard to conjure up the image of her late aunt Jasmine, who'd bestowed Penny the camper van upon her. But she saw nothing, other than the bright, sunflowery interior that still lived on in her aunt's honour – even if the rest of the van was trying its hardest to conk out on this trip. Well, that and mountains of boxes, some of which were stuffed with paperwork Lexie was too scared to look at.

Was she doing the right thing? Maybe she should take the hint and turn back. But no, there was nothing there for her now. She had no home in Manchester and she wasn't going to prove Drew's loser theory right by going back to sharing a bunkbed at her parents' house. She needed this job, and the money and sense of worth it would begin to restore. And, anyway, the clouds had definitely been clearing as she'd travelled away from that mess. Things were less grey, less ...

Dun dun duddla duddla dun ...

Lexie jumped as the *Hollyoaks* theme tune twanged through her headphones. It was the ringtone she'd set up for Sky, not least because a call from her younger sister generally signified drama.

'Hey!' Lexie tried to sound upbeat. She loved her sister, but having spent twenty-two of her twenty-seven years on the planet trying to steer Sky away from trouble, she never knew what to expect. And this was really not the time.

'Oh my God, Lex. Mum told me about Drew shagging that posh girl. I hope you're OK.'

Lexie winced. Her sister was never one for softening the blow. In fact the tactfulness gene had skipped her altogether – she'd been too busy queueing up for her head full of dizziness.

'Cheers for the imagery.' Lexie tried her best not to imagine her ex-boyfriend poking his manhood anywhere near Tabby and her Sidebottom.

'Yuck, did you actually catch them ...'

'No, Sky. They were ring shopping. Getting ready for some wedding I knew nothing about.' Lexie swallowed hard.

'Ooh, that's even worse, isn't it? *Ring shopping*. I mean, he never talked about marriage with you, did he? And you were together eighteen whole months. That's, like, a lifetime.'

'Yes, thanks for that.'

'Why didn't he want to marry you, then?'

Lexie pushed her foot down harder on the accelerator, for all the good it did. A silver Aston Martin sped past like a bullet and she tried not to roll her eyes.

'I don't bloody know. Maybe rich people are just ... rude?' It was as good an answer as any.

'So Mum says you're running off again. To Chew-something-or-other?'

'Tewkesbury. It's a medieval town in the south-west. All black-and-white buildings and *Rosie and Jim* barges, from what I've seen on Google.' A whole different world from the buzz of the city.

'At least it's not Asia this time, but Mum and Dad are still worried about you. And I can't believe you're going to fiddle your CV ...'

Lexie shot a nervous glance over her shoulder. 'That's enough.' Being criticised by her hopeless kid sister was doing nothing for her already plummeting self-belief.

'But you could go to jail for that. I heard about this guy ...'

'No, you cannot. And I'm not taking career advice from someone whose most impressive CV entry is three weeks at Greggs.'

'Four! Those sausage rolls were *the best*.'

'Anyway, I just need to get my foot in the door.'

Being a social media manager was surely the one thing she was actually good at, even if ... well, she would have to massage the facts a bit. What harm could a little truth-bending do?

'So what is this job?'

'It's doing social media stuff for a family-run paint

business. I love that idea – fresh paint, new beginnings. Like a wonderfully blank canvas.'

'Yeah, you loved art at school. Maybe they'll let you get creative.'

School. Lexie shuddered. Not all of it had been great. 'I'm not sure that's part of their plan.' Although who knew. 'It's just two guys interviewing me in some hall or other. I hope it's not too hideous. I just want to prove to myself that I'm not a disorganised, flaky loser.' She felt her voice start to wobble.

'Ouch. Is that what that dick from the band said to you? You're amazing at sticking your nose in and sorting out everyone else's business. Although ... you are pretty disorganised with your own crap. Ooh, maybe you should focus on your own life admin?'

A swish of sliding boxes in the back of the camper van tried to agree.

'Because you're such a successful grown-up,' Lexie countered.

'Actually, I am growing up. I'm moving into the commune with Billy-Bob next week. It's going to be *epic.*'

Lexie swerved onto the hard shoulder and screeched on her temperamental brakes. Penny bunny-hopped in protest before spluttering to a stop. Lexie cranked up the handbrake.

'You're doing WHAT?'

Was this the sign Lexie had to turn back? Surely she couldn't stand by and—

'Yeah, isn't it wild? I'm sharing a yurt with Billy-Bob, Indigo and Renata. Just like a proper family.'

25

'So they're, what, his kids? And isn't he about fifty? That's more than twice your age.'

'They're his other mistresses, silly. B-B practises free love. All the men on the commune do; it's totally—'

'Perverse!' Lexie snatched her phone from its cradle and bounced out of the van, raking her bitten nails through her sunshine blonde pixie cut with her free hand. 'It's just an excuse for Billy-Nob to stick his man parts in as many women as he chooses.'

'Just three. And at least it's out in the open – not like sneaky "I accidentally put my penis in Tabby" Drew.'

Touché. 'And you presumably stay faithful and cook the tofu?'

'Well, yes, we are meant to be vegan.'

Lexie kicked her deflating tyre and let out another sigh in support of its rubbery pain. She should head back north and put a stop to this craziness. 'You love sausage rolls. And you'll give Mum and Dad a heart attack.'

'Nuh-uh. They're always too busy worrying about you. "Will she ever settle? She's such a drifter."'

Lexie knew when her sister was quoting directly from the Book of Parent.

'Well, I guess Drew was never the one. Maybe it's obvious in hindsight.' She ploughed on before her sister could ask what hindsight meant. 'I'm broke. He's loaded. He's from a completely different class.'

'Oh, Lex, is that what you think?' She heard her sister sigh. 'I can't believe we came from the same sperm.'

'We didn't. That's not how it works.'

'You're the one who doesn't understand how stuff works.

Love doesn't care about money. Love will rock up and cast its spell wherever it wants to.'

Lexie exhaled. As if life was just that easy.

'You know, if you truly value yourself, bank balances don't matter. His or yours. Just saying.' Sky was probably just repeating some old rubbish from that cult. 'I'm giving all my money to the commune, in exchange for eternal happiness. Wealth is superfluous to us.'

I knew it! Lexie thought. As if Sky knew big words like that. And being skint certainly wasn't making Lexie ecstatic.

'They've brainwashed you. Don't you dare hand over a thing – I'm coming home.' Not that her sister had much to hand over.

'No, you're not, Lex. You do you, for once in your life. Stop putting everyone else first and ending up last.'

As Lexie let the concept filter through, another noise invaded her thoughts. A police siren. Oh God. And it was definitely headed her way.

She began a nervous pace of the hard shoulder. Should she even be on it if this wasn't an emergency? But the distant glare of a flashing blue light made her sweat for reasons that belonged even further back than Drew.

'Argh!' This was just her luck. If the police car stopped now, and started checking over her not-so-up-to-date vehicle records, she would never make it to this interview. Not to mention the trouble she'd be in. And would there be fines? How would she ever pay?

'What's that noise? Are the cops coming for you already? I said you shouldn't . . . '

'Sky! The police don't give a toss about the contents of my CV.'

As Lexie watched the white vehicle move closer, she realised this would be her final sign. If the police car stopped, her trip was doomed. But if it just sped by and left her alone . . .

And at that moment she realised just how much she wanted that job. How much she needed it. Damn it, she would even fight for the thing. Her sister was right. She did have to put herself first, for once. Or at least give it a try.

She shot a nervous glance at her phone. One hour until the interview and still forty miles to travel. She wasn't even dressed for it yet. Turning up in violet denim dungarees with a matching nose stud would make her look like a useless plum.

Her sister was still garbling something in her ear, but Lexie couldn't focus. As the siren got deafeningly close, she thought her head would burst.

Yet just as she thought she couldn't dig her nails any further into her clammy palms, the flashing blue light had passed. It was over. Lexie had been given the gift of time. She would get to this interview and do her best to bag that job. Then she would absolutely sort out her MOT. Soonish.

'Have they gone?'

Lexie shook her head, remembering her sister still had a hotline to her ears. 'Er, I think.' She barely dared believe it.

'Do they still make you nervous, after all that trouble with . . .'

'Yes! Now I need to get a move on. There's a blank canvas up for grabs.' She heard her sister give a cheer. 'But don't think this conversation about your foursome in the commune is over. Just stay put. I'll call as soon as I can.'

'Good luck with the interview! And watch out for the peacocks at that hall you're going to. I heard about this man in Mongolia who got clawed to death by his own pet. They can be super nasty when provoked.'

Peacocks. What was Sky even talking about? Out of the mouths of babes came utter nonsense. Or at least Lexie hoped.

Chapter 5

When Lexie pulled up to the gateway of Nutgrass Hall, her heart dropped. This was not what she'd been expecting.

The wrought-iron gates in front of her twisted in uninviting knots, like the pit of her stomach. The ironwork peaked at the top in angry spikes, which seemed to yell 'keep out'. Worse still, she couldn't see beyond because the iron was backed with thick wood.

What happened to the cosy village hall she'd been expecting? Maybe she should have researched better, although part of her knew she hadn't looked too hard in case she'd put herself off. She'd desperately needed to get away and find a job that didn't make her feel useless. And to earn some money to pay her way.

It had been a beggars-can't-be-choosers situation. But cowering in front of those imposing gates in her rust-bucket of a van, she was certainly feeling like the vagabond.

As Lexie fiddled with the handbrake, wondering whether to release it and reverse away, a screen near the gateway crackled to life. Oh great, they had intercom. And a camera. How grand was this place?

But before she could retreat, a murky shadow appeared on the screen.

'Am I pressing the right thing?' she heard an elderly lady ask. The voice then cleared its throat. 'If you're here for the interview, do come in.'

There. That seemed friendly, didn't it?

And with that, the iron gates yawned open to swallow Lexie inside. With a resigned sigh she let Penny chug forwards, praying that just for once the camper wouldn't backfire.

The gravelled driveway wove through a spread of perfectly striped lawns. Measured rows of bridal-white narcissi tilted their heads, as though curious at Lexie's intrusion. Even the hedges had been trimmed into seamless spheres, like great rows of cannon balls. Lexie gripped the steering wheel, trying not to overthink it.

At last, she caught sight of the house. Her mouth dropped open. It was like one of those mansions in a slightly spooky fairy tale. Tens of windows glared out at her from the beige stone walls. Vines entwined themselves around the bolted white doorway, and turrets sprouted majestically from the rooftop.

She did not belong here. Yet as she glanced over her shoulder, the gates were closing behind her. She pushed her foot against the brake. What was that approaching from the distance? A shimmer of something green and blue, like an iridescent army of eyes. Were they . . . *peacocks*? Yes, her sister had been right. The creatures were almost staring her down with their tailfeathers.

Lexie put a hand on her chest, forcing herself to breathe deeply. Her fight-or-flight instincts were having a party in her stomach, with the desire to flee winning the battle. What was this place? Did the paint family own it? Would she have to work here? That would be her worst nightmare, after everything with Drew. All this wealth, shaking its fancy tailfeathers in her face. Making her feel inadequate every single day.

Yet she needed this job and the money. Something she could be good at again, that was as far away from Manchester as possible.

Oh God, what was wrong with her? It was just work. She wouldn't have to live here. Maybe their office was somewhere else. Perhaps she'd be based in their factory, mingling with honest workers in overalls and inhaling the glorious fresh paint. Yes, she was overreacting.

Right. She should at least get out of the van. Releasing her white-knuckled fingers from the steering wheel, she switched off the engine and coaxed herself onto the gravel driveway.

And promptly wished she hadn't.

Penny the camper van was not impressed with the choice of venue and voiced her displeasure with a cannon-esque explosion. The engine had backfired.

Then the peacocks were upon her.

The phoenix-like birds advanced on Lexie with squawky open beaks and flaring tails, wailing screams of death. They jarred their angry necks towards her, red tongues darting. She scrambled back into the van and locked the door, puffing in panic. Thank God the lock was working. She'd underestimated these birds, and her sister's ornithological knowledge. The girl deserved more credit.

Clearly not done, two of the peacocks flapped onto her bonnet and pecked with fury at her already chipped windscreen. Lexie ducked in her seat, shielding herself with her arms. In one final reign of terror, the duo unzipped their bottoms all over Penny's vintage paintwork. Lexie gagged at the sight of the steaming gunk. Just as she thought she couldn't take any more, they blithely hopped down and slinked away, looking mildly disgusted at their own handiwork.

Lexie unfurled herself. What on earth? *Did that just actually* ...

She shook her head. She didn't know whether to cry with relief or laugh at the absurdity of it all.

Then something caught her eye. Two guys standing in the immense doorway of the house, craning their necks to get a better view of the fracas. Great. How long had they been there?

Lexie tried to suss them out. One looked like he'd be happier on a surfboard, with his Hawaiian shorts and sun-streaked knotty hair. At least he seemed entertained.

But the other one. Oh God. His square jaw was set into a look that was the opposite of amused. She eyed his neat dark hair and crisp, well-fitted suit. The pale perfection of his skin told her he didn't bask anywhere near sunlight, or perhaps even crack a smile. Humiliatingly handsome. So that's what that phrase meant.

Lexie guessed from her brief Google nosey that Frowny Face was her prospective boss. Or quite possibly not, after that shameful entrance. Maybe she should just reverse straight out of there and dream up another escape from her messy life. She'd be no better off playing second fiddle to this man than she had been living in Drew's wealthy shadow. He was probably rich and rude too. Even his peacocks didn't know how to behave.

As Lexie twisted her key in the ignition, her heart stopped. She was going nowhere. At least not without a tow truck. She banged her forehead against the wheel in frustration, half hoping she could knock some sense into herself.

Fate had made the decision for her. She would just have to get out of that van and show these people she was more than a peacock-scaring crazy woman.

What's the worst that could happen?

Chapter 6

L ike a purple pinstripe lamb to the slaughter, Lexie made her walk of disgrace across the driveway towards the intimidating house. She was fast regretting her trademark matching mascara and nose stud, but she hadn't had time for a full wardrobe change. A quick shimmy into her suit had had to do. At least she was going down in a blaze of Lexie-ness.

She fought to keep her back straight, even if her long frame was determined to curl up like a cheesy Quaver. It was as though her subconscious was willing her to bow to the sheer enormity of this building and the millions of pounds which must be tied up in its stonework. Would the stern guy try and steer her to a tradeperson's entrance? There was surely still time to leg it from this hideous interview ...

But no. She stuck out her chin. With more purposeful strides she landed at the arched white doorway, at the feet of the two men blocking her entrance. The bouncers to her future. Her churning stomach told her she wasn't sure she wanted in, but she had come this far. Going back was a far worse option – not that a girl with a broken van and no money for petrol had many of those.

Lexie took a deep breath and willed herself to be polite and friendly, even if the harsh guy's jaw was already set against her. Manners cost nothing, after all. It was just an interview; a chat about stuff. They were just people. It didn't even matter that one of them was frighteningly good-looking. She just had to skate around the CV issue and try not to balls things up. Simple.

Lexie gave her name and extended a hand, praying one of them would shake it so she didn't look like an idiot.

The surfer-type gave a little chuckle and grabbed her hand with both of his. 'Good to meet you. I'm Cory – the little bro who's too lazy to get involved in the paint emporium.'

'But interfering enough to set up interviews for roles the business doesn't need,' said the stern one in the suit.

'Hey, like I told you, a business that doesn't exist online is like a dead fish in the water.' Cory let go of Lexie's hand and held up his own in a shrug. 'Just trying to save your dying arse,' he directed at his comrade.

The warmth from Cory's hands had felt like the only thing keeping her there. Now he was shoving them back into his boardshort pockets, she could feel the spring chill creeping back into her. Or was it the cold front from the boss who didn't want her there? What was going on?

'Maybe I should just leave.' Lexie looked up at the

smartly suited man, whose name she knew was Ben. Not that he'd bothered to introduce himself.

Her eyes fixed on his as she waited for his answer. They were less dark than she'd expected. Blue flecked with green, like maps of the world. Why was he holding her gaze for quite so long? And why was it setting off a kaleidoscope of butterflies in her already nervous belly?

He blinked a couple of times and then seemed to reset himself. 'Right, well, you're here now. You'd better come in.'

Cory gave Lexie a conspiratorial grin. 'He's Ben, by the way. Excuse his manners; he's a loser around women. Anyway, give me your keys and I'll push that little beaut around the back by mine. Mum will do a kickflip if she sees it "littering the driveway".'

An angry-looking muscle twitched in Ben's jaw. 'Watch your tongue, Cory. And I thought you'd thrown *Mother dear* off the scent for today? She'd be even less impressed than me if she heard about your interfering. If she turns up, sniffing around . . .'

Cory held up his hands again. 'Look, she's meant to be at the polo club with the Fortescues or whatever they're called, but you know what she's like. If she gets a whiff of something, she'll be clawing her way over here, the old fox.'

He looked back at Ben and stage-whispered, 'This is the bit where you smile and shake hands. What's with you today? I thought you were good at this business stuff?'

Cory grabbed Lexie's keys from her sweaty fist, gave her an eyeroll and hopped barefoot across the pebbles, whistling as he went.

'Never work with children or animals,' said Ben through gritted teeth, as he watched his younger brother retreat towards the stool-splattered van. 'I . . . ' He cleared his throat. 'I'll arrange for your vehicle to be cleaned.'

Was that nearly an apology? But before Lexie could dwell on it, Ben moved back into the house and gave her a small nod to follow. She discreetly wiped her palms on her seen-better-days suit trousers and tiptoed in behind him.

And wow. Lexie tried not to looked fazed by the enormous entrance hall, which was bigger than the whole of her last flat. A wrought-iron staircase curved off imposingly to her right, like something from a grand film. Even the cream walls were dwarfing her, with their gallery of painted noblemen and horses that seemed to tower upwards forever.

But what was that funereal smell? It was like dust and history mixed with sadly wilting flowers. Lexie's eyes landed on a spray of white lilies in one of those tall pottery stands. A woman's touch.

Ben paced around, looking at his watch. Lexie guessed he was in his early thirties and she wondered if he'd spent all his years looking quite so agitated. She shuffled from foot to foot, her plastic ballet pumps squeaking embarrassingly on the cold marble floor. Perhaps she should say something polite.

'Impressive house. I should have Google-stalked better before I arrived.' She gave a nervous laugh. 'Rookie mistake.'

'Right.'

Did he even know what she was talking about?

Lexie looked back to the aristocrats in the paintings,

hoping for a friendlier face. But they seemed similarly scornful, their disapproving eyes following her every flinch. How did these people live like this? It was like being in an episode of *Scooby-Doo*. Her artistic eye squinted for a resemblance between the effeminate horsemen and her strong-featured interviewer. Hmm, it wasn't obvious.

He followed her gaze and shook his head. What did that mean?

And then, with a crunch of gravel, Cory arrived back at the open front door. He gave Ben a quizzical look, as though surprised to see them both still loitering in the hallway.

'So, fans, are we going to hit this interview?'

Cory was surprisingly laid-back compared to his brother. Why were they so different? She hoped he would play good cop to Ben's pain-in-the-arse variety.

Ben held up a finger, like he was still debating whether the interview would go ahead. 'You're a social media . . . ' His voice trailed off.

'Manager.' Lexie tried to straighten herself up. 'I breathe life into businesses by growing their social media following and adding sparkle to their online presence.' She tried to keep her hands under control, aware that she sometimes got overexcited when she talked about this stuff. 'I create content that really speaks to your audience and I get them talking back. Because an engaged audience means people are interested, excited, and getting ready to buy from you.'

Lexie looked at Cory and Ben, hoping her eyes weren't too full of dazzle. Cory gave a hearty clap, but Ben just raised his eyebrows.

'Sparkle.' He let the word hang awkwardly for a moment. 'And I just thought you'd be pinning chintzy photos and tweeting.'

Lexie filled her lungs and tried not to let Ben's words deflate her. Why did people belittle her job like it was pointless? It always felt like there was something to prove.

'Being a social butterfly is actually quite exhausting. And it would help if people didn't try to trample on my wings.' Her words came out quietly and she wished they hadn't. She knew it was unprofessional, but Ben's attitude was grating. Could she really work for someone who had no belief in her? It would be like the platonic version of Drew-gate all over again.

Cory coughed in an apparent bid to break the tension. 'Er, let's get to the interview room, shall we? If war's going to break out, I at least want a comfy viewing seat.'

Ben raised his eyebrows but Cory bulldozed past him, leading Lexie by a reluctant elbow. They moved through a long hallway of closed doors, with Ben following under a cloud of obvious antipathy.

Lexie took in her surroundings, hoping to get a feel for what made this family business tick. Part of her job – if she ever made it that far – would be sharing their story. Bringing it to life. But why was all the paintwork so *beige*? They were meant to be in the paint business. Who'd stolen all the colour?

What did they call this nothing shade? Lacklustre Linen? Haughty Horseradish? She thought back to her days in the art studio at school. Her sanctuary. This place needed some warmth, that was for sure. Although it sounded like the mother had her hand firmly on the paint pot. She wondered if she was in charge of the purse-strings too – like the pearl-clenching mother of a certain wealthy ex-boyfriend.

They reached a doorway, embellished with gold lettering. 'Private Drawing Room.' Lexie felt her muscles stiffen. She'd never been into a drawing room before – it sounded grand. The initials underneath read 'J. R. C.' Who was that? God, not the fox-like mother, waiting in her den.

'Maybe I should just . . . ' Lexie pointed back towards the exit. What was the polite way to say 'get the hell out of here'?

Cory laughed and patted her on the back. 'I won't let him bite.'

The drawing room, which was an office at one end and a lounging area with leather sofas at the other, had hardly seen a lick of paint. Shades of beige had been banished and wooden panelling ran the show. It was definitely a man cave. With a few candles and some burning logs in the fireplace, it could almost be cosy. But, anyway, she wasn't here to redecorate. At least not in the literal sense.

Ben installed himself behind a large desk with green leather inlay. Lexie could see her CV sprawled across it. She winced. And what were the other papers – more CVs? She wondered how many opponents were in the running. She needed this job. Hitchhiking home like a penniless failure was not an option.

But did she *want* this job? With grumpy Ben? She gritted her teeth.

Well, she was here now and she didn't plan to leave

looking like a numpty. She'd at least go down fighting and crawl out with a few shreds of dignity. Well, subject to Penny ever working again, and no further run-ins with the peacocks.

Her insides tightened. It was time to get the gloves out.

Chapter 7

As interviews went, Lexie could already tell this was going to be a strange one.

She tried not to squirm as Ben leafed through her CV. Should she try and distract him? Too many questions about its contents could end in disaster. She could do the job of social media manager with her eyes shut. But the advert had been firm that they'd expected a proper uni degree, rather than someone who'd taught themselves while backpacking and travel-blogging around Thailand. So maybe her CV wording was a bit on the creative side.

And if they ever learned the half of how that trip had ended up, then wow. They'd have two reasons to kick her out; that's if she ever got in.

A loud pop from the sofa made her jump.

'Sorry!' Cory winced before lounging backwards and delving into the bag of Doritos he'd just burst open.

Ben gave him an icicle glare. 'Manners.'

'Oh yeah, sorry!' He jumped up, wiped his hands on his shorts and held the bag out towards Lexie.

She got a whiff of Chilli Heatwave before having to duck to avoid the crossfire.

'Don't be absurd. Go and arrange teas, or something,' Ben snapped.

Cory rolled his eyes. 'What do you fancy? A pot of Tetley and some custard creams? Can you see why this old charmer is still single?'

'Er . . .'

'Not relevant, Cory,' said Ben, with slightly more sternness than was necessary.

Cory climbed to his still-bare feet. Oh crap, why was he leaving her with pain-in-the-arse cop?

'I'll speak to Mrs Moon.'

'You'll give her a hand,' said Ben.

There, that was kind. Wasn't it?

Cory grinned. 'He doesn't like Mrs Moon coming in here, otherwise he'd have to allow Mummy dear into the Presidential Office. Think yourself lucky. Not many ladies penetrate this far inside the mysterious workings of Carrington Paints.'

Oh great, mystery too. The Scooby-Doo gang would have a field day in this place.

When his brother had left the room, Ben put down the paperwork and stared at her across his huge leather-topped desk. His all-seeing atlas eyes seemed to pin her to her chair.

'So tell me why I need to pay somebody to chat with my clients on Facebook all day.'

Lexie clenched her fists in her purple pinstripe lap. 'You don't. You can do it yourself, if you prefer. But it's a full-time job, and a business the size of yours needs a presence on the social media sites where your clients are likely to be. Have you profiled your ideal client? Do you know where they hang out?'

'In business meetings, I shouldn't wonder.'

Being stuffy, and boring and *beige*? But she dared not ask that.

'I appreciate a lot of your paint might be sold to existing business clients, but you can't ignore the online world. You need a website, a blog, social media accounts. How will new clients find you? How will you share your story? How will you maintain a two-way dialogue with people, stay ahead of trends, move with the times?'

'We're doing just fine.' Ben crossed his arms over his chest, and Lexie wondered if that was the full picture.

'Are you doing as well as The Paint Guys? Paint by Numbers? Inspired to Paint?' Lexie had managed to research their main competitors. 'They've decorated the internet with their presence. Their audience is thriving and engaged, dying to buy. It's your call, but you know how business works. If you don't stay current, you'll be washed up. Like I said, you can do this with or without me, but don't ignore it.' Lexie shrugged.

Ben studied her, his eyes narrowed. 'And if all of that were true, why should I do it with you? Why you and not me?'

Lexie was sure Ben was astute enough in commercial conversations, but what was the polite way of telling him he was an anti-social tit?

'It comes down to time, money and skill-set.' There. Tactful and professional. She really wasn't too bad at all this. 'If your hours are better spent working on the things you excel at, and you can afford to employ someone better suited to being sociable, why wouldn't you? Do you do your own accounts? Run the machines in your factory? Make deliveries? Carrington Paints is surely a team.'

Did he just nod, ever so slightly?

'OK. And in the unlikely event I accept this role is necessary, why you and not the other candidates? You have experience, I presume? And the specified qualifications?' He shuffled the papers on his desk.

'Yes, of course!'

Well, yes to experience, at least. But qualifications? She hadn't even stayed on at that snobby school she'd got the bursary for, where she'd never belonged. She'd been desperate to start earning to help out her parents and Sky. After that, she and her second-hand backpack had followed her first boyfriend, Inkie, around Asia. But she'd set up a website, learned to travel-blog and starting acing social media. The university of life was surely a thing?

Lexie skated over those questionable years and told Ben about the social media work she'd done for a few trendy start-ups after her travels. Maybe her self-taught story wasn't so terrible, but the job advert had insisted on letters after her name and she just wanted to prove she was worthy of something. Lexie hated lying, but now was not the time to rock this already precarious boat.

'But all of this is not just about flinging snazzy words

and pretty pictures into the world. You need a social media strategy. And, with my experience, I can help you with so much more. Your website, your branding, your marketing. I've juggled it all. I love taking photos that capture the hearts and minds of your customers, and crafting words that inspire them to take action.'

Wow, she was even impressing herself at what she'd learned along the way. YouTube was a fine place.

'And what action would that be?'

'You want people to respond, to follow you, to visit your website and buy into the dream you've just sold them. To invest in your paints.'

Did one of his eyebrows just move in vague interest? Phew, this guy was a tough nut to crack. Lexie was longing for Good Cop to return with that nice cuppa; it was like she was singing for her life. What more could she say? Why was he eyeing her like that, and didn't he have any more questions? Maybe he'd had enough of her already. Damn it. When in doubt, waffle.

'I have so many ideas for blog posts. We could do exciting behind-the-scenes stuff, explore the story of how the business came about. Honest stories are so powerful.'

Oh God, she sounded like she was trying to sell him a drill. Was that a smirk emerging? Perhaps she should change tack.

'You seriously do need a website. I'm pretty handy with a widget!' She looked towards the door, willing it to open.

'Right.'

'And there's search engine optimisation, of course. We

47

want your website ranking on Google. When people search paints, we want them finding you before your competitors.'

'Hmm.'

Jeez, no one would be mistaking him for Chatty Cathy. It seemed like he needed someone to take charge of *all things* social, if only he could admit it.

Just as Lexie was wondering if she should just give up, something clattered against the door and made her insides flip. What if it was that fox of a mother, coming to sniff out her guilty CV secrets? Her eyes darted around the room. Was there a designated exit for liars with their pants on fire?

The door swung open and a silver tray appeared. China quivered on top of it as though it was as anxious as Lexie. And ... what was that lovely smell? Something lemony – a drizzle cake? Cory's body appeared behind the tray and Lexie let go of a long, tense breath.

The sight of a soft, spongy cake gave her a small sliver of hope. It looked home-made. Maybe there was some warmth somewhere in the depths of this place, after all.

Her stomach groaned. She couldn't remember how many hours it had been since she'd eaten her stale cornflakes, but it was definitely too many. All this flitting around the countryside, being pounced on by peacocks and withstanding interview interrogation had made her hungry. If she could just avoid choking on a cake crumb and coughing up her skeletons, perhaps she'd make it.

'Caught you, did she?'

Lexie squirmed in her seat. What? She looked at Ben, and realised with relief he was talking to his brother.

'Yep. Mrs Moon strikes again.'

Cory looked sheepishly at his now-slippered feet and back up at his tray of goodies. 'The housekeeper,' he explained. 'What can I say. At least somebody loves me.'

Did she imagine a tense look passing between the two men?

Cory cleared his throat. 'Anyway, your camper van's a doll. Vintage 1960s, isn't she? She must be worth a packet.'

Drew had always quantified Penny in terms of cash too. He'd nagged that if she sold Penny she wouldn't be so skint all the time. But the van was worth more to her than any money could buy. Penny was family.

'I inherited her from my aunt. She's ... she's precious.' Lexie felt a lump rising in her throat. Oh brilliant, was she going to cry now, too? 'I could never part with her. She's the very essence of Aunt Jasmine.' Right down to the flowery perfume she swore she could still smell on a good day.

Now Ben seemed to be swallowing something back as well.

'A bit like this office,' Cory replied. 'I reckon Dad's still ingrained in the woodwork. Some people will never leave you.'

Was he the J. R. C. from the gold doorplate? Ben coughed and shuffled more papers. Suddenly it seemed no one felt like cake.

After a few awkward moments, Ben cut through the silence and stood up, extending a hand to Lexie. Oh, was it over? But ...

'Well, Miss Summers, I think I've heard enough. Cory, did you have any questions? You're the one with the burning desire to see our lives spread all over the internet.'

Had she done nothing to convince him? Why was he still so cold?

'I've got a burning desire for lemon cake and a cup of tea,' Cory replied. 'Now, where are *your* manners?'

'I need to fully consider all applicants.' Ben was back in business mode, if he'd ever left it. 'I'll be in touch.'

Cory spluttered up chunks of the candied lemon he'd been nicking from the plate.

'What other applicants? Tewkesbury isn't exactly huge. You'll be lucky to find a queue of people with a degree in media and communications like Lexie. You'd better snap the girl up before someone beats you to it.'

Ben reddened. 'There are other applicants,' he said, firmly.

'Trisha from the Co-op?'

Ben appeared to be sucking in his words.

Cory turned to Lexie. 'Look, can you do the job?'

'Well, of course, I—'

'I have no doubt she's capable,' Ben conceded through tight lips.

He didn't?

'And can you start on Monday?' asked Cory.

'Well, I'd need to find somewhere to stay, of course ...'

'There are heaps of rooms here. Move in.' Cory waved a nonchalant hand like he'd just offered her a Dorito. 'There's loads of space now the old dragon lives in her town house and I'm off in the camper most of the time. Ben's just rattling around here with the decrepit staff and dust mites. You may as well keep him company.'

'No!' Lexie and Ben shouted at once, and then looked

50

at one another, apparently startled by the strength of their own protests.

'I have my own accommodation,' Lexie confirmed. 'I'll live in my camper van. I just need to find a campsite.'

'Our rooms are not suitable for guests. They haven't been lived in for years,' Ben added.

Lexie thought she'd probably die of beige-ness anyway. Or choke on their preposterous wealth. Hey, hang on. Did that mean she had the job?

'Well, that sounds like a yes, subject to logistics.' Cory slapped his brother on the back. 'Nice decision-making.'

'Wait, I didn't say that exactly; I ...'

Lexie tried to stifle a snigger. There was nothing like a younger sibling to throw you off balance, even when you thought you were the least messy one.

'What would Dad have said?' asked Cory, and they both looked towards the well-worn leather office chair.

There was a silence, and Lexie almost felt a small army of soldier ants prickle across her skin. When Ben spoke next, his voice seemed softer. Like the words came from a place in his subconscious.

'Dad would have said he liked her backbone. There's something entrepreneurial about her. And ... colourful.' Ben shook himself down and then looked slightly confused, as though he wasn't sure where any of that had come from.

'Woooo,' said Cory, with a playful air. She could almost imagine him making ghost noises and flicking the lights on and off if he'd been ten years younger. 'And would he also say you should be chivalrous and let the lady park up and live on the drive, to save on campsite fees?'

Ben's jaw seemed tighter now but, like a nagging younger brother, Cory wasn't giving up.

'What? It's an epic plan and it makes perfect sense. You work crazy hours, so why not have your social media guru on hand? Then Lexie can keep up to date with what's going on and get a feel for the place. And hell, Ben, the girl needs somewhere to stay. Give her a break.'

'Mum would be livid.'

'And Dad would say use that backbone of your own. Anyway, Mum barely visits. Put your foot down, golden boy. If you don't get used to saying no to her now, she'll have you marrying Cynthia Fortescue before you know it.'

'Not going to happen.'

Cory sniggered. 'You should hear about Mum's magnificent matchmaking, Lexie.'

'No, she shouldn't.' Ben's eyes shot lethal daggers at his brother. 'You've stirred up quite enough trouble for today. You've secured your contentious new employee. And even more controversially, she'll be camping out on our driveway. Mother will probably disembowel the three of us and hang our insides up to dry on Mrs Moon's washing line. And that's if she's in a good mood. Let's just leave it there, shall we?'

For once, Cory took his younger brother role seriously and had the grace to look suitably rollocked.

'Now, let me get a contract ready for Miss Summers to consider, before Mother gets wind of it and comes to blow this entire house down,' said Ben.

Cory shrugged and grabbed a couple of slices of cake. 'Guess we'll just have to deal with that crap-storm when it hits. Come on, Lex, we'll sort you out with an electric hook-up for the camper.' He turned to her and spoke more quietly. 'We can have a laugh about my brother's loser-ish love life another time.'

Chapter 8

Lexie was huddled with her laptop at the well-worn farmhouse table, tinkering with her new social media accounts for Carrington Paints. The kitchen, she had come to learn over her first weekend at Nutgrass Hall, was about the only part of the house where she didn't feel like a very underprivileged fish out of water.

Unlike the rest of the house, the kitchen was warm and modest, always filled with yummy baking smells from the huge, toasty Aga. Battered copper pans and ancient cookbooks lined the walls, and a blanket-strewn rocking chair swayed gently in the corner. This was very much Mrs Moon the housekeeper's domain.

'Her Highness never comes down here,' she'd whispered to Lexie, on her first visit. 'And don't tell her about my telly – she'll think I'm slacking.'

Lexie smiled now, as clandestine Nigella purred at a meringue-laden spoon from a screen in the corner cupboard.

Ben was taking Lexie to the factory later so she could take photos for social media and get ideas for the website and blog. She wanted to get a feel for the place and the family behind it, and hear people's stories. Of course, her nose was still twitching at the promise of that matchmaking gossip Cory had mentioned. There was something intriguing about the thought of Ben's love life, even if she wasn't sure why. But maybe she shouldn't pry if she wanted to keep her job and stay out of trouble.

'Now, keep your naughty fingers out of the mix,' Nigella warned from her hidey-hole in the cupboard.

Quite, thought Lexie, and then told herself off for sounding like one-word Ben.

Her first weekend at Nutgrass Hall had been a little odd. She'd steered clear of the main house, which still seemed so stuffy and imposing. It didn't feel like a home at all, more like a stale, beige museum, with little hint that life or love had ever existed. Lexie had stayed in her camper van as much as she could, although she had to admit it was a bit of a struggle. It was one thing to use it for a weekend festival. To live in it, with everything she owned crammed inside, was a totally different matter.

Cory had said she could use one of the spare rooms as her dumping ground, but she was determined to be as self-sufficient as possible. It already irked her that she was powered by an electrical cable running from her van to the kitchen, like a pathetic orange umbilical cord. Her leisure battery would only get her so far. Cory had laughed when she'd offered to pay her share of the electricity bill.

But the van was cold at night, and filled with condensation by the morning. Her clothes always smelt of burnt toast and she could never find anything. She was often running to the kitchen for fresh water and company, and her self-imposed march to the leisure centre for a shower was actually quite annoying.

Ben had mainly been in his office. She'd bumped into him a few times when he'd stuck his head around the kitchen door, although she could never work out what he'd wanted. He would just cough awkwardly and make a strange excuse. Did he feel a comfort at being near the glow of the kitchen too? He'd be too proud to show it, if he did. And Lexie still got the impression he hated her.

Yes, if Ben's office was the brain centre of the house, this room was like the heart. She shook her head, trying to forget the image Ben had painted of his mother stringing up their insides when she found out about her. Lexie hadn't met this notorious woman yet and she was in no hurry to.

Mrs Moon bustled in through the door in her frilly housekeeper's apron and bonnet; an oddly archaic look, which she seemed to wear with pride. Lexie had warmed to her instantly, with her squidgy pink-marshmallow cheeks and hair like one of those fluffy dandelion clocks. She just wanted to puff on her and make a wish. Sky used to say if you could blow away all the seeds in one breath, the person you loved would love you back. But then, Sky was a dreamer.

Beep, beep, beep . . .

Mrs Moon hurried to her ovens, batting the steamy air with an embroidered tea towel.

'Ooh, my lavender shortbread. I've made it specially to calm your nerves. Big day for you, lovey.' She rubbed Lexie's back as she rooted in a drawer for an oven glove.

Lexie smiled. She did feel anxious about her trip to the factory, but it was mainly being in such close proximity to Ben that would bother her. Maybe he'd be less abrasive on work territory.

Apparently nobody could resist the delicious fragrance of Mrs Moon's biscuits. No sooner had the elderly lady put them out to cool and opened a window, a head appeared in its frame. It sported a worn tweed cap, a shy gummy grin and seventy or so years' worth of friendly wrinkles, and it belonged to Tom the gardener.

'Ah, just in time for some of yer lovely bakin', Mrs M. 'Ave you got that kettle on?'

Mrs Moon straightened her bonnet and flushed.

'Tom, you'll make the poor girl jump, springing up like that. Now mind you don't get your grubby paw prints all over my windows.' She bustled over with a cloth. 'I was just about to make Lexie some soothing lemon-balm tea.'

Tom pulled his face into a mock grimace and set his muddy trowel down on the windowsill while Mrs Moon was distracted with a teapot.

'None of yer weeds in me tea, thankin' you. 'Tisn't no good for me insides. I'll 'ave some proper PG Tips.'

Lexie was still getting used to the gardener's West-Country drawl. She guessed Mrs M was well accustomed to it, after at least two decades of having him around.

'Honestly, I'm happy with normal tea if that's what

you're making. I don't feel that worried.' Lexie hated to be a burden.

The housekeeper gave her a sympathetic look. 'Prevention is better than cure, dear. Trust me, when Mrs Carrington-Noble gets wind of you, she'll be over here like a dog out of hell. And *then* you'll be nervous.'

Mrs Moon tipped a heavy dose of leaves into the teapot, took one look at Lexie's paling face, and scooped in an extra measure.

'Better stock up on those.' The housekeeper scribbled a note on her shopping list.

''Ere, young grockle.'

Lexie had learned 'grockle' meant someone from out of town. It seemed to be Tom's nickname for her. He said it nicely enough; it was almost touching.

'I managed to get that peacock mess off yer motor.'

Lexie cringed at the memory. 'Oh, Tom, that's so sweet of you. Honestly, there was no need. I would have done it if you'd found me a bucket. I'm not fussy.'

'It weren't no bother. Them's always up to no good. Probably just doing their matin' dance with yer. Not so often they see a pretty young thing like you.' He cleared his throat. 'Apart from Mrs M here, of course. Them's partial to a wave from Mrs M, and one of 'er lovely teacakes.'

He winked at Lexie while Mrs Moon hid her rosy cheeks in her herb cupboard.

Like another bee to the lavender patch, Cory shuffled into the kitchen in flip-flopped feet and sank into a chair near Lexie. He held up a hand in greeting.

Mrs Moon sorted out her chintzy crockery and slid a plate of shortbread in front of him. Lexie noticed she'd sneaked him a double portion. Mrs Moon had told Lexie she'd been the boys' nanny when they were younger. Ben had been ten when the Carringtons moved in and had been sensible enough not to want much fuss. But she'd looked after Cory since he was three, and she clearly adored him.

'How are things in the van, Lex?' Cory asked.

'Excellent, thanks.' She tried on her best convincing smile.

'Really? Because the weather's been shitty, and those vintage campers aren't that practical. You can use the showers here, you know. Or just move in; it's all good. Mr and Mrs Moon's old living space upstairs would be great with a lick of paint, now she's moved out to one of the garden cottages.'

'And Mr Moon,' the housekeeper reminded him firmly.

Lexie was glad she wasn't expected to share a four-poster bed with an elderly man she hadn't yet met.

'And Mr Moon,' Cory replied, with an eyeroll which was only for Lexie.

'I'm fine,' said Lexie, as breezily as she could manage.

'Lexie's off to the factory with Ben today,' Mrs Moon told Cory, as though she sensed the need for a subject change. 'To collect some *stories*.'

Cory grinned and craned his head around. 'Trust me, all the best stories are happening right here these days, with what Mum's up to.'

Lexie felt her gossip detectors flutter. She dusted crumbs from the wooden table onto her plate, trying not to look too interested. 'Oh?'

This was surely about Ben's mother's matchmaking. But no. She absolutely wouldn't snoop on the family's idiosyncrasies any more than necessary. Even if behind-the-scenes shenanigans would be more click-worthy than tales of beige-looking paintwork.

As Lexie looked up, she saw Mrs Moon's eyes dart towards Cory.

'Ben won't appreciate you talking about his personal bits and bobs. You know how reserved he is.' Mrs Moon looked over to Tom in the window, her eyes widening in some sort of SOS signal.

Tom tugged awkwardly at his ear. The worm on his trowel squirmed. 'Er, look, nipper. I'm not sure you should be tellin' tales.'

Cory shrugged. 'Now that Lexie basically lives here, she'd probably work it out at some point.'

'Gawd help us, Mrs Carrington-Noble will likely kill us all for lettin' the girl camp on her precious land in the first place,' said Tom. 'Without you airin' and sharin' Ben's private bizniz.'

'I don't know why he doesn't just settle for Cynthia,' Mrs Moon muttered, and then pursed her lips like she shouldn't have.

'My brother wouldn't date Cynthia any more than he'd go on a date with his own toenail.'

'Chalk 'n' cheese.' Tom nodded.

Cory pulled a face. 'Look, Lexie, I just wanted to give you a heads up,' he continued. 'Some of the things that go down in this place might seem pretty weird to an outsider.

I don't want you to be frightened off. But here's the thing. Ben is a loser with women.'

'Cory!'

'It's a fact. Like the sky is blue and like only death seekers surf Oahu's Pipeline. Ben Carrington sucks at love.' Cory looked directly at Lexie. 'And Mum's hellbent on finding him the perfect match.'

Lexie fidgeted on her stool. She wasn't sure she wanted to hear the intricacies of her boss's private life.

'When left to his own devices, he'd rather concoct a new shade of Carrington's beige than paint the town red. He's married to that business.'

So that explained the uninspiring paintwork.

'Mum's matchmaking is seriously not the best. Sometimes I wonder if she's more concerned about the family money and the future of the empire than what Ben needs in a woman.'

The house staff seemed to shrink away, as though unsure which side of the fence to fall on for minimal damage.

'Come on, guys, back me up here. Some of Mum's matches would make a vow of celibacy seem like a tasty alternative. What about senseless Sindy and that amoeba of a pooch?'

'Ah, that rat of a thing that worried me peacocks,' Tom joined in. 'And the dog weren't much better.'

'And St Frances the stern nun.'

'Cory, don't speak about the poor girl like that.' Mrs Moon busied herself with the plates. 'Frances was a very nice girl.'

'Ben pretended he was into devil worship so he didn't have to go on a date with her.'

Tom gave a toothless snigger from the window.

'And I don't know what the sudden rush is, but Mum wants Ben married off by the end of the year. She's keen to get the business signed over to him as part of the deal. Probably trying to avoid inheritance tax, or something. Maybe she's feeling her age.'

'Cory!'

'She's laid down the law that she's got to approve his choice. She wants to be sure he doesn't fritter the family fortune on some "gold-digging riff-raff". I think that was the phrase.'

Mrs Moon's lips were pinched again.

'Mum's a massive money snob. She'd love Ben to upscale and marry into even more cash. That's why she's got her beady eyes on the Fortescues. Their family interior design empire will be a good mix with our paints, so she reckons. Excuse the tacky pun.'

God, these rich people really were strange. Lexie downed some of her nervous tea.

'And if Ben doesn't meet this end-of-year deadline?' She couldn't believe she was even asking. It was ludicrous.

'Mum has threatened to sell the business to the highest bidder and spend the money on cruising the world with her toy boy, Carlito. Anything to avoid letting the taxman have it, after how hard Dad strived. Working all those hours probably sent him to an early grave. Not that he didn't love it.'

'That mother o' yours is what sent 'im to an early grave, poor bugger,' muttered Tom.

Mrs Moon made frantic mouth-zipping gestures at Tom

62

before turning to Lexie. 'Ben would be devastated to lose that business. He was helping his dad with it for as long as I can remember. Following him around with his little brief-case and getting involved with all those meetings.'

Cory sniggered.

'So wait.' Lexie needed to get this straight in her head. 'He won't marry Cynthia, but he needs to marry someone. It must happen by the end of the year and the woman has got to be rich – or he loses his precious business?'

'Exactly!' Cory slapped the table.

'And you're telling me this, because ...' Lexie thought for a moment. 'Oh, wait ... no!' She felt her face flush. 'I'm not sure what's going on here, but let's lay down some boundaries. I'm not dressing up in a Cinderella ballgown and pretending to be loaded so Ben can fool his mother. And there's no way I'd marry him. No way! I mean, you know. No offence.'

They all immediately started laughing.

'What? It's a ridiculous idea! Look at me. I could never pull off posh. And I wouldn't even want to. I'm perfectly happy with my lot, and Ben and I ... well. He's far too ... '

Rude? Standoffish? Irritatingly wealthy?

'*Different*,' she concluded, diplomatically.

Cory burst into full-blown laughter. Was he actually crying with amusement? What was all this about? Lexie wished someone would just spill the bloody beans.

Chapter 9

Mrs Moon rushed towards Lexie with the rest of the pot of nervous tea and started pouring. 'No, no, dear, you're getting it all in a pickle.' She rubbed Lexie's arm. 'Nobody's asking you to marry Ben. Mrs Carrington-Noble would never have it.'

'I dunno. I think they'd be all right together,' said Tom, scratching his head. ''E could do with jazzing up a bit. I'm sure 'e didn't used to be so serious.'

'Thomas! Lexie's staff, like us. Now get your head out of the clouds.'

Tom shrugged.

They were still in the kitchen in the throes of the world's strangest discussion about Ben, and he was likely to appear at any moment. Lexie tugged at the ends of her pixie cut, which were feeling as frayed as her nerves.

Cory finally stopped convulsing. 'Don't panic, Lex. My point in telling you this was exactly the opposite. If you see Mum parading fancy women around the place and trying to foist them onto Ben, it's best to smile and pretend it's perfectly normal. And don't go looking too friendly with Ben. If she sees you as a threat to her master plan, she'll turf you out. We're on dodgy ground as it is, getting a new employee without her say-so. And no mentioning any of this on the socials, as juicy as it sounds.' He gave Lexie a wink.

No getting friendly with Ben. Well, that bit should be easy enough. And as for meddling. Well, she'd driven one hundred and twenty-five miles, fought peacocks and convinced the world's most reluctant employer for this job. She didn't want to lose it now, or the home her broken-down camper van was squatting on.

'I can manage unfriendly and discreet.' Lexie nodded. In fact, the sort of man who couldn't be bothered to pick his own wife sounded infuriating anyway. 'Wouldn't he be better off arranging his own love life?'

Cory waved a hand. 'Searching for a suitable match is like unnecessary admin to Ben. He'd happily stay single, if it didn't involve losing the business. I'm not sure he even believes in love.'

Lexie gasped. That was the saddest thing she'd ever heard. Not that she wasn't completely off love herself for a while, of course. She couldn't see herself falling for another guy until at least the day Mrs Moon retired from baking and dyed her hair green. But what kind of person thought of love as *unnecessary admin*?

She gave a small harrumph. Someone cold and beige

with a stupid bag of cash where his heart should be. Someone like Ben.

'Why doesn't he just stay single and buy the business himself, if that's all he wants from life?' Perhaps money addled the brain.

'Neither of us has any real money unless Mother waves her magic wand. She owns the house and Carrington Paints. Ben never takes much of a salary, because why bother if you're an antisocial workaholic? Mum will probably shove some feel-sorry-for-the-drifter money my way if she gives Ben the business. But, really, I couldn't care less about cash. I'm happy with my surfboard and the camper.'

Cory looked off into the distance with a quiet smile, as though imagining some far-off wave. 'But Ben. Ben's different. Ben needs this.' He held his arms upwards, as though signifying the whole of Nutgrass Hall. 'He's a home bird. He's lost enough without Dad, let alone snatching him away from Dad's sacred office and their joint venture. And I'd actually just like to see my bro happy, you know? Laughing once in a while. Less narky. So I hope the right woman does appear.'

Was that a tiny twinge of sympathy tugging at Lexie's heart? Maybe it was her instinct to support a lost cause. Ben, the dark-suited emperor penguin, facing extinction. She tried not to giggle.

Well, she just hoped she could steer clear of this parade of wealthy women. A memory flashed up and made her wince. Her so-called boyfriend's mother lording it among the diamonds rings, gawping at her like she was their cleaner. This was exactly the kind of thing she'd just escaped from.

Lexie shivered and downed her cup of scaredy-cat tea. But before she could get lost in her downward spiral of thoughts, she heard footsteps marching down the hallway. All eyes swivelled towards the door. Even the worm cocked its head. Or was that its tail?

Ben burst through in a cloud of urgency, scowling at his watch and pulling his waistcoat like a white rabbit who was late for a very unwelcome date. He looked at Lexie like she was an inconvenient toilet stop on his important journey.

'Are you ready?'

'We were just explaining to Lexie about Mum's match-making thing,' said Cory, apparently unfazed by his brother's extreme business mode. 'So she doesn't wonder what the hell's going on. And don't worry, she knows not to interfere.'

Ben held up his hand like an official stopping traffic. 'It's a shame you don't. Miss Summers, I'll meet you at the car.'

Ben glared at his brother and retreated from the group with even more strident steps. Great, now he was in a worse mood than before, if that was even possible.

Cory rolled his eyes.

The kitchen door slammed and Lexie jumped to her feet, worried she would miss her ride. She let out a tense puff of air, grabbed the flamingo raincoat she'd found to replace her duckling one, and steeled herself for a stormy first morning at Carrington Paints.

Friendly, but not too friendly, she reminded herself. Collect stories, but not the wrong kind of stories. And don't scupper anyone's matrimonial plans ...

What on earth was she getting herself into?

Chapter 10

'You keep your filthy hands off her. You're nothing but trouble!'

Lexie snatched her own hand back from the kitchen door, uncertain whether to enter. She was sure that was Mrs Moon's raised voice inside. Should she back away? But she was going to be late for her first end-of-week meeting with Ben, and she only needed a few bits. Lexie cleared her throat and gave a loud knock.

She heard scurrying from within, followed by some clattering.

'Come iiiiiinnn!'

Lexie entered gingerly. What the hell had been going on in there? But she saw nothing, other than a slightly red-faced Mrs Moon rearranging her bonnet.

'Is everything OK?'

'Just tidying up, dear, don't mind me!' She checked her watch. 'Goodness, look at the time. Mr Moon will wonder where I've got to!'

Lexie's brow furrowed. She still hadn't seen this fabled Mr Moon – he really must be a hermit. But, like most things in this place, it was best not to ask too many questions. Her *odd* sensors were on overdrive, though she was kind of getting used to it.

Lexie clanged in cupboards, looking for some half-decent crockery. Her first week working for Ben had been pretty intense. Everyone at the paint factory had been welcoming, but she could see she'd need to insist on a lot of changes if they were to bring Carrington Paints up to date. And tonight was the night she'd have to break all that to Ben.

'Here we go!' Lexie pulled out some plates. She just hoped the night wouldn't end in Ben smashing them over her head.

Because the business branding was like something from the dark ages and their marketing probably still involved carrier pigeons, there was no point in Lexie fixing the company's online mojo if none of it tied in with what was happening on the ground. Their messaging needed to be consistent; she would have to go deep. Stuck-in-his-ways Ben was going to *hate it*. And, of course, her. If he didn't already.

Strangely, the factory staff all seemed to look up to Ben. Perhaps she was missing something, but she wasn't sure what. He was still as cold as an icicle with her. She was hoping to thaw him with a cheap Thai meal she'd grabbed from a takeaway in town with her first pay cheque. At least he'd agreed to pay her weekly, otherwise she'd have been eating dust until the end of the month. Maybe that was a sign he wasn't the devil.

'Having your meeting in the house somewhere, lovey?' Mrs Moon asked.

'Nope.' Lexie gave her a cheeky grin. 'This is my Friday night and if I have to bloody work, I'm not standing on ceremony in his wood-panelled man cave.' Or his mum's stuffy beige house. 'We're holding the meeting in Penny.'

By some fluke she'd managed to catch Ben off-guard, otherwise he surely wouldn't have agreed to it. As a small concession she was gathering non-disgusting plates, as all of hers were chipped and unmatching.

'Your camper van?' Mrs Moon raised an eyebrow. 'That'll be cosy, dear.'

'No, it really won't.' The spotty orange upholstery was almost threadbare, and Ben didn't seem like a man who appreciated bunting. Or indeed much.

'Ooh, what's that pong? Is something off in those sweaty bags of yours? The bin's over there.' Mrs Moon pointed a helpful finger.

Lexie laughed. 'It's Thai food; it's meant to smell like that. Does Ben eat Thai?'

Mrs Moon looked at her strangely. 'Food from Thailand? Hmm. I'm surely it's lovely if you say so, dearie. But do you know Ben? He's about so high, dark hair, usually wears a suit.' The elderly housekeeper's puzzled look lingered.

Lexie put her bags down in dismay.

'You can give it a go, but it's as much as Cory can do to persuade him to touch takeaway pizza. And he'll only have a number five Margherita; not too much cheese. He won't even entertain a chunk of pineapple. Even Mr Moon isn't scared of a Hawaiian. Pineapple's good for your bones, they say.'

Urgh. Stuck-in-the-mud in all areas of his antisocial life. This did not bode well for their evening of discussing change.

'Well, he's got Tom Yum, green curry and sticky rice.'

Mrs Moon looked doubtful. 'Best of luck, lovey. There's a nice cottage pie in the Aga if he pooh-poohs your sticky green Tom.'

Mrs Moon edged her way around the contentious steaming bags, plucked her coat from its peg and shuffled off into the night.

Ten minutes later and Ben was knocking at the door of the vintage orange camper van, which was parked on the driveway of Nutgrass Hall.

The purposeful banging made Lexie jump, and she edged open the fraying floral curtains to double-check it was him. She still hadn't encountered his mother, Mrs Carrington-Noble. She was apparently living in a Cheltenham town house with her toyboy, Carlito, but she'd surely get wind of Lexie's existence any day and blow in like a formidable gale. Lexie gave a sigh of relief when she saw Ben's square jaw through the darkness. The lesser of two evils.

She screeched open the cantankerous sliding door and Ben winced and shook his head.

Lexie jutted out her chin. 'Are you coming in?'

He paused for a moment before folding his reluctant limbs into the vehicle. Lexie tried not to cringe as she saw him adjusting his eyes to the bright colours and sunflower pictures that Aunt Jasmine had découpaged everywhere. Then his nose took over and screwed itself up against the smell of Thai curry. She busied herself with plating up as he grappled with the door, gritting her teeth against his lack of appreciation.

'Right. I thought we were having a meeting.' He'd finished with the door and was staring at her zebra-print slippers. His eyes moved up to the two plates of food on the counter.

'And I thought it was Friday night.' She gave his formal grey suit and briefcase an equally quizzical look and grabbed a plate. 'Help yourself.' She pointed to the other plate as she sank into one of the spotty bench seats either side of the rickety table. 'If it's not too far outside of your comfort zone.'

They eyed each other across the cramped interior of the camper van like two cats in a chintzy orange standoff. Perhaps she should be less spiky – this wasn't even like her. But for some reason, Ben always got her prickles up. She tried to ignore the steam from her defiant breath dancing across the cold air in his direction.

He straightened his jacket as though trying to assert some authority, before grabbing the second plate and establishing himself at the table opposite her. A bag of prawn crackers made a greasy barrier between them.

Lexie winced. Ben was taller than her; of course he was. When he sat down, the socks hanging from the makeshift washing line above their heads dangled right in his line of view. Ruddy typical. She'd had the sense to quickly dry her knickers with a hairdryer and shove them into a drawer before he arrived, but socks took ages. Living in a rusty old van was becoming a pain in the arse, but she wasn't going to admit it.

He cleared his throat and rearranged his position so the socks weren't touching skin.

'You're welcome to use the tumble dryer in the house,' he said quietly, as though mentioning unmentionables wasn't entirely polite.

'No, thank you. I'm managing perfectly well.'

'So I see.'

Lexie tried not to cringe as she saw him do a quick visual sweep. Maybe she should have organised things better before he arrived, but there just wasn't room. Boxes of junk she couldn't be bothered to deal with were stacked precariously on every available surface, most of her clothes were still stuffed into her battered suitcase that just wouldn't shut and ... oh God ... had he just noticed the moss that was growing on the window frame? She hadn't had the heart to make it homeless.

But all this was fine. Just fine. She wasn't here to prove she could organise her own life, after all.

As though trying valiantly to cut through the silence, the room's one dim lamp began buzzing and flashing like it wanted to die.

'And I'll pay for any electricity I use.'

'That's not necessary.' Ben ducked to avoid a bright yellow sock as a draught blew through the van. 'I'm just concerned this way of living isn't entirely ... *practical*.'

Lexie glared at him and speared a prawn with her fork. She'd bloody felt that. 'So you think I'm impractical?' Just

73

like Drew had said. These ill-mannered rich folk were all the same. Just because she didn't sleep in a four-poster and eat foie-sodding-gras for breakfast.

'I didn't say that. It's just ... well ... you don't even have a lavatory.'

The lamp buzzed even louder, swarming Lexie's thoughts. It was perfectly normal to use your employer's toilet, and all of this was just temporary. She would save up some money, and then ... urgh. Whatever.

'If it would be easier for you to move yourself into the house ...'

'I'm not moving in!' Her face was beginning to burn, tears of frustration stinging the backs of her eyes. Desperate to relieve the heat from herself for a moment, she cleared her throat. 'Anyway, you haven't touched your curry. Is it too spicy?' He surely wouldn't miss the element of dare in her voice.

'Of course not. I just don't usually ...'

'Eat anything that isn't beige?' She pushed the bag of spare rice at him. 'Don't worry, this is pretty bland.'

Ouch. Was she giving him the tail-end of the storm that was meant for Drew? The lamp give a final defiant buzz before giving up and throwing them into darkness.

'Shit.' Lexie leaned across and gave the counter a loud smack. It was a manoeuvre she had to carry out at least five times on a normal night, but that had felt especially pleasing. The light coughed back to life and dingy lighting resumed.

They looked at each other anew. Did she see a hint

74

of compassion in his eyes? Or was he just feeling bloody sorry for her?

Ben cleared his throat. 'Let's begin again, shall we.' He moved his plate and spread out some papers from his leather briefcase, which looked like it was worth more than Lexie's entire camper van. 'How have your online projects been progressing this week, and what are the next actions?'

Hmm, so he'd restored himself to business setting – his natural home. They did need to talk shop, but for some reason she found it more amusing when he was a little off balance. Prodding him seemed to ignite a hint of colourful flame.

Then to Lexie's surprise, Ben began eating the curry, forkful by tiny forkful, even though she could see he wasn't used to the heat and some might say it looked a bit pond-y. Should she grab him a cold Singha beer? Not yet. It was fun to watch him flounder in her world, when she was usually trying her best not to drown in the riches of his.

'I've been working on the website, but I need to know more about your story,' Lexie finally felt brave enough to reply.

Unsurprisingly, Ben dived into some automatic spiel about paint manufacture that Lexie had probably heard before.

She nodded and tried not to roll her eyes, understanding why he absolutely shouldn't be left in charge of creating buzzworthy social media posts. And this was probably the reason he needed his mum to find him a date.

Lexie grabbed her battered laptop from behind her seat and pushed Ben's dull paperwork out of the way. It was time to get brave and show him the first draft of the new website.

The screen wobbled to life and she took a deep breath and pulled up her handiwork, together with the new social media profiles. She'd spent time at the factory chatting to the staff and getting a strong sense of who their clients were, and she hoped she'd chosen colours and words that would really draw them in. Everything was beautifully consistent, bright and energising. What Ben would think of it was an entirely different matter.

She watched his face with trepidation as the screen's reflections of wild streaks of paint lit up his orderly face. It was probably time to crack open the beers that had been stashed in Penny's fridge for God knew how long. Lexie grabbed a couple and quickly popped them open, praying messengers didn't actually get shot.

Chapter 11

Ben eyeballed Lexie's work-in-progress website, his face almost unreadable. He swigged his cold beer more quickly than Lexie was expecting. 'It's very ... *intense.*'

'You're a paint company.' She was sticking to her guns on this. She wanted him to be happy with the outcome, but her instincts were telling her if she let him lead the way, they'd end up with something bland. 'Shades of beige just won't cut it.' She cocked her head in the direction of the neutrally painted house.

'It's Toasted Camel. Mother's choice.'

'Whoever toasted a ruddy camel?' she muttered.

'You obviously haven't met her.'

Lexie shook off a sudden chill. 'Look, I've been speaking to your customers online, and they actually aren't all that stuffy. In fact, if you're not careful, they'll be nipping off to your competitors before they die of boredom. I'm just trying to help.'

She held his gaze, determined to show she was serious about her job, she knew her stuff and she actually kind of cared. More so about Mrs Moon, Tom and Cory, of course. If the paint ship sank, they'd all go down with it. 'Just trust me, OK?'

His eyes flicked around Lexie's living quarters, and his raised eyebrows said it all. *How can I trust you to organise my business when you can't even sort out your own mess?*

'I'm on top of this,' she said, perhaps too defensively, as Ben batted a sock out of his face. 'I am!'

'Quite.'

His sarcastic one-wordish-ness was infuriating. As though sensing the blood boiling up towards her head, Ben continued in less confrontational tones.

'OK. I can see you're extremely … creative.' His gaze landed on a box of paperwork that was spilling its contents all over the floor. 'But if I'm to trust you with my online life, maybe I can assist with some of your offline paraphernalia.'

'It's under control,' she insisted, her jaw getting tight. 'You don't need to micro-manage my life. You pay me for the work I do. No additional favours are required.'

He shrugged. 'Well, if you ever want to move some of these boxes into the house to give yourself space …'

'No. Thank you.' She thrust out a leg and shoved one of the offending boxes out of sight. 'I have plenty of room.' Out-of-date bills and papers from a life gone by spumed out and said otherwise.

Keen to deflect the heat again, Lexie moved the topic back to the new branding she was determined to fight for.

She broke the news that if the business was to embrace the new online look she was creating, everything must change with it. From signage to stationery to the artwork on the cans of paint. Lexie could almost see Ben's hackles rising. He snatched up some of his paperwork, holding it like a barrier against this unwanted upheaval.

'There's no need for you to get involved in anything outside of the virtual world.'

'There absolutely is. We can't leave your clients feeling confused – consistency is key. Anyway, didn't you just say there was no point in having your online life in order, if real life wasn't?'

'There is nothing wrong with my *real life*, thank you, Miss Summers.'

'Well, there must be. Otherwise your mother wouldn't have to hook you up with a woman.'

Oh God, how had that popped out? It wasn't even relevant. And why did she keep coming back to that thought? She just wanted to rewind. Preferably to some point before she'd invited him to have their first business meeting in a cramped, steamy van, which really did smell of curry.

He was gripping onto his papers so tightly, she could see the whites of his knuckles.

'Can we just stick to the agenda. Please?' He rubbed the back of his neck.

Something about his tone told her the subject was closed. She was already on shaky enough ground this evening, without causing any more tremors. Although the whole thing was strangely intriguing . . .

79

Ben shook out his papers with an irritated flourish, bringing her back to the present.

'You talked about starting a *blog*.'

Why did he have to say it with that disbelieving tone?

'Yes,' she replied, feeling like an indignant teenager but determined not to cross her arms. 'A blog is a real thing, you know.'

'I'm sure. So sell it to me. What will it be about?' He took another long swig of his Singha and she instinctively grabbed him another one

'Lots of things.' She wanted to stay huffy, but she had so many simmering ideas she knew she'd struggle to contain her excitement.

'Enlighten me.'

The temperamental lamp flickered again and Ben leaned over this time, giving the worktop a firm tap. Hmm, did he usually wear that much aftershave? The strong woody scent teased Lexie's nose and she got herself another beer. She was just being observant, of course. *Smelt good* was about all that could be said for him right then.

'I actually have heaps of ideas for the blog, although you'll probably hate most of them.' She paused for his cutting remark, but it didn't come.

'People love real tales that tug at the heartstrings and bring your family business to life.' She could feel the thrill building inside her. Painting pictures with words was one of the best things about her job. It warmed her right from her fluffy-slippered toes to her belly.

'I want to take your clients on emotional journeys that

will change their hearts for ever. Stories that will have them flocking to you, investing in the magic of your paints.' She was leaning towards him now, the warmth from her enthusiasm radiating into the chilly van.

'When you wrap people up in a story, when you pull them in and cosy your soft blanket of words around their skin, make their senses dance with the woody scent of the breeze, you produce chemical reactions in their brains. You change the very make-up of their bloodstream.'

Their faces were inexplicably close now. He must have leaned in too, drawn in by her stream of energy.

Suddenly all too aware, she shook her head and they both moved backwards.

'Er, sorry. I got a tad impassioned. Not sure where that came from.' And what the bloody hell was that thing about woody scents? He surely knew that was inspired by his aftershave. This was her boss! And mostly an annoying one.

'No problem.' He loosened his collar. 'Very spicy, all this Thai food.'

'Yes! Anywaaaay.' Right, what was the rest of it? 'Maybe I could blog about home makeovers.' She glanced towards the house. 'Gorgeous images to make you Insta-worthy and pinnable.' Great, she was back on track.

'Right. Well, I can do without the earache from the old fox if you start tarting up her precious walls.'

'Maybe you could introduce me to clients who've done big makeovers with your paints?'

'I'm not sure I want to . . .'

'It's important!' She watched as he wrote it down with three question marks next to it.

'You also need to keep me up to date with the industry, so I have plenty to shout about on social media.'

He looked pensive for a moment. Was he dreaming up more excuses?

'Well, there is an event coming up, but you would thoroughly hate it. I'll update you afterwards, if you're desperate.'

'Afterwards is no good; social media wants the gossip as it happens. Don't push me out.' She took a swig of her beer and clopped the bottle down on the table for effect.

He sighed. 'It's the Paint Association weekend conference in London in a few weeks. It's generally a room full of balding old dullards wittering on about the latest technology in coatings. It's unlikely to be your scene.'

'Sounds perfect. I'll take loads of photos and jazz it up somehow. That's my job.'

'I wasn't inviting you.'

'Oh.' She sank backwards in her chair. This was exhausting. 'Are you always going to put up a fight? I can't do this if you're not with me. I thought you took your business seriously.' She was beginning to learn he responded best to a challenge – much like herself.

'I just can't see us ...' He appeared to be picking his words carefully. 'Spending a weekend together without murdering each other.'

She glared at him across the dimly lit van, still not sure when he was exercising his dry sense of humour or when he was just being a pompous twat.

'There are at least two reasonably sharp kitchen knives in this camper van and I haven't killed you yet.'

Was the edge of his mouth trying not to twitch into a smile?

'Anyway, it would be the perfect chance for you to tell me all about your mother's matchmaking,' she dared to quip.

The twitchy smile turned flat. 'I'd rather extract my own eyeballs with a curry-covered fork.' He pushed his plate away, knocking the bag of prawn crackers so its jagged contents began to spill. 'That nosey brother of mine is as bad as our interfering mother. He should start wearing Chanel No. 5 and palazzo pants.'

'Is it true? You need to marry a suitably rich woman by the end of the year, if you want your mother to hand over the business rather than sell it to a stranger?'

'Right. So you know all of that.' His neck was starting to redden. Maybe he thought it was ridiculous too. 'Well, I don't want you blogging about it.'

'As if I would. I mean, as long as you keep me in the loop on the world of balding men wittering on about topcoats, I won't need to delve into anything too personal.'

It was cheeky, but she got the feeling she would have to be. And if she could just topple this small domino . . .

'You actually want to come to the paint conference?'

'Why not? We can get networking and show off the new branding. You'll have updated business cards by then, and . . . ' She could feel the wind beginning to lift her sails again, in the chilly damp of the van. She stopped herself mid flow, concerned he might try to snatch it.

'Branding.' He let the word hang. 'Did I agree to that?'

She grabbed a handful of prawn crackers and filled her mouth before she swore at him. And why was he looking at her like that? She thrust the bag back in his direction. Two shiny blue foil packets rolled out.

He looked at the packets and then back up at her eyes. 'You say branding is all about consistency?'

'Yes,' she replied carefully.

'And you're big on consistency.'

Was that a dig? 'What do you mean?'

The twitchy smile was back now, at both edges this time. 'Your nose stud always matches your mascara.'

She touched her nose, a little self-consciously. Her theme was blue today, although she hadn't purposely coordinated with the fortune cookies.

'It adds a bit of anticipation to the day, wondering what your latest colour scheme will be,' said Ben.

Lexie pursed her lips, unimpressed he was finding such sport in her careful accessorising. What was wrong with having a bit of order among the chaos? Well, she could add *observant* to the list of things she was learning about His Standoffish Highness. Along with *didn't smell bad* and *eyes that looked a bit like little globes*, now she came to think of it.

Lexie reached across the table and collected her fortune cookie, pulling it out and throwing the offending blue packet towards the bin. She'd always loved the messages in these things, but she felt silly reading hers in front of Ben.

'Go on. I'm intrigued.' He nodded to the sugary shell in her hands. 'What's your fortune? Will you get your own way, or not?'

She let out a huff. 'I don't know. What does yours say?'

He took the other packet and opened it, tidying the shiny blue foil into his pocket. They held their shells, not taking their eyes off each other, as though guarding against cheating.

'Ladies first,' said Ben.

'We'll open them together.'

They cracked their shells, and Lexie wondered what she was even wishing for. She wanted her own way about the home makeovers, branding and going to the conference; but a weekend with narky Ben? On the other hand, it might be better than hanging around here, waiting for his mother to rock up and rollock her.

With a mutual nod they opened their hands, uncurled the tiny slips of paper and read aloud.

'*Alone you are weak, but together you are strong*,' they said in unison.

'Are they meant to say the same thing?' asked Ben.

'Not really. But, you know. It could happen.' Lexie believed in signs, but she wasn't going to be laughed at. 'So I guess we're meant to go to London.'

'Because a piece of mass-produced paper says so? Hardly. Anyway, it's getting late.' He gathered up his paperwork, not looking at her now. Was he in a mood again? It was always so hard to tell. He was antisocial, and hanging around with her for a weekend was never going to be his thing. But it was for work; maybe he'd come around.

Lexie stood up from the table and busied herself with tidying away the plates.

'I'll take those to the dishwasher.'

'No need; I'll manage.' She dropped them onto the draining board, noticing that neither of them had eaten much with all the tension of the evening.

He held up his hands in surrender.

As he bent to retrieve the foil from her fortune cookie and place it in the bin, an idea struck her. Colour schemes. Consistency. Together we are strong. A concept for the first blog post was beginning to quiver to life. She would draft it tonight while the thoughts were still fresh, and hit publish on the website while the beer was giving her courage. It was time to get this ball rolling.

They said their stilted goodbyes and she hurried him out of the door before her muse grew wings and disappeared. And he definitely wasn't that muse. Was he?

Chapter 12

Lexie was sitting in her camper van feeling like a girl on fire.

She'd survived her first Friday night meeting with Ben. And, despite all the awkwardness of the encounter, it had fuelled her imagination for Carrington Paints' first blog post. She'd worked well into the night, finalising the website, writing the blog and pressing publish. It had been both terrifying and exhilarating, and she was buzzing on double-strength tea and stale doughnuts as she worked to promote the blog post.

Ben had surely given her a greenish light to get on with things last night. Anyway, this was her domain. He'd probably never even look at the website again. There was no harm in getting on with her job. She passed off the strange internal jittering as elation and excess caffeine.

Lexie pulled back Penny's dog-eared net curtain and smiled out at the sunshine. Yes, it was a beautiful day. Nothing could possibly go wrong.

She looked back at her laptop and smiled at the stats. The blog post was doing well. She'd been posting it all over social media and drumming up excitement. It was driving traffic to the new website, and people were staying to have a look around. And more importantly, they were being inspired to buy paint. Those precious numbers would hopefully keep Ben off her back if he launched into another of his doubt-fests.

Yes, this was the part of her job that made her feel alive. Worthy. And now that feeling was starting to seep back into her, she didn't want to lose it.

She read the post again, still excited by the angle she'd taken. She'd written the blog from her own point of view, as the newcomer. The inexperienced Alice in this Wonderland of paints. That way, readers could come on this journey with her. She'd be their multicoloured fly on the beige-painted walls.

Consider me your woman on the inside.

It added a kind of intrigue that she hoped would build a loyal following.

The first blog was about her colourful arrival at Nutgrass Hall. The peacocks, the explosions, the rebellious orange van. Her bright and simple existence in this luxurious but muted realm. Her dreams of injecting some colour of her own. And then the fortune cookie.

'Together you are strong.' Could it be a sign, wonderful readers? Should I throw my inspired thoughts into the mix? Because

88

next week I hope to share exclusive photos of clients' home makeovers (think palatial!). And then how about we go behind the scenes at the London Paint Conference? Wish me luck ...

Her brave promises were hooking in new subscribers. Now all she had to do was convince Ben.

She ran her fingers along Penny's flaking paintwork and her eyes flicked to the Carrington Paints brochure on the table next to her laptop. She'd nabbed the brochure from the factory and now that her creative brain was awake, she was awash with wild thoughts. Could she tempt Ben into adding some new shades? Or even completely new ranges. A bit of Cheeky Cherrybomb, or La La Lemon? And chalk-style paints for furniture ...

But no, that was definitely the sugar talking. She swiped a stray blob of jam from her plate. New colour schemes were way out of her domain and Ben would never accept it. Not to mention ... Urgh. She shuddered. The brothers' notorious mother. Now the website was public, it was only a matter of time before Lexie would have another stubborn face to prove herself to. At best.

The sharp *Hollyoaks* ringtone from her mobile made her jolt.

'Sky!' she shouted, to no one in particular. Her errant little sister hadn't been answering her calls for the entire week and a half that Lexie had been freezing her bum off at Nutgrass Hall. Her chewed giraffe-print nails bore testament to her nerves about the whole Billy-Bob commune situation.

Lexie swiped to answer. 'Thank God. Where have you been? Talk about stressing me out!'

Sky treated Lexie to the usual sarcastic groan.

'Jeez, Lex. Give me a break. There's, like, hardly any signal here in Phoenix Fields. I live in a yurt, not some fancy-pants mansion.'

'I camp on the drive.' Lexie stood up in protest, swiftly banging her head on the old metal roof. At least the socks were hanging outside today. 'And why did you move in? I told you to stay put until we'd talked about it.'

Lexie felt her cheeks flaming pure Cherrybomb. And much like a bomb, her head was nearing explosion. Since she'd heard from her parents that Sky had moved out, it had taken all her energy not to go back up there and rescue her.

Her sister sighed. 'Just because you're shit at love, doesn't mean I have to be. It's my life; stop trying to strangle it. If you stifle our sisterly bond, it will never thrive. Let me breathe, Lexie, so our relationship can flourish like a rose bush.'

Lexie's face froze into a gawp. Sky had almost started to sound convincing until the thing about the rose bush. Those were not her sister's words. That had *scary cult brainwashing* written all over it.

'Anyway, I didn't have a tantrum when you and Inkie-pants flew off to Shanghai with your smelly backpacks. I never rang to have a go at you for leaving me with our loopy parents.'

'They're not loopy! Mum's just … *different*. And it was Chiang Mai, not Shang-bloody-hai.' She let out a sigh, her colour draining back to Eggshell. 'But I see your point. When I was your age I was kipping on a beach with only two

T-shirts and a pair of flipflops.' And ending up with a tattoo she feared would never really suit her skin. She tugged the strands of her pixie cut. 'I suppose you should make your own mistakes.'

Lexie thought of the cock-ups that plagued the end of her own first adventure and winced up at the skies. 'Just don't come back in a police car.'

'I promise. And hey, nothing ventured comes to those who wait, as they say.'

Lexie was pretty sure nobody said that, but she had long since stopped trying to unravel her sister's jumbled sentiments. So her little Sky bird was flying the nest. Living with zero money in even less luxury than a rusty old camper could only end badly; but who was she to lecture right now?

'Look – any problems, call me. OK? Or send smoke signals, or whatever you do. And don't catch crabs.'

They said their goodbyes, and Lexie set her sister free to do whatever communal folk did of a Saturday morning in spring. Gathering leaves for toilet paper, and the like. She shuddered. Or who knew. Maybe Sky would actually be happy. At least she wouldn't find her bloke ring-shopping with Tabby what's-her-bottom, and there surely couldn't be any snobbery about money.

Just as Lexie was folding herself back into her faded orange seat, another dreadful noise made her bounce back up. What the hell? It sounded like tyres screeching across stones, and then ... squawking? Then the angry beep of a car horn, constant, as though a fist had punched it and wasn't giving up.

Lexie twitched back the net curtains, almost too scared to look. Nutgrass Hall had been relatively peaceful since her arrival, and she kind of liked it that way. But deep down she'd known trouble would turn up at some point. Trouble always did.

An expensive, pearly white four-by-four skidded to a halt on the driveway. Lexie winced as its tyres sprayed up gravel like bullets. It was one of those pretentious off-road vehicles that had probably never seen the likes of mud.

'Those DRATTED biiiiiiiiiirds.'

The voice erupted through the opening car door like a war cry, followed promptly by its owner. It could only be the notorious chief, Mrs Carrington-Noble. Mother to Ben and Cory, and owner of the manor. Lexie gulped.

She was much taller than Lexie had expected, although she carried her bony frame in a stoop, as though a heavy weight was forcing her down from the shoulders. It was a shame for her well-cut linen suit, which didn't quite know how to sit. The jacket flapped open like the terrible wings of a buzzard.

And bloody hell, she was coming Lexie's way. She strode across the drive like a woman on a mission, unperturbed by the gravelly stones trying to shrink away beneath her pointy court shoes.

The peacocks had caught up with their assailant. Lexie cringed back behind the curtains, wondering if they were going to commence one of their frenzied attacks. Would they give themselves a colonic irrigation all over that sparkling white Range Rover? Or would Mrs Thingy-Noble pull out a hunting rifle and splatter their guts all over Tom's neat lawn? Lexie ducked down, one eye peeking through the netting.

But the peacocks fanned out behind their mistress like an exquisite army, marching onwards towards the camper van, a turquoise show of solidarity. Mrs Carrington-Noble shooed them with jutting arms, just a few determined stragglers skulking in her shade.

'Benediiiiiiiiict!'

The woman was shrieking over her shoulder towards the house, where some of the windows were open to invite in the fresh spring air. Well, at least it had been fresh until this fog of bother swept in. And who was Benedict? Lexie prayed he was the person this venom was directed at, and not . . . oh God.

The mother was hammering at the door of the van. What should she do? There was nowhere to hide if this woman meant business.

Lexie slid off her bench seat and cowered under the table. How was she going to deal with this?

Chapter 13

Lexie's stomach was tying itself into a new knot with each bang on Penny the camper's poor old vintage door.

Lexie knew she should get up and face Mrs Carrington-Noble, but the longer she left it the more awkward it became. Lexie was a squatter on this driveway, and an employee Mrs Carrington-Noble had not even sanctioned. The brothers had insisted their mother rarely interfered in the day-to-day running of the business, but she was throwing herself all in now.

As Mrs Carrington-Noble thundered around the outside of the van, Lexie's ears were on high alert.

'What are these dreadful rags?'

Damn it, she'd found her makeshift washing line.

'And this?'

Mrs Carrington-Noble was pulling at her umbilical cord – the orange electrical cable that was tying Lexie to the house like a pathetic foetus. Quaking on the floor of the van,

Lexie felt about as small as she had in that jewellery shop; surrounded by pompous haters and diamonds when she'd been dripping wet and dumped.

Maybe she should start up the van and chug out of there. Living on this grandiose drive like a second-class misfit was never going to work. Who had she been trying to kid? And maybe Sky really did need her.

Lexie forced her weak legs to stand, yanked the plug on the electric cable and pushed the end back through the window until she heard it thud onto the gravel. At least the noise had distracted Mrs Carrington-Noble.

But, damn it, those peacocks were pecking at the thrift-shop woollens she'd left drying on the clothes horse outside. She would have to leave them. She clambered over the seats into the front of the van and searched for her keys. Just as she was twisting them in the ignition and praying Penny wouldn't backfire, Lexie heard another war march across the stones.

'Benedict! What in God's good name is going on here? And why do I have to hear about family business second-hand from *factory staff*?'

Lexie craned her head, intrigued to know who this mystery Benedict was. When her eyes landed on all six riled feet of Ben, she couldn't help but guffaw. She'd assumed he was a Benjamin; no wonder he shortened it. Mrs Carrington-Noble really did have illusions of grandeur. What on earth was Cory short for?

'Mother, don't yell. Come inside.'

Lexie should drive off and leave these not-so-noble

people to their bunfight. But there was something quite captivating about a stern Ben in an open-collared white shirt. She was unexpectedly transfixed.

'Why would I want to go inside? The travelling circus is clearly out here. Who is this girl and why the hell is she spreading our business in *blog posts*?'

Oh crap, she'd seen it. Well, that explained the bewildering dawn raid.

'Because that's her job,' said Ben, with a firmness that was almost touching.

'Says who?'

'Says the person who's in charge of giving people jobs,' he replied.

'We'll see about that. Now where is she?'

'Lexie?' Ben made his way around the van, squinting into windows as he called her name.

Lexie tried to duck in the driver's seat, but it was futile. He could see her shrinking down. He looked through the window and down to her hand, which was clamped onto the keys in the ignition.

'The gate's locked,' he shouted through the glass. 'So you may as well join us.' He lifted his palms towards the skies. 'It's lovely weather for it.'

Mrs Carrington-Noble had seen Lexie too; there was no escaping it. She only wished she wasn't wearing her sari fabric pyjamas and a bobble hat that made her look like the guy from *Where's Wally*. Well, the van had been chilly. Lexie forced open the rusty door with a screech and tried to look businesslike as she lowered her zebra slippers onto the stones.

Ben's mother paused in her fight with a peacock over one of Lexie's woollens and gave her a pointed stare.

Lexie felt the return of Cherrybomb to her cheeks. She couldn't have felt more out of place in the shadow of this Downton Abbey of a house, with these people who dressed so bloody formally for this early on a Saturday.

Mrs Carrington-Noble moved her foxy, glaring eyes to her son. 'You cannot invite stray women to live on our grounds, nor delve into our private business, without my say-so. What will people think?'

'Which people, Mother? The precious racquets club?'

There was a short silence. Lexie held her breath.

'You know full well I don't play racquets anymore. Not since ...' The woman's voice faltered.

'Sorry, it's the polo club we're aspiring to impress these days. My mistake.'

There was obviously some personal battle going on, which Lexie had no desire to be a part of. 'I should just ...' She pointed a bitten giraffe-print nail at the van.

'Not so fast.' The vulture-faced woman strode across the gravel, sending tremors through Lexie's bobble hat. She landed in front of Lexie, her neat auburn-and-grey bob trembling like her indignant cheeks. 'Who are you, exactly?'

Lexie gave a feeble wave and introduced herself. It was clearly no time for a friendly handshake.

'And why are you camping on my driveway dressed like a vagabond?'

The peacocks tried to gather behind their mistress, but Ben shooed them away.

'Lexie's our new social media manager. She pins and tweets, and pokes people on Facebook—'

'Poking's not a thing anymore,' Lexie whispered.

'She's also in charge of blogging and trolling—'

'No! Definitely not trolling. Trolling's a bad thing,' Lexie corrected him. 'You see why he needs someone to sort these things out?'

She threw a hopeful half-smile at Mrs Carrington-Noble, slightly disappointed at her compulsion to please this mean lady. But she was the gatekeeper to Lexie's precarious fresh start, and she'd been beginning to enjoy her new role. In all honesty, she needed it. Because what else did she have?

But the smile was met with a scowl so frosty the woman would have looked at home with a carrot as a nose, if the weather had been any cooler.

'And why do we need such interference?' The woman addressed her son.

'Because it's the twenty-first century, so Cory keeps telling me. The business will apparently die without an online presence. Lexie's here to save us.' He gave a sarcastic salute.

Oh right. So Ben was standing up for her to wind his mother up rather than because he was starting to believe in her. She'd thought it was too good to be true, but she'd take what backup she could. Those peacocks were still eyeing her from a distance.

'So you published a blog post?' Ben asked Lexie.

'Yes!' Lexie was glad of the change of tack. 'It's all about … colours.' Oh Christ, that was feeble. She was fast beginning to feel like fox food.

'And about how you bothered my peacocks, duped my sons and invited yourself to set up a gypsy camp on my driveway.'

Lexie gulped. 'That wasn't exactly my message, it was more about . . . ' But she couldn't arrange her thoughts.

'How she's here to inject some life into us all,' Ben added.

So he had read it. Did she sense some irritation in his voice? But he hadn't marched out here to tell her to take the post down. Nor the colourful new website.

'And you can't say she's not doing that.' Ben swept his arms around the scene. A bright orange camper van, a trail of half-chewed woollens, a quaking Lexie in bobble hat and PJs, and two grumpy peacocks shaking their tailfeathers in distaste.

'Is this thing even roadworthy?' Mrs Carrington-Noble slapped Penny's ancient paintwork and Lexie tried to stifle a gasp.

'My paperwork is very much in order,' said Lexie, with at least two fingers crossed behind her back.

Ben raised an eyebrow.

'Well, this heap of metal is making my estate look shabby.'

'If you disapprove of her taking up temporary residence on the gravel, we have enough spare rooms to solve the refugee crisis.' He waved an arm towards the house. 'But I'll warn you, she grumbles a lot about beige and I wouldn't trust her near a paintbrush.'

'I forbid you to redecorate my house!' Mrs Carrington-Noble glared at Lexie.

Ben seemed to be enjoying himself now. 'Oh, really?

That's such a shame because I do hate all those pompous heads and imposing horses.'

'You will not disrespect your ancestors,' his mother rasped through tightly pinched lips, her red lipstick leaking bloody lines along her wrinkles.

'Ah, the *ancestors*.' Lexie could see Ben's twitchy smile. 'Lexie would soon have your paintings posing on a feature wall of shocking pink. She tells me bright colours are all the rage.'

'I will not have it!' Mrs Carrington-Noble stamped a court shoe into the gravel and the stray peacocks made their final flap back to the safety of their pride.

Then, as if knowing exactly when to bring imminent disaster back from the brink, Ben tapped his mum's arm jovially.

'I totally agree. Let's leave Lexie out on the driveway, where she can't make too much trouble.' He gave Lexie a swift look. And was that a wink? 'I'm taking her to see some of our best clients on Monday, so she can interfere with their makeovers instead.'

Ooh, did he just agree to letting her have her own way about something? It was probably only to wind his mother up, but still.

'Now, let's get you a nice cup of tea. Mrs M has probably got some weed or other for times of stress.' He rubbed his mother's tense shoulders and began to manoeuvre her away from the fracas.

The stooping woman almost looked frail next to the masculine frame of her son, as he led her by the elbow towards the house. Mrs Carrington-Noble's feet were suddenly less steady now on the wobbly stones, as though the adrenaline was seeping from her. Although something told Lexie she wouldn't be deflated for long.

Did Lexie have the energy for this fight? She'd been trying to run away from being made to feel small by folk who valued money over manners. Had she just jumped right from the frying pan into the fire?

And yet she was desperate to prove she wasn't flaky. If she fled now, Drew would be right. And what impression would it give to her little sister, when she was trying to demonstrate the importance of holding down a proper job? Plus she needed the money, and somewhere to park her worldly belongings. She wasn't exactly a woman with options.

She would stick it out. For now. At least Cory had given her the heads-up on Mrs Carrington-Noble's curious matchmaking, so she didn't accidentally get in the way or look too jolly with her precious Benedict. If this was the trouble one parking space and a blog post could cause, then who knew what the woman was capable of.

And mini hooray – Lexie had won the battle with Ben over visiting clients. Monday might even be pleasant if Ben wasn't too standoffish. She'd just have to pray that Mrs Nosey Fox Carrington-Noble didn't come back and snoop while she was gone.

Chapter 14

'What. The. Hell?'

Those were the only words Lexie could think of when she and Ben arrived back at the gates of Nutgrass Hall on Monday evening, after a day out taking photos of clients' home makeovers.

'What. The. Actual. HELL!' The words kept going round her head on a loop, while her stomach tried to flip its contents into her gasping mouth.

'Lexie, I'm terribly sorry. I don't know what to say.'

As they stood on the gravel looking down at the pile of junk that blocked their entrance, Lexie didn't know whether to cry or scream. Penny the camper van had never looked so small – probably because she had never been so small. She was about the size of a coffin, which was perhaps a suitable description. Because Penny the camper van was dead.

'She's been murdered. Ransacked and bloody well murdered!'

The rest of Lexie's life had been unceremoniously dumped next to the crushed cube of a van. Boxes of overflowing paperwork, with a few strays frolicking in the breeze. Her battered suitcase containing her thrift-shop woollens. A few pots and pans. And . . . oh. Delightful. Some threatening paperwork about fines for Penny's seriously overdue MOT, unroadworthy condition and invalidated insurance. Not to mention a bill for vehicle crushing, sanctioned with the signature of Mrs Carrington-Noble. Money really could arrange anything, no matter how unorthodox. And perhaps without it you were screwed.

Ben put his coat around Lexie's shivering shoulders and pressed the intercom buzzer on the gate.

'I'll call Cory to come and help me with these boxes, and I'll ask Mrs Moon to get the kettle on. Her chamomile tea is going to take a hammering.'

In a daze, Lexie felt herself being shepherded through the grand gates towards the house. The neat rows of white narcissi bowed delicately at her passing, not a single head out of place. Tom was on his hands and knees tending to them, and he tipped his cap at Lexie when he saw her.

'Lovely job, Tom,' Ben said, pointing at the flowers.

'They always pop out to say 'ello in spring. New beginnings, ya see.'

And with that, Lexie let go of the tidal wave of tears that had been building in her chest, and Ben ushered her across the driveway and into the house.

Ten minutes later and Lexie was huddled in a huge beige armchair in the exceedingly beige living room at

Nutgrass Hall. She had three of Mrs Moon's hand-knitted blankets around her and the log fire was on in defiance of Mrs Carrington-Noble's regulations, but she still felt cold to her bones. That dreadful woman had arranged for her home to be towed away and crushed, presumably by flaunting her money for favours judging by the speed it had all happened. Lexie and Ben had only been out for the day.

Poor Penny was now a sorry cube of steel probably destined for a future as a batch of baked-bean cans. And exactly what Lexie's future would be was suddenly under hot dispute. Mrs Moon was plying her with raspberry ripple sponge, Cory was full of his usual easy surf-dude smiles and even Ben was trying his best to be affable. It seemed they had a common goal in mind, and Lexie was running out of fight to resist it.

'Just move in, Lex. There's plenty of room,' said Cory.

Ben cleared his throat. 'Yes, it does seem like the best suggestion. It's the least we can do, under the circumstances.'

'Mrs Carrington-Noble will hit the roof,' said Lexie.

A wicked smile crossed Cory's lips. 'Exactly! And it would serve the old fox right.'

'I told her if you weren't living on the driveway you'd be in the house. She had fair warning and she's brought it on herself.'

Ben was right, of course. But Lexie didn't feel any joy at the thought of living even further inside that woman's unwelcoming womb.

'She'd kick me out as soon as look at me.'

'I can assure you, once I've had firm words with her she absolutely won't.' Ben's jaw was quite possibly the squarest Lexie had ever seen it.

'If you go, we all go,' said Mrs Moon, handing Lexie another slice of cake. 'And I'll tell her that myself.'

To Lexie's surprise, Cory, and even Ben, were nodding.

'I know she seems like a mean old huntress at times,' Mrs Moon continued. 'But she just worries about losing things.' She looked across to Ben with a small sadness. 'Again.'

'She clings on too tightly,' said Cory.

She strangles things, thought Lexie. She remembered Sky accusing her of the very same. Perhaps she could almost relate, as much as it irked her. Sky should give Mrs Carrington-Noble the lecture about letting love grow like a rose bush, or whatever it was.

The others were having a conversation about which part of the house would be best for Lexie.

'Hey, I haven't even agreed to live here. I'm just not sure I'd feel . . . comfortable.' She looked around at the grandiose room with its high ceilings and cold marble floor. It was beautiful, but just so intimidating. Those enormous gleaming chandeliers were a far cry from the paper lampshades in the three-bed council house she'd grown up in; she and Sky sharing a bunkbed while Aunt Jasmine nabbed the spare room when it was too chilly to sleep in Penny the camper. Lexie swallowed a threatening sob.

'You could share Mrs Moon's cottage,' Cory suggested.

'But what about Mr Moon?' the housekeeper replied.

Lexie still couldn't work out why they looked at Mrs M so strangely whenever he was mentioned. Perhaps they really disliked him.

'You could take our old quarters here in the house,' said Mrs Moon.

'Or I can pay for you to stay in a hotel in town, if you prefer,' said Ben. 'But it won't be practical to take all these boxes with you.' He pointed to her various piles of life. 'If your stuff is going to be here, you may as well inhabit a room with it.'

She did want to keep an eye on her papers, that was for sure. She couldn't have people digging into her past. And she didn't want Ben paying hotel fees for her. Forking out for hotel rooms herself wasn't an option either, especially with these new fines and crushing fees on her back.

'Maybe we can even sort some of these papers out,' said Ben.

'It's all in perfect order!' said Lexie.

Ben looked out of the window at the hunk of metal that used to be Penny.

'OK, maybe not *perfect* order.' Lexie crossed her arms over her chest.

Cory stood up. 'Look, I'm going to put some of this stuff in Mrs Moon's old quarters upstairs before we have an open-fire disaster.' He nodded towards the crackling fireplace. 'If you choose to sleep up there with it tonight, then whatever.'

He made it sound so easy. Lexie watched as he began moving boxes, and Ben rolled up his sleeves and joined in the production line.

'Well, hey, just because I'm a woman ...' Lexie jumped up and rolled up her own sleeves, not wanting to be out-muscled. Moving a few boxes upstairs for now couldn't hurt, and it was getting late. She didn't have anywhere else to put them, or even anything else to transport them with, other than her skinny arms.

As they trudged up and down the stairs, Lexie felt some of her lost adrenaline creeping back. Some of the fight that had drained from her since finding her life in a heap. Ben and Cory were right. She was homeless from their mother's own doing. Mrs Carrington-Noble owed her a roof over her head and if it got on the woman's nerves, that served her right too. And it would only be temporary. Once Lexie had paid these fines she'd have money to pay proper rent some-where. In the meantime, she could give Ben a contribution for staying here.

Plus she'd have a new camper van in a few weeks' time. Ben was going to replace it and charge it to his mother – Lexie had agreed to that much. But Lexie wanted it to be equally vintage – as close to her darling Penny as possible. It would need to be sourced, which would take time.

Ben had also offered to pay the fines, of course. But Lexie had reluctantly concluded that that mess was of her own making. If she wasn't so disorganised with her life, so rubbish with money and fearful of paperwork, Penny's doc-uments would have been up to date.

'If you're moving in and having to put up with Ben for even more hours, we should probably give you a pay rise,' Cory joked. 'You'll be like a fly on the wall.'

More hours with Ben. Wasn't she meant to be staying out of the way and not ruffling Mrs Carrington-Noble's match-making feathers? Fly in the ointment, more like. This did not bode well.

Ben dropped a box inside Lexie's new room and let out a huff. 'Am I that dreadful that we have to pay people to put up with me?' he asked his brother.

'Well, Lexie probably wouldn't choose to hang around with you. The girl's got better taste.' Cory thrust an arm in Lexie's direction.

Ben seemed to contemplate her for a long moment as she stood in the doorway. She felt self-conscious in her purple pinstripe suit trousers, her top half stripped down to her vest top after all the heavy lifting. Her face must have been pink with the effort and there was a definite sheen across her chest. Why was he looking at her like that?

'Her taste is very . . . consistent.' Ben nodded towards her nose stud, which perfectly matched her mascara and tied in with her vest top. 'She's amber today.'

Lexie tried her best not to change to red. Why did his scrutiny cause such a sudden heat?

'I don't want a pay rise,' Lexie said firmly.

'There you go, mate. Maybe you're not so bad.' Cory slapped his brother on his white-shirted back, and she noticed for the first time Ben's loosened tie was actually quite colourful. And he looked pretty chiselled under the well-fitting cotton.

She shook herself down. Maybe it was a good thing his mother was concentrating on finding him a woman. Getting hot under the vest top about her totally unsuitable boss was not part of this already ludicrous situation.

She kicked the final box over the threshold and vowed to find herself a seriously cold shower.

Chapter 15

There was no mistaking it: that peacock was definitely glaring at her. Lexie had noticed it more and more since Mrs Carrington-what's-her-chops had first shown her face the other day. The day when she had undoubtedly decided to wait until Lexie was off the premises and have her camper van towed and turned into a hexa-bloody-hedron.

Lexie stuck her tongue out at the peacock's haughty pointed face from the safety of her new living quarters, and adjusted her tie-dye headscarf. She'd heard Mrs Moon mutter that the spots on the peacocks' tails were like the boss lady's all-seeing eyes, and it wouldn't have surprised her. Mrs Carrington-Noble had probably installed bird-cam.

The woman was on the prowl again today, of course. Lexie knew that from the peacock fanfare and screeching tyres she'd heard earlier on. In the few days since Lexie had moved into Nutgrass Hall, Mrs Carrington-Noble had been creating increasingly more absurd excuses to stalk over and mark her territory like a passive-aggressive cat. The woman was on a warning from Ben to be civil, but she was finding novel ways to make Lexie feel like a veritable pig in a poke.

So, Lexie would just stay out of the way. She was determined to make this room her sanctuary, for the short space of time she'd vowed to be here. A safe place to get on with her work, stay out of trouble and earn her living as a respectable and non-flaky employee until her new camper van was ready and she could go and camp elsewhere. Easy. She had no interest in being dragged into anything else.

She settled herself at the long table, which she'd pulled across to the window and draped in a length of bright orange-and-pink Thai silk from her travels. Lexie had commandeered this as her desk, and it was the only pop of colour in the room. She was getting used to her new space, with its huge four-poster bed at one end, and a living area with cream sofas and a coffee table at the other. And it was a huge relief to have her own en-suite bathroom, rather than legging it to the leisure centre for a sneaky shower.

But it was all so pale, and she'd never liked that fussy damask pattern. Its pompous little leaves seemed to form part of a club that would never unfurl enough to let her sort in. Not that she wanted to be in, of course. Out was perfectly acceptable. Out was where she belonged; just minding her own quiet business.

Boooonng. Well, OK. Quiet apart from that grandmother clock in the corner. The one that made sporadic tick-tock-tutting noises at her, interspersed with ferocious bongs that made her skin jolt. Lexie checked the time. Fifteen minutes until she'd need to creep down the stairs for her work catch-up with Ben. In the meantime, she was in planning mode. She had her laptop open and was looking at the photos she'd taken of the Carrington Paints makeovers, from her field trip to rich clients' houses with Ben.

Yes. She could turn this into a fantastic blog post, and use lots of fun quotes for social media posts too. She wrote down ideas on multi-coloured sticky notes and stuck them along her desk. The houses they'd visited had been impressive, and yet . . .

She ran her fingers over the Carrington Paints catalogue, which she had open beside her laptop. Something was still lacking. The sad thing was that none of its colours were that interesting in isolation. Perhaps with a bit of mixing and a dash of something else. A sprinkle of colourful inspiration from a far-off land, a spice-filled souk or a riotous sunset . . . She eyed the lifeless walls for a second. No. All of this was just temporary, and she had no business making her mark. She was just employed to spice up their online world, and she was only hanging on to that much by a beige thread and a few white fibs.

Big ideas were for people who cared about big money. And she didn't intend to be one of those. So why were her hands busy cutting out swatches of coloured material and paper-clipping them to the pages of the Carrington Paints book? Urgh. Wandering minds could get into all sorts of mess.

'Alexiiiiiiiiiis!'

Lexie jumped out of her seat with an overwhelming urge to hide. It was Mrs Carrington-Noble's voice barking through her door. Damn it! She'd thought she was safe here, but the insistent knocking warned her otherwise.

'Ermmm.' Oh help. What was she meant to do about her creativity corner? Not that she was doing anything wrong just yet, but if idle minds could be read . . .

Before Lexie had time to stash anything, her uninvited guest burst into the room. She was holding a wodge of papers to her chest like an inspector with a clipboard.

'A-lex-is.' Mrs Carrington-Noble stamped out the beat like a huffy horse as she moved towards Lexie.

Alexis wasn't even her name. It seemed she had a thing about getting it wrong on purpose, and wouldn't be persuaded that Lexie wasn't short for anything.

Lexie gritted her teeth and ignored it, to save her precious breath. 'Can I . . . help you?'

Mrs Carrington-Noble stopped and looked around the room, blinking. 'Just keeping a check on my grounds, as a landlady is entitled to do. What are you up to in here? What's different?' Her foxy grey eyes squinted around. 'You know you're not allowed to redecorate or change anything?'

Get off my land or I'll wee on you, was clearly what the woman wanted to say. Lexie hovered in front of her multi-coloured desk of sin, hoping she could save it.

'I don't think you're meant to be in here,' Lexie said with a sigh, although she'd come to learn that arguing didn't get her very far.

'What's all this about?' asked Mrs Carrington-Noble, making a move towards the desk. 'Is that my paint catalogue?'

Tick-tock-tuuuut. The grandmother clock spat out one of its unexplained, impromptu warnings which seemed to surprise the older woman. She took a step backwards.

'Anyway, I was looking for Benedict.' Mrs Carrington-Noble sniffed the air, as though searching for traces. Lexie wondered how she could smell anything over the richly overpowering layers of Chanel No. 5 she must have bathed in. No wonder she was always coughing.

'Well, you won't find him in here. But I'm due in a meeting with him now, so if you'll excuse me.' Lexie turned around and grabbed her laptop and paperwork. As she made her way towards the still open door, praying her intruder would follow, Mrs Moon and Cory appeared in the doorway.

Mrs Moon made some excuse about inviting Lexie to elevenses, but Lexie was sure they'd come to the rescue. Lexie just wanted to escape.

'Can I, er . . . ' Lexie was pointing to her exit, but her new visitors were too busy looking over her shoulder to see what Mrs Carrington-Noble was up to. And before Lexie knew it, she was hustled back into the room.

Mrs Carrington-Noble had installed herself on a throne-like Queen Anne chair, and was looking out of puff. Lexie still hadn't decided if this was an act she put on for sympathy, because it certainly seemed to work. Mrs Moon fussed over her and even Cory poured her a glass of water from the jug on the coffee table. Mrs Carrington-Noble placed her papers down to take a sip.

What were they? They looked like a pile of letters with photographs attached. Photos of well-heeled-looking ladies.

Were they part of her strange matchmaking shenanigans? Lexie tried not to roll her eyes as she wondered if Mrs Carrington-Noble was flaunting them on purpose. She peered nervously at the clock. She was late for her meeting with Ben, but she dared not leave this mob here, as much as she trusted two of them.

Just as she was wondering if she should text Ben, he appeared in the doorway too. Of course. Why did she ever expect anything less than the full circus in this surreal place?

'Do come in,' Lexie said to him, through sarcastic lips. 'You may as well join us.'

Ben stood awkwardly in his smart navy suit, like he'd never been invited into a girl's room before. But when he caught sight of his mother holding court, his brother lounging like a jester in his seal-sanctuary T-shirt and the housekeeper pretending to dust the sideboard, he cleared his throat and stepped into the show.

Chapter 16

'Mother. What on earth are you doing in Lexie's private quarters?'

Mrs Carrington-Noble looked squarely back at Ben. 'I could ask you the same thing.'

'We had a scheduled meeting,' he answered.

'In her bedroom?'

Ben's jaw was set, like he had no intention of lowering himself to this conversation.

'Anyway, I was looking for you. I have a selection of suitable matches for you and I want to hear your thoughts.' Mrs Carrington-Noble spread out her bounty across the coffee table.

So much for trying to stay out of their curious business, thought Lexie, feeling an odd heaviness pull down inside her chest. She couldn't help but notice one of the glamorous faces pouting out from a photograph, looking airbrushed to perfection. Cascades of chocolate brown hair slinked over one shoulder and her golden skin shimmered like an oasis.

She was so flawless, Lexie could barely look. It made sense, she supposed. Lexie couldn't always vouch for Ben in the manners department, but she had to admit he was a treat for the eyes. When he bothered to crack a smile.

'I'm not interested,' Ben told his mother. 'You can sort it out.'

Why bother to involve yourself in the mundane task of choosing your own wife, Lexie thought with a huff. What was wrong with these people? Or maybe even perfection wasn't good enough for Monk Benedict.

Cory pointed at the same brunette who'd caught Lexie's eye. 'She's not bad, bro.'

'Then she's all yours,' said Ben. 'Lexie, are you ready for our meeting? We can go through the stats in my office.'

'Alexis, what do you think?' Mrs Carrington-Noble croaked her interruption, seemingly keen to stop her prized son and his meagre employee making their escape. She waved her arm across the photos lined up on the table.

Lexie was certain the woman had no interest in what she thought. And Lexie wanted no part in this outrageous *X Factor*-style process for finding Ben a wife, even if this did look like that fun episode with the judges' houses. The idea of selecting a life partner based on their blow-dry and bank balance was all a bit sickening.

Lexie shrugged. 'Don't ask me – I'm a fish out of water.' More accurately she felt like a crappy sardine in a sea of rich mermaids.

Mrs Moon gave Lexie a discreet shoulder squeeze. Lexie gave a tiny smile. She guessed the housekeeper would have years of experience in swishing around the outskirts of these circles.

'Let's just go through some stats here, Lexie. I'm far too busy to bounce around. I have some papers in my briefcase,' said Ben, with his usual air of impatience.

Cory whistled through his teeth. 'You know how to excite the ladies.'

'Cornelius!' his mother snapped.

Lexie tried not to giggle. Was that his real name?

Cory grabbed a beanie from his back pocket and pulled it sheepishly over his head until it reached his eyebrows.

'A Bulgari Serpenti!' Mrs Moon yelped, as though trying to create a distraction. She was pointing to the snake-like chain around the brunette lady's neck. 'Rose gold, demi-pavé diamonds. Well, that's worth at least fifty thousand pounds.'

Cory and Lexie gawped at Mrs Moon. Where was she getting this left-field knowledge of bling?

Mrs Carrington-Noble narrowed her eyes at the photo. 'Quite right. How would you know such a thing?'

Mrs Moon looked flustered and rearranged her bonnet. 'No reason. Lucky guess!'

'And your point?' asked Ben, looking unimpressed, as he pushed his mother's paperwork aside to make space for his own.

'Well, look at the woman's description,' Mrs Moon continued. 'It says, "Job title: lady of leisure. Hobbies: collecting eligible men." And jewellery she hasn't paid for, I shouldn't wonder. She sounds like a professional gold-digger.'

'After my money!' Mrs Carrington-Noble squawked. 'I'll have no such thing. Good work, Mrs Moon.'

'But, Mrs M, how on earth . . . ?' Cory began.

From the housekeeper's tight lips, it was clear the conversation was over.

Mrs Carrington-Noble swept Ben's stats to one side and laid out her next top trump. 'How about this one? Thoroughbred and local.'

They all looked at the fresh-faced, sporty-looking beauty in the photo. All except Ben, who'd stalked over to Lexie's brightly decorated desk with his papers. He seemed distracted by Tom, who was out on the lawn trying to shoo off the peacocks.

Cory began fiddling with the hem of his T-shirt. The room went unusually silent, other than the tut-tutting of the grandmother clock in the corner.

'Well?' asked Mrs Carrington-Noble.

'Erm, not her, Mum.' Cory lowered his voice. 'I may have surfed that wave already.'

Mrs Carrington-Noble harrumphed. Mrs Moon straightened her apron and pretended not to hear.

Unsure which was the rock and which was the hard place, Lexie took the chance to creep away and join Ben by the window.

'All I wanted to do was talk stats,' he muttered towards the window, his voice deflating. 'Even social media audience figures and website traffic news are preferable to this.'

'I was just trying to mind my own business,' Lexie replied, their joint breath making a patch of steam on the window. Lexie resisted the urge to draw a sad smiley in it.

As the steam cleared, they saw Tom doing an elaborate shooing dance with the final peacock.

'I should have insisted Mother take those pretentious birds with her when she shuffled off to live with Carlito. But she'd probably have them turned into a pie, and Tom has grown quite fond of them. Nice to have a bit of colour, I suppose.'

Ben spread his paperwork out across the orange-and-pink makeshift desk covering, and Lexie added some of her coloured sticky notes in solidarity. Was that his twitchy smile again? Why was he watching her like that?

'I think you're more suited to a plain girl.' Mrs Carrington-Noble's voice hit them from across the room.

Ben appeared to shake himself from his thoughts. 'I'm sorry – what?'

She waved a photo at them. 'Like this one.'

The lady in question had black hair scraped into a no-nonsense bun. She wore thick-rimmed glasses and reminded Lexie of the type who'd suddenly become stunning in one of those makeover films.

Cory and Mrs Moon were poring over the woman's details.

'What's a coleopterist?' asked Cory.

'Oh dear, Mr Moon had one of those, do you remember? They put a little camera right up his . . . '

'Not a colonoscopy,' Mrs Carrington-Noble barked.

Cory laughed. 'You know, this would make an awesome blog post, Lex.'

Ben fixed Lexie with his atlas eyes, which seemed to have taken on a sudden worldwide storm. 'Miss Summers. My private business is not for social media. And the blog is not to be used for affairs of the heart.'

Why was she getting the brunt of his rage? So much for maps; there was no reading this maddening man.

'Coleopterist. It's someone who collects beetles,' said Cory, after a quick check on his phone.

'No, no.' Mrs Carrington-Noble shook her head. 'Parts of my house are already starting to look like a flea market.' She scowled at Lexie's flamboyant desk space, swimming like a tropical fish in a sea of beige. 'I don't want any more unwelcome critters.'

Ben snatched his paperwork up, bits of Lexie's sticky notes reluctantly swept along for the ride. 'Right, that's enough. Mother, let's get you out of here.'

It was clear he wasn't taking no for an answer, and Mrs Carrington-Noble looked too shell-shocked by his outburst to argue.

Within moments he'd eased her up from her throne and ushered her out, photographs of moneyed hopefuls being scattered in their wake.

Why couldn't Ben just go on Tinder like everyone else, Lexie wondered. More money, more bloody problems.

Boooonng. The grandmother clock seemed to agree.

Lexie let out a long tense breath and went to join Cory on the sofa. Mrs Moon was still standing on ceremony, but Lexie waved her to sit down.

'Will you have to marry someone suitably loaded, Cory?'

Lexie asked. She couldn't imagine someone as down to earth as him putting up with this charade.

'Nah, I doubt it. I don't suppose Mum gives two hoots what I get up to. Ben's the golden boy and the natural choice to inherit the business, seeing as he basically lives and breathes the thing. She gave up on trying to mould me years ago.'

Most people would surely have been bothered, but Cory seemed relieved.

'She loves you both the same,' Mrs Moon insisted. 'And I'm sure she'll give you a nest egg too, if Ben inherits the business.'

'What would you do with it?' Lexie leaned forward, her people-organising skills already twitching. As if she didn't have enough madness to deal with.

'I'm happiest catching waves in Newquay. I'd love to set up a surf school down there, or something. Give something back.'

'And maybe save a few seals!' Lexie pointed at his T-shirt, feeling suddenly excited.

'Yes, Lex, now you're talking. Nothing would rile Mother more than if I spent her hard-snatched pennies on something actually worthy.'

'Well, if you ever want to brainstorm ideas,' Lexie offered.

'Money.' Cory waved a hand. 'I'm not sure I'd even take it. It can't buy the important things.'

Now he was sounding like her sister. She hoped he wouldn't hand his over to a commune and cosy into a love quadrangle with a twat called Billy-Bob.

'If you mean money can't buy love, then that's not true for Ben,' said Lexie. 'It looks like he can take his pick, beetles and all.'

'It'll take a special woman to crack Benedict's heart. Some days I'm not entirely sure he's human. He still thinks of this as a business arrangement, poor guy. He'd happily hide from life behind his desk, with his briefcase as his shield.' Cory laughed, but Lexie could tell it came from a hopeful place. That reminded her.

'Cornelius, by the way! I had no idea.'

'That's our mother for you,' said Ben.

'And she doesn't like names to be shortened,' Mrs Moon added.

'Yet another thing I'll never understand,' said Cory.

'A housekeeper never tells.' Mrs Moon tapped her nose.

Lexie had come to learn that mysteries and oddities were part of the stonework at Nutgrass Hall. They hid in suits of armour. They peeped out through the eyes of creepy paintings. And sometimes they violated your living space and stirred you in all sorts of unexpected ways.

Chapter 17

Lexie needed fresh air. The walls were closing in on her in this big stuffy house and, after having her room invaded by Mrs Carrington-Noble and her godawful match-making circus, she was beginning to feel like nowhere was sacred. She was navigating tricky waters, and Captain Aloof was about as much help as a shark with no bite.

So it was time to get back to things she could control. She would do some brainstorming for her social media strategy, and outside was surely the place to find the perfect hidey-hole.

Somehow the world had crept its way into May, and Lexie hadn't even properly explored the grounds. It had been easy enough to close the curtains and pretend the grandeur didn't exist when she'd been in the safe haven that had been Penny. But now she'd been thrown into this mayhem, she may as well get welly-deep.

Dressed in her bright flamingo mac, she squeaked her

way along the hall, past Ben's office, and fought with the heavy front door until it finally let her through into the sunlight. She closed it with the least amount of possible clatter, which was still in fact a lot.

Lexie scanned the grounds in front of her. She needed space to think, and to map out some questions to tackle with Ben. Carrington Paints was a family business, and potential clients would want to know more about the people behind the paint pots. But what did she really know about Ben, the antisocial butterfly? Once she'd jotted some thoughts in her notebook, she'd knock on the door of his scary wood-panelled office and extract what she needed. Even if it would be like pulling teeth.

The rest of the house would be occupied with afternoon tea in the kitchen. Ben would be busy working, and she hadn't heard the peacock fanfare all day. She'd be safe to find a quiet corner. What was that archway in the distance? Still conscious of the peacocks, she tiptoed across the immaculately striped lawns, hoping not to rouse the birds. They were probably tucked up in their spoilt-brat shed, which was largely more impressive than Lexie's old flat. Other than it was full of scary birds, of course.

Once she'd crossed the first stretch of lawn, Lexie dipped under the archway into a more enclosed area of the gardens. It was less exposed and she breathed a sigh of relief, letting her shoulders melt downwards. She followed the neat pathway through Tom's green-fingered handiwork. Although the peacocks were off duty, the place still prickled with Mrs Carrington-Noble's presence. The flowers were a battalion of ivory, all orderly and funereal. The fussy white hyacinths were lined up with military precision and even the birdsong could have been piped.

The garden was doubtless a thing of beauty, but Lexie couldn't help but feel sorry for it. It was being suffocated. Why did Mrs Carrington-Noble cling on to everything so tightly? What was her obsession with keeping up appearances?

Beyond the part that looked like a bleached version of the Chelsea Flower Show, Lexie stumbled into an orchard. Now this was more like it. The apple trees were in full, fragrant blossom. Their outstretched limbs, costumed in powder-pink petals like ladies at a ball, beckoned her onwards.

There were two small cottages tucked inside the orchard, huddled together for moral support. They were plain but pretty, with neat window boxes and matching green doors. Was this where Tom and Mrs Moon lived, side by side, in defence of chaos? The lights were on in one, and she thought she could hear music. That must be the elusive Mr Moon. But it wasn't the day to introduce herself.

At the end of the orchard, Lexie found a high wooden gate. It had a rusty old padlock, but it looked as though someone had forgotten to fasten it. Should she really be that nosey?

She whipped her head around. Yes, she was alone. Not that she was snooping, as such. Nobody had mentioned anything being out of bounds. Maybe she'd find something exciting to blog about. Perfect. She was here on business.

Lexie cocked an ear. No footsteps. No peacock cries. So

she snuck up to the gate. Her hand wavered over the handle; what if it was something dodgy? Or Mrs C-N's private nudist escape? She might be in there with her toy boy, their naked bodies being fanned by a poker-faced butler. Maybe *that* was what Mr Moon did all day!

Just as Lexie was giggling to herself and starting to turn away, she heard a burst of birdsong. It seemed to be calling her, inviting her in. Well, it would be churlish not to. And she had been looking for a peaceful escape. Before she could change her mind, she pulled open the rickety gate and stepped over the threshold.

What met her on the other side of the boundary couldn't have been more different to the forced elegance in the rest of the grounds. This was the great outdoors in all its riotous beauty. Wildflowers sprouted from every inch of space; colours clashing, stems intertwining, vibrant petals clambering excitedly for headroom. Bushes bustled from cracked terracotta pots and plants poured over the sides of a mossy old wheelbarrow. Lexie's heart swelled. This was how a garden ought to look. It reminded her of one of her late Aunt Jasmine's canvases: a fresco of unkempt blooms, unbridled and exciting. She'd never seen this garden before, but already it felt like part of her. A streak of colour in a painfully plain kingdom.

In a far corner she spied a greenhouse, the odd cracked pane patched up with heavy tape. Falling apart at the seams, but pulled back together with determination and love. Was it Tom's? She expected he was from a time of 'waste not want not', which was unlikely to tie in with Mrs

Carrington-Noble's quest for superficial perfection. Hmm. So the padlock was probably to keep the boss woman out rather than to deter the likes of Lexie. There. She needn't feel too ashamed about exploring. She made her way to the shiny structure, interested to know what else Tom might be nursing back to life.

As she eased back the reluctant door, the warmth flew out to greet her, carrying a tempting herbal fragrance on its wings. She inched her way inside, trying to make out the delicate plants sheltering within. There were all sorts of potted vegetation in varying shades of green. Some with long whiskery tendrils, others with tiny budding flowers. Each had its own distinctive texture and aroma. She couldn't help brushing her fingers against them to encourage up the scents. What were they for? Mrs Moon ordered her herbs from the supermarket – Lexie had seen them on the list.

Then, as if to remind her of her small intrusion, a bee buzzed at her ear.

'OK, OK. I'll get out,' she told the disgruntled insect as she shook herself and climbed out of the greenhouse.

'Oh!' Her hand flew to her chest as she tried to still her heart. 'Ben. You made me jump.'

It was starting to be an occupational hazard in this place.

Chapter 18

'What were you up to in Tom's greenhouse? He's cagey enough about his secret garden.'

It was Ben in a grey tweed suit, looking more like he was going to a wedding than scuffling about in the bushes. Couldn't a girl get any peace in this place?

'Nothing, I ... You're wearing wellies?' God. Why did she always come out with something dumb in his presence? Maybe his awkwardness was rubbing off on her.

'Top marks for observation, Miss Summers. I live on a country estate. I can't always wear a formal shoe.'

Of course he had to point that out, as if she didn't already feel out of her depth here. She'd grown up on a council estate, where the main function for wellies was to splash in poorly tarmacked puddles. She clutched her notebook to her chest.

'I was just ... er ... going to make some notes. About you, actually.'

He raised an eyebrow.

'You know, to build up a picture of you to share with the followers. Nothing too *private*. Just a bit of fun – to help people get to know the people behind the business. Anyway. I needed somewhere quiet to think.' She waved a hand. 'Maybe you can help me.'

'Hiding among the wildflowers, thinking about me. I'm charmed.' The corners of his mouth were doing that annoying twitchy thing again. He was trying not to smirk.

'Not in that way, just . . . Oh!' Why was she starting to feel off-balance? She looked down at her feet as they began to be swallowed by a patch of wet mud. She splayed her arms out to stop herself falling.

Ben stepped forward and grabbed her free hand, pulling her from the dirt. His touch was warm and firm, and took her by surprise. She tried to steady herself, although something inside her felt strangely less steady than before.

'Thank you,' she muttered, tugging her hand away. Maybe he had more manners than she gave him credit for. But, anyway, she didn't need his help. 'What were you doing following me?'

He cleared his throat. Did he look a little embarrassed?

'I don't believe I'm barred from any part of the gardens. I heard you clattering along the hallway and wondered where you were off to. I needed to stretch my legs, in any case.'

He waved down at his, as though she might not know what legs were. At least she wasn't the only one making an idiot of herself.

'There's a bench over there. Maybe you want to sit, and

we can *think about me* together. I steal out here sometimes too, when the beige gets too much.'

He strode off and, suddenly intrigued to know more about this boss who occasionally showed a hint of raspberry ripple through his vanilla, Lexie found herself following him.

When they arrived at the promised bench, Lexie realised it was one of those kissing seats which curved around in an 'S' shape, and was totally unsuitable for most things other than kissing. How were they meant to have a proper conversation if they were facing opposite directions? She plonked down and tried to twist herself so she was looking at the side of Ben's head. Was that even stranger?

He turned to face her too, and then realising their faces were disconcertingly close they apologised and turned back to face their contrasting views. Ben was facing the big house, which was some way in the distance beyond the overgrown garden, and Lexie was looking towards the boundary wall edging the dirt track beyond.

'So what do you need to know?' he asked.

'Share some of your personality with me.'

'You'll be disappointed; there's not much to tell. If I had one, perhaps I'd know how to chat on social media myself. And indeed, find my own wife.'

'Oh, I . . .'

'Just ask your questions.'

Ben had a way of making even a bit of sociable fun feel like business. His tone of voice was fit for chairing a meeting. Lexie flipped open her notebook and straightened it out on her lap. Well, two could play at that. She was just here to take the minutes.

'Hobbies?'

He turned to look at the side of her face, but she refused to look back at him.

'What are we, twelve?' he asked.

'No, but . . .'

'Well, being twelve wasn't much better.'

Lexie sighed. 'Look, these are the things I need to know if I'm going to build a human being out of you. People will be more compelled to engage with you and invest in you if they get to know the face behind the paint. Maybe that could be a lesson for you in dating, too.' She sniffed. 'I've been here for two weeks and I haven't seen you do anything that didn't involve a briefcase, so excuse me for asking.'

She could see in her peripheral vision he was trying not to baulk at her sarcasm, but she wasn't far from the truth.

'Actually, sorry, there was the one Friday when you came to my camper van and pretended to eat a Thai curry.'

'I'm not accustomed to spicy food,' he snapped. 'Anyway, having your underwear hanging in my face was putting me off.'

'They were just socks!' She thought back to the haphazard washing line and was glad he'd turned back in his own direction and probably couldn't see her blushing.

'Squash,' he said.

'I'm not your bloody drinks maid!'

'I like *playing squash*.' He rearranged his jacket. 'When I have a partner. And I use the gym, up in the house. Maybe

132

if Dad had used it more his heart wouldn't have ...' His voice was cracking.

Lexie felt a sudden flush of something, and turned to squeeze his arm.

'I'm so sorry. I didn't realise.'

He didn't look back. 'No reason you should. A man's heart can strangle him in the end.' He laughed a little strangely. 'Although I suspect Mother played her part.'

What did that mean? The woman was wicked, but surely ... Lexie was dying to quiz him, but it didn't feel right to push. She let go of Ben's surprisingly toned biceps and resumed her position. Now was not the time to assess his guns.

'So, you're sporty. That's good!' She tried to sound upbeat, keen to lift the mood from those curious undertones. And, anyway, well-maintained bodywork was a pretty good selling point for when he came to select this wife of his, though she wasn't going to admit it.

'Is it good? Or is it just boring?' Ben asked.

His voice seemed almost deflated, and Lexie wasn't sure whether he was thinking out loud or if he actually wanted an answer. She floundered, conscious of her wayward thoughts.

'Working out isn't boring, it's just ...'

'You've encountered more flamboyant men. Your ex-boyfriend was, what, in a band?'

Had she even told him that? She'd mentioned it to Cory when they were discussing music one day, but ...

'And the guy before that was a tattoo artist who travelled the world?'

133

Maybe she had mentioned Inkie, although in hindsight that had been a rookie mistake. She prayed Ben would never delve into how that ended up.

'Well, I haven't been much further than Jersey. I can't sing, dance or play the ukulele, and I'd rather eat an apple than risk a Pot Noodle. So there isn't much to say about my *personality*. Either for your social media project or for my mother's ludicrous matchmaking.'

Lexie was surprised by his sudden outburst. He'd just confessed more about his personal life than she'd ever heard him say. Was it the ambience of this magical garden making his usually clamped-up leaves unfurl? Was it that they were almost on neutral ground here, away from the house and among this flurry of colour? Or that they were staring in different directions, for once not locking horns.

'Look, I'm not here to advise you about finding your perfect match. I can't even sort out my own. But if it helps ... urgh. You're not trying to impress a girl like me. So it doesn't matter about those things. Maybe your ideal woman would go crazy for a game of squash.'

'It's honestly not that thrilling. And is that what I should be looking for? A woman who likes all the same things as me? A Benette to accompany my Ben. Should she favour beige and go to business meetings and be a little bit socially ... inept?'

Lexie tried not to gawp.

'I don't know all the answers; I'm just here to sort some stuff for Facebook.' She waved her pad feebly.

'Yes, apologies. You're right. This finding-a-match

nonsense really isn't your problem. And I didn't believe I cared much about it myself until ... ' His voice trailed off. 'Recently.'

'Right.'

'I was just willing to let Mother get on with it. But imagine if there's more to it than that.'

'I know. Imagine.' Lexie discreetly rolled her eyes.

'I mean, it's interesting to be ... challenged. To be faced with a different outlook, a fresh perspective.' They stared on in their opposite directions. 'Like that funny little pattern on your top.'

He couldn't see her top from there, could he? It was a tatty old thing from her travelling days, and the pattern was so small. It was Yin and Yang. The circle with the 'S' in the middle. Two opposing energies, two opposite colour schemes, coming together as a complimentary whole. Or perhaps like a kissing seat. But it was just coincidence. She was running out of clean washing.

Lexie pulled her mac around herself, even though she was starting to feel uncomfortably hot. 'It's just something I picked up from a market stall in Beijing.'

'Beijing,' Ben repeated, like it was the most exotic word. 'Impressive.'

'Oh, you should go one day; it's something else. The colours, the smells. It's a real attack on your senses. A whole different world.'

He was quiet for a while, and Lexie contemplated his situation. She'd always assumed that money opened up a person's world to everything, and yet here was Ben seeming as though his had been so much more sheltered than hers. Maybe the contents of your wallet didn't dictate as much as she'd thought; but what did she know.

'And can I ask what delights you ate in Beijing? Fortune cookies?'

Lexie laughed. 'I think the fortune cookies are a Western thing, but the street food over there is amazing. Deep-fried scorpions are good.'

She sensed his face crumpling into a grimace. 'Only joking. I didn't try them. There's plenty of other stuff. Oily bean curd, rolling donkey – which is not what you might expect . . . '

'I think I'd pass.'

Lexie was enjoying this gentle tease. She really couldn't picture Ben that far out of his comfort zone.

'Is that how a person gets more colourful – by going to these places? I fear my current CV of squash and deadlifts is as uninspiring as Nutgrass Hall's paintwork. Maybe I've been stuck on life's treadmill.'

The last time Lexie had been on one of those evil things, she'd got her footing wrong and had been ejected off the back. He was one up on her.

'I'm sure a few brushes with far-off lands would add a bit of colour to your palette. Maybe it would inspire you to perk up the shades in Carrington Paints' catalogue too. I keep thinking something is lacking.'

She turned to face him, feeling a tickle of excitement. Apparently drawn by her sudden energy, he moved to face her too.

'I see you slinking through spice-laden souks, ambling

through Amsterdam, hitting the carnival in Cape Town...'
She gave a little shimmy, ignoring his surprised chuckle.

'You make it sound so easy.'

'But it is! You just grab a backpack and a few essentials, and get on a plane. Or, you know. Get the butler to fill your Mulberry cases.'

He tutted at her. Of course she knew he'd never had a butler. He didn't even like Mrs Moon doing things for him, although he also didn't like to deprive her of her sense of purpose. It was actually quite sweet.

'Is it as easy, as say, going through your paperwork and making sure your homelife is up to date?'

She crossed her arms. 'Maybe we all have our comfort zones.'

'And if we try and cower inside them, sometimes life has a funny way of throwing us out,' he said, as though the thought had only just dawned. 'Like a woman who ignores her out-of-date documents, causing her home to be crushed, so she's forced to move into her own worst nightmare.'

Lexie grimaced. Maybe he had a point, even if she did want to whack him around the head for reminding her about poor Penny. 'Hey, you could whisk some of your compatible dates away to foreign destinations.'

He seemed to consider it. 'I'd be more at ease on home territory.'

'But off-balance Ben is so much funnier!'

'I'm glad my incompetence amuses you. Perhaps you'd like to tag along with your notebook and take notes for some excruciating blog post?'

'Being piggy in the middle while you date some beetle collector chosen by your mother? What a treat,' she scoffed. 'Anyway, I don't have the money for that kind of stuff, in case you hadn't noticed.' Or a passport. But were those the only things holding her back? After the near-disastrous end to her travelling days with Inkie, she was pretty sure she was just too plain scared. Maybe her world had been shrinking more than she cared to admit.

'Then perhaps one day you'll show me the world by way of a business trip, and you can charge it to expenses. If the Carrington Paints colour chart needs spicing up, and you recommend travel as the best way to gather inspiration . . .'

'Well, it was just a thought. None of my business, or anything. But I'd love to see some travel-inspired ranges. Or maybe that's just silly.' She shrugged.

'Not silly at all; you're an entrepreneur. You should have more faith in your ideas.'

'I'm sure your mother would be delighted with me interfering with colour schemes, as well as brightening up your online presence. And having business field trips with you. What could she possibly crush next?'

'She's not as bad as all that. Look, she even paid a visit to your living quarters the other day. Maybe she likes you?'

'She all but called me a fleabag! And she was only there to rub my nose in how crummy I am, compared to all of your rich and exquisite matches.' She sniffed. 'God knows why she thinks I'd be bothered. Anyway, I'd get on your nerves if we went abroad together. I always seem to.'

Somewhere in the distance, a peacock cried. And

with that, the magic spell of the secret garden seemed to be broken.

Ben checked his watch and stood up. 'Quite. Well, any time we spend together is just a temporary inconvenience. I'm sure Mother will have her way soon enough, and you'll probably be off to more suitable climes.'

What did he mean by that? Another reminder that she didn't belong? As she saw him pull a face at the mud beneath his feet, she wondered if he was back to no-nonsense Ben. The man who was far too busy to find his own wife and didn't want his suit to get dirty.

'Right, well, I'll get back to my Facebook faffing. Thanks for the gripping info. Maybe you should share some of that with your mum to help her bag you that perfect wife,' she said through gritted teeth.

'Indeed. Well, she has some interviews planned to pluck out the most suitable. Maybe you can keep an eye on what she's up to, now you know all about me. My own schedule's far too hectic.'

Interviews. For the position as wife? Was he having a laugh? But before she had time to question him he was off across the garden towards the house, like a man who'd said too much.

Lexie gave a sarcastic salute to his back and wondered if the military-precision flowers weren't his after all.

Chapter 19

Some weeks were definitely stranger than others, but Lexie was fast learning that all weeks spent at Nutgrass Hall would be verging on the edge of ridiculous. Odd was most definitely the norm, and the sooner she accepted it the easier life would be.

Lexie marched across the orchard, checking her watch and cursing the lateness of Mrs Carrington-Noble's pina-fored partner in crime. Mrs Moon might not feel like this morning's preposterousness, but Lexie was liking her role as unofficial gofer even less. And she didn't even want to delve into all of the reasons why this whole business felt so wrong.

Two weeks had passed since her weird little chat with Ben in Tom's secret garden. Since then it had all been going on. Mrs Carrington-Noble had turned up and had actually been vaguely civil. Lexie suspected she'd been coerced into politeness by Ben, and no doubt some emotional blackmail had taken place. The woman had even muttered an apology about *any perceived hostilities*, whatever that meant. Albeit through gritted teeth, stained with blood-red lipstick.

There had been something offbeat about that meeting, Lexie recalled as she stomped across the wet grass. For starters, Mrs Carrington-Noble had apparently just returned from an exotic sunny holiday, yet she'd looked peculiarly pale and dare Lexie say it – fragile?

But now the *grande dame* was back with a vengeance and organising this charade. The spectacle that Lexie had been trying her best to play no part in, culminating in this morning's crude interpretation of *The X Factor* live auditions.

Mrs Carrington-Noble would apparently be starring as a less orange Simon Cowell, with Mrs Moon pushing the tea trolley. They were holding interviews to find a suitable wife for Ben. Suitably rich, suitably accommodating of this absurdity, and suitably accustomed to beige.

Lexie was becoming adept at suspending her own disbelief at how the other half dared to live. Did having too much money allow you to be excessively eccentric? Suddenly it became OK to wear mustard cords, grow your hair like Boris Johnson or have your mother line up potential wives so you could inherit the family business without too much bother.

'Urrrgh!' Lexie narrowly avoided a puddle but skidded on a pile of wet leaves.

Why was she even getting dragged into this? She'd just been flitting along the hallway, when Mrs Carrington-Noble had all but grabbed her by the collar and started bossing her about. Of course, she hadn't strictly needed to pass by the ballroom on her way to nick a slice of fruitcake from the kitchen, but perhaps she was just a little intrigued to have a backstage nosey. Next thing she knew she'd been tasked with collecting Mrs Moon, so the new Simon Cowell didn't get her court shoes mucky.

Well, Lexie was trying to embrace the greater good. At least if Ben were married off, Mrs Moon and Tom would be more likely to keep their home. Word had it that Ben would get Nutgrass Hall as a little wedding gift, and he'd surely never turf them out. There. Lexie did hate to think of any creature being stranded.

Lexie finally reached Mrs Moon's cottage and hammered on the door. Apparently the candidates would arrive at any minute, and heaven forbid Mrs Carrington-Noble would have to arrange her own tea and biscuits.

As Lexie paced from foot to foot at Mrs Moon's door, her yellow pixie boots trying not to get swallowed by mud, she had one of those curious *déjà vu* moments. What was that racket going on inside, and why did she feel like she'd heard it before? It was like ... arguing? Mrs Moon's voice was one of them. Could that be Mr Moon rowing with her? Should she intervene?

Lexie stuck her face against the front-room window, but the fussy net curtains blocked her view. Of course. This was just like her first Friday night at Nutgrass Hall, when she'd heard that fracas in the kitchen. When she'd entered, Mrs Moon had looked flustered and had straightened her bonnet.

And there she was again, opening her front door and doing much the same.

'Oh, sorry, dear. I'm late. I was just ... Never mind. I

should really keep my voice down or I'll wake Mr Moon. Then we'll all be in trouble!' She slammed the door behind her with a force that was sure to wake anybody, and made off across the grass towards the morning's show.

Chapter 20

Lexie wanted to be involved in the 'suitable wife' inter-rogations like a turkey wanted to be stuffed.

She'd been hoping to nip off and work on some blog posts, just as soon as she'd deposited Mrs Moon into Mrs Carrington-Noble's care. Yet, when she saw the elderly housekeeper being dumped with a list of jobs before the lady of the manor swanned off to have her bob tonged, she felt too guilty to leave Mrs Moon struggling. Lexie tried not to think of the joy Mrs Carrington-Noble would get from keeping her in her place.

'Why do the Carringtons have a room dedicated to balls, when Mrs Carrington-Noble has surely never been jolly enough to cha-cha?' Lexie hissed at Mrs Moon as they dragged another pot of white lilies from the main house into the high-ceilinged ballroom, where the tomfoolery was due to take place. 'And why does she still insist on ordering flowers for the place when she doesn't even live here?'

They were hoping the scent of the flowers would detract from the fusty smell that hung in the air, but in fact they'd just made it smell even more like a funeral. Perhaps that was fitting.

'Oh, nobody's danced in here for quite some time,' Mrs Moon replied. 'Sad, really.'

Lexie could quite believe that, from all the last-minute dusting she'd felt moved to help Mrs Moon with. Sad was exactly the word. The decadent gold leaf that seemed to adorn every cornice had lost its happy sparkle, and even the huge grandfather clock had stopped bothering to tick. It was like a room without a heart. Which was apt, thought Lexie, as she batted another image of Ben from her mind.

When Mrs Carrington-Noble returned with her well-coiffed mane and installed herself on an extravagant chair, Lexie and Mrs Moon escaped to the hallway to oversee the queue of hopefuls.

'Oh, you get yourself away now, dear. You've done more than enough.' Mrs Moon puffed as she began wheeling her tea trolley up and down, serving refreshments.

As much as Lexie felt icky shuffling around these well-to-do women in her thrift-shop jumper dress, poor Mrs Moon looked exhausted. And what if a fight broke out? Some of these women looked as keen as vultures. Who knew what could occur if they got their claws out.

'I'll stay,' Lexie insisted, taking over the handles of the trolley to give her comrade a break. Besides, she quite fancied a snoop. She just hoped curiosity didn't always kill the cat.

It turned out to be a bit of a wild morning. But then, if they insisted on lining the ballroom walls with actual gold they could expect a few gold-diggers. Lexie was sure she'd never been more right about money turning people ugly. It was like the old days in her snobby senior school all over again, with rich girls peering down their noses at her. Well. She was glad not to be part of their world.

The morning had brought bitching and bickering, and Lexie had been bossed around like a handmaid. At one point she'd even had to play bouncer, when two so-called ladies descended into a cake-flinging match.

What a waste of Victoria sponge.

It was just as well Lexie had stuck around, at least for Mrs Moon's sake.

And as much as Lexie was willing herself not to get sucked into the pantomime like some floor-sweeping Cinders, she couldn't help sizing up the players. Just out of sheer boredom, of course.

'There's the lady who collects those funny bugs,' Mrs Moon hissed. 'She's made a packet selling rare ones.'

Lexie tried her best to spark up a conversation, but concluded that hanging around with dead stuff had killed the woman's sense of fun.

'Is that one wearing mourning clothes?' whispered Mrs Moon, pointing at a lady who looked like a spidery black widow.

Had she just killed and eaten her husband? Ben could be annoying, but Lexie didn't want him murdered for his fortune.

And then a honey-haired twenty-something breezed into the waiting area with the elegance of a very pretty swan, but none of the show-offy-ness. Lexie couldn't help falling a little bit in love with her swishy orange skirt, which looked vintage in a very designer way.

'I'm Grace,' she said, waving away Lexie's hand and going in for a hug. 'Sorry, shaking hands makes me feel nervous. I just needed some love.'

Lexie smiled.

Grace. It suited her.

Within moments, Grace was raiding the trolley for cake and insisting on serving some up to Lexie and Mrs Moon too. Well, it had been a long morning.

'Ooh, she looks like you, dear,' Mrs Moon whispered as Grace was busy with the cake slice. 'If you'd won the lottery and grown your hair like a proper lady.' The housekeeper nodded at Lexie's pixie cut, the ends of which Lexie had recently dyed blue in a rebellion against goodness knew what.

'Don't be silly,' Lexie murmured back. 'She's got far better genes.'

Lexie had to admit, Grace had far better everything. From her zebra-print boots to her perfectly matching manicure, this woman was flawless. As Grace started pouring tea and nattering away about what a lovely place Nutgrass Hall would be with a lick of colour, Lexie couldn't help but warm to her.

When Grace told them who her family was, Mrs Moon mouthed 'multi-millionaires' at Lexie. Grace shared stories of her travels and adventures, and Lexie soon wondered with a pang if Grace was the perfect Yin–Yang opposite for Ben. But why the painful twinge?

Lexie gave herself a shake. Surely it was just that she wanted to keep Grace all to herself. Yes, exactly. It definitely wasn't from a reluctance to see Ben paired off.

'Ben doesn't really travel much, but he should,' Lexie heard herself divulging.

Grace rolled her eyes. 'Too busy making the money, hey?' She looked around at the décor, a quizzical look on her face. 'And you say their business is paint?'

Lexie tried not to giggle. 'I know what you're thinking. Why all the ... '

'Beige!' they said in unison.

'It's their mother's choice,' Mrs Moon added.

'Isn't it bloody always.' Grace tutted and then put her hand over her mouth. 'Oops, sorry. I'm sure she's perfectly nice.'

'Hmm,' Lexie answered.

And they both laughed again.

'I should be better behaved if I want to find a husband, so my parents keep saying,' said Grace, and then lowered her voice. 'I'm only here to keep them off my back.'

'It must be tricky finding a suitable rich guy.' Lexie checked around and then lowered her voice too. 'It feels like the more money some guys have, the less manners they've got. Don't you think?'

Grace pulled a strand of hair through her fingers as she appeared to give it some thought.

'Honestly, I don't think money makes much difference.

If a guy's a nob, he's a nob. The jerk-gene fairy doesn't ask about bank balances when she comes waving her wand.'

Lexie laughed. 'I guess.' She remained to be convinced, although Grace would know a lot more rich men than she did.

'But, anyway, I don't have to hook up with someone wealthy just because my parents are loaded. People are just people.' She shrugged. 'Love turns up where it wants to. Just like friendship.'

And on that note, Grace was ushered into the ballroom for her interview with the potential mother-in-law from hell. She was the day's final contender.

Twenty minutes later, Grace was helping Lexie and Mrs Moon tidy up the ballroom. Mrs Carrington-Noble had gone to update Ben, who hadn't shown up. Lexie assumed he hadn't deemed it worthy of his trouble. It was only the trifling matter of marriage, after all. Maybe he was just as bad as his queue of pampered hopefuls.

Even Grace had shown more effort in the day's proceedings. She'd insisted on staying to lend a hand, after hitting it off with Lexie and falling in love with Mrs Moon's array of sponge cakes.

Just as Lexie and Grace were dragging out the last pot of wilting lilies, music began to fill the ballroom. The women looked around and Mrs Moon pointed to some dusty speakers, which were creaking back to life.

Lexie knew from watching too many YouTube videos on South America that this was tango music, and there was something irresistible about its beat. It was dynamic, as though it demanded to be stomped to. Grace, a woman so different and yet somehow so in tune with Lexie, seemed to feel it too. She extended her hands to Lexie and Mrs Moon.

'Shall we?' Grace's eyes sparkled with a delight that was infectious.

Lexie grabbed Grace's hand and pulled Mrs Moon's sleeve.

'No, no, lovey. It takes two to tango, not three! You go ahead. God knows, this tired ballroom needs some life.'

The lily leaves seemed to wave their approval and, within moments, Lexie and Grace were clutching each other and spinning around the room, making up a dance that probably resembled nothing the formal ballroom had ever seen.

But who had started the music? And why? Ben was surely more of a waltz man, although he did keep surprising her. Was he on his way? Grace interrupted Lexie's musings.

'So what's this Ben actually like?' she asked as they sashayed around the floor. 'Seeing as he's too important to show up. His mother wasn't exactly a bag of fun.'

Lexie threw her head back and laughed, euphoric from the music, before gathering her thoughts. 'Well, he's … handsome, I guess. You know – tall, pretty muscular. Neat chocolatey brown hair that always looks fit to ruffle.' She ought to try and do him justice.

'Eyes?'

'Hmm, unusual. Like globes, or something. He doesn't even get out much, yet when you look into them …' Lexie shook her head. 'Sorry. Blueish, with a bit of green. Just normal, really. Two of them.'

'Oh, OK. Two is always handy. And personality?'

Now that was a tough one.

150

'At first, I thought he was quite annoying. And he can definitely be standoffish.'

'Are you trying put me off?' asked Grace.

'No, of course not! I hope he finds his sparkling match.' Well, maybe. 'So, yeah ... ' She thought back over the last month they'd spent together. It was strange, now she tried to piece it together. He irritated her and they were nothing alike, and yet ... what was it? There was just something. Like a funny little pull. A compulsion to be near him, even though he prickled her skin.

'Lexie?' Grace was waiting for an answer. How long had she been thinking?

'Right, sorry. Er ... ' Lexie stopped spinning for a moment, feeling dizzy enough. She was conscious of Mrs Moon, almost perching on the edge of the seat she was resting on. Why would she want to hear? Mrs Moon knew Ben's mysterious personality better than Lexie did. 'He's ... actually quite amusing. And chivalrous.' She thought back to him trying to yank her out of a puddle. 'And interesting, when he bothers to say stuff. Plus his staff all seem to like him, although I'm not always sure why.'

Mrs Moon nodded.

'And there's even the slight possibility that he might be charming, although I've not seen it with my own eyes. You could work on it,' said Lexie.

The pair chuckled and linked arms again, continuing their spin around the room. As Lexie and Grace chatted about the surreal kind of day it had been, one of the double doors creaked open and a draught swept through the room.

All heads turned in its direction to see Ben filling the archway, his crisp black suit immaculate as though he was going to a ball himself.

Grace gave a low whistle. Lexie couldn't blame her.

Ben was considering the once-dancing women with a look that was surprisingly intense. Lexie wasn't sure she'd seen it before, or certainly not that strong. It must have been aimed at her dance partner, who was an absolute vision in shades of peach and tangerine, full taffeta skirt bustling as though destined to tango. Lexie imagined the two of them together, so finely turned out and smelling intoxicatingly expensive. They would be like something from a formidable dream, all luscious locks and well-groomed skin. And Lexie was right here, giving them a helping hand. Maybe Mrs Carrington-Noble would even thank her.

Wow. She should bring this dazzling pair together and bow out of the dance.

She gulped down the prickly thing that was rising in her throat and offered Grace's hand to Ben.

Chapter 21

'**Y**ou fancied her.'
'I did not!'

Lexie and Ben were walking along Tewkesbury High Street the Friday after the *Find Ben a Wife* interviews, arguing like a pair of schoolchildren. Lexie had explored the market town several times, but this was the first time she'd been here with Ben. She was surprised he'd agreed to leave his office so early.

'Yes, you did. You got all shy when I tried to give her hand to you. You wouldn't even dance.'

'I'm not very good at dancing.'

'You chose the music!'

'I thought everyone would have left by then.' He pulled his collar loose as they trekked past the crooked timber-framed buildings.

'So who were you expecting to dance with? Mrs Moon?'

'Nobody! I was just … checking everything was still working. It's been a long time.'

Lexie tried not to raise her eyebrows.

It was a sunny May afternoon, and Lexie had managed to talk Ben into having their weekly planning meeting early. Her sneaky end goal was to bag herself an invite to the paint conference in London. If Ben was swanning off, she didn't want to be stuck at Nutgrass Hall, waiting for Mrs Carrington-Noble to show up and order her to sweep ballrooms and serve Earl Grey, or whatever nonsense. Surely he owed her one after that fiasco?

Anyway, Lexie had promised her followers she'd blog about this conference. She couldn't let them down.

So Lexie had told Ben it was criminal to stay cramped up in his wood-panelled office when the weather was so nice. He'd reluctantly agreed to a business lunch by the river, probably to avoid Lexie plying him with spicy Thai takeaway later on.

The high street was surprisingly busy and they weaved in and out of meandering shoppers. Medieval flags flapped above their heads, happy streaks of colour against the black-and-white Tudor constructions.

'Ooh!' Lexie just managed to stop herself tripping over a display of old furniture that was arranged outside a shop front.

'Load of old junk.' Ben tutted. 'Look, even the neighbours think so.' He pointed to the people from the shop next door, who seemed to be emptying their wares and moving out.

'No! Not at all.' Lexie pulled him back to look. 'That's what I love about this place. So many vintage shops and once-loved items. It's full of such promise.' She always did get enthusiastic at the thought of a bargain.

He looked at her quizzically as she tried not to bubble over with excitement.

'Tatty brown coffee tables. Go on, enlighten me.'

'But they don't have to be brown, or beige, or any boring table colour. With a splash of paint they could be any shade you want.'

He looked at her in her yellow sunflower-print jumpsuit, her electric-blue thrift-shop cardi matching happily with the blue tips of her hair.

'Indeed.'

She flapped her arms in frustration. 'For someone in the paint business, you don't have much vision. You've probably never even heard of chalk-style paints. They're far too cutesy for you.'

They moved to avoid the vacating neighbours, who were struggling through their door with brimming boxes.

'And I'm sure some new, exciting business will set up its home here soon. Isn't it always great when someone new moves in?' she said, treating him to a wink.

'Thrilling.'

Lexie was still never sure when he was being sarcastic good or sarcastic bad, so she gave up the debate and strode on towards the river, with Ben shrugging and pacing along behind.

They soon arrived at Ben's chosen restaurant and picked a table outside by the water. Lexie felt a little flutter of something as Ben pulled out her chair and checked she was comfortable. Then she tutted at herself, realising he was probably just trying to appease her after their set-to in the street.

Lexie settled back into her chair and took in the view. The water trickled by peacefully, making its way towards the old stone bridge. The trees were shimmying their late-spring leaves. There was every danger she might see a duck. This place was too quaint for words; maybe Ben wouldn't be so terrible at dating after all.

Despite all the loveliness, Lexie couldn't help feeling a hint of rebellion in the air. It was like one of those hazy school days when the teachers went wild and took lessons outside on the grass. If she were wearing a uniform she'd be making her tie into a headband and tying a jaunty knot in her shirt.

'So was Grace the top contender in the potential-wife parade?' Lexie enjoyed making him squirm on this topic, even if she wasn't quite sure why. Was she hoping for a confession? If so, what did she want him to confess?

She shook off the thought. No. She wasn't playing a grown-up version of 'my friend fancies you'. And did Grace even like Ben?

'Don't be ridiculous. There were surely other reasonable options. What about the lady with the bugs?'

'Plain Susan?' Was he being serious? 'I mean, not to do the woman a disservice, but she did actually describe herself as a little bit boring when she asked Mrs Moon to scrape the jam off her sponge.'

'There's nothing wrong with being dull.' Ben shifted in

his seat and waved for a non-existent waiter, clearly trying to avoid eye contact.

Lexie gave an exaggerated gasp and leaned across the table towards him. 'You still think you're boring, don't you?' she stage-whispered. 'You think you'll have nothing to talk about other than spreadsheets, so if you end up with Bug Lady at least you'll be marginally more interesting than her dead centipedes.'

Lexie wished she was sitting a bit nearer, so she could poke him in the ribs and giggle. 'Is it because I call you beige?'

He flashed her a glare. 'You know I didn't choose the paintwork at the house.' At last he caught the attention of a staff member and signalled for the wine menu.

Lexie had to concede that was probably true. Mrs Carrington-Noble's presence was painted into the very stonework. 'So what colour would you have chosen?'

Ben let out a frustrated huff as though dealing with a disruptive toddler. 'I don't know – you're the creative one. How about something from your proposed new range. Something exotic.'

Lexie laughed. 'Coming from the guy who thinks having pineapple on his pizza is a step too close to crazy, I'm not sure you could handle exotic.' She folded her arms across her chest, leaned back in her chair and eyeballed him, a twinkle of defiance in her eyes.

'So put your proposed palette together and we'll see.'

Ooh, was that a double dare? She was surprised he'd even remembered her mention of a new range of colours for Carrington Paints. He must have sensed before that she didn't trust herself to actually pull it off. Well, maybe she'd triple dare him back.

'If you're so wild you should try a date with Grace. Perhaps she's just the streak of colour you need.'

He winced.

'What?'

'She's just too . . .' He seemed to be picking his words carefully, so as not to cause offence – which was unusual in itself.

'Vibrant, captivating, full of life?'

'Well, yes, I'm sure all of those things,' he said.

'Which is good?'

'I suppose it could be, but . . .' The wine arrived and he engrossed himself in watching it being poured.

'But what?'

He was giving her the stop-being-a-tricky-toddler look again. 'She's just too familiar, that's all. She reminds me of someone.'

Lexie rewound her thoughts to the queue outside the ballroom.

She looks like you, dear.

Isn't that what Mrs Moon had said? Lexie felt the heat of embarrassed blood cells rushing to her chest. She pulled her blue cardi around her to hide the little traitors.

'I see.' She took a glug of her wine with her free hand. 'Somebody unsuitable, who kind of gets on your nerves. I get it.'

Now it was his turn to test out one of his twitchy smiles. 'I do enjoy it when you're vexed.'

'I am not vexed.'

A trio of ducks swam by and seemed to giggle-quack at the pair of them.

'Your ruby-red neck says you are. Can I interest you in a Hawaiian pizza to go with your Beaujolais? Or are you more of a Margherita girl?'

'You'll never find this wife of yours if you're too scared to go on a date.' She stared at him across the table.

He shrugged. 'Then let's start now. Tell me about yourself. We can hardly describe you as a little bit boring.'

'Not with me, you fool. Obviously, you're never going to slum it with Lexie from the block.'

He studied her again. 'Your financial situation really bothers you, doesn't it?' His contemplative look irked her even more.

'Absolutely not!' She tried to ignore the sudden draught through her jumpsuit, which had seen slightly better days. 'There's nothing wrong with living modestly.'

He nodded slowly, as though he'd never really thought about it. 'It suits you.'

She felt like a cartoon character whose eyes were in danger of popping out of its head on stalks. What did he mean by that? Seeing her expression, he looked surprised and tried to backtrack.

'Oh hell, did that sound wrong? You see why I'm no good at these things. What I meant was ...' He waved a hand in her direction. 'You look fine as you are. Although I do wish you'd organise your own affairs as well as you organise everyone else's. It wouldn't hurt to get on top of your paperwork and to sort out some rainy day savings.'

'I don't need "rainy day savings". I don't want to have money – it does nothing for your manners.' She swallowed down a memory from her snooty senior school with a long swig of wine. It had only been reinforced by the bitching and mayhem outside the ballroom.

The waiter arrived to take their food orders, which was probably just as well. Lexie was sure she'd end up sacked if she continued on her 'rich is rude' tirade. What she wanted to say was, it was *his* financial situation that bothered her, not hers. She'd spent her teenage years at that awful posh school, and the girls had been nothing but mean about her lack of money and make-do-and-mend clothes. Maybe her current wild wardrobe was a rebellion against all things conventional.

'And you, madam?'

The waiter was staring at her, waiting for her order as though he'd been asking for some time.

'Er ... ' She flicked quickly through the menu, decided it was stupidly over-priced, and opted for nothing. 'I'm not hungry.' She slapped it shut and gave the waiter a tight smile. 'Thank you.'

Maybe she shouldn't have given such a big chunk of her wages to that seal sanctuary, but the picture on Cory's T-shirt had looked so cute.

'It's a business lunch. You don't have to pay,' said Ben, apparently sensing her awkwardness.

Was he mocking her now? She didn't need to be paid for. And just because she was only his employee ...

He reached a hand across the table and placed it on

hers, which seemed to be shaking. What was that – anger? Nerves? Or just that late spring chill?

'It's OK. I owe you for various dubious takeaways, which you keep thrusting upon me against my will. The least you can do is let me repay you with a cheap and cheerful pizza.'

He had a point, although to her these prices were definitely not cheap. But whatever had just been bubbling up inside her had genuinely put her off her food. It was weird, and slightly irritating.

'Want to share my Hawaiian? All that pineapple might be a bit too crazy for me anyway. I'll probably need your help.' He gave her an annoyingly sweet frown of apology, and she found herself nodding.

She did feel a bit guilty for getting narky. It wasn't strictly his fault he had a better bank balance. Although, maybe she would speak to him about giving some away to those seals. They really could do with more help.

But first, she should have a word with herself. What was wrong with her today? It wasn't like her to be so topsy-turvy. The main task on her agenda was to convince Ben to let her tag along to the paint conference. She had no idea why she kept poking the hornets' nest that was Ben's sorry dating situation. Was it that the sooner he shacked up in his marriage of convenience, the sooner she'd feel safe from that irksome internal fidget she couldn't quite place? Because if they were going to spend the weekend in the same hotel, there would be a lot less confusion if she knew he was tied up with someone else.

A single swan floating along the water pulled her back to the present.

'Grace,' she heard herself saying. Grace was perfect for him. Wasn't she? If those two got together, Ben would surely inherit his kingdom, and the employees of Nutgrass Hall would live happily ever after. And Lexie would be safe from a danger that, however unlikely it had once seemed, was now troubling the edges of her subconscious.

The danger that if she didn't tread with caution, she might stumble heart first into the nightmarish world of money and pretentious bad manners. Again.

Chapter 22

When the waiter had disappeared and Lexie had spent enough time pretending to be fascinated by a swan, Ben made tentative steps back to their conversation.

'So. It would cheer you up if I went on a date with Grace?'

Would it? Or was she just using lovely Grace as a human shield to protect her soul from whatever she'd started to feel when Ben had walked into that ballroom? Lexie sighed. 'This isn't about me.'

He was doing that twitchy smile again.

'What?' said Lexie. 'You need to find a rich and vaguely interesting wife before you turn into a pumpkin. Grace is an incredible catch. Maybe the sooner you sort your life out, the sooner your mother will get off your back. And mine. She clearly sees my presence as some kind of threat to her master plan, although goodness knows why. Let's just say she's not exactly my bestie.'

Ben's face lit up with a smile. 'I said you were shrewd. But don't take it personally. Mum's never been one for besties. She's not motivated by friendship.'

You mean she's not very nice, Lexie thought. But she decided against saying that, second glass of wine or otherwise.

'She's not been quite herself lately.' He exhaled strongly and seemed to gather his thoughts. 'She took it hard when Dad died. I think maybe she . . . blamed herself, for various reasons. For a while she tried to cling on to Cory and me so tightly we thought our heads would explode. Then by some miracle she fell for her new man, Carlito, and things changed. She moved out and bought herself a little pad ten miles away. Can you imagine.'

The part Lexie still couldn't picture was the stern Mrs Carrington-Noble cavorting around with a hot young Spanish guy. She wondered if he'd passed her strict financial tick-list.

'Of course she never fully let go,' Ben continued. 'She still owns the place.'

And parades around her creepy peacocks, fills it with funeral flowers and turns up at intervals to spring-clean other people's lives from the driveway, thought Lexie, trying not to grimace.

'But lately, she's been acting strangely. First this insistence to get the business off her hands and to ensure I marry someone rich to inherit it. Then her behaviour towards you and your camper van. It's all rather . . .'

Outrageous? Offensive? Stark raving mad?

'Clingy,' Lexie settled on, impressed at her own diplomacy.

'She did seem to approve of Grace.' He rubbed his jaw, which was always so impressively smooth. 'And the money adds up.'

'Of course. I mean, what else is there?' Lexie tried to hide the sarcasm from her voice. 'And will you be happy if the bank balance is a match?'

There was a splashing in the water as two ducks flapped to safety, trying to avoid a yacht that was gliding towards them along the river. The proud vessel seemed out of place against the pretty painted canal boats moored along the water's edge.

'Money is my only saving grace, Lexie. We can't all be naturally flamboyant.'

Flamboyant. Hmm. Did he just mean trashy?

But the pizza arrived like a great steaming barricade between them, and Ben was saved by the pineapple. Maybe they would always belong at opposite sides of the table, but it was fun to watch him trying to tuck in with his hands when she knew he was desperate to pick up his knife and fork.

As they negotiated the gooey pizza, they went through their usual weekly updates. How the blog was going, what the stats were like for the website, what had been happening on social media. Things were looking positive. Perhaps that was why Mrs Carrington-Noble was just about putting up with Lexie's presence. Drawing in and nurturing clients improved revenue, and the woman couldn't resist more pounds in her Chanel-lined pocket.

As Lexie watched Ben handle his wildly brave lunch, she couldn't help thinking that with each meeting, he seemed to relax a little. Was he beginning to trust her judgement? Maybe it was a good time to tackle him on her next issue, while he had his hands full.

'We'll be in London for the paint conference when our next weekly meeting is due.'

'Did I even agree to you coming?' He narrowed his eyes.

'You were saying we should do a field trip abroad when we were chatting in Tom's secret garden. Consider London your trial run.'

'But . . . '

Lexie held her hands up. 'Feel free to do your own social media promotions if you prefer. Or waste a massive opportunity to showcase what you do to your audience.'

He nodded cautiously, his mouth full of pizza.

'Maybe you can entertain me with the gossip on your matchmaking dates while we're there. You'll surely have been on at least one by then?'

Ben quickly swallowed his mouthful. 'What? Why? Doesn't this count?' He gestured between them.

'We find each other aggravating and I'm thankfully too skint to meet the criteria, so, no, actually.'

'You're not always aggravating,' he conceded.

'But I am always poor.' She didn't wait for the inevitable awkward silence. 'If you want my opinion, I'm vetoing Bug Lady. I can't see that you have anything in common other than money in the bank and a lack of things to talk about, and your mother doesn't want all those dead critters in the house.'

Lexie gave him a moment to fight for his queen of the

166

cockroaches, but he just gave a disinterested shrug. Well, that answered that question.

'Anyway, I'm vetoing Grace,' he responded.

'You're suddenly so fussy that not even Grace is good enough for you? What's your big problem?'

'No big problem,' he said. 'I just don't want to marry her.' His tone was nonchalant, as though they were discussing what to have for pudding.

'Of course you don't – you barely know her. Maybe you just need to spend time with some of these women.'

'Sounds exhausting.'

'Maybe your mother could do that bit for you too.' Lexie flicked her eyes skywards. 'And don't even bother doing that twitchy smile thing.'

He raised an eyebrow.

'I mean it.' She pointed a finger at his mouth.

They held their position for a moment, Ben clearly trying hard to keep his mouth still, and Lexie feeling sure she could see that sneaky smile peeping through his eyes instead.

'You don't just see someone and decide you want to marry them. It doesn't work like that,' Lexie said, returning her digit to the rest of the pack and grabbing her wine.

'It doesn't?' he asked, with his best innocent look.

Lexie thought back across her past landscape of failed relationships. She'd never quite believed she'd marry Inkie or Drew, so how could she say what a proper match was meant to look like? Maybe she was out of her depth trying to advise anyone.

'Then how do you know when the right one arrives?' he

continued. 'Will there be some sort of sign? Will she arrive in a great puff of diesel smoke, with a fanfare of peacocks?'

'Yes, very funny.' She could do without being mocked. 'Maybe your princess would arrive in a Bentley dressed like she was ready for the ball. Although if you don't keep your eyes peeled, you won't even notice.'

'If you're so keen on Grace, maybe you should go out with her yourself.'

'Maybe I will,' said Lexie, grabbing another slice of the communal pizza.

'If you haven't decided to dislike the poor woman just because her parents have money.'

'I would never ...' But she let her voice trail off. OK, so she did tend to judge. But only based on her past experiences.

'Oh, please, you're a money snob in reverse. You're prejudiced against wealth – no wonder you do your best never to have any. Don't think I haven't noticed your "rich people are rude" stance.'

'I'm not prejudiced against anyone!' When he put it like that, it didn't sound nice. She hadn't intended to be that sort of person. 'I'm sure the perfect match will be somewhere among your mother's fine collection. Who knows what magic sparks could fly.'

Ben gave her a strange look. 'I'm not looking for Harry Potter. Anyway, you said most of them were gold-diggers or rich-husband murderers. Excuse me for having standards.'

She guessed she couldn't argue with that. He got on her nerves at times, but she didn't want him dead.

'And, quite honestly, I'm not sure I want the kind of woman who would let herself be interviewed for the role of potential wife. Don't you think it's a little ... odd?'

Lexie's mouth fell open. 'You allowed your mother to set up that whole charade and you let poor Mrs Moon get blisters pushing her tea trolley up and down your queue of cat-fighting prima donnas. And even I ended up being bossed around by your mother and looked down upon by your potential princesses. And now you can't even be bothered to consider a single one of them?'

He let the words hang for a moment while he chose his own. 'Why are you so keen for me to go on a date?'

Lexie pushed herself up to standing, the legs of her chair making a belligerent growl as they scraped across the stones. Were those tears prickling at the backs of her eyelids? 'I don't know.'

And, truly, she just wasn't sure. Was she putting everyone else before herself again? Or was something deeper at play?

'I need to get back. Take my share of lunch out of my wages,' Lexie said as she snatched up her bag. 'I can pay for my own.'

She wondered if he'd even bother to touch the *exotic* pineapple now she was gone.

Chapter 23

'Honestly, everything is fine with me and Billy-Bob! I just came to say hi. And to check out my sister's posh new home. Twit-twoo!'

Lexie narrowed her eyes at Sky, who'd arrived at Nutgrass Hall earlier that day pretending not to be in a flap. Lexie had received a call from her first thing that morning, asking her to transfer some money so she could catch the train from the commune.

'Nobody travels one hundred and sixty miles to say hi,' said Lexie, who remained to be convinced by anything her younger sister said – ever. 'And me living here is an extremely temporary measure. Much like you living in a yurt with a guy who bones two other women, I seriously hope.'

Grace, who was also sitting cross-legged on the floor of the living room with the two sisters, spat out a mouthful of green tea.

'Does he really?'

Grace had arrived to help Lexie with a few work things, and Lexie was glad. She was also secretly relieved Ben had vetoed Grace from the wife hunt, not least because she got to keep Grace to herself. It absolutely wasn't due to any desire to keep Ben single. No way.

Sky fidgeted on her cushion, chomping on her fourth Greggs sausage roll of the afternoon. Lexie had known she'd make a rubbish vegan. 'It's not exactly like that. We take it in turns.'

'Noooooo! How does that work? Do you use a timer? Or is it more of a rota system?' Grace seemed genuinely intrigued.

Lexie held up a hand. 'Enough. It's too weird.' People could do what they wanted in the privacy of their own sleeping bags, but she'd prefer it if they didn't involve her perpetually naïve sibling.

'Not as weird as getting roped in to serve cake while your boss's mum holds interviews to find him a wife.' Sky pouted. 'At least my love triangle was brought together by fate, not by a meddling posh lady with a clipboard.'

'I'm not in any love triangle! And anyway, four people make a quadrangle,' Lexie corrected her. She could see from Grace's face she was trying to work out the logistics of Sky's yurt bed-shenanigans.

'Anyway!' Lexie pushed the laptop to Grace. 'We were meant to be talking about this.'

Grace ran her eyes over the screen for the second time that afternoon. 'Lexie, honey, it still makes zero sense.'

'But why?'

Lexie had been drafting another blog post for Carrington Paints, inspired by her feud with Ben. Of course she wasn't going to tell the world he was a pedantic sod who made everything difficult; her writing was sufficiently cryptic. She should probably give him credit for the fact he'd since offered to let her come to the upcoming conference as a sweetener, but she still felt decidedly like a sourpuss.

'You say clashing colours should be avoided at all costs.'

Lexie tugged the fraying sleeve of her favourite yellow jumper. 'That's true.'

'Although what you really mean is your boss has pissed you off,' said Grace.

'He's annoying.' Lexie sniffed.

'But you told me he was beige,' Grace continued. 'How does beige clash with anything?'

'Urgh, he's not actually that beige. He just thinks he is.'

'Really? That's the saddest thing I've ever heard.' Grace rearranged her elegantly scruffy top-knot, which was now streaked with blue after she'd insisted on experimenting with Lexie's hair dye. 'Maybe you should help him see his own true colours. Coax him out of his hermit-crab shell and get him painting the town red!'

'No! I've seen his true colours, and they're more or less the shade of a bank note. He can bugger off. We totally clash. It's there in black and white.' Lexie waved at her laptop screen.

Grace leaned over and pressed delete. 'So rewrite it.'

Sky and Lexie gasped.

'Oi! It took me all bloody morning to write that.'

'You were never going to post it. It was a passive-aggressive rant, and it would have got you the sack.'

Lexie glared at Grace.

'Anyway, you love clashing colours.' Grace pointed at Lexie's outfit, the dalmatian print on her jumper looking admittedly odd against her wildly striped shorts.

'So do you,' Lexie muttered.

Grace was wearing one of Lexie's thrift-shop jumpers – one of the many things she'd fallen in love with from Lexie's wardrobe. Lexie had to admit, Grace was like her sister from a richer mother.

'The only Carrington I'd want to get clash-y with is the surfer one.' Grace wiggled her bare toes, which were still drying from Lexie's bargain orange nail varnish. 'Can you hook me up?'

'Ooh, yeah, he's hot!' Sky shook her head and seemed to remember herself.

'Stop it, the pair of you! No more matchmaking.'

Grace looked at Lexie and lowered her voice. 'Hey, we should matchmake you with Ben.'

'Yeah, you totally blush when he's around.' Sky giggled.

Grace threw herself backwards onto a mound of cushions and kicked her feet with joy. 'You'd make an excellent lady of the manor.'

Lexie threw pillows at both of them. 'That's ridiculous. Anyway, I'd never feel at home among all the finery, horsey paintings and shades of bloody snooty.'

'So you'd make it your own,' Grace replied.

'Stop it! The financial criteria are extremely strict, anyway. I'm from a totally different world.'

Grace sat bolt upright. 'But you like him?'

'Absolutely not! When did I say that?'

'You didn't say you didn't – which says it all! Want me to share some cash?' Grace offered.

Lexie pursed her lips.

'What? Money is just stuff, Lexie. You share your things with me.' Grace shimmied in her borrowed jumper.

'Not the same.' Lexie crossed her arms.

'You'd be surprised.'

'I wouldn't.' Lexie tried to keep her voice level as the memory of being the girl with hard-up parents bit again. 'I went to school with a bunch of rich girls. I managed to get a bursary for less well-off kids because of my talents in art, but I never really belonged. So they kept pointing out.'

'Ahh, Lex.' Grace leaned across and grabbed her hand. 'Were they cruel-arsed bitches?'

Lexie couldn't help but laugh. 'Yeah, kind of. I just always felt different, you know? Not good enough. The one with the slightly odd clothes, who would probably never make it because she couldn't afford uni.'

'Wow,' said Grace, rubbing Lexie's hand. 'This is deep. So you repel money, in case you end up like one of the meanie bitches.' She nodded sagely, seeming pleased she'd unravelled all of Lexie's problems in the space of a minute.

'I do not repel money.' Lexie pulled her hand back and fiddled with her sleeve. It was all very well Grace unpicking her problems, but then they'd end up with a massive pile of tangled wool. How was that better?

'I didn't know the girls at your school were nasty,' Sky said quietly. 'You didn't say.'

'Hey, it wasn't so bad.' Lexie pulled her sister into a hug, always keen to protect her. That was part of the reason Lexie had got a job instead of borrowing money for uni. She wanted to help out, so Sky never got laughed at for being the girl with crappy trainers. Not that she'd ever confess that. 'You know me. If people joke about my clothes, I dress even more kookily.' That much was true. She'd never felt like a victim – just *different. Less*, perhaps.

'Maybe it would be better if you didn't keep having to bail me out,' said Sky. 'I'll pay you back for the train ticket.' She sniffed and pulled away from the hug.

'No you won't, silly. You'll always be my favourite project.'

Grace wiped a tear from her eye and cleared her throat. 'Anyway! You can rewrite this ranty blog post later. Because right now, we have something more important to fix.'

Chapter 24

'Like what?' Lexie asked Sky, wondering what the little minx was so interested in fixing next.

'Like you,' Sky replied simply. 'And your crazy theory that money builds walls around hearts.'

'What was it that rapper guy said?' asked Grace. 'More money, more ...'

'Problems,' Lexie concluded.

'I gave all mine away to the commune,' Sky told Grace, like it was the winning formula. 'Not that I had much. But now everyone is equal.'

And nobody can afford to get the train out of there, thought Lexie. But she didn't want to make her sibling feel bad.

Grace shrugged. 'Honestly, I've been out with guys from all walks of life. I can't say money makes much difference. It's how they behave that matters. And how they make you feel.'

'Well, rich guys make me feel poor,' said Lexie.

'And poor guys screw you over and try and land you in jail,' Sky added.

Lexie shot her a warning look. This was not about her stupid ex Inkie, either.

'Incredible!' said Grace. 'You two have so much fun. You've got to tell me ...'

'No, we don't,' said Lexie, through tightened lips.

'So tell me about you and Ben then,' said Grace. 'Because if I didn't know better, Lexie Summers, I'd say you had a thing for that boss of yours.'

'Completely,' Sky agreed, like some kind of relationship oracle.

'I do not!' Lexie replied, her voice a few octaves higher than she'd expected. She cleared her throat. 'I do not have designs on Ben "I want my mother's money" Carrington. I don't.'

A chorus of angry peacocks somewhere in the distance seemed to disagree.

'I beg to differ,' said Grace. 'And he gave you a pretty intense look in the ballroom that day too. There was something going on behind those mysterious eyes of his.'

'He was looking at you,' said Lexie.

'Nope. He'd already given me an awkward nod; then his gaze suckered onto you. His eyes were more like magnets than globes.'

Lexie tried not to think of those eyes. 'Like I said. Even if I had any thoughts of that nature – which I absolutely don't – they'd be irrelevant. I'm not the same.'

There was silence for a moment, as though the three

girls were chewing over their thoughts. Grace was the first to speak.

'It makes me sad that you think you're not as good as those women, just because of a bunch of numbers. It doesn't matter that they buy their shoes from Harvey Nic's. You're just as fantastic as they are, Lexie. You're a real career woman with talent and vision. Hell, you could even make your own fortune,' said Grace.

Lexie screwed up her face.

'You just have to trust yourself. To believe in your ideas.'

Where had she heard this before? Was Grace conspiring with Ben, or something? It wasn't Lexie's job to have ideas, outside of orchestrating social media and the like. Big ideas were always followed by trouble.

'And if you did save a bit of money, instead of squandering it all on seals in need,' Grace continued. 'It wouldn't make you ugly. In fact, in life you've got to secure your own parachute first. If you don't save yourself, helping others won't even be an option. You'll just be hurtling towards the pavement, ready to go splat like a big old pot of red paint.'

'Nasty,' said Sky.

Lexie considered it. 'I guess if I had more money, I could definitely save more seals in the long run. And stranded sisters.' She still sensed there was discord in Sky's not-quite-paradise.

Grace rolled her eyes. 'Both noble causes, I'm sure. But you're doing it again. Putting yourself at the back of the queue. I'm asking you to value yourself, Lexie. To believe that you are good enough for whichever path you choose. And that goes beyond money.'

'Definitely.' Sky grabbed her sister's hands. 'Give it all away, Lex. Come and live in the commune.'

Lexie snatched her hands back. 'No bloody way!' If anything, her sister was an advert for getting a truckload of ISAs. She got to her feet and began pacing, full of tense energy that she needed to shake off. Why was everyone getting on her back? 'So you think I don't believe in myself?'

'Well, do you?'

Lexie trailed her fingers across the furniture as she traipsed circuits around the room. 'At times I have,' she said hesitantly.

'And then?'

'And then ... *life*.' She swallowed back her thoughts. Whenever she tried believing in herself, it only ever came back to bite her.

Grace waved a hand. 'The past is done, Lex. We don't live there anymore.'

She had a way of making everything sound so simple.

'What would you do right now, if you believed in yourself?' asked Grace. 'Go on, tell us. No judgement here.'

Lexie stopped, her hand hovering above a coffee table, which was far too mahogany for its own good. She knew exactly what she would do if she believed in herself. It had been popping into her thoughts often enough.

She picked up the table and dragged it to the centre of the room, where Grace and Sky were sitting.

'Paint this.'

Grace and Sky looked at each other and started laughing.

'Pfffff – that's the best you've got? You'd paint an ugly brown table?'

'Hey, you said no judgement! Anyway, I'd paint other stuff too.' Lexie looked at the walls, which were still far too beige. But it wasn't *these* walls, exactly. 'It's more of a feeling, really. That things need shaking up.' She fought for the words, which were still a bit jumbled. 'If I had my way, I'd be choosing the colour schemes. Metaphorically speaking. I'd be painting a new palette. Something more exciting.'

Sky scratched her head. 'So what, you'd be a painter? Like Aunt Jasmine?'

Lexie had loved painting at school, but this was something more. This was about ideas. Ideas that always blossomed when Ben was around. Like his confidence in what he did rubbed off on her, or maybe his surprising words of encouragement gave her wings.

She thought of the factory, with its conveyor-belt production of slightly-too-tame shades. Was she here to brighten it? What the hell – this was just a fantasy.

'I would rewrite the colour book.' Lexie waved her arms like a magician, finally getting into the spirit of daring to dream.

'And get rid of that horrible Mrs Carrington-thingamajig,' Sky added.

There was a clattering somewhere in the distance. The walls in this place really did seem to have ears.

'Shh!' Lexie giggled. 'You'll get me into bother!' She draped herself belly first across the long coffee table and kicked out her legs. 'Then I'd bring out a range of chalk-style paints. Paints for real people, who like to make do and mend, to create new beginnings.' She grabbed a nail file from her back pocket and pretended to rub it over the varnish, as though sanding away the dullness.

Caught up in the moment, Grace sprang to her feet and began pirouetting with a net curtain. 'You could take over the empire, make bossy Ben your employee and demand that his mother finds you a suitably rich husband!' She blinked at the girls from behind her makeshift veil.

'I still think Cory is better.' Sky jumped onto one of the sofas and braced herself in a surfing-the-waves position.

'The Carrington guys are hot!' Grace squealed, through a room full of raucous laughter.

As the three girls threw shapes in their unlikely game of roleplay, there was an almighty metallic clunk against the doorway, then a crashing of delicate china. A tea trolley sped into the room, followed by a panting Mrs Moon and a red-faced fox of a woman.

Chapter 25

'M rs Carrington-Noble is here!' Mrs Moon announced, shoving her trolley to safety on the living-room rug with one hand and rearranging her bonnet with the other.

But Lexie could hardly mistake her. She gulped, praying that the woman hadn't heard the bit about her sons being hot.

'What on earth?' Ben and Cory's mother glared at Lexie, Sky and Grace in turn, seemingly deciding which one to tear apart first. Her eyes landed on Lexie. They were angry and grey, and looked nothing like Ben's comparatively agreeable atlases.

The girls stayed frozen in their now-quite-ridiculous poses – Sky surfing the sofa, Grace camouflaged by a net curtain and Lexie wishing she hadn't belly-flopped onto a table better suited for morning coffee.

'Get. Off. My. FURNITURE!'

Lexie and Sky didn't wait to be told twice. They

scrambled to their feet and lined up with their backs to the fireplace, like two of the children von Trapp. Lexie couldn't even argue; they'd been acting like love-starved chimpanzees. Although the absence of Grace in the line-up made her quake at the threat of rebellion.

Mrs Carrington-Noble coughed into her hand, almost winded by the effort of shouting, before straightening her jacket and composing herself. 'Alexis.'

'It's just Lexie.' Her voice came out as a squeak and she saw Mrs Moon grimace.

'Alexis. I have put up with you squatting under my roof. *In the circumstances.*'

'In the circumstances of you having had my van crushed,' Lexie muttered, somewhere in the direction of her slippers.

'But if you're going to announce on *social media* that you're moving in your assemblage of *sisters,*' she hissed the final word, looking back and forth between Grace and Sky, 'then I'll have to rethink my position.'

'Sister,' Lexie mumbled. 'I only have one, and she's just visiting.'

Lexie pointed towards Sky, and tried not to cringe as Mrs Carrington-Noble appraised her. Sky was looking particularly 'hippy commune' in a brown floaty dress, with scraps of ribbon braided through her henna-dyed hair. The woman let out a huff before turning her attention on Grace, who was still swishing around in the net curtain, face veiled like an obstinate bride.

Lexie dared to glance back at Grace. Of the unlikely trio, her friend was the only one who didn't look fazed.

Lexie could have sworn she heard her chomping on imaginary gum.

'Who is this?' Mrs Carrington-Noble directed the question at Lexie, as though the blue-haired woman in the borrowed thrift-shop jumper did not deserve to speak. 'And why won't she remove herself from my bobbinet swags?'

'Grace,' her new friend said. 'Not short for Gracious, Cornelius or anything fancy. Just Grace.'

Oh God, oh God, oh God. Lexie could feel Sky's shoulders beginning to shake with laughter at her side. And why was Mrs Carrington-Noble wearing some kind of screen-goddess turban? This was too much.

'*Not-Gracious* who?' Mrs Carrington-Noble screwed up her forehead as though the name was vaguely familiar.

Mrs Moon fiddled awkwardly with her tea trolley, fishing bits of broken china from her Victoria sponge. Lexie tried not to think of the time the housekeeper explained that the Patricia Noble of her school days hated her name being shortened, or in fact extended – to Patty Cowpat.

'Does my surname matter?'

Lexie could see Mrs Carrington-Noble's pointed chin beginning to tremble with annoyance.

'Young lady, if you are in my house, leading a merry dance with my silk bobbinet fabrics and making lewd comments about my offspring, you can at least identify yourself.'

The woman had ratcheted up her accent to the highest level of posh. Lexie really was going to have to try hard not to wet herself.

'Very well,' said Grace, over-exaggerating her own

184

pronunciation. She stepped out from behind the netting and gave a bored-looking shrug. 'It's Montgomery.' She let the name settle for a moment, before adding the final embellishment. 'Daughter of Magnus and Mirabella.'

Mrs Carrington-Noble's glare narrowed in on Grace's features and then she did a double-take.

Lexie didn't know much about shape-shifters, but she was pretty sure Mrs Carrington-Noble was embarking on an excellent impression of one. As the penny dropped, the double-barrelled show-off switched from uptight lady of the manor to shameless suck-up in a matter of moments.

'Oh, *Montgaaaawwwmery*. Of course, of course! Why didn't you say, darling girl? We've met already. Mrs Moon, pour the tea. Do take a seat.'

The transformed woman rushed to the sofa and began fluffing up cushions for her esteemed guest. Lexie was still trying to stifle her laughter.

'Who's *Montgaaaawwwmery*?' Sky hissed in her ear, her sweet northern accent not quite getting it.

Lexie elbowed her in the ribs.

'My surname shouldn't make a difference.'

Mrs Moon hurtled towards them with the tea trolley, always keen to fix a situation with cake. She stopped in front of Grace, who waved a hand and began serving Sky and Lexie.

Mrs Carrington-Noble looked horrified that the daughter of one of the richest couples in the county was serving cake to her unwanted squatters, but seemed too surprised to intervene.

'In fact, I was just explaining to Lexie that financial status shouldn't matter. I mean, it's not as though I'd look down on anyone for being *nouveau riche*. Would you?'

Mrs Carrington-Noble mumbled something and re-arranged her funny turban, like her crown had just been knocked.

Lexie was too busy pinching her giggling lips together to bother deciphering their alien subtext.

Mrs Moon ducked in, secured her mistress a slice of sponge and helped her sit down.

'And to what do we owe this pleasure?' Mrs Carrington-Noble addressed Grace. 'Have you come to see Ben? I can send for him ...'

Grace shook her head and took a bite of cake. She chewed slowly, and Lexie could tell she was brewing up mischief. She just prayed whatever Grace came out with wouldn't land her in more trouble after the joke-dust had settled.

After an excruciating wait, Grace answered.

'To be honest, Ben's not my cup of tea. I get the impression he's more interested in Lexie.'

Mrs Carrington-Noble baulked and began choking on her jammy sponge.

'Oh, Pat! Don't panic,' Grace said, going over to rub Mrs Carrington-Noble's back. 'Lexie's far too good for Ben. He's really rather beige.'

When the old fox's breathing had returned to normal, Grace gave Lexie a wink. 'Although I'd keep your eye on Sky, over there. She's got room for two more concubines, and she's definitely got one of her eyes on your Cory.'

Oh, gee whiz on a moped. As much as Grace meant well in standing up for Lexie, she knew she was absolutely going to pay for this at some point. And remembering Mrs Carrington-Noble's van-crushing rampage last time Lexie went on a field trip, she just prayed the woman didn't come sniffing out trouble when Lexie was away in London with Ben.

Chapter 26

As the lights of the London skyline blinked at Lexie through the indigo night, she thanked her lucky stars for the chance to flit away from Nutgrass Hall. After her awkward run-in with Mrs Carrington-Noble, she was sure the old mare would be nipping at her behind again at some point. At least Sky had saved herself and gone back to the commune – although who knew which was worse.

But right then, Lexie was free. It was the weekend of the paint conference and as she sipped cocktails at a bar in the Shard with Ben, she tried to pretend it was only the cocktails that were making the evening sparkle.

'Did you learn anything today?' he asked, a mischievous glint in his eye. He'd warned her it would be as dull as watching paint dry, but she'd been determined to brighten it up.

She pulled out her notebook. 'Yep. I know all about nanocoatings and poly-something-or-others.' She pointed to some words that she'd definitely misspelt.

'Anything else?'

'Might have picked up some ideas for a little side project.' She tapped her nose.

'Oh, the chalk-style paints for renovating furniture? Yes, I overheard. You should try it. We could play with some ideas at the factory.'

Damn it. And why did he always make everything seem so easy? 'No need! It's probably silly anyway.' It seemed like he already knew too much. If she failed spectacularly as a paint mixologist, she wanted to do so in the privacy of her own living space – borrowed as it was.

What he didn't know was that she'd felt a strange tingle of *something* when she'd watched him work that conference room. It was as though a spark had come alive in him; she could barely tear her eyes away. For someone who couldn't arrange himself a date, he had no problem charming potential business contacts. It was just a shame they were mostly ageing, overfed men with questionable comb-overs.

'Your ideas aren't silly. In fact, they're often annoyingly astute. Anyway, for a lady who's got her deep purple claws into everyone else's business, you don't accept much help in return.' He pointed to her varnished nails, which matched her full-length tube dress. It was one of her favourites from the bottom of her suitcase, but it made sliding on and off her high bar stool feel like a bit of a gyrate-athon.

'I do accept help.' She sniffed and pulled her Manhattan towards her. 'Just not from you.'

'Ah, yes, the illustrious Grace.' Ben's eyes rolled towards

the stars. 'Is she also the reason I had a rollocking from my mother about being besotted with you?'

His gaze lingered on Lexie for a moment too long and she felt her face flame.

'Which I'm not,' he clarified, taking a swig of his own drink.

Had he felt that burning too? A bit more air-con wouldn't have gone amiss. Ben's choice of exclusive cocktail bar was so high up that Lexie was starting to feel heady. At least she hoped that was the reason. The view of the capital by night was spectacular, but that really wasn't the only sight which was magnetising her attention.

'Of course not.' She dismissed the idea with her hand. He probably only had eyes for the Queen's head on a banknote.

'And thanks to that, I was forced to go on one of Mother's horrendous dates to keep her off my back and avert suspicion.'

Suspicion? He made it sound like he and Lexie had something to hide. Did they? No, surely . . .

She shook her head. 'Er, yes, you mentioned. So tell me more about . . . Amanda?'

'I was hoping to forget.' He rubbed a hand across his face.

'Oh dear. That bad?' Lexie reached over and squeezed his forearm, which felt remarkably firm through his crisp white shirt. 'You'll find someone.' She should really let go of his arm, but the little flutter in her chest was willing her not to.

'I just don't know,' he said. 'On paper, it should have worked.'

On paper. Lexie pulled her hand back. He could keep his fluttery stomach charms. 'Well, you must be extremely difficult to match,' she hissed across the shiny bar. 'I mean, what kind of guy says his favourite fruit is an apple? An apple!' She pointed to the scribbles she'd made in her notebook that day in Tom's secret garden.

'What's wrong with apples? I've seen you eating them.'

'Of course you have. Everyone eats apples, but they're not my *favourite*. You need to branch out. Be a pineapple, or something.'

She was expecting to see hackles, but he just countered her with a mildly amused face.

'I'll leave the crown wearing to you.'

That didn't even deserve an eyeroll.

'So, come on, what was so terrible? She drove the wrong sort of Rolls-Royce? She didn't bank offshore?'

'Lexie, don't be so crude. I didn't vet her finances.'

'No, of course not. Your mother did that for you.'

Ben released a frustrated huff. His breath was warm and smelt of sweet maraschino cherries. She was absolutely ignoring it.

'If this matchmaking process was going to work, Amanda seemed perfectly suitable. At least, for most of the date. And yet … I had no interest in an amalgamation.'

'An amalgamation? You make it sound like a business merger! Or something gloopy to do with paint.'

'Which was exactly what this was meant to be. A transaction of convenience.'

Lexie tried not to bristle. 'And now?'

'It feels like that's not enough. I want more.' He fixed her with those atlas eyes that made her feel like anything was possible.

'Like ... physically?'

Ben laughed. 'By the end of the date, Amanda had made it pretty clear that was on the table if I wanted it.'

'And did you want it? On the table?' Lexie blinked. Oh, *what*? 'I mean ... not on the table, but generally.' Why had she asked such a thing? Did she even want to know?

'With a woman who was all but trying to prise my trousers off to see what I was using to pad out my Calvin Kleins?'

Various thoughts buzzed around Lexie's head, and she wasn't sure where to start. The thought of Ben in a tight pair of Calvins, or the chance to get down and dirty with him on a table.

Mmm, that suddenly sounded appealing. She'd heard him taking a long shower in his neighbouring hotel room that morning, and the enticing thought of it had been springing up ever since. She knew they were totally unsuitable as a long-term prospect. But sex ...

'Lexie?'

Shit, what was wrong with her? This was Ben. This was work! She shook her head back to the present and tried to look innocent.

'Er, right. Sorry! As if you'd need to pad out your boxers.' She gave a nervous laugh and willed herself not to look at his trouser region. Which was really bloody difficult now the thought had crossed her mind.

He gave her a strange look.

'Oh God, not that I've checked. I mean, I have no idea if you'd need to beef up your briefs. I'm just assuming. Anyway, it's not even a thing, is it? Not like girls padding their bras.' She cupped a boob by way of panicked demonstration.

She. Cupped. A. Boob. What the hell were her crazy limbs doing? She pulled her hand away from her chest and tried to ignore the frisson of excitement as she saw his startled eyes glance there.

No, he surely hadn't meant to.

Lexie fanned her face. The air-con was seriously unreliable; she needed a moment.

She slithered off her too-high bar stool, trying her best not to look like a seductive snake-woman, and disappeared in the direction of the ladies' before her thoughts could get her into trouble.

When Lexie returned from the loo five minutes later, Ben had taken off his tie and loosened his collar. Damn it, she'd just been trying to cool off. She could do without him looking a notch more handsome. Maybe he was feeling this extra heat too.

'Tell me what I should do,' he said to her, as she tried to manoeuvre her bottom back onto the world's trickiest bar stool. 'I'm no good at these dating matters. I thought Mother's plan was straightforward enough for a plain, apple-loving man like me, but ...'

'Actually, I think you're faking it,' Lexie declared when her bum was safely back on fabric.

He swished the orange peel around the burnt amber liquid in his glass and she wondered what he was thinking.

'I mean, you say you don't get out much,' she continued. 'And that your dating life is a disaster.' She looked around the bar with its tantalisingly dusky lighting and shimmering walls of glass. 'But I don't think you need my advice at all.'

He smiled at her, but there was a sadness somehow. As though he'd grappled over the thought before.

'Quite the opposite, Miss Summers. I'm beginning to notice I need you more than I could ever have bargained for.'

Miss Summers. *God*. It had really wound her up when he'd first called her that, like a teacher speaking to an unworthy pupil. But now … She grabbed her cocktail stick and popped her maraschino cherry into her mouth before she let out some sort of involuntary moan. And how did he need her? Like, *need* need? Or just the need for a bit of advice on finding his rich wife? Yes, surely the latter …

'You did an impressive job of choosing the dinner venue too,' she managed, once she'd swallowed her cocktail decoration. Why did her voice sound so husky?

After the paint conference, Ben had shepherded her to possibly the best Thai restaurant ever, outside of Thailand. He'd clearly done his homework. The menu had been as gloriously sweet and spicy as Ben's efforts to skate outside his comfort zone. Lexie had struggled once more to ignore that surprising feeling – her poor, unsuspecting heart being warmed.

'Well, I had my work cut out to beat your breakfast venue. Peanut butter, bacon and banana on a waffle. Who knew?' he said, with a smile.

'Who knew there were still living humans who'd never

tried waffles.' She returned his grin, glad of their familiar banter. 'I was impressed you ordered the Elvis. A brave move from your usual Mrs Moon's homemade crumpet.'

'Which is why I need you.' He winked. 'Broadening my horizons.'

She laughed. 'Although I'm deducting marks for the lack of after-dinner fortune cookie.'

'You said fortune cookies weren't authentic.'

'They're not, but I like them. Much like you, you big faker.'

'Duly noted.' He nodded. 'But don't give up on your fortune cookie just yet. As for the fakery, Miss Summers, we're all just winging it. In life, money, business. There's no real magic.'

She considered it for a moment. She knew he was just trying to make her feel better for being the only one in the room in a seven-year-old tube dress and wildly scuffed pixie boots. His efforts were touching, nonetheless.

'And in love, Mr Carrington? Are we all just winging it there too?'

'Love.' Did his smile just tighten? 'I'd never been a believer. Perhaps now it's a luxury I can't afford.'

He picked up his glass and downed the rest of his Manhattan, in a 'case closed' kind of gesture. By the time he'd got the attention of the barman and ordered more drinks, Lexie felt there was no way of clawing the conversation back.

Chapter 27

As the barman strode off to make two Singapore slings, Lexie gave Ben a low whistle. 'Get you and your cocktails from around the globe.'

'After spending half of dinner being mocked for the lack of action in my passport, I thought I'd try and look a bit worldly. Have you been to Singapore?'

'Yes, way back in a different lifetime.' She exhaled, wishing it hadn't been with Inkie, the complete waste of epidermis, and regretting the artwork she'd let him adorn her with. Not that it wasn't beautiful in its own way, just that it was meant to be symbolic of something she always seemed so far from achieving. Now the tattoo just reminded her she was perpetually stuck in the mud.

'You should go. At night, parts of it look almost like this.' She waved an arm towards the vista beyond the window, the deep purple fading to black. The curiously shaped skyscrapers stood like dark dominoes, blinking with electrical

196

bulbs. 'Singapore's a quirky little island with a mix of Asian influences. Some say it's where Buddha keeps his teeth.'

'Handy. I must drop by. Is there anywhere you haven't been with that tatty suitcase of yours?'

'Plenty of places! You know, I've never actually been out in London, so this is a first. You're broadening my horizons too.' She gave him a wink.

'Am I really? I like that idea. Where else could we go that you haven't been?'

'Nowhere! I'm saving up. I can't go squandering my hard-earned money on jolly holidays. I'm a person with an ISA now. Does that make me boring?' She laughed. She'd set one up after Grace's small stop-repelling-money kick up the butt, although she still hadn't done much with it.

'Yes, completely. I'll be forced to start calling you beige.'

Lexie gasped in fake horror and put a hand to her chest.

'Looks like I'll have to do all this research for the travel-inspired paint ranges myself,' he joked. 'What was it we talked about in Tom's garden? Souks, spices . . . ?'

'Don't you dare go to Morocco without me! I haven't been.' Oh hell, had she just invited herself on an imaginary vacation with him? These cocktails were strong. She picked up the glass from her previous Manhattan and swished around the dregs.

Ben took it from her and held it up to the candlelight. 'It's a tempting colour. Maybe we could do a range of cocktail-inspired paints.'

She joined him in inspecting the beautifully rich shade.

'Amber,' she said, more to herself than anything. Not far from red and yet a world away from green. She shook her

197

head. 'Anyway, did you just have an idea? As in, an artistic one, and nothing to do with spreadsheets or profit and loss?'

'Mmm,' he said, as they continued to let the tawny, candlelit liquid mesmerise them. 'I've started having the odd one lately. It's a bit strange. Like there's been something in the air, inspiring me.'

She could see the corners of a cheeky smile twitching on his face, and she gave his arm a nudge. 'Idiot!'

The barman placed two rose-pink Singapore slings on serviettes in front of them and backed away.

'It's not a terrible idea,' Lexie continued. 'We could have luxurious Espresso Martini shades, bright Fuzzy Navels . . .'

He raised an eyebrow.

'Or we could just keep it as beige as a Mad Monk Milkshake.'

He nodded. 'We're not a bad team when the ideas start flowing. Although you're going to have to accept I'm not responsible for the beige walls of Nutgrass Hall.'

'Telling women your mum chose your colour scheme is no more impressive. And you'll have to ask her to stop ordering funeral flowers for the place too, if you're hoping to move a wife in. And maybe start buying your own underpants.'

'She does not buy my underwear! Anyway, I'm more concerned about her choice of wife. She's on my back again about going out with Cynthia since I shunned Amanda and turned my nose up at her other finalists.'

'Oh, the Fortescue woman? So what's wrong with . . . ?'

'No bloody way. Too much history.' He shuddered. 'As for Mother selecting the colour scheme, I'm just a bloke. If she elects to kit the place out in shades of bland, I let her get on with it. Anyway, it's still her property, so if she wants to paint it black and turn it into a hovel for devil worship there's not much I can do.'

'Or, you know, you could just move out, like normal people.'

He took a gulp of his Singapore sling. 'That wood-panelled office is where the magic happens. If I'm not sure of the way forward, it's like Dad is in there, channelling the answers through the woodwork.'

'And your ancestors in the creepy horsey paintings.'

Ben scoffed.

'Maybe your new wife will inspire you and you won't need your dad's guidance any more.'

He looked like he was mulling it over. 'Tom and Mrs M would be redundant without me and Cory. Mum would turf them out on their ears and trade them in for fancy new ones, given half the chance. Or just sell the place.'

'You really are a home bird, aren't you?'

He shrugged. 'That house and the business are under my skin, or maybe even part of it. They're surely all I need.'

'And a loaded wife to secure it with.'

Ben pulled a face. 'I'll have to stick her in a granny annex like Mrs Moon if she ends up annoying me as much as Mum annoyed Dad. To death.' The last two words were more of a whisper.

Would there ever be a good time to ask what all that was about? No. There were more pressing issues.

'Ben, you can't live like that for ever. No love, just money, work and a wife you've confined to an outhouse. You'd end up old and bored.'

'Yep. I'm just boring Ben.'

She could tell he was trying to be nonchalant, but it wasn't quite working. Did this *boring* thing go deeper than her jokes about the beige?

'Anyway, maybe I'll speak to her about those ghostly white flowers.' His voice was more upbeat again, thank God. 'I think they remind her of Dad. I'm working on her, but I haven't got the heart to tear out her roots entirely. She does have a soul in there somewhere, beneath the rhino skin and layers of woolly Chanel.'

Lexie giggled. In fact, these cocktails were making her feel far too giggly. She hoped she wouldn't be staggering all over the place when they came to leave.

'What about you, anyway? You're always wittering on about the importance of this so-called *love*, but I don't see you out there looking for your own perfect match.'

She waved a hand. 'I'm off men. They're a bloody nightmare. The guys I choose always seem to be selfish dicks who are motivated by pound signs.' She thought of Drew tossing her aside for thoroughbred Tabby, and Inkie being so keen to make a fast buck he could have landed her in a prison jumpsuit. Maybe there was something to be said for Sky's money-free world. God, she really must be tipsy.

'And if you were on them?'

She rewound their conversation, everything starting to feel hazy. On what? Pound signs? Dicks? She tittered into her cocktail. No. Sensible Ben did not mean dicks.

'Men,' he clarified, as though noticing her thoughts were in a tangle. He waved at the barman for a jug of water. 'If you were *on men*, in a purely hypothetical and non-physical way, who would you see as your perfect match?'

She pointed a wavering finger at him. He raised his eyebrows further.

'Yooooooou, Mr Carrington ... '

'Me?' He looked surprised.

'No, not *you*, you. I mean yoooou must learn to behave yourself. I'm the social butterfly around here. Don't you go worrying your pretty face about me.' Did she just call him pretty? Hell, but he was though. Well, manly pretty. *Hot.*

He leaned over the bar and grabbed a pencil, ready to write on his serviette. 'Maybe I'll have to find you someone. Now, tell me about yourself. Favourite fruit? And don't you dare say apples.'

'Bugger off!'

'Kiwi fruit.' He pointed at her. 'I've seen you peeling the hairy little things for your breakfast. I tried one the other day. Not bad.'

She sniffed. 'Probably.'

'Favourite colour?' He leaned slowly towards her face. What was he doing? Going in for a kiss? And why were her lips involuntarily willing him in?

'Purple.' He was focusing on her eyelashes and pointing at the tiny jewel in her nose.

She unpuckered her lips, embarrassed. Bloody traitors. They were as bad as her boob-cupping hands.

'Purple,' she conceded. 'You know too much. Or maybe

it's because you're choosing the questions, you big old cheat. Anyway, perhaps none of that really matters.'

'What, you can't match two people by whether they both prefer kiwi fruit? Who would have thought it. So what is your theory?' he asked. 'If Mother can't just find me a woman who likes beige, and be done with it? What does draw two people together to make a complementing match?'

She shrugged, staring down at her scuffed, purple pixie boots that looked completely out of place next to Ben's polished brogues, but which she wouldn't have swapped for the world.

'Maybe a clash could also work?' She looked up at him questioningly.

'It could certainly be interesting.' He nodded. 'I mean, if both of you went crazy for kiwi fruit, who would eat all the Granny Smiths? Your fruit bowl would be in disarray.'

'Exactly! And you don't want someone who would eat all the green triangles in your Quality Street. You need someone who prefers that rubbish fudge one.'

'I quite like the fudge one.'

She looked at him, surprised. She couldn't even imagine him eating a Quality Street. Maybe he was semi-human after all. 'Oh, I don't know. It's all a bit of a jigsaw.'

'You may have a point.' He pushed his serviette alongside hers. 'Because that's how jigsaws work. Each has a part that the other piece needs to help them fit together.'

She studied the two squares of paper, which did not stick together because they were too alike. If the air-con worked properly they'd probably blow away.

'One has a sticky-out bit, and the other . . .' She pulled a face. Oh, this was getting confusing. The other had a sticky-in bit. Maybe jigsaws were only good at sex – which was quite possibly the strangest thought that had ever crossed her mind.

She stood up. 'I seriously need some air.' And to stop thinking about jigsaw sex. Ever. Again. 'Walk?'

'Absolutely.'

Ben stood up and put some cash on the bar. Lexie rifled in her bag and did the same.

'Jigsaws should be equal,' she said, still not sure what she was rabbiting on about.

'The same, but different.' He nodded, as though she was talking perfect sense.

'Things would be a lot clearer if we hadn't missed out on our fortune cookies.' It was as good a drunken theory as any.

'Then I know where we're going next.'

He took her hand, which was definitely just to steady her, and they made their way through the winking lights of the bar, towards the equally knowing lights of the big city.

Chapter 28

'Fresh air is . . . lovely,' Lexie declared to the cool London night, for want of a better description. Those innocent-looking cocktails had a way of sneaking up on a girl.

She reached her arms up to the stars, letting the breeze tickle around her. It was a welcome sensation after the warmth of that bar, although she was pretty sure most of her heat had been caused by a certain square-jawed boss.

He came towards her, pulling her lightly by the waist and taking hold of one of her arms to link through his. No, hang on, rewind a bit. She'd liked that waist-holding thing. His hands had felt so firm and strong against the soft material of her tube dress.

'Lexie, you're in the road.'

Oh.

He shepherded her back to the safety of the pavement, keeping her arm linked with his.

'But London's soooo . . . '

'Lovely?'

'Yes, lovely! How did you know? You always know. Which is weird, isn't it? Because at first we seemed so different.' Was she gabbling? The night air really was intoxicating.

'We should get a cab. I think you need some sleep.'

'You're the voice of reason,' she said, cosying her head into his neck. Hmm, it felt good – she should try it out for a bit longer. Most men weren't tall enough for it.

'Thanks, Lexie. You make me sound so exciting.'

'A taxi. You're probably right.' Experience told her this was the moment when they should call it a night, go back to their separate hotel rooms and definitely not drink another drop. She had a snuggly complimentary dressing gown and there would be plenty of trashy movies on TV. And yet . . . 'Hey, didn't you promise me something? Up there?'

Lexie lifted her head and pointed back up towards the glassy pyramid skyscraper they had just walked out of. She replayed their conversation. What was it now? Morocco? Pineapples? 'A fortune cookie! You see, you are exciting.'

'It must be your influence.'

She sensed the smile in his voice and gave his side a congratulatory squeeze, which only seemed fair. He'd grabbed her waist just moments ago, hadn't he? Now they were quits – although he definitely had more muscle. What were those things called? Obliques? He had good obliques.

'Come on, then, before I change my mind,' said Ben, looking down at her feet. 'Good, you're wearing flat boots. Then we'll walk the scenic route. I think you need the fresh air.'

After what felt like far too much walking, they made a

snake-like path onto Tower Bridge, its blue-and-white steel arms outstretched to welcome them. Apart from the buzz of azure light, which seemed to encircle it like a halo, it reminded Lexie of Nutgrass Hall, with its majestic stone turrets. She wondered if it too was the gatekeeper to many strange secrets.

Lexie had been so busy absentmindedly appreciating Ben's profile, she nearly missed the view. But when they reached the middle of the bridge and he twirled her around to take in the sapphire glint of the Thames, fiercely guarded by its towering buildings, it took her breath away. The gleaming edges of the Shard cut through the night like a golden-tipped sword, rising high above the lights of London. Lexie had seen some cities, but this was immense. She squeezed Ben's hand. For all her travelling, she'd barely seen London. For once, Ben was showing her the way. A little part of her liked it.

He squeezed her hand back and she felt a happy sigh float out from her lungs. Sometimes his quietness was refreshing. Like he didn't feel the need to fill the air with profound but pointless words. The view was overwhelming, but a recipro-cal hand squish was communication enough.

'Not boring at all,' she whispered, silently happy they'd taken the long route.

They walked onwards across the bridge, back onto dry land, and began weaving through the city's side streets. The long trek and chilly night air seemed to be fuelling her gid-diness rather than sobering her up. Or was she just looking for an excuse to huddle into Ben's side?

'Let me show you this,' said Ben, steering Lexie towards the floodlit dome of St Paul's Cathedral. It stood tall, quiet and confident; another stunning sight she'd never seen.

Lexie's eyes settled on the statue of Queen Anne, which stood fierce guard outside the pillared front. 'She looks just like your interfering mother. Come on, let's get a picture! It's probably the closest the three of us will ever get to a family portrait.'

Lexie hoiked her tight dress above her knees, climbed onto an abandoned crate and pulled a protesting Ben up after her. They wobbled for a moment, their feet hopping like tap dancers as they tried to find their balance. Lexie wrapped her arm around Ben's shoulders to steady herself and angled her phone to take in their faces, with Queen Anne scowling between them in the background. She took the shot.

'We should try one without her,' said Lexie, resting her cheek against Ben's. The touch of light stubble against her skin made her nerve endings tingle. He was usually so polished, but this tease of late-night roughness was throwing a party for her senses. A wave of goosebumps rushed over her, and she shivered against him.

'Are you cold?' She felt his cheek move against hers.

'No!' she squeaked. She could not let him start stripping off his layers for her; she'd fall off the bench in a lusty quiver. Those bloody cocktails. Trying not to overthink how perilously close her lips were to his, she tilted her phone screen until the angle was perfect. Although if she moved her head just slightly . . .

Flash. She took the photo before her mind could start wandering off in all sorts of directions, the destinations of which she might never have clawed her way back from.

They stayed freeze-frame for a moment, as though realising how easy it would be to slip into a kiss. And then Ben moved his cheek away, coughed awkwardly, and stepped back down to safety. Just as Lexie was reasoning it was probably better not to break her neck on the wonky crate, he lifted his hands up to her waist and lowered her back onto the floor next to him.

Wow. She loved the chivalrous self-assurance a few cocktails gave him, not to mention the feel of his fingers so close to her flesh. But before she could close her eyes and dissolve into his heat, his hands were gone and he was rearranging his jacket.

Was he just being polite? Whatever was going on, this whole forbidden-fruit situation was getting frighteningly arousing. Noticing the tips of his ears were turning red like they did when he was embarrassed, she fiddled with her phone to give them a moment. God knew what she'd do if she didn't.

Their selfie looked surprisingly good, although she couldn't help noticing the original version with the disgruntled monarch between them.

'Three peas in a bed . . . er . . . pod. I mean, we definitely wouldn't . . . ' Lexie flapped a hand, wondering what the hell Freud would say about this. Meh. Well, she didn't speak German anyway.

Ben looked up at the statue. 'Somebody would probably chop our heads off.'

When his gaze drifted back to Lexie, she was sure she'd caught an unfamiliar glint. What was that – rebellion? A 'let's do it and see'? Or was that just what she wanted to find, in her cheeky gin-fuelled mood?

He linked his arm through hers and pulled her close again, in the warm glow of the old-fashioned streetlamps. 'Well, this is almost romantic,' he conceded.

It would be all sorts of other indecent-in-a-public-place things if she didn't keep her mind on track. She needed to cool it. This was her boss. He belonged in a world where she would only ever be *staff*, and when they weren't softened by alcohol they generally found each other annoying.

Didn't they?

Anyway, he was rich. He was invariably rude. She did not intend to be slept with like common people until his Princess Sidebottom came along.

As though sensing the need for a dousing of flames, Ben added, 'Don't worry, this place with the not-quite fortune cookies is not going to sweep anyone off their pixie boots.'

They moved towards the aptly named Cheapside and back into the side streets, Ben leading the way. Lexie was expecting a little restaurant, and laughed when they landed in front of the intermittently buzzing, cracked sign of Sinbad's Corner Shop. Or Corner Ship, as the crack would have them believe. This would be the most down-to-earth place she'd ever seen her well-heeled boss enter.

Inside, Sinbad looked as miserable as the proverbial sin. Lexie gave him an over-exaggerated thumbs up and he shoved his head back inside the paper he'd been reading.

Ben steered Lexie towards the back of the shop, past the bottles of gleaming alcohol that she tried to ignore. There was nothing like artificial strip lighting to make a girl realise quite how drunk she was.

'I really need crisps,' she hissed at Ben. 'And maybe a pasty. Have you ever eaten a pasty?'

'I have been to Cornwall,' he whispered back. 'And, indeed, Waitrose.'

'*Waitrose*,' she mouthed sarcastically behind his back. '*Get you*.'

She had to admit she enjoyed this joshing between them. It set off little sparks of excitement, like being a kid and prodding the boy you quite fancied. Not that she fancied Ben, of course, but . . .

He gave her a quick look over his shoulder, his suit jacket pulling taut across his back.

Argh, she sometimes did. But she would not grab any part of his rear area. That was just not polite.

As they neared the back of the shop, which had felt like the longest 'trying to walk in a straight line and definitely not ogle anyone's derriere' journey, it seemed that the strip lights had given up hope. It was invitingly dark here, apart from the glow from a large arcade machine.

Lexie gasped. 'Zoltar. From *Big*! What's he doing here? I love that film — how did you know? Wow, does it work?' She rattled Zoltar's glass box a little too enthusiastically, making his bearded chin clatter.

'He won't tell us anything if you break his jaw off.' Ben removed her hands to a place of safety. 'And I heard you chatting to my crisp-munching, telly-addict of a brother. Growing up with him, I've endured more cheesy films than you can imagine.'

She gave him an exaggerated wide-eyed look and poked his shoulder gently.

'Ooh, you might just be human.'

'I try. Anyway, I couldn't let the night end without your fate being decided by a scraggy piece of paper. It's your favourite tradition.' He pulled out a pocketful of change. 'Ladies first. If you're not going to wallop me for offering to pay, that is.'

'I'll pay the price for your fate, and you for mine.'

'It's a deal.'

Chapter 29

Lexie's heart flipped with delight at Ben's small Zoltar-shaped gesture. He'd said she wouldn't be swept off her pixie boots, but once again he'd underestimated himself. They were in the darkened end of Sinbad's shop, and Lexie, for one, was intrigued to discover her fortune.

She selected the shiniest coin from Ben's hand, blew on it for luck, then rolled it into Zoltar's eager possession, hoping for something magical. Or at least that she wouldn't turn huge and hairy overnight, and burst right through her outfit like Tom Hanks in *Big*.

Zoltar's eyes flashed red and wild as he accepted the payment and considered Lexie's fate. He gawped and groaned like a beast possessed, his hands encircling his crystal ball, his turbaned head lurching forwards.

'*Mwaaa haaa ha ha haaaaaaaa.*' With one final shudder, as though he'd just given birth to a particularly bothersome egg, the fortune teller released Lexie's fortune down the spout and into her outstretched palm.

She held it for a moment, eyes tightly shut, willing good energy into the ball. Then she gave in to temptation, prised it open and unfurled the scroll.

'What will you say, O wise one?' She took Ben's hand and he squeezed it, oddly supportive of her little quirks.

She scanned the paper quickly, drew in a breath, and then read the words out loud.

'*Worry not, sweet girl. You are rich beyond wealth, and wise beyond learning. Follow your instincts; dance from your heart. Open your petals to the sun, for you are the summer.*'

Her eyes widened as she let the words settle. 'He knows me,' she whispered through the dark to Ben. 'Zoltar really knows me. Look, he knows I'm female, that my name is Summers. He knows ... everything.' She held the paper to her chest and swayed to an imaginary beat, wondering what she would do if she was brave enough to open her petals to the sun. But she was sure she already knew.

She turned her eyes on Ben. He was leaning casually against a shelf, his usually neat hair ruffled from the walk. He didn't normally do casual. Which was just as well because it was outrageously attractive. As was the small smile on his face, which seemed to say 'you're nutty but I like it.'

God, they should get out of this dimly lit corner before she got too many strange petal-opening ideas. She shook herself down.

'Er, your turn. Zoltar insists!'

They looked at the plastic genie, who in fairness did seem to be nodding. Alternatively his head was just wonky after Lexie had given his glass such a shaking.

'I can't wait to hear what he thinks I should do with my petals,' said Ben, mock-sagely. His voice seemed to have taken on an after-midnight huskiness that was doing nothing for Lexie's willpower.

Lexie dug her hand into her leather jacket and pulled out some coins. Ben humoured her, followed her blow-it-for-luck ritual, and sacrificed it to the gods of fortune.

The mighty one trembled and undulated with such vigour Lexie was sure he was about to deliver triplets. Finally, Ben's future tumbled down the birthing canal and landed in her eager grip. She kissed it and locked her hands with Ben's, his message from the wise one incubating like a tiny egg in the warmth between them.

'I can't look,' he said, their faces only inches apart. 'What if the mighty Zoltar knows too much?'

She tried not to giggle, but she really was intoxicated. 'You're not taking this seriously.'

'Oh, but I am.' There was a definite teasing note in his voice. 'I agree to do whatever the mighty one tells me.'

'Anything?'

He had a quick look around, as though securing their territory. 'Anything.'

His voice was so low she had to study the shape of his lips to hear it. It was just one word, but suddenly it was the most tempting one ever. His tone was light and yet the word so full of potential, the anticipation of it

214

fizzing between them. Lexie couldn't help being swept along by the thrill of being there with Ben in that rare, unguarded moment.

As he gave her hand a final squeeze, a wave of goose-bumps shivered over her as though every part of her skin was willing him back. But it was time to find out what *anything* meant. He unclasped their hands and read out the words.

'*You crave money, but without love you will never be rich. Give in to your deeper desires. Taste the exotic fruit. If only for one night . . .*'

They stared at the paper, both aware that as soon as they moved their eyes, anything could happen. And any-thing probably would. The words were frivolous, but it felt as though they were meant for them. Like it really was a sign.

'Is a kiwi exotic?' Lexie whispered, her eyes daring to move up to meet his. She could almost hear a crackle of electricity dancing between them.

'Mm hmm,' he responded, as though barely trusting himself to speak.

'And do you . . . desire one?' Something was pulling her in towards him, their limbs now touching and beginning to entwine.

His next word sounded like a groan, deep and feral against the flesh of her neck, and so sexily defenceless. She could feel his body weakening against hers. She pressed into him, wriggling off her jacket as she moved. There was no room for gratuitous material; she wanted to feel everything.

215

'Then what the hell,' she growled into his ear. 'It's only for one night.'

And with that, she pushed his firm but willing body against the cold glass of the fortune-teller's box and melted against him, her lips finding his in a desperate flurry. They were warm and inviting, and moved against hers with a rhythm that was almost hypnotic. She felt her whole body slipping into the flow. The machine behind him continued to undulate, sending endless vibrations through them.

'Oh God, just touch me,' she moaned into his mouth, frustrated by the politeness of his hands against her back. '*Anywhere*.'

And at last he did. She felt the heat of his hands slide across her body, one finding her buttocks and pushing them deliciously into him, the other moving slowly towards her breast. She grabbed hold of it and encouraged it on its way. If they only had tonight, she did not want to waste a second.

Every part of her body seemed to be pulsating now, as though six weeks of frustration was writhing its way out of her. Six weeks of secretly wanting this. The deep woody smell of his aftershave rubbing onto her skin, the rough sensation of his hair gripped tightly in her palm, the warmth of his solid frame against hers. It was a full-blown orgy of the senses.

And yet, was it enough?

'I want more, Ben.'

He was groaning in agreement, his hands moving over her curves. Urgent. Emboldened. Seriously bloody hot.

'Hotel,' she managed to squeak, the possibilities already

raging through her imagination like wild, uncontrollable beasts.

'*Anything.*' His voice was now so husky he was barely intelligible.

'Be careful what you wish for,' she murmured back.

Chapter 30

Lexie awoke with a start. It was still dark, and yet it felt like morning. Her head was – dizzy? She spread her limbs out around her. She was in a bed. It wasn't hers, although the room felt familiar. Of course, her hotel bed. She was still in London. And she was alone.

Actually, no, that was wrong. Because something was there with her. It felt hot and heavy, and it was sending her into a panic. Oh God, what was that? It was so weighty it made her want to hide under the duvet and cry. She shuddered, as though alcohol was trying to escape her body in great surges. Oh bollocks.

It was *shame*.

That horrible, post-drunken sensation when she was sure something reckless had happened, but she couldn't fathom what.

She flicked through her memories of the night before. Ben. A nice restaurant. Then being high up in the Shard.

Cocktails, more cocktails. Oh hell. She hung her head over the side of the bed and dry heaved.

She spied her boots on the floor, and her dress neatly folded on the chair next to them. Odd. She was not a tidy drunk. And what was that scrap of paper? She pinched it towards her.

Open your petals to the ... oh, Jesus, Mary and Joseph on a trike. Zoltar. A darkened shop. A pretty steamy taxi ride home. What had she done?

Her hands ran over her body. OK, she was still wearing underwear. Her matching good set, at that. And her tights. Phew. She would not have opened her petals to anyone's sun and then faffed around climbing back into her ten-deniers.

Anyone. Who was she trying to kid? There was only one person who made her feel like tearing off her tights these days. The same person she had inadvertently dressed for in her lacy black undies, long before any of those cheeky cocktails had passed her willing lips. Ben Carrington. Her rich and unattainable boss.

Because she'd known he was unattainable. To her, at least. And she hadn't even admitted to herself that she had had any designs on attaining him. And yet the lace did not lie. And neither did her 'Shakira, Shakira' hips in the rear of Sinbad's shop, for that matter. Hell, if her hips had had their own way, they'd have a certain man clamped between them right now, instead of a ridiculously uncomfortable thong. She eased herself back under the covers and groaned into her hands. Oh God, what had she done? What exactly had happened after 'try not to be too indecent in the back of a taxi'-gate, and where was Ben now? Had she completely disgraced herself? Had he run for his life?

There was only one human-shaped dent in the bed, and the sheets didn't smell like him. But her skin did. His woody aftershave against her neck. His lips, his … Urgh, she had to get out of this bed before she had any more indecent thoughts. She needed a shower to wash off this mess. Whatever this mess actually was.

She climbed gingerly from the bed, her head pounding like the inside of some terrible disco. Waiting a moment for the furniture to stop moving, she swayed towards the bathroom in search of water. There was a glass next to her bed, but it was nearly empty. Who had put that there? The inebriated Lexie she knew would not have organised herself so well. Had Ben been here? Was that his scent she could smell in the air? She wished she could just remember.

As she fiddled with the taps in the bathroom, she heard some commotion at the door of her room. A rattling? A knocking? Maybe she had drunkenly ordered room-service breakfast on her way through Reception last night. Arranging hangover food did sound like something wasted Lexie would do. Where was that complimentary dressing gown?

She inched her way back to the bedroom. 'All right, all right!' Why did people have to make such a noise? She stopped to steady herself, the room still spinning.

'Lexie?'

How was the door opening by itself? And why did it know her name? Before she could work out the answers to life's conundrums, a shape appeared, weighed down by two bags.

'Ben? Jeez, I'm nearly naked! What are you doing here? And shut the bloody door.'

She grabbed the nearest piece of material to cover herself. It was a discarded hand towel splodged in last night's make-up; it was not hiding much.

'I just took the key to go and get you breakfast. I was worried you might die without sustenance.' He shrugged as though it was obvious, and closed the door behind him.

'So you ... stayed?' She turned back to the bed to count the dents again – just one – had they slept in it together?

Then she squeaked, realising she was revealing her thong-clad rear to him, covered in barely-there tights. She turned back to face him, squirming behind the towel.

'Don't worry, I've already seen the show.' He pointed to her not-much-of-an outfit. 'You were very insistent I should see your best matching underwear before ...' He looked towards the bathroom.

What the hell had happened in the bathroom? Lexie ran a hand through her scruffy hair.

'Look, I can't remember much. Past the ... taxi stuff.' She prayed she didn't have to elaborate.

She was talking to the floor, she realised, and backing towards the bed. She shuffled her bottom back into it, pulled her knees up to her chin and dragged the covers around her shivering shoulders. Shame was an ugly, ugly thing.

'No, I imagine you don't.'

Did his voice sound unimpressed, or was she being paranoid?

'Don't worry, nothing much happened when we got back to the room.'

'Other than me stripping off my clothes and doing something or other in the bathroom.' That sounded like more than enough to her.

'You were pretty drunk. More than I'd realised.'

He was still standing near the doorway, radiating awkwardness and a very interesting bacon smell. But now was not the time to discuss sandwiches.

'I put you to bed and slept in the chair. I was worried you might croak it.'

'You put me to bed,' she repeated. It did not sound sexy, or becoming of her one good pair of undies.

'Just after you insisted on the striptease.'

Lexie felt the last morsel of dignity cave inside her and her shoulders slumped forwards until she was curled up in a foetal ball.

'Striptease,' she repeated dumbly, still processing her thoughts. She winced as some of the highlights leapt in. Which was most mortifying? The fact she'd lunged mouth first at her boss in a convenience store (which suddenly felt particularly inconvenient), that she all but ordered him to fondle her or that he took one look at her tacky efforts at bedroom seduction and decided the armchair was more appealing.

Who had she been kidding that he'd consider her good enough? She had no money, and now she'd taken to behaving as though she was cheap.

Lexie let out a long sigh. Maybe she was just being hard on herself. There had been something there to start with, hadn't there? A fire between them that she surely hadn't imagined.

'So you just went off the idea when you started to sober up,' she heard herself blurt out.

He paused for a moment. 'I do have ... standards.'

Ouch. 'I don't need reminding of your stupid criteria,' she mumbled. Or that she would never meet them.

'For example, I expect a woman to be sober enough to make an informed choice.'

And to be loaded, boring and good enough to please your evil mother, Lexie couldn't help thinking, with a meanness she wished would just bugger off. 'I'm a big girl. I can make up my own mind.'

'You barely tolerate me when you're sober. So if we're discussing criteria ... '

'Which we're not.' She put her hands to her throbbing head. It was all so confusing, but she did not need him to list her inadequacies. She felt shitty enough as it was. A game of 'how will I never love thee, let me count the ways' was not her idea of hungover fun.

'Miss Summers ... '

She held up a hand to stop him. Last night it had made her heart thump when he'd called her that, but this morning it just felt belittling.

'And the thing about the bathroom?' God, why was she even asking? Hadn't she tortured herself enough?

'I was just taking off my jacket. You ran to the bathroom to be sick.'

Sick. That was the polar opposite of the classy,

impress-one's-snooty-mother material he was looking for. No wonder he'd turned his nose up. He'd probably brought her P45 in one of those bags.

She studied him through her knees. Was his face reddening? Christ, he was embarrassed for her. Embarrassed about the whole sodding thing. And what if he did want to get rid of her after this humiliating encounter?

Her aching heart sank. As weird as the whole situation had been at first, she was enjoying her job with Carrington Paints. And Mrs Moon, Tom and Cory were starting to feel like an admittedly odd family. She didn't want to be booted out.

Right, she would have to iron out this awkwardness. Nip the entire ill-judged situation in the bud. Make clear she wasn't an untrustworthy nymph who was after Ben's money or his manhood. From then on she'd be a reliable employee, eager to get on with her job and not cause fuss. And the sooner Mrs Carrington-Noble sorted out a suitable wife for him, the better. Then Lexie would be safe from any more ridiculous temptation.

'You should cooperate with your mother and find yourself a respectable wife. And please. Forget about this.' She waved a hand over the detritus of the room. Discarded clothing. Towels covered in make-up. Was that an unopened packet of . . . God.

'And that's what you want?'

'Absolutely,' she responded, her voice suddenly several shades closer to fake bright and breezy. 'You asked for my dating advice last night, and that's it. Trust your

224

mother – she'll do a sterling job. Perhaps she and I are just kindred spirits.' She gave a phony laugh. 'Both great at organising people.'

Although Lexie wasn't so hot at organising herself, so everyone kept pointing out. And looking at the mess of this place, they weren't wrong. But hell knows, she would need a distraction. Maybe she'd start working on her own crap for once. Or maybe not. No need to go crazy.

At last, his awkward body seemed to loosen and he took a long, deep breath. There. He looked better about the whole thing already. Thank God. They would just have to soldier on past it, like the iffy drunken liaison it had been.

'I'm sorry about last night. It should never have happened.' Lexie squirmed inside the covers as she spoke.

'Right,' he replied. He put the bags down on the floor as though they were suddenly too heavy. As he straightened himself he ran a hand over his face. He looked tired. 'It was . . . a regrettable situation. Please accept my apologies for letting things get out of hand. I'm meant to be your employer.'

He sank back into the chair he'd slept in. 'You'd be within your rights to . . .'

There he was again, setting out the boundaries. Drawing a mark around himself in the sand. She wished he'd just pass the bacon to her side of the line and leave her to scrub off the shame with the free hotel toiletries.

'Rest assured, I won't let it happen again,' he continued. 'I'll show willing with Mother's matchmaking as soon as we get back to Nutgrass.'

His words were businesslike, but Lexie couldn't help

225

noticing he didn't seem as tough around the edges as usual. Sitting hunched forward on the chair, he reminded her of a Steiff bear who'd had the stuffing knocked out of him. She'd embarrassed him as well as herself. Nice work, Lexie.

'That's settled then,' she said to her knees. They were unlikely to disagree. 'Brilliant. Your mother will be thrilled.'

'And maybe she'll stop asking absurd questions about you.'

'Absurd,' Lexie repeated, her concurring knees echoing the word back at her. That was the last time she was treating them to a tube of Veet.

Somehow, the bear in the chair seemed to rearrange his stuffing and he stood up, finally looking purposeful.

His mouth pulled itself into a smile which didn't bother to inform his eyes. 'Then we have a plan. Excellent.' He brushed down his suit trousers. 'I'll ... leave you to it. Take the day off, or something. Get yourself back in order.'

Lexie cringed as his gaze moved round the room, settling on various piles of mess.

'OK, you can go now,' she said, keen for this to be over. There were only three things she needed to deal with humiliation and a hangover, and none of them was Ben Carrington.

He lifted the bags from the floor and she winced at the thought of her bacon disappearing. Perhaps she did need him for one of the things.

To her relief, he pushed a pile of make-up to one side and set it down on the side table next to the kettle, which he flicked on. OK, maybe that was two of the things. Damn it.

'I'll tackle today's conference alone. We'll leave this evening, if you're up to it.'

'I'll be up to it,' she confirmed, matching his efficient tone. Just as soon as she'd fixed up the third thing, which was finding her battered laptop and choosing a cheesy film to curl up with. After the Zoltar debacle, maybe she'd even watch *Big*. There was nothing like immersing herself in someone else's troubles to help her forget her own. At least she hadn't woken up six foot and hairy.

And yet, after last night, something had definitely shifted. Could she ever go back to being the person she was before that kiss? Or had her fortune, or lack thereof, already been decided?

Chapter 31

'**G**et out o' thur, you bloody blighters!'

Tom was on his hands and knees on the front lawn. Lexie wasn't quite sure what he was up to, but it seemed to involve a trowel and a lot of West Country swear words. He wiped the perspiration from his forehead with a muddy forearm and squinted as she approached.

'How be, young grockle? Nice to see yer back. You kids enjoy yer trip?'

Lexie fiddled with the cuff of her flamingo mac.

'Er, yes, thanks, Tom. It was ... how shall I put it? Enlightening.'

Although in truth, she felt more like a mushroom in the dark. The drive back with Ben the night before had been sombre, as though something had died a humiliating death. Had he been disappointed with her drunken behaviour? It was hard to tell, but he'd since been avoiding her. At least being ignored gave her plenty of time to catch up on social media admin. The point of the trip had been to give her plenty of material, after all. It was just a shame most of it was not for sharing.

'Anyway, how are you?' She crouched to Tom's level. As kooky as this place always was, she felt a strange comfort at being back with her trusted inmates.

'Fair to middlin'. Just trying to get this ruddy nut grass out o' my lawn. It's a right pest, make no mistake. Gets its tough roots in, then runs amok, sending out its 'orrible underground claws. I can't get rid of it fast enough.'

Lexie grimaced. 'Oh. Is that why this place is called Nutgrass Hall?'

'That's right, me love. Although how it got here, I'll never know. It's not from round these parts. And why they'd name the place after this frightful weed is anyone's guess.'

As he dug cautiously around the stiff spiky blades, Lexie wondered how many hours it would take him to get through this immense lawn. She dreaded to think. Feeling a stab of pity, she grabbed a spare pair of gloves and a trowel from his gardening box and tried to mirror his actions.

Tom gave her one of the toothless grins she'd come to know and love, his warm brown eyes twinkling with gratitude. He must have been handsome in his day, before the tooth fairy struck gold and before he began rebelling against false teeth. She wondered why he had never married, although, like everyone in this place, he didn't give much away.

'Tom?' She worked her trowel gingerly around a stubborn root, taking care not to slice it. 'Have you ever repainted anything here?'

His warm look melted into worry. 'Why, what yer plannin'? 'Er 'ighness won't like it.'

Lexie still wasn't sure what she was planning, but after the London mess she felt like she needed to regain a scrap of control. Channel her energies into something useful. Experiment with these brainwaves she kept having instead of filing them away in the 'big ideas are not for numpties' box. Or maybe just keep her idle brain from wandering onto Ben-shaped territory.

'Don't worry, I'm not going to start painting over the beige.' Much. 'I just wondered if you had any old kit I could borrow. Paintbrushes, dustsheets; that sort of thing.'

He scratched his cap-covered head. 'I'll have a look in me shed later on. Bound to 'ave somethin'.'

They continued amiably with their digging.

'So is that your secret garden down there, beyond the orchard?'

Lexie sensed the air change, and Tom's gaze didn't budge from his patch of roots. It was what always happened here when she asked too much.

'You know, the other side of the gate with the rusty padlock?' She tried to sound casual, although she was itching to know.

Tom rearranged the peak of his cap to keep the sun's glare from his face.

'Secret garden? Not sure what you mean. I got a few bits down there, out the way. Mrs Carrington-Noble ain't partial to no mess, so I keep it separate. No 'arm in that.'

Tom put down his tool, gripped the spindly neck of the weed he'd been working on and began teasing it out.

'No harm at all. It's beautiful. The wildflowers are as pretty as a picture. Not that the rest of the garden isn't immaculate. But there's something special about things growing as nature intended, don't you think? When the seeds land where they want to and the petals bloom in defiance?'

She was sure she saw the old man's weathered cheeks reddening like two plump berries.

'You got it, young maid. Nature don't look its best when it's all structured and fussed about with. It's like love, ain't it? It lands where it wants to, and there's not much we can do about it.'

Tom began sniffing and pulled a cotton hanky from his pocket with a muddy hand. 'There. Must have this new-fandangled 'ayfever, or summit. Silly old fool.' He looked at the embroidered initials before wiping the corner of his eye and shoving the handkerchief back into his pocket.

Lexie took a few deep breaths, trying to swallow a sad-ness that had suddenly tried to burst up her throat. What was this funny wave that had just washed over them? What was in these intoxicating roots?

'Anyway, Mrs Carrington-Noble likes her garden 'ow she likes it; can't argue with that. 'Er 'usband never dared to, so you won't see me interferin'.'

And there was another mystery no one ever wanted to talk about. But she couldn't just come out and air her suspicions on that one. What would she say? Excuse me, do you think the posh lady bumped her husband off? As if anyone would tell her if they knew.

'So, what are you growing in your greenhouse?' Lexie asked instead. Surely that was safer ground.

Tom rubbed the back of his neck and inspected his sprig of stubborn nut grass.

'Are they herbs, or something? They smell wonderful.'

''Erbs?' He said the word like it was entirely foreign to him, still fixating on his work.

'Mmm, you know. Like mint, or parsley, or ...'

Tom cleared his throat. 'Look, whatever you might 'ave sin. Well, s'probably best if you pretend like you haven't sin anythin'. It don't do if everyone knows everythin' in this place.'

'Of course. I get you.' Lexie gave an awkward cough, although she wasn't sure she did understand. Why was he getting so edgy about the greenhouse? It was only ... oh God. What if it wasn't only herbs? Or, more to the point, what if it was dodgy herbs?

She gave him a quick sideways glance. No, surely not. He never looked stoned. Did he? Gardeners were just naturally calm. Although anything was possible in this surreal place. With Mrs Carrington-Noble on the prowl, maybe a nifty joint in the potting shed was just what an old guy needed.

Anyway, she was sure she'd remember the heady smell of illegal weeds from her days of putting up with Inkie. Whatever it was, Tom was entitled to his privacy so she'd keep it under her hat. It wasn't as though she didn't need a particularly large beret to hide some of her own past indiscretions.

As though on a mission to break up the interrogation,

Mrs Moon came wobbling along the path with a tray of refreshments. Tom gave his root a final yank, threw it into his wheelbarrow and climbed to his feet to relieve Mrs Moon of her charge.

'Hello, Lexie, love. Good to see you back. Lovely time in London?'

Lexie pasted on a thin smile. 'Er, yes. Great. Very informative. Who knew the world of paint could be so . . . gripping.'

Was she rambling? Tom and Mrs Moon exchanged looks.

'I made some rose tea to cheer you up.'

Mrs Moon had set up camp on a white metal bistro table that Tom had dragged over. She was pouring pink liquid from a chintzy teapot.

'Thanks. But what makes you think I need cheering up?' Lexie was still pulling at a nut grass stem that wouldn't budge.

'Woman's intuition, dear.' Mrs Moon tapped her nose. 'It's all been very quiet since the two of you got back. Both shuffling around the place staring at your feet, your smiles all upside down. And don't think I didn't notice you didn't have any breakfast. Anyway, we'll speak no more of it.' She straightened herself up. 'Victoria sponge?'

Lexie felt a genuine smile begin to battle with the fake one. 'Thanks.' She nodded, her stomach rumbling in agreement.

Tom began tidying the muddy equipment and pulled over a hose to clean their hands. Mrs Moon handed him warm towels and busied herself with crockery. The pair worked in effortless tandem, as though they'd performed this routine a thousand times. They probably had, Lexie thought, with a ripple of warmth.

Trying not to upset the careful symphony, Lexie joined in by bringing garden chairs. They sat down for what Lexie had come to know as elevenses. She was always touched when she was welcomed to join – Mrs Moon needn't have worried about the happy tea.

'So what have I missed, Mrs M? What have you been up to?'

Mrs Moon smiled and flattened down her apron.

'Well, the weather's been lovely. I've been able to get out and about a bit more with Mr Moon. I don't take him out when it's too chilly, but he does love the sunshine.'

The elderly lady's face lit up like a carnival when she talked about her husband, but Tom's expression was a little odd. Was he . . . jealous? Or maybe his gums weren't coping well with all the sticky jam. Who could tell.

'Now, Tom, you will remember to save me some of the nut grass root?'

Mrs Moon pointed to the gnarly brown knots in Tom's wheelbarrow. They were ugly things, like scum-sucking catfish with long twisting whiskers. Why on earth would she want them?

'They're good for the epidermis,' Mrs Moon responded to her puzzled look. 'It's the latest thing in skin lightening technology. Should work wonders on my age spots. Certain folk use it for weight loss too, but I'm not into all that kerfuffle.'

Now Lexie really was baffled. Sometimes the housekeeper came out with the strangest little insights.

'Oh, you know. I saw it on … something or other.' Mrs Moon stood up sharply and began clattering the crockery back onto its tray. 'Anyway, must dash. Something in the Aga.'

And with that, the housekeeper rattled back up the path, her short legs moving surprisingly quicker than before.

'Is she OK? Should I go after her?' Lexie asked Tom.

'Ah, no, she's all right. Probably still in a tiswas about the boss woman sniffin' around while you were gone. Collecting post and snatchin' papers from Ben's office. But Mrs Moon don't like to tell tales.'

At least someone's post had arrived. Lexie was still waiting on the package for her little paint-mixing experiment. She'd have to order more.

'It's her business too. She's allowed to check the paperwork.' Although Lexie knew as well as Tom that Mrs Carrington-Noble only seemed to look for trouble. She'd probably been dying to find some after that incident in the living room when she, Sky and Grace had been caught twirling, bride-like, in the *bobbinet* curtains and calling her precious sons *hot*.

Tom drank the rest of his tea. 'And Mrs Moon is still worried we'll be 'omeless by Christmas if Ben doesn't marry one of these fancy Cynthia Forty-skew types.'

'Don't worry.' Lexie reached across and rubbed his arm. 'I'll encourage him to persevere with the rich-wife plan. We can't have you all homeless.' Although surely any new woman wouldn't want Lexie hanging around – not even on the driveway in her new van, whenever that would turn up. She should chase it, and put some money in that new ISA.

'Mrs Carrington-Noble is praying on some fancy weddin' to marry their empires. Upkeep of this place ain't cheap.' He tapped his nose. 'Not that I likes to tell tales.'

Lexie put on a mock-serious face. 'No, of course.'

Hmm. It surprised her that people with heaps of cash would still worry about it. But then, money didn't grow on trees for anyone.

Maybe Carrington Paints could still work with the Fortescues' interior design business somehow. Of course, there was the trifling issue of Ben's aversion to Cynthia. But who didn't enjoy a bit of trifle?

Tom interrupted her thoughts. 'Like I said, I don't like to gossip ...' He lowered his voice, gossip clearly imminent. 'But it's best to keep yer 'ead down in this place. The mistress ain't keen at 'avin' an unknown nipper on her patch – especially not such a purdy young thing. Just be careful.'

Lexie shivered. Did one of those nut-grass tentacles just twitch? 'Right, well, anyway.' Lexie stood up. 'Haven't we got some roots to dig up?'

'Yup. These root systems are terrible if you let 'em take hold. Now, what does that remind me of?' He gave her a wink and eased himself up too.

'I wonder.'

Lexie helped Tom with weed-extraction services for the rest of the afternoon. It was strangely cathartic, and it gave her time to think.

Her unrequited London striptease had left her feeling flesh-crawlingly cheap; it was time to start proving her worth.

Not to the likes of the Carringtons, but to herself. She was a creative woman with bags of ideas. She ought to let the poor things out before they suffocated.

There'd been a time when she'd trusted her instincts, travelled the world and forged a new career from the contents of her backpack. She'd taught herself so much and earned her own good living – not just as someone's employee. Yet something even more artistic was brewing.

Mingling with Ben and the other entrepreneurs at the paint conference had given her hope that her concepts were good. It was encouraging, inspiring; like little seeds being planted. Could she dare to help them grow?

Perhaps the first step was to stop cowering in someone else's spare room, drowning in boxes of paperwork she was too scared to look at. It wasn't just other people she needed to organise anymore.

And it sounded like she might need her own wings again soon. If Her Highness kept digging, she might unearth more than one reason to evict her. In the long run, she'd be forced to take flight and leave Ben and his new wife to make their nest anyway, even if the thought made her queasy. Feather by feather, Lexie would have to get ready to fly.

Chapter 32

O
h, those unnerving eyes – they were definitely watching her. At least ten pairs of them, looking down their snooty noses, trying to make her feel inadequate from their lofty, gilt-framed positions.

She stopped on the staircase, laden with paint pots and brushes, and stared back at the paintings. Actually, no. She wasn't having it. She had full permission to be here, overalls and all. They could just bugger off. And anyway, didn't the moving eyes in the *Scooby-Doo* cartoons belong to the bad guys?

'You don't belong either,' she whispered at them. 'You probably died centuries ago.' She poked her tongue out and was sure the effeminate posers looked a little more shocked than before.

'Nice horse,' she added, before stealing up the rest of the staircase and back to her room.

Lexie breathed a sigh of relief as she closed her bedroom door with her back.

Her newest friend Grace was waiting on a sofa, looking

like the world's most stylish decorator in her AlexaChung overalls, her beautiful caramel locks tied in a messy bun and swaddled with a spotty headband.

Lexie would ordinarily have felt a bit crap next to her, in the tatty blue overalls she'd borrowed from Tom, complete with knee patches lovingly stitched on for him by Mrs Moon. But Grace had a way of making everyone feel at ease, like an excited child with sunshine for a smile.

'Paint!' Grace jumped up and gave a little dance. 'I'm seeing this wall in La La Lexie, which would definitely be a shade of yellow.'

Lexie guided her friend back to the sofa and sat her down, placing her hands neatly onto her knees. 'We're not painting any walls; we're just mixing. Getting ideas for a potential new range of colours, which Ben hasn't even agreed to. Now, I don't want you getting dirty.'

Grace pouted. 'You wouldn't have invited me here if you were in the mood for playing it safe. You're ready for rebellion, I can tell.' She looked at Lexie's hair, which now had even more streaks of riotous blue dye. 'That's if you haven't rebelled already.'

Lexie coughed and busied herself arranging pots of the Carrington Paints range on top of dust sheets and taking some shots for social media. 'In my mind's eye I see souks lined with spices, heaped in wicker baskets in a hazy sunlight. I want warmth. I want to almost smell the paprika and cumin when I look at these new colours.'

'But what you've got is Mangy Mustard and Just-About-Ginger.' Grace screwed up her nose. 'I see why the

239

Carringtons need you – and not just to help with their online world. There's no point in polishing a poop. The company must have been stuck in the dark ages before you came along. Or maybe the dull-shades-of-crap ages.'

Lexie laughed.

'All your work with their new website, blog and social media stuff has been making them pretty cool. Although they absolutely need better colours.'

Wow. Were people starting to see the business in a brighter light because of her efforts? Lexie wondered if the mean mother would hate her a bit less if that were true. Or maybe a bit more. She shuddered. It wasn't worth thinking about it right then; bridges should be crossed when you got to them. Or never. Never was good.

Lexie and Grace arranged themselves around the paint pots like good witches around a cauldron. They stirred and scooped, and tried their best to make magical colours from shades of dull. Then they splashed each other, played noughts and crosses on the dust sheet and redecorated their overalls with multi-coloured handprints. But inspiration did not come.

'We need music,' Lexie declared with a huff.

Grace wiped her hands with an old towel, grabbed her phone and flopped to the floor. 'You're right, this is tough.' She pulled her best thinking face as she swiped across the screen. 'How about . . . Muse? Perfect.'

'Oh God, don't let Mrs Carrington-Noble rock up when we're blasting out "Uprising" and flicking sickly beige all over her carpet.'

'Bring. It. On!' Grace bounced up into her best cheer-leader impression, Lexie opting to ignore the droplets of paint which flew off her arms.

But after more mixing, playing air guitar and poking their concoctions with sticks, the girls had to admit that two wrong shades really didn't make a right.

Lexie pulled her pixie cut in frustration. 'I can't seem to turn these sorry hues into anything vaguely vibrant. Maybe I need to start from scratch.'

'Some brand-new recipes, or whatever they call them. Yes! Research trip.'

'To the factory?'

'To the souks.' Grace swept her hand in an elaborate arc, as though painting the scene. 'Consider yourself an explorer, going out into the world to gather inspiration.'

'Or I could just pop to the spice aisle in Tesco?'

'Lexie! What about your spirit of adventure? Are these people making you drab? I thought you loved travelling.'

'I did.' Lexie's eyes flickered to the boxes of junk, which had been shoved to the outskirts of her bedroom. She'd definitely sorted some of them. Well, one or two. 'But anyway, I don't even have a current passport.' She hadn't dared to renew it after what had happened at the end of her travels with Inkie. It would surely be fine but . . . still. It was easier not to. She rubbed the tattoo, which was hidden on her back.

'So we'll get you one, stupid.' Grace jabbed the screen of her phone and fiddled for a few moments. 'There – I've sent you a link explaining exactly how to arrange a fast-tracked passport just in case *adventures* come your way. Simple. We'll get you booked in quickly before you change your mind.'

Lexie expelled a huge lungful of breath she hadn't realised she'd been holding. 'Wow.'

Anyway, whatever. She probably wouldn't be going on any adventures, fast tracked or otherwise. She didn't have money to burn, and who would she even go with? Ben? After the messy London trip, that seemed unlikely. Foolish, even.

Grace followed Lexie's gaze to the rows of boxes she'd found herself staring at.

'What is all that crap, anyway? Shall we just sort it out?'

And before Lexie could argue, Grace was dragging the boxes to the mixing station and sorting through as though it was child's play. She made one neat pile of anything useful and began drowning the rest in the vats of ugly shades they'd concocted.

'So much better than a shredder,' said Grace. 'This claggy paint wipes your slate clean.' She pulled out a sheet of paper, which was now completely saturated in paint and dripping from the corner. 'Blank canvas.' Grace winked.

Lexie filled her lungs with a fresh, if not slightly paint-fume-ridden, gasp of air, and joined in the life admin renovations. It actually wasn't as scary as she'd thought. It was just ... history. Old bills she'd been avoiding but had somehow paid in the end; letters from charities thanking her for donations she really couldn't afford. Receipts for expenses she definitely should have included in her tax returns back when she was self-employed, but had probably forgotten.

'You pretty much hide from anything to do with money,' Grace concluded, as she submerged another batch of ancient bank statements.

Lexie felt her hackles rise.

'It's not a dirty word, you know. I mean, you love me, don't you?' Grace gave Lexie her big teddy eyes. 'And I saw you checking out my AlexaChungs.' She pulled at the chest of her overalls. 'Have them if you want. I prefer yours anyway.'

They looked at Lexie's fraying knee patches and giggled.

'You're not the poor kid at posh school anymore,' Grace continued. 'That was flipping years ago. You're whoever you want to be, Lex. You're whichever picture you decide to paint.'

Lexie shrugged and let her hackles flatten again. 'Maybe.' She was coming to learn that people with money weren't always that terrifying. Or that different. Which reminded her. 'Do you know the Fortescues?' Grace seemed to know everyone in the right circles.

'Yeah, I love Mrs F's interior design stuff. She did some of Mum and Dad's place. Cynthia's a bit stuck up though.'

'Oh. No wonder Ben won't consider a date.'

'I think the feeling's mutual, although she doesn't mind his potential bank balance. I heard she dull-shamed him at a summer ball years ago – in front of everyone. Told him to stop talking about work like a boring sod. That's probably why I've never seen him on the social circuit. Pretty sure he kept to himself after that.'

'Ouch! He's actually not boring at all, if you scratch the paintwork.'

243

Grace raised her eyebrows and jabbed Lexie in the ribs. 'And have you?'

'No!'

'Which blatantly means yes! I wish you'd tell me about London.'

'It was all polymers and pigments. I'll show you my notes.'

'I saw the official version on social media,' said Grace. 'But I'm determined to find out what happened off screen.' She made smoochy face impressions which Lexie did not care for.

'We decided Ben needs to work harder with his mum's matchmaking, is what happened.'

'And you resolved to busy yourself with random paint-mixing projects to distract you from what's really going on in your head.'

Lexie fiddled with her knee patches as she tried to withstand the heat of her friend's stare. 'Anyway, they can sort their own silly matchmaking. But whether or not Ben and Cynthia would be a good match, I can't help thinking the two businesses could work together. Is that too wild?' She lifted her gaze.

'Interiors and paints? It makes sense to me. Although you'd need to jazz things up.' Grace waved an arm over the uninviting shades. 'With a nice exotic range, and maybe a research field trip.' She winked. 'Want me to speak to Mrs F?'

'Hmm. I did meet her once.'

Lexie recalled the day she and Ben had visited to take photos of Mrs Fortescue's downstairs toilet – the only room she'd deemed fit to coat in a shade of slightly dull Carrington Paint. Could Lexie persuade Mrs F that the new paint range, which the Carringtons hadn't even sanctioned yet, would be exciting enough for her to endorse? Maybe Lexie could even kill two birds with one stone and convince Cynthia that Ben was not boring beige either. Hell, she'd even have Mrs Carrington-Noble on side at this rate. Then perhaps the old fox would stop hounding her.

Lexie drummed her fingers against her leg, to the beat of Muse's 'Time is Running Out'.

'So you'll be brave enough to call Mrs Fortescue,' Grace said. 'She's great. Just like me.'

Lexie couldn't help smiling at the cheeky twinkle in her friend's eye.

And then, as though the bell was trying to save her, a ringtone made them both jump. Lexie quickly arranged the screen of her laptop to take the video call from her sister. It was about time she got the latest on the Billy-Bob debacle, if only to take the spotlight off her own sorry love mess.

Chapter 33

'Sky!' Lexie and Grace waved frantically at the laptop screen.

'You managed to sneak out from the commune with your contraband phone?' Lexie was still narked that Sky had returned to the brainwashing fold, but she was trying not to be all Carrington-Noble control freak about it.

Sky screwed her face up at the screen. 'I think it's just a Samsung. Ooh, but look at you with the paints out. Aunt Jasmine would have loved that. You're like a chip off the old goat.'

Lexie laughed, although she had no idea what the goat was about. 'She would. Anyway, how are you?'

'Amazing! Honestly, things are so great here since I got back. Billy-Bob has been extra nice.'

Even Grace tried not to baulk at that one.

'Really?' asked Lexie.

'Life is perfect,' her sister confirmed. 'Well, you know.'

She lowered her voice. 'I could kill for a sausage roll. I love being vegan or whatever, but I wish they ate more meat. Vegan sausage rolls are *not* the same.'

'And you'd prefer it if phones weren't banned?'

'God, yes, and wi-fi I have to walk for ages to sneakily check Facebook. And it's a bit boring having to listen to uku-lele music all the time, and those scratchy hessian dresses ... But apart from that.'

'Completely perfect!' Lexie concluded, through tight teeth.

'But what's wrong with you?' Sky squinted. 'Like, why have you dyed your hair even bluer and started listening to miserable rock tunes? Are you having man troubles? Because I remember when Archie Geldof dumped you and you got into Led Zeppelin and piercings.'

'I did not!'

'It can't be Drew; you binned him ages ago.' Sky paused, looking almost pensive. 'Wait a minute. Are you listening to "Stockholm Syndrome"? Shit, Lex. What did they do to you?'

Grace exploded with laughter. 'She won't tell me either! But I swear something went down in London.'

'Shh, Jeez, both of you! Look, if you must know, there was an *incident*. But it was just an embarrassing mistake and there certainly won't be a repeat performance. I'm going to concentrate on my job and myself, and forget all about it.'

'An *incident*. Like what? Because you know she basically ended up on *Crimewatch* after her travels with that Inkie guy?' said Sky, aiming the final sentence at Grace.

'Piss off, Sky, I was not on bloody *Crimewatch*,' Lexie hissed at her sister, standing up to reduce the volume on her blabbering mouth. 'Ben and I had a kissing situation, if you must know. I got a bit tipsy and leapt on the poor guy. It did not end well.'

Sky's surprised eyeballs appeared large on the screen.

'I knew it!' Grace shrieked, with a barrage of unnecessary pointing.

Lexie wished Grace had a volume button too. 'And you wonder why I'm reluctant to tell you this stuff! Be quiet, seriously. It was nothing.'

'My God, you have to tell us what happened. You HAVE to!' said Grace, clearly failing at being less shrieky.

'Totally have to.' Sky nodded, from her field somewhere in Lancaster.

Lexie felt her skin sweating under two pairs of interrogative eyes as she tried to concoct an edited version. 'We had too many cocktails – things got a bit intense. There was this strange lingering moment and for some reason . . . ' She inhaled a shuddery breath as she was transported back to the moment. 'I . . . just couldn't help myself.'

'You find him *irresistible*!' said Grace, as though it had been obvious all along.

'No! I . . . urgh. It was just for that second.'

'Was it good kissing?' asked Sky, with far too much innocence for someone shacked up in a foursome.

Lexie tried to keep her breath even and prayed her face wasn't as flushed as it felt. This was surely just the tail end of all that humiliation.

248

'It was ...' Oh God, why was it so hard to talk about it? 'Hot?'

'Hot!' the other two all but screeched.

Lexie regretted the word as soon as it escaped her mouth. 'But just for that moment. You know, like a release of frustration or something. We were caught up in a kind of magic. And then it was over, like someone waved a wand and ended it. By the time we got back to the hotel, he'd sobered up and realised it was a dreadful idea. That was pretty much it.'

They didn't need to know she'd given him a striptease, he'd turned his nose up and she'd puked all over the bathroom. She'd never hear the end of it.

'Did you talk about it?' Grace asked.

So much for curbing the interrogations.

'He brought a bacon sandwich to my room the next morning and we decided to pretend it never happened and that he should continue with the matchmaking.'

'Woooow,' said Sky, her eyeballs still impossibly huge. 'I'd kill for a guy who brought me bacon.'

'This is Ben Carrington,' said Grace. 'Crap at communicating, even worse at finding himself a woman. How do you know what he's thinking if the sum total of your discussions involved charcuterie and something awkward about his mother's bloody matchmaking?'

'It wasn't awkward.' Lexie slumped down on a dust sheet and started fiddling with the hem of her overalls. It totally had been awkward. 'And I don't want to discuss it any more.' That much was true.

After a few moments of trying to ignore Sky and Lexie's swivelling eye communications, Lexie composed herself.

'Right, Sky. Why did you call?'

'Ooh, yes, me,' her sister replied.

Sometimes Lexie was grateful for her sibling's gnat-sized attention span.

'I wanted to invite you to my commitment ceremony with Billy-Bob.'

'Your *what*?' Lexie jumped up, a sudden anger propelling her to her feet. 'But you don't even ... whoa ... whoa!'

But it was too late. Lexie lost her footing amid the detritus of paint pots and stumbled backwards. Grace tried to get to her but she wasn't quick enough. Lexie wobbled desperately on one leg, arms flailing, before landing butt first in a vat of sludgy home-brewed paint.

'Shit!' It was bloody typical. And probably symbolic of just how helpless she felt with this whole sister-in-a-cult situation. 'A commitment ceremony?' She wriggled like a slippery eel, Grace pulling at her arms. 'Because Billy-Nob is ready to promise himself to just the three women? What a dick.'

'Who, me?'

The door pushed open and Cory's curious face appeared, followed by Ben's. Of course. When was life ever going to give her a break? Lexie made one last struggle, streaks of paint slopping all over the dust sheets, before at last Grace managed to yank her to her feet.

'This is definitely one for Instagram,' said Cory, pulling out his phone.

Ben put his hand over his brother's screen. 'Give the lady

some dignity. Not all of life needs to be played out for the world to see.'

Lexie felt a gush of blood rushing to her cheeks. She wasn't sure if it was caused by flailing around like a pig in paint, Ben's unexpected arrival, or because he'd just called her a lady. Not that she was going to start wearing pearls or anything, but still. Maybe he didn't think of her as a complete hotel-room hussy.

Ben looked around at the paint disaster, saw Sky gawping at them all from the laptop screen, and cleared his throat. 'Right, well, I was hoping to talk to Lexie about a few things, but this looks like a bad time. Maybe you and I can schedule something in?' He raised his eyebrows at Lexie.

'Sure.' She tried not to look flustered, even though the thought of them alone together made her feel flappier than when she'd been trying to wriggle out of that paint pot.

'Lexie's got a proposal for you too, so that works out well.' She felt Grace arrive at her side, a tower of strength against her jelly-like frame.

'You're going to propose to him?' a confused voice yelled from the screen. 'I thought you said what happened in London was an awkward mistake?'

Lexie whipped her head around to glare at her sister's face, wondering how one human being could actually be so stupid. It was as though she opened her mouth before her two brain cells could stop and have a chat.

Cory let out a long whistle. 'Oh, bro, what happened in London?'

Lexie gulped, praying that in gossip terms, what happened in London would absolutely stay in London.

Chapter 34

'Nothing happened in London,' Lexie and Ben managed to exclaim in sync.

'Just an ... awkward mistake.' Ben repeated Sky's words in an annoyingly unreadable tone.

'So nobody's proposing?' Sky continued. 'Because Billy-Bob kind of proposed to me!'

Lexie exhaled in relief at her sister's propensity to boomerang the conversation back to herself.

'I was just inviting Lexie to our commitment ceremony. It's in Mum and Dad's back garden. Next week.'

Next bloody week? 'Can't make it,' Lexie blurted out. 'My replacement camper van hasn't arrived yet and the train will cost a fortune.' A fortune she didn't want to spend watching her sister do something sublimely dumb. What was a commitment ceremony anyway? If it wasn't an actual wedding, she surely didn't need to go.

'I'll drive her,' Ben confirmed to Sky's distraught face.

'It's the least I can do. It's my mother's fault she's without transport. Lexie will be there.'

'I'm busy,' Lexie interjected, annoyed at Ben's interference. 'Working.'

'I haven't even told you what day it is yet,' said Sky, with a pout. 'And I really want you to be there.'

'I'll give her the time off,' said Ben. 'She worked enough extra hours in London.'

Lexie felt herself bristle. What was that supposed to mean? Like the cocktails-and-kissing fiasco was part of her working day? If he dared pay her overtime . . .

'That's amazing! I can't wait to see you both.'

'Ben isn't invited,' Lexie said firmly. If she was going to endure hanging out with her sister's bloke's two other girlfriends in her parents' crumbling council house, she didn't want Ben there, tailored to perfection and making her feel even more hopeless. She wouldn't even be able to drown her sorrows in gin, in case she accidentally snogged him.

'No, of course. I won't intrude. I have some business associates in the north I can catch up with. The trip will be handy for me too,' said Ben.

A six-hour, stuck-in-a-car round trip with Ben. Lexie had to find a way to wriggle out of it before next week. 'I don't approve,' she said, in a clipped tone that made her feel a tad cruel.

'She doesn't mean that,' said Ben to the screen, as though sensing Lexie's words didn't suit her. 'It's a pain in the proverbial when someone tries to dictate who you should and shouldn't fall in love with.' He wavered for a second, pulling the cuffs of his shirt as though recharging himself. 'If you believe in all that romantic palaver. Anyway, the one you've fallen for reciprocates your feelings. You haven't been written off as boring. You should celebrate.'

Lexie noticed Ben's shoulders slump a little, as though his battery life was dwindling again. Was Grace right about Cynthia calling him boring? Maybe that was why he protested so much about her. Maybe he'd liked her once, and deep down he was hurting. Not that he'd ever admit it.

Perhaps there was a spark of hope for Mrs Carrington-Noble's matchmaking efforts after all. Lexie swallowed down the painful lump that was rising.

'Anyway, I'm waffling,' said Ben. His brother's eyes were on him and he seemed uncomfortable under his gaze. 'I'll bow out here. Lexie, we'll ... catch up.'

Ben gave a salute and retreated from the room. Lexie should have felt relieved, although somehow she almost wanted him to come back. But anyway, it was just that they had work things to discuss. She was probably just excited at the bubbling up of ideas.

When Lexie turned her attention back to the room, she felt as though she'd just walked in on the unlikeliest of threesomes. Cory, Grace and Sky were chatting about nothing in particular, but the flirty tension in the air was palpable. Even her vaguely betrothed sister was fluttering her eyelashes. At least she was taking her open relationship seriously.

Lexie wondered at the possibility of Grace *Montgaaaawwwmery* and Cory. Mrs Carrington-Noble would probably have Persian kittens if those two hooked up, as well as Ben and Cynthia.

But the idea felt odd. Grace was like a well-high-heeled version of Lexie, and Cory was more like . . . well, Sky.

'Was my big brother just talking about love?' Cory interrupted her thoughts. 'Jeez, what did you do to him in London?'

'I . . . er.' God, she was floundering again. Like the flappy flatfish that liked camouflage.

'Did you brainwash him, or something?'

'Ha ha, yes, probably!' There, that was much safer. Brain over badly behaved body. 'I think he secretly likes Cynthia after all.'

'What?' Cory rubbed his stubble.

'Yes, I'm sure he let it slip,' Lexie lied. But it was just a little white one. She needed to divert this heat. 'Anyway, can I help you with something?' she asked Cory. Presumably he hadn't turned up in the hope of taking photos of Lexie falling butt first into a pot of paint and emerging like a chacma baboon.

He gave a shy shrug and plunged his hands into the pockets of his shorts. 'I just came to chuck around some ideas for this surf-shop thing you've inspired me with, but I guess it's a bad time.' He looked at the messy boxes and explosions of paint.

'Oh, Lexie loves organising people. That'll be right up her alley,' said Sky from the screen. 'One of these days she might even organise herself.'

'On it!' said Grace, waving a scrap of discarded paper in the air and dunking it into one of the mixtures.

'So, now I'm helping myself, I'm officially allowed to help you too,' Lexie confirmed, as Cory pulled out some sheets of crumpled A4 from his back pocket.

'Cool. What do you think?'

He laid his papers out on a side table, and soon Lexie and Grace were inspecting Cory's drawings of his longed-for surf school and shop, with Sky's head bobbing up and down in the background.

'Wow, these are great. You're a bit of an artist,' said Lexie. 'And you did all this since our little chat a few weeks ago? Do you think you'll go for it?'

'Yeah. Nah. Not sure, to be honest. Probably just bum around drawing more dumb pictures and waiting for my next wave. But, you know. It's good to have dreams.'

'It is good to have dreams,' Lexie repeated, feeling excited for him.

'Have you got the financials mapped out?' asked Grace, less nervous of the potential pound signs. 'Bank of Mum?'

'Nah, definitely not.' He waved an arm. 'I've got some savings from the surf lessons I've been doing for years, and I'll get a proper bank loan for the rest. It's nice to do something for yourself, you know? Dad built his own fortune, and Ben's been entrepreneurial too. No reason I can't have my own venture. I don't want to be answerable to anyone else.'

Lexie nodded. 'I get you.' It did sound nice, and she had been her own boss once. That pull was nagging again. She glanced at the side table they were leaning on, and back at her mess of paints. There was still the idea of her own kind of paint empire, now her replacement package had arrived.

A scary voice inside her kept telling her to prepare for being thrown back into the wilderness. Especially if Ben was going to be married off by the end of the year. She couldn't outstay her welcome.

'So, let's talk venues, budgets ...' Grace was counting Cory's requirements with her fingers.

'We should write up a proper business plan,' Lexie added. She'd seen it done, and there was always Google.

'I'd love to learn to surf.' Sky joined in. 'I could buy a new wetsuit and everything.'

'Says the girl who gave her money and worldly belongings to a commune to live a simpler life.' But Lexie couldn't help a smile. For once, she really hoped her sister's thing with Billy-Bob was just a fad. Because Sky had never seemed like a sausage-free, hessian-dress kind of a person.

Could she talk Sky out of that stupid commitment ceremony within the next week? Or was it time Lexie learned to live and let cry ...

Chapter 35

She wasn't going to steal anything, exactly. Ben probably wouldn't mind, and surely his mother wouldn't even notice. They had tons of furniture. And some of it was so drab, it was crying out for a makeover. She'd be doing them all a favour, and she'd absolutely put it back when she was done. Only then it would look a bit brighter.

Lexie was stalking around the living room at Nutgrass Hall, still in her paint-splattered overalls after her mixing experiments with Grace. Inspiration was bubbling after their paint-themed discussions. Even Cory was showing the spirit of adventure with his new surf-shop idea. His passion was almost infectious, and the three of them had enjoyed thrashing out the beginnings of a business plan for him, with Sky cheering them on from the laptop screen. All this paperwork wasn't half as scary as Lexie had thought.

Better still, she'd found a box of vintage magazines among

the stuff she'd been clearing out with Grace. She knew hoarding things wasn't always bad. Some of the beautiful images had danced off the page. She could imagine them découpaged on furniture. Pieces she would bring back to life with her own handmade range of chalk-style paints, then paste eye-catching pictures to. Just as Aunt Jasmine had crafted her own sunflowery versions on Penny the camper van's cupboards once upon a time.

It was hot work, all this scoping out, and Lexie had peeled down the top half of her overalls, revealing her thin yellow vest top. Her paintbrushes were tucked into her waistband like a western gunslinger, and an indie rock tune about world domination was blasting through her earphones.

Just as she was bending over to inspect a side table, a piercing voice made her jump.

'Well, I say!'

Lexie froze, mid heist.

'Is that a . . . *tattoo*?'

Bloody buggering bollocks. There was only one voice as condescending as that around these parts, and it only ever turned up when it was particularly inconvenient. Her stupid music must have drowned out the peacock alarm. Lexie pulled out her earphones and whipped herself around to face Mrs Carrington-Noble. She straightened herself up, hiding the body art she still didn't feel worthy of and hoping the woman hadn't noticed her baboon-bottom paint stains.

'I will thank you to keep your skin and its garish pond plants to yourself while you're under my roof.'

259

'It's not a ...' Lexie's voice trailed off. She was sure she wasn't usually such a wet jellyfish, but Ben's mother was so unnerving. Appearing from nowhere like a mystical beast, eyes narrowed for the pounce.

'And where do you think you're going with my occasional table?'

Surely it was always a table? But Lexie had the feeling it was not the time to split hairs.

'Er. Borrowing it?'

Mrs Carrington-Noble's eyes darted towards Lexie's fingers, which were involuntarily twitching over her waistband.

'Paintbrushes. I might have known. Does this have anything to do with those dreadful paint-mixing photos you've been posting all over social media? Because if you change anything in this house by one single shade ...'

Lexie waited for the full force of the threat, but it didn't arrive. The older woman took a step backwards and grabbed an armchair for support. Being that mean must be draining.

'My things are precious, Alexis.'

'Actually, it's just Lexie.'

'This table is a Louis the Fifteenth antique.'

And what was Ben, a Queen Anne dining chair? But Lexie dared not say that.

'And you do not have permission to touch my walls.' She pointed an angry finger at one, as though someone as meagre as Lexie might need clarification.

'Noted,' said Lexie, trying to be polite to the woman who was ultimately her boss, but feeling a veiled hint of sarcasm creeping up. 'I know you prefer beige.' Oops.

Lexie tried to keep a straight face as the pale skin on her opponent's face began to quiver.

'This room is Emperor's Ivory.'

'Of course.' Lexie nodded sagely. Why wouldn't it be?

Mrs Carrington-Noble let out a huff of frustrated air and began rifling through her overpriced handbag. 'Anyway, I didn't come here to seek your approval on my colour schemes. I will conduct my affairs as I see fit, and my members of staff will keep their ideas to themselves.'

'Quite.' Lexie reminded herself of Ben, with his one-word responses that didn't seem to match his sentiments. Maybe a lifetime of this woman could do that to you.

'I came to discuss this.' Ben's mother slapped some papers down on the so-called precious table between them. Perhaps it was *occasionally* less treasured.

Lexie lowered her head to look, a wave of recognition roaring up and slapping her in the face. Oh hell, it was her CV, covered in angry red pen. Was this what Mrs Carrington-Noble had been pinching from Ben's office when they were in London? By all accounts, the woman didn't trifle with paperwork unless she wanted to make trouble. And there was plenty to be found in Lexie's colourfully embellished CV.

Lexie swallowed down a lump of rising panic and straightened herself again, trying to look as authoritative as she could in Tom's old overalls and a vest top that even the moths couldn't be bothered to eat.

'Yes, what about it?' There. Perhaps she could still style this out.

'This curriculum vitae is as fabricated as your shocking blue hair.'

Damn it. How much did she know? Nerves began to crawl through Lexie's stomach.

'It's a perfectly good document,' Lexie confirmed. That wasn't a lie – it was perfectly good. Just not strictly true.

'Most of it is utter tosh.'

'That's a very impressive history,' said Lexie. She was getting good at this bending-the-truth business, as much as she hated it. But now wasn't the time to look guilty.

Mrs Carrington-Noble picked up the CV and shook it towards Lexie's face, as if she could read it any better when it was flapping like a shameful flag.

'You did not attend Manchester University, Alexis Summers. You do not have a degree in anything. I have checked. Even under the name *Lexie*.'

Oh God, oh God, oh God. Lexie stayed rooted to the spot, too afraid to twitch in case she accidentally scratched her nose and gave herself up as a liar.

'Well?' Mrs Carrington-Noble glared at her, the angry red veins in her eyes all but bursting for a response.

Should Lexie continue with the pretence, or would that make it worse? She hadn't signed a consent for anyone to check her records, but Mrs Carrington-Noble had probably doctored something. Or pulled some more money-buys-everything strings, like when she'd arranged for Penny the camper van to meet her hasty end.

Lexie's limbs were quivering with panicky tension; this was excruciating. The eyeballs were blinking at her like a computer egg timer, counting down to who knew what. An explosion? An attack of outraged peacocks? Or would she just be sacked and thrown out. The woman was within her rights.

'Look,' Lexie began, not quite knowing where she would end. 'I . . . urgh. I may have added a few sequins to the facts. You know, a tiny bit of *décor*. But I wanted this job, and I knew I was capable. I just didn't have the fancy qualifications to prove it. I . . . couldn't afford to go to uni.'

'So you thought you would lie to get your cheaply shod foot through my door. You deceived my sons with your big doe eyes and strange bright outfits. You pretended you belonged in the job. And then what? Were you planning to fudge your way into Benedict's bed?'

'No! I . . .' Lexie pulled at the ends of her pixie cut. 'I've never had any intention of getting into Ben's bed.' OK, so maybe that one night. But she wasn't saying that. 'Pretending to have a degree was a terrible idea, I admit that. But haven't you ever made a mistake? Haven't you ever completely messed up and then wished with all your heart you hadn't?'

The air was still for a moment. Was Mrs Carrington-Noble actually looking pensive? Lexie could barely breathe as she tried to read the woman's face.

Mrs Carrington-Noble cleared her throat, still leaning on the armchair with one thin arm. 'We all make mistakes, Alexis. But are you sure you've only made one?'

Bloody hell, what else did Patricia Poirot have up her sleeve? Lexie felt like she was in a game of who blinks first, as the two of them eyed each other over the unfortunate table.

Lexie could see Mrs Carrington-Noble's free hand rummaging in her bag, as though getting ready to flash her trump card. What the heck could be in there?

A package appeared and Mrs Carrington-Noble let it drop onto the table between them. A bag of white powder. OK, so it didn't look good. But Lexie could absolutely explain.

'Is this yours?' Mrs Carrington-Noble demanded.

Lexie couldn't deny it. It would have arrived in a box with her name on it. 'Well, yes, but it's honestly not what you think.' The powder itself wasn't going to kill anyone, but if she'd been doing any digging . . .

'And what on earth is it?'

'Seriously, it's nothing illegal.' Lexie held her hands up. A girl could buy a lot of handy things on eBay, but she was pretty sure class A drugs was not one of them.

'So my contact at the constabulary assures me.'

Lexie could sense an air of disappointment. Or was it more of a force-nine gale? 'It's calcium carbonate. Chalk powder for making a chalk-style paint – to renovate ugly furniture.' She deserved that last quip for stealing her post.

Mrs Carrington-Noble narrowed her eyes. 'Tell me why the next item out of my handbag shouldn't be your P45, Alexis. And don't think my background checks on you are finished.'

But the exertion appeared to have finally got the better of the older woman, and she manoeuvred herself around the armchair and sank back into it with a puff. Did she look ... dizzy?

'Can I help?' Lexie found herself saying.

Mrs Carrington-Noble took a few more breaths and blinked a bit. 'I'm not sure anyone can.'

'Oh, I ...'

Lexie moved towards her but was flapped away.

'Don't be ridiculous, girl. I'm fine. I just have a lot on my plate.'

'I see.' Not that she did, really. Lexie wished she didn't care, but that wasn't in her nature.

'Look.' Mrs Carrington-Noble was gripping the arm of the chair, like she was seasick on a small boat. 'I don't flit about trying to make people's lives a misery. I just ... want things to be right. It's a lot of responsibility. History ought not repeat itself.'

What history? That thing with Ben and Cory's dad? Maybe she hadn't bumped him off. It wouldn't make sense that she was worried about accidentally murdering her sons too. Whatever the case, now had to be the time to get the lady on side. While there was the slightest glimmer of light through the chinks of her armour, Lexie should grab hold of it.

'It can be exhausting, fighting against things all the time,' Lexie began, tiptoeing over the words like they were tiny eggshells.

Mrs Carrington-Noble gave Lexie a strange look, but she refused to let it faze her.

'Maybe if you accept that I want the same things as

265

you, we can work together,' Lexie added, barely daring to breathe. She could tell from the rich woman's pointy-faced appraisal that being grouped into the same team as Lexie wasn't high on her list of life goals, but she did look knackered. One less battle would surely do her good.

Mrs Carrington-Noble waved a royal hand. 'Go on.'

'You want the business to do well. You want Ben to find a suitable wife. I'm willing to help with both of those things – there's no need to fight me.'

Lexie watched as the woman chewed over her thoughts, staying still all the while like a mouse facing a cat.

'How do I know you don't want these things for yourself? My business? My son? You've already moved yourself in and now you want to change the very colour of my walls.'

'I don't believe you can see me walking up the aisle with your son any more than I can.' Lexie gave a weak laugh and held her arms out, highlighting herself in Tom's old overalls, hair full of wild dye and pockets full of nothing.

'Granted.' The other woman shrugged. 'But how can we reach a mutually agreeable conclusion? We don't have the same ... *taste*.'

There was no time to take offence. Lexie ploughed on.

'Cynthia!' The word popped out before Lexie had really decided upon it. Maybe it had decided upon itself – but that was surely a sign? 'And the Fortescues. I think I can persuade Ben and Mrs Fortescue to get the businesses working together. It would be an exciting collaboration that would make you both money. Your paint empire with their interior design world.'

Mrs Carrington-Noble seemed to be mulling it over. 'You? Hmm. Well, if in doing so you can engineer some alone time for Cynthia and Benedict ...'

Lexie winced. The plan didn't sound at all appealing when she said it out loud, but if it would keep Mrs Carrington-Noble on side and stop her delving into her business ... Well, at least she might keep her job, dignity and home for a while longer. And who was she to interfere with whatever was meant to be?

'Good.' Mrs Carrington-Noble nodded, looking pleased for the first time Lexie could ever recall. 'Because even if you did have designs on my Benedict, he's savvy enough to know where his bread's buttered. And he does like jam on it.'

Just as Lexie was pondering the wisdom of a response, the woman bit through her thoughts.

'And even if Benedict did take leave of his senses and fall for a member of staff, he would soon change his mind if he found out their past was a litter bin of lies and goodness knows what.' The mother's eyes looked brighter now. She was clearly pleased with her brilliance and was looking at Lexie as though expecting a pat on the back.

Goodness knows what indeed, thought Lexie. But Mrs Carrington-Noble wasn't wrong. Ben already didn't want her, but he'd be furious if he knew she'd conned him about her CV and hidden that other big hole in her history.

'So, you'll need to get a move on. I want him married off by the end of the year, so that whatever happens ...' She coughed a little. 'I can rest safe in the knowledge that things are taken care of.'

'Right.' Lexie scratched the back of her neck, wishing she could feel more *right* about it. 'Well, my role would be to get the businesses working creatively together. Who Ben marries is out of my remit. I can't really promise . . . '

'He does care for Cynthia in that stubborn heart of his. And for reasons I can't quite fathom, he listens to you. Help him to help himself.'

'Oh. He does care for her?' Why was she letting herself get pulled into this nonsense again? Organising other people was becoming less and less appealing. And she didn't even want to consider whether she was just using Cynthia as her latest human shield against her feelings for Ben. Well, maybe Cynthia was welcome to him. Who'd want Mrs Carrington-Noble as their dragon-in-law anyway. Lexie would never feel good about herself again if she had that woman breathing scorn down her neck for all eternity.

'And I'll hurry things up with your replacement van. You'll need your own living space when Benedict moves his new wife in. If you help to facilitate a union of businesses and hearts, I'll stop digging around in your past and your secrets will be safe. We all have things we'd rather keep buried.'

Lexie gulped. She knew what was lurking in her own past, but she still wasn't sure what, or perhaps who, Mrs Carrington-Noble was keeping interred.

'I'd even let you keep your little job on the internet, with no more questions.' Mrs Carrington-Noble flapped a hand as though arguing over a few Instagram posts was altogether too trifling. 'Maybe you could even pitch up your camping-mobile in the bushes, over by the peacock shed.'

Urgh. Lexie Summers and her bloody bright ideas. Maybe there *was* something to be said for sorting out her own parachute first. But until then, she would have to just nod, smile and try to stay out of trouble.

Chapter 36

'You should have seen Mother's latest suggestion. Her earrings were bloody terrible,' Ben shouted across the top of the car at Lexie.

She rolled her eyes and they jumped into Ben's Merc and belted up, ready for the drive to Lancaster for Sky's commitment ceremony. Ben had promised he had some business to attend to and Lexie was hoping he'd drop her off at a safe distance from her parent's tatty council estate.

'Sounds like you're being unreasonably fussy,' Lexie replied, as she searched her bag for road-trip M&Ms.

Ben had spent the past ten minutes systematically bull-dozing his way through his mother's updated list of matches, discarding each with a cutting remark.

'They're so heavy they're giving her spaniel ears. Pat Butcher would have been proud of those.'

Lexie tutted, although she couldn't blame him. It seemed like Mrs Carrington-Noble had picked a particularly odd bunch, presumably so Cynthia Fortescue would look like a comparative lottery win. How Lexie was going to broach the Cynthia subject with Ben was another matter. She had a three-hour drive and a hell of a lot of chocolate to help her with that.

Ben's car crunched across the gravel driveway, past a pride of beady-eyed peacocks, and out onto the open road.

'I can only assume she has a low opinion of me,' said Ben as they finally hit the motorway.

'Hmm?' said Lexie, disturbed from her train of thought. She'd been watching the landscape in the distance, feeling like she was experiencing her drive down here all those weeks ago, but in reverse.

'I mean, I had zero in common with most of those so-called *matches*. Call me choosy, but if I must go through with some charade of a wedding, my opposite number should at least be someone I could feel vaguely connected to.'

'With respectable earrings,' Lexie muttered. 'They are removable, by the way.'

'But dodgy taste in accessories is not.'

He was probably right on that point, but she wasn't going to openly concede it.

'You make it sound so unromantic,' said Lexie. 'Why are you giving me a lift to the other end of the country if you think weddings are a charade?'

'I didn't say all weddings. It's just not something I would have chosen for myself. Being superglued to the same nagging human for the rest of my life until they finally peck me into an early grave.'

'It's not always like that, if you find the right person.'

'The right person according to whom?'

Ben's face was angled away from her, but she could still see the tightness in his jaw. He was becoming irritable, and in the small space of the car it was quickly contagious.

'Well, you agreed to her bloody matchmaking. There's no need to chew my ear off about the standard of people's jewellery.'

'Apologies. I should keep my private affairs to myself.'

'Apparently so, after London.' Oh God, where had that come from? She hadn't meant to poke that ugly bear, twenty minutes into the world's longest drive. He wasn't even talking about that.

'I'm extremely sorry about London. It was . . . regrettable. It won't happen again.'

Oh. Maybe he did mean that. Which was fine. Wasn't it? As if she wanted any of that Shakira grindy hips awkwardness with her too-good-for-anyone pompous arse of a boss. A small flutter in her chest was trying to argue with her, but it could just bugger off.

'You're right. It won't happen again.' Lexie heard her voice echo. Now the words were out there and she couldn't hoover them back.

'If I just stick to the suitable-wife criteria, it will be easier for everyone. It's just business, after all. A means to an end.'

'As all good love stories should be,' replied Lexie, making no effort to quell her sarcasm. She didn't need to be reminded of his *criteria* or how she didn't fit them. Not that she even wanted to. Maybe he and snooty Cynthia belonged together.

Lexie grabbed her headphones from her bag, tuned herself in to one of the businesswoman podcasts she'd recently started binge-absorbing, and drained half a packet of peanut M&Ms into her mouth. Before she knew it, she was drifting into a calorie-induced coma, and she couldn't have been gladder.

'Fortune cookies!' Lexie woke from her sleep with a start, pulling out her earphones. 'Should I have brought some for luck?' Then remembering what had happened in London after their last brush with fortune, she felt her cheeks flame.

'I thought you wished them doom? Anyway, you're making a lot of effort for a ceremony you don't believe in.'

'I believe in most ceremonies, just not this one.' Wait, hadn't they had a similar conversation earlier, or had she dreamt that bit? She'd definitely had a dream about what could have happened in a certain hotel room in London, and it had been getting even steamier than Ben's car. Being in an enclosed space with a man she'd recently kissed was dangerous. Her poor brain was getting carried away.

She opened the window and prayed she hadn't uttered anything weird in her sleep.

'But you've arranged a singer for them. And a photographer.'

'Mia and Jake are friends. I helped to get them together, in fact. Anyway, they're not charging anything. The hippy couple have requested non-consumerist presents.'

'Quite the matchmaker, aren't you? And hippy or happy?' Lexie scoffed. 'My matchmaking was certainly happier

273

than some I could mention, but my sister's union probably won't be.'

She decided to call a truce of sorts and shoved the half-empty bag of M&Ms onto Ben's lap. A flurry of excited energy passed through her as her hand brushed against the heat of his firm leg. Wow. Would her beloved sweets melt there? Perhaps she should just reach back and save them . . .

'Peanut?' Ben asked.

'What? I didn't mean to touch anything, I just . . . '

'I used to prefer the chocolate ones, although you're talking me round.'

'Oh, peanut!' Lexie buzzed the window fully down. Hell, it was getting out of control. Why couldn't they have a normal conversation, like two not-even-into-each-other adults, without her mind or body charging off in a completely inappropriate direction? Maybe she should take a leaf out of this matchmaking book and sort out her own bloody love life.

Eager to steer things back to less risqué ground, Lexie let Ben sweeten himself up with her M&Ms before moving on to other pressing matters. She told him about the new colours she'd been unsuccessfully trying to mix with Grace. She was keen on the idea for the new travel-inspired paint range, but the inspiration still wasn't quite there.

'Then we should travel to find it.' He gave the answer as though it was completely obvious. Phew.

'And maybe . . . further than Cornwall?'

'Very funny, Miss Summers. I have a passport. And you?'

'Well, nearly.' She'd sorted out those forms and been cajoled by Grace to book a fast track appointment, as though life was too short to wait. But it wasn't her she was worried about. 'What about . . . if Cynthia came?'

'What?' He gave her a confused double-take, making her glad he had to revert his focus to the road. 'Why?'

She explained her proposal to get Fortescue Interiors to work with them in designing the new range, and how they would endorse it and use it in their customers' grand properties. It would also be exciting for Carrington Paints' social media and the blog. The photo opportunities would be phenomenal.

Lexie had already run the proposal past Mrs Fortescue, and she'd shown an interest. Even more so when Mrs Carrington-Noble had gushed about using it as a way of matchmaking their reluctant offspring. It seemed Mrs Fortescue was keen to see her pernickety daughter off the shelf too. The pushy mothers had suggested a jolly holiday as quickly as Ben had. Now Lexie just had to convince him that three heads were better than two, even if she didn't strictly believe it. But she deserved to see her ideas blossom, and at least she wouldn't accidentally pounce on Ben with Cynthia *in situ*.

'The collaboration will be a fantastic way to breathe new life into the business, and lucrative too. But Mrs Fortescue wants Cynthia involved every step of the way. She'd have to come with us, or I'm pretty sure it would be no deal.' Only a small exaggeration.

Lexie held her breath as the cogs in Ben's brain

churned it over. There was probably a calculator in there, working out the potential profits and weighing them up against losses.

'You'll be there too? And it's all just business?'

'Just business,' Lexie chirped. Well, it wasn't her job to be flipping Cupid. She hadn't exactly promised Mrs Carrington-Noble that she would bring Ben and Cynthia together, and it wasn't her problem if the pushy woman had inferred it.

'Always preferable to have a chaperone, I suppose.'

Ben looked at the sweaty mix of M&M colours on his palms before buzzing down his own window. Lexie wondered whether it was her or Cynthia as chaperone. Ben's half of the car had become steamy for the first time since they'd set off, so perhaps there was something in this secret desire for Cynthia theory. Or perhaps she was going stir-crazy in this car.

'Right, I'll get straight on it.' And before Lexie could stop herself, her yellow-painted nails were all over her phone screen arranging dates with the Fortescues and booking three flights to Marrakech. Well, none of them could back out now, could they?

Before long, they were a few miles from her parents' house. Lexie was just trying to think of a suitably distant place for Ben to drop her off, when a call rang through on Ben's hands-free and an older man's voice filled the car.

'Ben, Ben, Ben ... Was it today we were meeting? Something's come up. Can we make it another time?'

Lexie stiffened. What? Who was this buffoon, and didn't he know about manners? You didn't go cancelling plans willy-sodding-nilly and leave people stranded. What was Ben going to do for five hours? Sit in a layby?

'It was today, Malcolm. I'm nearly there, in fact.'

Ben ought to be outraged, but he seemed almost pleased. Was his mouth twitching into a smile? Who would be happy about driving for three hours to be stood up by a joker named Malcolm?

'Never mind,' Ben continued. 'I have a backup plan. I was invited to a commitment ceremony, so I'll crash that instead.' He dealt with the usual niceties and hung up on Mr Stand-up.

Lexie did not feel nice. The cruel hand of panic was tightening around her neck.

'Well, this will be even better,' said Ben, seeming distinctly more chipper than he had for the last hour. 'Sky did say I was welcome, and I'd love to meet your parents and see where you're from.'

Lexie swallowed hard; she could not think of anything worse than Ben pulling up outside her folks' zero-class home in his S-class Mercedes, wearing an absurdly smart designer suit. Urgh. Why was he even wearing that? He looked more like he was attending a special occasion than meeting no-show Malcolm. Had he planned this?

'Maybe I don't want you to,' Lexie said to her window, trying to hide the wobble in her voice.

'What? Why?'

Lexie took a deep breath. Was it really that difficult? 'It's just ... embarrassing.'

'What are you, ten years old? Who cares about their

parents being embarrassing? It's just a given, isn't it? Look at my mother. She's a haughty bloody monster, but I don't hide her in a cupboard.' He scratched his head. 'Although maybe I could?'

'It's not that they're my parents.' Lexie was ignoring his stupid jokes, even if his mother really did belong in a cupboard. 'It's just that we're from different worlds. Worlds that don't exactly mix.'

'Right. Then you're embarrassed of me?'

'No! I don't think I'm embarrassed about anyone in particular. Maybe just myself. My past. Our different roots.'

Ben laughed and Lexie became even more conscious of their surroundings. They'd entered her parents' council estate. How did he even know the way? And what was so funny?

'Are you mocking this?' she asked him, turning her body around to face him. Surely not even he would be that rude. Not in front of her, anyway.

'Did you ever even ask about my roots, Lexie?'

'No,' she conceded, her bottom lip jutting out.

'Well, maybe you should.'

And with that, he pulled up a few doors from her parents' house and jumped out. 'Now, it's down here somewhere, isn't it?'

Lexie clambered out too and eyeballed him across the roof of the car. Oh, for the simpler times of three hours ago, when all they had to dispute was a pair of Pat Butcher earrings.

'You should always Google stalk your destination before you set off – rookie mistake not to. I do believe you taught me that on the first day we met. You're a lot savvier than you give yourself credit for.' He winked at her and beeped the lock on the car doors.

Lexie reluctantly conceded it was time for her worlds to collide. She only wished she'd brought a crash helmet.

Chapter 37

'Do you, Sky Trixibelle Summers, promise to unite your soul, spirit and heart with the soul, spirit and heart of Billy-Bob Heavenlybody, in a truly soulful, spirited and heartfelt way for the rest of your days, or until one or other of you prefers not to?'

Lexie had purposely chosen a seat towards the back of the commitment ceremony, as she didn't trust herself not to bounce up and protest. She hadn't banked on it being quite so hilarious. She was clinging on to Ben's arm, trying to hide her laughter behind his shoulder.

'Do you think that's his real name?' She giggled, crossing her legs so she didn't actually wee herself.

Ben gave her an admonishing look. Fancy him being the one taking this 'vague effort at commitment' ceremony seriously.

'And where do his other two girlfriends fit in?' Lexie whispered.

Mia Ricci, sassy half-Italian singer and girlfriend of her old boss Jake James, was sitting on the other side of Lexie. Mia gave Lexie a playful poke in the ribs, by means of a 'behave nicely' warning. Jake was busy at the front taking photos, and probably thinking lovey-dovey thoughts about Mia. It couldn't be long before he asked Mia to tie the knot, although Lexie hoped he wasn't taking any notes from this circus.

In fairness, Lexie's parents had done a lovely job of the garden. The weather was as grey as this questionable union deserved, but they'd filled the space with wildflowers, painted bright murals across the rickety fences and made colourful chair covers from an eclectic mix of chintz. It was perfectly bohemian; the sort of thrown-together look other people probably paid a fortune for, but that her artistic mother no doubt achieved on a shoestring. Lexie wouldn't ask which public garden she'd 'borrowed' the flowers from.

'And, Billy-Bob Heavenlybody, do you undertake to treasure Sky Trixibelle Summers as though she was one of the greatest pearls in the ocean, but no more or no less great than the other pearly women in your life, namely Indigo Dreamcatcher and Renata De La Soul?'

Even Mia's shoulders were politely trembling at Lexie's side now. Who had made up these vows, and what did they really mean?

After what felt like an unnecessary amount of vacuous promises and cheesy readings about rabbits that loved each other, Sky and her three-timing suitor were declared husband and third pretend wife. Lexie was just pleased Sky's commune didn't believe in the sanctity of legal marriage. Small blessings.

The clouds continued to loom as some awful non-alcoholic herbal concoction was served on the lawn, from a selection of mismatched crockery. Jake flitted around with his camera and Mia was singing something soulful in the background, trying to embrace the collection of bare-footed men with tambourines who'd decided to accompany her in a completely offbeat fashion.

Despite the odd set-up and dodgy canapés Lexie was actually enjoying herself. Ben was doing his best to cheer her mood and was being a delight to everyone they spoke to. She needn't have feared any awkward, clash-of-worlds divide. Oddly, he seemed to fit right in. He obviously wasn't as bad at being human as either of them had thought.

'Lad!' Lexie's dad appeared and slapped Ben on the back like they had been friends for ever. Surprisingly, they'd been getting on like a house on fire before the ceremony, when Lexie had been fussing with Sky and their mum. 'The shirt looks great on you.'

The shirt was a riot of orange and brown flowers, and had a huge 1970s collar. Much to Lexie's horror, her dad had been keen to lend it to Ben when he'd felt overdressed in his formal suit. But, somehow, Ben did look good in it. It fit snugly across his firm chest and matched his neat hair perfectly. Well, it had been neat until Lexie had given it a ruffle. And he hadn't even complained.

'Anyway, you were telling me about this factory.'

Lexie's dad, Graham, beamed at Ben's question, the wrinkles around his eyes turning into happy smiles as he began describing his prized factory. He'd been a caretaker there all his working life. Objectively it was a lowly job with meagre pay and unsuitable hours, but he was proud of it and probably didn't get to talk about it much. Most people didn't show an interest.

'Ooh, isn't he a bobby dazzler in that top.' Lexie's mum, Hazel, arrived at her side, speaking in not-quite-hushed-enough hushed tones. Lexie gave her the customary keep-your-voice-down glare. She didn't want Ben to overhear.

Lexie's mum was a worry. She always meant well, in her swathes of purple tie-dye, smelling of homemade rose perfume. But she was just so ditzy. She never engaged her brain before speaking, and who knew what would tumble out. She was like a very colourful truth bomb just waiting to go off. And there were still so many things Lexie didn't want Ben to know.

'But he is a cutie.' Lexie's mum poked her in the ribs, which in fairness had already had enough poking. 'And you know it.'

Lexie expelled a frustrated sigh. There was no point in even trying to keep her mother under control. Hazel lived in an alternative floaty universe where trifling conventions like behaving yourself didn't matter. As much as Lexie loved her mum, she'd spent most of her growing-up years feeling a tad embarrassed about what she might say or do. She'd come to learn it was easier to live at a safe distance.

'We're not suited,' Lexie hissed back. 'Now shh.' Although she knew it was futile.

'On the outside you two looked very different, when you arrived.' Hazel nodded, as though she was particularly wise. She was not wise. 'But the ones you usually turn up with . . .' She began counting them on her fingers. 'That Inkie the tattoo scoundrel, and then rock-wannabe Drew from the band. You looked all matchy-matchy on the outside. Arty and interesting, with a streak of rebellion. But underneath it all, you didn't match them at all.'

'Right,' said Lexie. She was not even going to ponder this. Her mum had a head full of rose-scented air. And she'd probably pilfered the roses.

'Anyway, it's not all about matching.' Hazel was on a roll now. Lexie tried not to roll her eyes. 'Look at me and your dad.'

Lexie did look at him, as he inexplicably rubbed Ben's shoulder. He was salt of the earth, with his big bear hugs and fuzzy grey curls. There was nothing tie-dye about him, and he usually wore overalls when his wife didn't sweet-talk him into a strange Hawaiian shirt.

'Stilton doesn't need more Stilton,' Lexie's mum continued. God knew what she was talking about. 'Stilton is at its most delicious with a cracker.' And with that, Hazel gave her daughter a wink and bustled off into the crowd, her cheap bejewelled flipflops clapping with glee beneath her.

'Certifiable,' Lexie muttered, before elbowing herself into the bromance between Ben and her dad. She guessed Ben was missing his own father today.

284

After a few minutes of listening to the two of them rave about the importance of an honest day's work, Lexie felt like a bit of a spare part. She noticed Mia and Jake were taking a break, so she wandered over to hang out with them under an archway of pretty tissue-paper flowers. They did look a picture and she felt almost rude to interrupt. But she'd had a hand in matchmaking them not so long ago, so she deserved to relish her own handiwork.

'I always said you two were perfect together,' said Lexie, pulling Jake's camera from around his neck and taking some photos of them under the arch.

'Looks like we're not the only winning couple,' Mia replied, trying to tame her long brown waves so they didn't look too frizzy in the shots. She'd jettisoned her usual rock-chick style for a floaty green dress, albeit with DMs and a lot of red lip gloss.

'Sky and Billy-Nob?' asked Lexie, shocked they would even think it.

'Lexie and Ben,' Jake replied, thankfully with a hint of discretion. 'And you can get rid of that protesting pout. I remember the world of denial; it's a big old waste of life.'

Lexie was starting to feel heavy with the weight of people getting on her back today. Why was everyone so obsessed with her and Ben?

'He's my boss, Jake.'

'So make him not your boss.' Jake shrugged. 'Other jobs are available. Or be your own boss. You were a great help when I was setting up JakePix and the shop; you know the ropes. And weren't you an online entrepreneur once?'

'Massive exaggeration,' Lexie replied. Although she did secretly keep fancying herself as her own boss again. 'Anyway, he's loaded, whereas I come from this jumble sale.' She waved her arms around her. The garden admittedly looked better than usual, but nothing could hide the simple property in its questionable state of repair.

'So? What is this, Jane Austen times? Who cares what dowry you come with?'

Lexie flicked her eyes skywards. 'Tell your boyfriend to stop being a sarcastic twat,' she said to Mia. Although she couldn't help thinking it did sound a bit foolish when he put it like that.

'Rich people are annoying, anyway. I mean, Ben's all right when you get used to him. But I'm not sure I could marry into his world.'

'Money is the root of all evil,' Lexie heard a female voice muttering nearby. She peeked over her shoulder to see a commune dweller in what looked like a hessian dress, preaching to Lexie's great aunt Mabel. 'We renounce money and all its malevolent trappings.'

OK, so that sounded pretty odd too. Would she start wearing itchy hessian and handing over her beaded purse to the gods of whatever, if she carried on thinking like this?

'So you've had a few sneaky thoughts about marrying him!' Mia squeezed her arm.

'Obviously not,' Lexie lied. In truth, she had played out a few possible scenarios. But it had always ended in her feeling silly. 'Anyway, he's got to marry a suitably rich woman or his mum will screw him over. He won't inherit the business, and she'll probably kick him off the family estate and murder the peacocks.'

Mia gasped.

'Sounds like a massive charade,' said Jake. 'When you clearly like each other.'

'Why is everyone saying that?' Lexie flapped her arms in frustration.

'Because they've got eyes?' Jake shrugged. 'Anyway, if he feels the way I think he does, he won't give a toss about the money.'

'Urgh. I don't really know how he feels,' Lexie conceded. She was running out of fight.

'Someone gave me a pep talk on this very subject once,' said Jake. 'She came banging on my darkroom door, red faced and hair like a pixie. Do you know what she said?'

Lexie knew this was about her, when she'd been persuading Jake to make a play for Mia when he'd been sure all was lost. 'Can't remember,' she muttered.

'It was something about not being afraid to make a fool of yourself for love. To say how you feel or live a life of regret. Then you called yourself Paddy McGuinness and booked me a flight to Fernando's – well, Venice – to tell Mia that I loved her.'

'Oh.' Well, she'd booked flights again, all right. Three flights to Marrakech. But who knew who would be declaring their love to whom. *Ménage à* bloody *trois*.

'Make sure it's not always other people's lives you're sorting out though, Lex,' said Jake.

Seeming to sense that Lexie needed cheering up, Mia

interrupted. 'Hey, if it makes you feel any better, Drew left the band.'

Mia was the singer in the same indie rock band as Drew, although Mia had always been vocal on how slutty she thought Drew was for cheating on Lexie.

'It was probably for the best,' Mia continued. 'I couldn't like him after how he treated you. Anyway, better still. He was forced to leave because his new fiancée Tricky Tabby didn't want to marry someone who was in a "crappy band" as she so politely put it. He had to cut his hair and start wearing a suit to work in Tabby's dad's boring investment business. So marrying someone from the same wealthy background isn't an instant ticket to eternal happiness either, in case you were wondering.'

Lexie couldn't help grinning at that little gem. She was past caring about Drew, but she had always believed in karma. Sometimes it was a beautiful thing.

And when Ben appeared through the crowds of hessian and tambourines, Lexie smiled even more. Jake took back his camera and angled Ben and Lexie under the tissue-paper flowers for some photos of their own.

'And a few for the social media accounts,' said Lexie, handing Jake her camera phone.

After the photos, Lexie left Ben with Mia and Jake while she went to freshen up. She'd given them both her best don't-say-anything-stupid eyes before she'd left, but who knew what the cheeky pair would get up to. She couldn't play bouncer to Ben all day, or she'd never get to pee.

Anyway, she'd only be five minutes. What could possibly go wrong?

Chapter 38

When Lexie returned to her parents' garden, Ben was chatting amiably with her mum. Could this commitment ceremony get any worse?

Lexie's chest was pounding as she rushed across the grass to them. Her mum saw her coming and gave her an innocent little finger wave before shimmying off in a different direction.

'What was she talking about?' Lexie asked, half panting, but trying her best to sound casual.

Ben smiled. 'Nothing important. This and that. She's a sweetheart, isn't she? So honest and carefree. She really wears her heart on her sleeve.'

'And her mouth,' Lexie mumbled.

'You shouldn't be so hard on her.' Ben rubbed her shoulder, seeming to notice she was tense. 'She means well, and at least she has a more caring way of showing it than my old dragon.'

Well, at least Ben was still talking to her. Presumably her mum hadn't dished too much historical dirt.

Ben pulled over two of the non-coordinating garden chairs that Lexie guessed had been borrowed from various neighbours, and they sat down under the ceremonial archway. The paper flowers rustled around them, as though trying to whisper something.

'It's all just a bit ... cringeworthy,' said Lexie.

A barefooted teenager arrived, wearing a dress probably made of old curtains. They nodded politely as she handed them cups of grassy tea and disappeared.

'You should never be embarrassed of where you're from, Lexie. Or where you're at now, or even where you're heading. It's all part of the pretty picture that is you.'

Lexie tried to hide her flushing cheeks behind the steam from her cup.

'And you never did ask where I was from,' Ben added.

'I've seen it,' said Lexie. 'It's a crazy estate ruled by nut grass and peacocks.'

Ben tried his dubious tea and appeared not to hate it. 'No, it's not, actually. You just assumed that. We moved there when Cory was little, but I was about ten. Before that we lived in a fairly normal house.'

'Really? Wow. I mean, I remember Mrs Moon saying you were a bit older when you moved in, but I had you pegged for a rich kid, born and bred.'

'Not at all. I grew up on Micro Machines and Monster Munch too. We didn't always have money. Dad made his own fortune with the business and a few lucky windfalls. He bought the disused factory for a song when the market was low and worked damned hard to build it up.'

Ben stopped for a moment, and Lexie could have sworn his eyes looked a little teary. She had a million questions, but it didn't seem the time to bombard him. Ben cleared his throat.

'He was a man of ideas. Like you, but not the man bit.' Ben looked at her and smiled gently. 'He never let anything get in the way of them.'

'Ah, that bit's not so much like me,' Lexie said softly.

'We all have our weaknesses. Dad's was probably Mum.' He gave a small laugh. 'I'm sure he would have been happy living in our old house, but Mum pushed and pushed. She was so keen to climb the social ladder.'

'Did she ...' God, it was a stupid question. Of course Mrs Carrington-Noble hadn't got fed up of her husband and bumped him off.

'Put him under too much pressure? Probably. Cause him to have an early heart attack? No, I don't think that's how the science works. But she does feel guilty about his death. She believes she should have been looking after him better. Keeping her clutches on things at home, rather than flitting around the racquets club making eyes at young Spaniards. Perhaps.'

Jeez. No wonder Ben was reluctant to find a woman of his own. His mother hadn't given him the best impression of marriage. But hang on ...

'What about all those effeminate horseman paintings at Nutgrass Hall?'

291

Ben laughed. 'Nothing to do with us. Strangers. They came with the house. I actually feel more comfortable here, now I think of it. More relaxed. More myself.'

'Here?' Lexie put her hand against his forehead like he must be suffering from a fever. 'In Smallpenny Road, sitting on a mismatched chair under an archway of paper tat?'

'With you. And your parents. Everyone. You're all so hugely welcoming, so full of warmth and colour. You can't put a price on that feeling. The feeling of home. I miss it.'

Lexie put down her weedy drink and grabbed his hands. 'But Nutgrass Hall is your home. It's amazing. I know I take the mick out of the beige walls and funny suits of armour, but Cory, Tom and Mrs Moon make it home. All that cake and kerfuffle.'

He laced his fingers through hers and squeezed them. 'It's all right. I'm not having a breakdown.' Lexie had never been more pleased to see the corners of his twitchy smile. 'I just feel different today. Like I can be myself here. Like anything goes.'

Lexie looked around at their surreal surroundings and laughed. 'Anything pretty much does go. Although I'm glad you didn't take my dad up on his offer of the brown sandals. I am enjoying your company today, but I draw the line at hanging out with your toes.'

Ben finally joined her in laughing. 'You're right. I should keep my toes to myself.'

But his hands were just fine where they were, she couldn't help thinking. Wrapped up in hers, and, for this surreal moment, on this strangest of days, it felt safe. Maybe they were existing in a parallel universe, and tomorrow would be different. But there was no need to overthink it.

'You know, I love the business, and Nutgrass Hall feels like it's under my skin now. With the memories of Dad, and everything. But I've never felt any sense of belonging in Mum's world of snobby friends. Or in the private school I went to as a teenager. I always felt more comfortable in our old life. Maybe that's why I kept myself to myself a bit. Stayed busy helping Dad with the business. Didn't bother making real friends.' He shrugged. 'I got the impression they all thought I was a bit dull anyway. But this . . .' He nodded to the garden shenanigans. Sky and their mum playing limbo with a couple of their cousins. Their dad hiding among his runner beans, pretending he wasn't drinking a beer. 'This makes me feel like life's worth celebrating. Like someone's taken a paintbrush and splashed me with colour.'

Lexie stole a look at him then as he took in the scenes playing out around them. His eyes were alight and his whole face radiated happiness. She didn't even think there was anything intoxicating in that herbal tea. She felt warmed by him. Not just hot to rub up against him like she had that time in London. But something deeper. Maybe she was his splash of colour. But he made her feel good about believing in rainbows again too.

'Sausage rolls,' Sky hissed, manhandling Lexie and Ben to a space behind the garden shed. They'd been stretching their legs and finding a place to discreetly pour away the dreadful tea. 'Cover me,' Sky said to Ben, shoving him in place like a great flower-power shield.

Sky opened her beaded silver clutch bag, which had apparently been hand-stitched by small commune children, and let the smell of warm, sweaty pastry escape into their hideaway.

Lexie laughed. 'Rebelling on day one, you little troublemaker?'

'I did not make any promises about sausage meat. Well, not today, anyway.' Sky shoved a handful of sausage roll into her mouth before offering some to Lexie and Ben.

'So what's been frying?' Sky asked, in between mouthfuls.

'Not a lot,' said Ben, seeming to understand her misquoted saying without worrying about correcting her.

'Did you make all that chalky-paint stuff yet?' she asked Lexie.

Ben raised his eyebrows.

'Er, nope,' said Lexie, fiddling with the hem of her short, yellow hippy dress.

'I checked it out on Insta,' said Sky. 'Doing up your furniture with chalk-style paint is huge. I get what you mean though – people need more vibrant colours. I'm so over dove grey and chicken egg.'

'Duck egg,' Lexie replied. 'And I thought you weren't allowed to use devices or access the internet.'

Sky shrugged, her mouth too full of banned meat products to answer.

'Didn't you mention the chalk-style paint thing before? Don't ignore your ideas if they're still vying for attention,' said Ben.

'It's just something I've been toying with.' Lexie nodded slowly. 'Possibly a bit wild for your taste, but I like it.'

'Then make it your own venture. Your inspiration deserves space of its own. Carrington Paints shouldn't prosper from all of your brilliance.'

'I could help you!' Sky enthused. 'Like a family industry.'

'You live at the other end of the country,' Lexie reminded her. 'And you've just committed yourself to a four-legged partnership in a commune that doesn't believe in people doing work for money.'

'Oh, yeah.' Sky looked disappointed as she swigged from a miniature bottle of clandestine gin, which she'd pulled from her clutch bag.

Not for the first time, Lexie wondered how long this Billy-Bob fad would last.

'Skyyyyy.'

Talk of the devil. Sky gave a small squeak of panic as she heard her new not-quite husband's voice and shoved the bottle of gin into Lexie's hand.

'There you are, my darlin'.' Billy-Bob's head, with its long grey beard and red bandana, appeared around the corner of their hideout. He was approximately twice as old as Sky, and scarcely half as nice. In fact, Lexie liked him about ten per cent less with every word he said. In his phony American accent.

'Just having some family time.' Sky squeezed Lexie and Ben's hands, and then gave them both a cheesy fake smile Lexie had never even seen before.

Billy-Bob lifted his beak-like nose. 'What's that I can smell?'

'Foxes!' Sky blurted out.

It made zero sense to Lexie, as she stood there reeking of pork and pastry, with a bottle of Asda's London Dry in her free hand. But, then, not much about this surreal day did.

'Anyway, gotta dash.' Sky let go of their hands and barrelled into Billy-Bob, who gave Lexie a narrow-eyed look before he was woman-handled away.

'I do not like . . . ' Lexie began, through gritted teeth.

'His dirty-looking beard, bogus accent and the way your sister morphs into a completely different person every time he appears?'

'Yes! I mean, call me fussy, but bloody hell. What do those two even have in common? They might have handed over their worldly belongings to allow them to be equal, but that doesn't make them the same.' Lexie took another swig of the gin and then reminded herself she was not meant to be getting drunk. She couldn't stop fantasising about touching Ben again, since their unexpected finger-entwining moment earlier. But if anything was going to happen between them, she wanted to at least be sober. And preferably not hiding behind a shed.

'Should two people be the same for love to work?' Ben asked.

He turned to face her, his atlas eyes wide with question. He was suddenly so close. Why did it feel so teasingly good?

'I . . . ' Did he just say the L word? Lexie felt almost dizzy, like she wasn't really sure of anything. 'No, I guess not. More . . . '

'Complementing?'

He knew all the answers today. They were almost in sync.

296

'Comfortable?' He tried out another word when he didn't get a response.

And suddenly Lexie knew that was exactly how she felt. Even though they'd spent weeks rubbing each other up the wrong way, it was as though all the rubbing had turned them smooth. Like two glassy pebbles on the beach. Her fingers unfurled from the bottle almost involuntarily. It dropped to the muddy floor.

'Can I kiss you?' he asked.

'For someone who I initially wrote off as rude, you can be frustratingly polite,' she murmured as she felt herself drawing nearer to him.

She lifted her hands to his solid jaw and pulled it down towards her until their mouths met in a gloriously warm, soft kiss. Their lips moved together in perfect time and she pushed her body close to him, keen to feel his heat. His hands slipped around her waist, his fingers resting excitingly close to her bum. But it was nothing like London. If that had been fiery and charged and full of frustration, this was like a gentle voyage. A meaningful embrace between two lost hearts that were ready to be found. As Lexie looped her arms around Ben's neck and let her head fall back, his mouth tickled deliciously across her throat. And she tried not to think of what would happen when it was time to leave this wonderful parallel universe. She tried to simply be.

Chapter 39

C ynthia Fortescue had extremely large feet.

That was the one thing Lexie couldn't help noticing as she sat with Cynthia and Ben in the back of the Fortescues' Bentley on the way to the airport. Not that Lexie wanted to be mean about anyone's feet, but she had to take her mind off the awkward atmosphere by thinking about something.

It had been a week since Sky's commitment ceremony, when she and Ben had kissed behind her parents' shaky old shed. The drive back from Lancaster had been so full of electrical charge she'd felt like they'd been in a bumper car. There had been an abundance of leg grabbing and longing looks. Luckily, or perhaps unluckily, Cynthia was now wedged between them, looking like she'd just stepped out of a Moroccan fashion feature in *Vogue*. She was draped in orange-and-gold sari material, her long, slender feet encased in pointy leather slippers covered in what were quite possibly real diamonds. They'd probably get mugged.

'M&M?' Lexie asked the other two, through a mouthful.

Ben took the opportunity to reach across and take the packet, accidently-on-purpose brushing Lexie's hand as he did so. A tingle ran up her arm, and she tried not to giggle like a stupid teenager. It had been like that since they'd got back from Lancaster. Snatching secret moments together, behind closed doors, to lock their bodies into each other and recreate that moment of lust. Each meeting was getting just a little hotter. It hadn't felt right yet to fling their clothes off and get down to more meaningful business – but they both kept hinting about Morocco. And Lexie had absolutely packed her slinkiest undies.

They hadn't talked about what this heat between them actually meant. It was the elephant in the room. Perhaps like their third Bentley bedfellow, although she was more of an elegant white tigress. Anyway, Lexie was trying not to think about the logistics. She didn't want Ben to sacrifice everything for her, and she wasn't even sure if she wanted to shack up properly with her boss. But she was happy to enjoy this while it lasted.

Lexie heard Ben mildly groaning at the other side of the car as he filled his mouth with chocolate. Cynthia sniffed and looked at them both like they were pigs. Her hair was black and poker straight, tied back in a tight bun that made her cheekbones look severe. But she could rock it, Lexie thought, with something approaching envy. Cynthia did look catwalk-chic and rich, even if she did know it.

Lexie should have cancelled this charade, of course. Or at least confessed to Ben what it was originally about. She knew Mrs Carrington-Noble had high hopes of Lexie trying to shove Ben and Cynthia together on this trip, and she hadn't done enough to put her straight. Maybe Lexie would never have lowered herself to meddle anyway, but there was zero chance of it now she was getting hot and oh-so bothered with Ben herself. Lexie tried not to think about the tricky secrets from her past that Mrs Carrington-Noble could delight in revealing now Lexie wasn't quite playing ball.

Ben would hit the roof if he found out Lexie had been entertaining his mum's wild matchmaking ideas. And now Cynthia would probably go mad if she worked out there was something going on with Lexie and Ben. Cynthia's mother and Mrs Carrington-Noble had obviously been egging Cynthia on, and she'd made clear to Lexie before getting in the car that she was looking forward to the challenge of snaring herself a husband. And for someone with a good upbringing, Cynthia had made some particularly explicit hand gestures to signify exactly what she was hoping to achieve with Ben that weekend. Urgh.

Cynthia pulled a packet of Harvey Nichols Honeycomb Dips from her bag. Trust her to have styled the packaging of her snacks to match her radiant outfit. Matching is not better, Lexie reminded herself, thinking of her mother's weird Stilton and Stilton theory. Anyway, those sweets were just fancified bits of Crunchie bar in an overpriced bag. Lexie tried not to get territorial as Cynthia offered one to Ben. And not her! The cheek.

'No, thanks,' she heard Ben reply. Was it childish to feel a small buzz of satisfaction? 'I prefer peanut.'

'Oh, don't worry, darling. So do I.' Cynthia turned to Lexie and gave her a sly wink. Lexie wanted to poke her eye clean out of its socket. Only she did the peanut jokes around here, and then it was only as a blunder, not some sleazy come-on. This was going to be one long weekend.

Lexie flip-flopped through the cool marble foyer of the hotel in a favourite pair of purple sequined harem pants from her travel days. Her vest top and arms were covered with a bright floaty shawl. It had been so long since she'd even dared to travel. She felt a fizz of excitement at the way Ben was inspiring her. And as for the thought of the unknown territory they'd discover together . . .

Ben was at her side, his chest puffed out more proudly than usual. She would not be moaning that he looked too beige in his chinos, with his white shirt pulled taut across his torso. That personal gym of his was a thing to be celebrated.

'Shall we go and explore?' he asked, giving her hand a quick squeeze.

'I can't wait.'

And she really couldn't. An afternoon with hot Ben in this Moroccan heat would turn her insides to jelly. Could they sneak in a dip in the pool afterwards to cool off? Although who knew what the sight of him in shorts would do to her.

For now, they were deliciously alone. Cynthia had opted to slink off already, more interested in checking out the hotel's spa facilities than in seeing Marrakech. Annoyingly,

Mrs Fortescue had insisted on booking the hotel, and had bagged Ben and Cynthia stunning neighbouring suites, with jacuzzi baths and rose-petal-strewn beds.

She'd shoved Lexie in a bog-basic room on the opposite side of the hotel, from where she could see the other two on their balconies basking in the sun. Lexie wasn't fussy about what sort of room she had – it was practical and clean, and who really needed their towel shaped like a swan? But it would irk her seeing Cynthia and her greedy claws so dangerously close to Ben. Cynthia was from the *desirable* class and was undeniably stunning, and with one little 'I do' she could secure everything Ben wanted. His father's business, which he'd given his all to, the family home, future financial security. The very things that too much of a connection with Lexie would snatch away.

Although, as Lexie and Ben stepped blinking into the radiant sun, Lexie felt as though the warmth was melting their problems away. For the moment. She readjusted her shawl to cover her head and they began their winding journey through the side streets of the medina towards the main square.

'Wow.' Lexie soaked up her surroundings. 'This is exactly it, don't you think? The kind of inspiration we're looking for. These colours; this charm?' She could feel it already, like some kind of Moroccan magic, seeping into her skin.

They stopped and looked around them, Lexie spinning slowly like a child in a wonderland of treats. The buildings were beautiful and yet modest in their terracotta simplicity, draped with hand-woven rugs in glorious shades of cerise, burnt orange and midnight blue. All the colours of the rainbow seemed to shimmer around them through the hazy, hypnotic sun.

Lexie felt like her soul was on fire with anticipation. She was desperate to hug Ben with the sheer joy of it, but, out of respect for the culture, she didn't want to display too much physical affection. She shook herself down, trying to ignore the tingle in her fingers to touch him. By the end of their walk she'd be fit to pounce.

He smiled at her, like she was the most enchanting thing. 'It's beautiful,' he said. 'As are you.'

'Mr Carrington, we're on a research trip. Do behave yourself.'

'I will behave myself all day.' He crossed his heart and gave a small bow. 'But do I have to behave myself all night?'

With Lexie's agreement, he'd managed to convince Cynthia he'd be in his room all evening working and he wasn't to be disturbed. In truth, he and Lexie were taking a taxi to a quiet restaurant in the High Atlas Mountains. She smiled at the image of an evening alone with him, enjoying his handsome features across the flicker of candlelight. And when they were back at the hotel ... *mmm*. There'd been plenty of insinuations, and she was sure that part would be the most delicious of all.

As they moved on through the old town, the ancient buildings packed tightly like a dusky orange maze, Lexie marvelled at everything they saw. Old-fashioned pharmacies selling everything from exotic perfumes to cooking spices; tiny shops where craftsmen worked hard with wools and leather. Locals rushing by on bicycles and donkeys, offering to take them to places for a few dirham. Everyone was keen to make, sell and barter – and they hadn't even reached the souks. Lexie could sense there was no abundance of money, but the people had a keen eye for business. And yet they were jovial and welcoming, with Lexie teaching Ben the polite but firm stance.

'Nice handbag, madam?'

'Two hundred dirham for these shoes, sir.'

'Come inside and try some wonderful mint tea.'

Once they hit the souks, there was no mistaking it. The labyrinth of market stalls was almost too mesmerising for words. The alleyways were lined and piled high with wares of every colour and description. From dazzling Moroccan lamps to beautiful bejewelled slippers to spices that filled the air with a thousand tagine-like fragrances.

Sunlight filtered down to them in lazy strobes through the makeshift wooden slats overhead, making the colours dance with even more opulence and spreading a warm leathery smell.

Resigned to the fact she couldn't touch Ben for a while, Lexie wanted to stroke and breathe in everything. Although with the market traders keen to pull them this way and that, she had to play it as cool as she did with the real object of her desires. It was as though she'd been dipped in a land of temptation and forced to behave.

With Ben tantalisingly close behind, she slipped through an archway into one of the shops, knowing full well if she touched anything, it would be as good as bought. Showing the slightest interest, daring to let her fingertips trail across anything she craved, would begin a process of hard bargaining that would not stop until the thing was hers – at whatever price.

As she felt the caress of Ben's warm breath against her ear, innocently asking her what she wanted, she wondered whether tonight would be much the same. She closed her eyes and tried not to melt on the spot, aware that this was really not the place. This feeling would have to wait.

Before Lexie knew it, they'd been bustled from stall to stall, caught up in the magic of the place. The tickle of materials against her skin; the way the light dazzled through the reds and greens of the glassy lamps; the taste of cinnamon in the air. It was as though everything was conspiring to whip her up into a sensual frenzy. She was being seduced in every sense of the word.

And it seemed as though Ben was struggling with temptation too. Her firm instructions not to buy anything had melted in the muggy heat.

'It's research,' he told her in hushed tones, as he hustled for a brightly coloured rug to go with the armfuls of other quirky items. 'We need sample colours to inspire this new paint range of yours, don't we? And isn't it about time we spiced up some of that beige at Nutgrass Hall?'

Lexie tried not to laugh at the thought of Mrs Carrington-Noble's plush cream sofas being draped with loud Moroccan throws.

'You just can't help doing a bit of business, can you?' she teased him, as he made his purchase and they left the pressure cooker of the souks. Watching him lock firm but friendly horns with the stallholders had fanned her flames for him even more. 'Who would guess you're so far out of your comfort zone.'

'It's so much more thrilling than Cornwall,' he teased back. 'Although I dare say the pasties aren't as good.'

As they moved into the blazing heat of the main square, Lexie drank up every inch of it. It was everything she had read about and more. The Jemaa el-Fna was a huge open space overlooked by a towering mosque, but filled with rows of covered markets and floods of people busying in every direction. It was a place of pure hustle, and locals vied for their attention, keen to help them spend their money in creative ways.

Lexie and Ben had no particular place to go, and yet they knew to look purposeful and try not to be swayed. They moved briskly around the square, making concentric shapes towards the middle, like they were riding a helter-skelter in reverse. There was a buzz of excitement that was completely infectious, as they danced to avoid people offering to dress them with snakes and paint them with henna.

'This place smells fantastic,' Lexie whispered to Ben, as they wove past stalls cooking kebabs, the smoky flavours wafting out at them and clouding their way.

Every other stall seemed to be piled high with juicy oranges, winking at Lexie like forbidden fruit. Lexie's mouth was dry, and yet she had a strange sensation that she needed to wait. That it was too early to give in to whatever it was that made her want to touch and taste everything.

And soon they were at the heart of the square, where people thronged and owners of makeshift eateries tried to tempt them to sample their menu. Lexie felt almost swayed by the current of people as Ben turned to face her with a questioning look. Would they eat now, or save themselves for later? But the thought of everything to come made her almost too jittery for food.

'I can wait,' she said, knowing full well that she would have to. Because the thing she desperately wanted was out of bounds until they were somewhere discreet. And when that moment finally came, she knew it would be worth it.

'Then let me get you an orange juice before you melt,' he replied.

But she already was. As he looked at her, waiting for her nod of agreement, she felt like the moment was almost perfect. If she could just reach up and kiss him, this memory would be complete. Men hurried around them, robed in billowing beige among the stalls of vivid colours. It was like this place was combining them both, on its own unique canvas. And tonight. Tonight would be the time when their colours would truly merge.

'Yes,' she replied. 'That would be perfect.' As he turned away from her, she tried not to imagine the luxurious feeling of two yearning souls becoming one.

Chapter 40

Lexie shimmied into her best black lace undies, wondering where she would be when she took them off. Not that their date would just be about that, of course. She was hoping for a heart-to-heart with Ben, to see where they stood. It felt almost implicit that something deeper would come of their relationship. Not that she was looking for promises of diamond rings, or anything crazy. And she knew she still had lurking skeletons to deal with. But what they had was surely something more than furtive fun. She didn't want to be an appetiser before his main event, and, once they'd agreed that, she'd be on fire for whatever fun awaited.

Lexie sprayed her neck with perfume, letting the musky fragrance settle coolly on her skin. It wasn't often that she bothered with her bottle of Black Opium, but she wanted to feel wildly decadent. Today had been a tease for each one of her senses and she wanted the heightened awareness to last. The trip was going well; her colour palette ideas were coming to fruition. She was remembering her creativity; how she loved to travel. And the closeness to Ben, even if some of it had to take place in her imagination, was a sheer delight.

She slipped into a long blue silk dress that Grace had insisted on swapping with her for a bunch of tatty thrift-shop junk. Lexie knew her friend was just trying to kit her out in great clothes for the trip, in a non-charity-case kind of way. Although Lexie's savings were looking better now. Maybe she'd be treating herself soon enough.

The dress hugged where it touched and tickled against her skin. She swished around in front of the mirror, feeling like an almost-princess. Was that music playing outside? The hotel was gearing up for the evening and she thought she could hear pipe players out by the pool. With a tingle of excitement she pulled open her balcony door, keen to soak up everything the starry night had to offer.

As she smiled into the moonlight, the fresh evening air embracing her skin, she noticed Ben on his balcony across the other side of the water.

'Hi!' She waved frantically, although of course he couldn't hear.

He seemed to see her, though. But why was he looking straight through her? Was he ignoring her? He was on his phone. He looked ... annoyed? Disturbed? Definitely not pleased, anyway. She wondered who he was talking to. But she shouldn't overthink it. They'd discuss it later; it was probably nothing.

Lexie retreated to her room but kept the door open in case Ben finished his call and tried to wave back. She busied herself with filling her handbag for the evening. Key, purse, make-up. But she couldn't shake off the nervous feeling wriggling in her stomach. There'd been something cold in Ben's look. Realisation, perhaps? Did he know something? Had he been speaking to his mother? God, that could be it. Who else would he speak to on holiday? It wasn't like he had heaps of friends, and it was unlikely to be work at this time.

But why would his mother disturb him? And what would cause that look on his face? Had Mrs Carrington-Noble heard back from her police spy person? Did she know Lexie had no intention of matchmaking Ben and Cynthia, and was she dishing the dirt on Lexie's past?

Oh God. She sank down onto the bed, her legs beginning to feel shaky. It would be just her luck for things to go wrong for her. Suddenly she felt ridiculous in her almost-princess dress. The fishtail swam around her ankles. Was it a sign she was out of her depth? She kicked her feet with agitation, as though trying to stay afloat.

Right. She grabbed her phone. She actually had no idea what was going on and she should try to find out. Maybe it was just self-doubt talking. She couldn't let it eat at her before she even knew the facts.

Lexie craned her head to get a view of Ben's balcony. He was gone. She would ring him. Easy.

Her heart was in her mouth as she pulled up his number and pressed call. That green light for go, when she didn't know where she'd end up. But his mobile was engaged. Damn it. She swiped her screen, found Mrs Carrington-Noble's number and did the same. It was ringing. There.

Perhaps he hadn't been talking to his mother at all. So, shit, what was she going to say? Should she ... oh, too late.

'Yes?' The stern woman's voice came down the line, and she did not seem happy.

'Er, hi! Just thought I'd check in, and ... ' God, she was waffling. She was a bag of trembling nerves.

'And what? Tell me the truth for once?'

'No, I ... Well, I mean, I always do anyway, but ... '

'Cut the crap, Alexis. I know exactly what you are now. And so does Ben. He wants you out of our business and out of our lives as quickly as I do. You're a liar.'

Was it the distance, or did Mrs Carrington-Noble sound different? Still angry but almost ... at the end of her tether?

Lexie pulled at the neck of her dress, the heat suddenly suffocating. 'But we already discussed the situation with my qualifications. You said it would be fine.'

'I was willing to overlook it if you were going to encourage my son to form a union with Cynthia. But from what I hear from Ben, you've been busy trying to help yourself to him.'

He'd told tales on her? Why had he done that? What was he, twelve?

'Ben and I are just ... ' But what were they, really? That was something she'd been hoping to talk over on their date. Over candlelight; beneath the stars. They were going to explore their relationship and ... urgh. Had this stupid dream always been hopeless?

'Finished, is what you are. If you ever even started. My son does not want to be associated with a criminal and a junkie.'

The words, spat so cruelly into her ear, seemed to smash against her delicate eardrum and shatter into a million shards. Just like her heart. Ben knew – her lie was out. Her past was finally catching up with her to drip its oily colours all over the fresh canvas she'd been naively trying to repaint. Because that was what lies did, in the end. They caught up with you and exposed you for who you really were. Who you'd always been. Just a hopeless trier with a head full of air and a pocket full of nothing.

'I'm not a junkie,' Lexie whispered into the phone. 'I don't take drugs. Never have.' That bit was true, other than the odd experimental puff that had given her a nasty headache. 'Nor a criminal. Not really. The charges were dropped almost immediately. It was a horrible mistake.' But still on her record. She could have applied to have it removed, if only she hadn't been so bloody scared of paperwork. Maybe that was why she was scared. It had been skulking in there for far too long.

'A mistake that you arrived back from your travels with a suitcase full of class A drugs?'

'Not full. It was just one packet. And it wasn't mine.' Lexie tried to hold her chin up, for what it was worth. But the traitorous thing was quivering.

'It was your boyfriend's. Same thing.'

'No! I didn't know anything about it.' Sodding Inkie and his desperate attempts to get rich by any means. Money truly could turn people grotesque. She would never forgive him for that, even if seven years had passed.

'So you say. And so the police seemed to believe, with

312

your fluttering eyelashes and your dizzy fake smiles. But don't think for a second that Ben or I will trust you again. You've lied to us, and we've no proof you didn't lie to the police too. I knew I should have got that pack of powder you brought into my house properly tested.'

'That was chalk. To make chalk paint! You can test it to your heart's content.' Lexie stood up, feeling a glimmer of hope that all of this was ludicrous. Ben would surely believe her. He had to. She wasn't going down as easily as this. 'We can talk about it when we get back.'

'There will be no more *we*, Alexis Summers. I suggest you pack your bag and leave that hotel immediately. Your replacement camper van has arrived at Nutgrass Hall. You will take it and you will never return.'

Lexie pulled her phone away from her ear and stared at it. Who was this woman, speaking to her as though she was the queen of the tossing world? No. She could just piss off.

'I'll speak to Ben,' Lexie told her. They would find a way.

'I wouldn't waste your breath; he'll be otherwise engaged. With Cynthia. He knows what's expected of him if he's to inherit what he wants.'

And then the phone went dead. That bloody woman had hung up on her. And what was she talking about? Ben wasn't her puppet. Lexie stormed out onto her balcony to look for him. Who had he been on the phone to after his mother? Because if Lexie had just been talking to the old dragon, he must have been ringing someone else.

Aha – yes! Lexie felt a wave of relief as he walked back

out onto his balcony. She gave a hopeful wave, but he didn't see her at all this time. He still seemed hassled. And … what? Who was that woman joining him? Lexie narrowed her eyes. Cynthia. Was his awful mother right?

Why had Ben let Cynthia into his bedroom? Onto his balcony? She had her own room. Is that who he'd just been calling? Lexie felt her stomach drop as she took in Cynthia's black satin dressing gown. There was surely no mistaking what she was up to? And yet Ben had let her in – just like his mother had said.

She watched as Ben turned around to face Cynthia, so Lexie could just see his back. Her throat felt tight. What the hell was going on? And suddenly it became excruciatingly clear. Cynthia flung her arms around Ben's neck, and Ben's whole body seemed to sag into hers with sheer relief. Jesus, that was exactly the way she'd imagined him sinking into her tonight. How could this be happening?

But neither Ben nor Cynthia was letting go. They were clutching one another as though they'd been waiting years for that moment. Lexie could not believe what she was seeing and yet she couldn't tear her eyes away. Something inside her was still clinging to the hope that Ben would throw Cynthia off in outrage. Not that she could hear a thing against the maddening noise of those pipe players, their repetitive snake-charm music gathering speed by the second.

And then, at last, Cynthia let go of Ben, her bright red nails disappearing from the back of his neck. He walked purposely towards the bedroom without looking back. Cynthia let her black dressing gown fall to the floor and followed Ben inside, wearing a skimpy black teddy that was absolutely not daywear.

She closed the balcony doors behind them.

Chapter 41

Lexie was frozen to the spot, staring at Ben's closed balcony doors, desperate for them to open and for the whole scene to be rewound and played back differently. But, deep in her wretched heart, she knew it was hopeless. The evidence had been there, right before her. Mrs Carrington-Noble had warned her and now she'd seen it with her own eyes. Behind those doors, Ben was with Cynthia. Wearing not very much and doing what he needed to do to secure himself a rich wife and get his hands on his mother's cash.

Somehow she'd fooled herself into thinking that he'd changed, but he hadn't changed at all. When it came down to it, he was just like her cheating ex, Drew. He couldn't steer himself away from the promise of wealth. In fact, he was no better than her first ex, Inkie. Money had made him grotesque.

Or maybe it was just her. She was the common thread, after all. The idiot who kept falling for men who valued money more than her affections. Maybe she wasn't as good as having pockets full of cash. Maybe her sister was the wise one after all, in her commune full of simple values and hessian.

As she stood there on her budget balcony in the clammy evening heat, the pipe players whipping the air into a frenzy, she had never felt colder. It was as though the blanket of happiness and hope that had been cosying around her had been suddenly snatched away. She looked down at her bare arms – a sea of goosebumps. She was shaking. A sob fought its way up her throat, but she swallowed it down. Now was not the time to cry. She had to pack.

Her arms and legs took over, as though they knew what to do in times of crisis. She felt herself moving back into her room and closing the balcony doors. Just like Cynthia had done, although with less of an entitled look on her face. It was a look Lexie remembered well enough from her school days. All those rich girls who knew that wealth was their legacy and the world their shiny oyster. They'd been right.

Lexie moved around her room in a trance, stuffing things into her broken-wheeled suitcase. She was not sticking around to be jettisoned for Cynthia and her collection of Fendi swimsuits. Each item she shoved away tried to summon the threatening sob, and each time she gulped it back. This charade did not deserve her tears and she had no time for them. She wanted to be out of there before anyone noticed. Although, judging by Cynthia and her flaunty black satin , no one would be giving a shit where Lexie was right now.

She blinked furiously as she pushed that afternoon's outfit into her suitcase. The spotlight above her head caught the harem-pant sequins in a taunting peacock tail of colour. They were stupid trousers and she should have thrown them away after her travelling days. She pulled them out and hurled them into the bin. As she snatched up various designer items she'd borrowed from Grace, she tried not to chide herself for pretending to be someone she wasn't. She would give it all back. These clothes. Those dreams.

And then she felt one last pathetic hope crawl into her. She hated herself for it, but she could just give it one last try. Just a quick double-check that she hadn't been mistaken. God, did she enjoy being kicked in the teeth? Looking at the clock, she realised her date with Ben should have started fifteen minutes ago. They'd agreed he would knock on her door. He was never late. She still had her dress on; maybe it was a sign. Maybe he would just answer his phone and tell her he was on his way.

Against her better judgement, she grabbed her mobile and called his number. He would surely answer. Tell her he was not with Cynthia, and he hated his mother, and ...

'You're through to the voicemail messaging service ...'

Oh God. Lexie's futile hopes were stopped dead in their tracks. His phone was off. Ben Carrington's phone was never off, just like he was never late. Business never stopped for him. Unless ... But she couldn't even bring herself to imagine the one intimate thing that would cause him to be uncontactable. When he was meant to be here with her.

Lexie looked down at herself, her legs still quivering

under the ludicrously expensive dress. She didn't belong in it any more than she'd belonged in Ben's world. He had only ever used her for a bit of sneaky pleasure. In the back of a crappy shop; behind her dad's bloody shed, for God's sake. She was just cheap to him. He was probably even paying her for the time they'd spent groping.

With a flurry of rage she pulled off the silk dress and watched glassily as it floated to the floor, leaving her bare flesh exposed. Craning her neck to see what she could throw on instead, she caught sight of herself in the mirror. The tattoo on her back. The dark inky stain seemed to catapult its reflection off the mirror and hit her in the face. And at last the tears came. Thick and fast, they rolled down her cheeks, taking streaks of borrowed La Prairie make-up with them.

Even her own skin embarrassed her. Or maybe she was an embarrassment to her skin. Her pale, can't-even-afford-a-decent-holiday face under Skin Caviar that wasn't hers. And that tattoo. What a joke. It was a lotus flower, symbolic of growing up through the mud to bloom. Seven years later, she still wasn't worthy. It was nothing more than a badge of her naivety. She couldn't stand to look at it.

That was it – she was getting out of here. Away from this mess. And as soon as she got back to England, away from Nutgrass Hall. She grabbed a wad of toilet roll from the bathroom and blew her nose violently. Throwing on her giraffe-print jumpsuit, she gathered up Grace's dress and did a final sweep of the room. She stood for a moment in the doorway. Her mobile clutched tightly in her hand, she realised there was one more thing. One more cord tying her sorry self to Ben and his surreal world.

She uncurled her shaking fingers and pulled the back off the phone. The handset was hers, but the bills were paid by Carrington Paints as she'd used it for work. She didn't want them paying for her and she didn't want them to get in touch. Nor vice versa. She knew the important numbers by heart or would be able to find them. But she hadn't memorised Ben's and she didn't want to know it. She plucked out the SIM card and dropped it into the bin, its small golden face disappearing under tissues and her discarded purple harem pants.

She'd suspend her social media accounts too, when she got back to her laptop. She wouldn't even need the online world if she wasn't going to be anyone's social media manager. And what would she want to share about her own life right now? Precisely nothing. She was as un-Insta-worthy as it got.

So that was it. Time to get to the airport and see how quickly she could fly out of that place. And then who knew what. As she dragged her suitcase along the darkened hotel corridor, she tried to ignore the dissenting screech of its annoying broken wheel.

Chapter 42

'Wooooah!' Lexie jumped about a foot in the air, her hand flying to her heart to check it was still beating. 'What the ... ?'

Her suitcase tumbled to the floor, and the thing in her bed that had made her yell started screaming back. Lexie fumbled for a switch.

When light illuminated her bedroom at Nutgrass Hall, the scene before her still made little sense. Her sister huddled on her bed amid pyramids of crumpled tissues and empty Greggs wrappers, wearing a zebra onesie and watching Bridget 'my love life's a pickle' Jones.

'What are you doing here?' Sky had the cheek to ask when she got her breath back. Her sister shuffled to the edge of the bed and Lexie could see her eyes were puffy.

'I live here,' Lexie stage-whispered, shoving her suitcase fully into the bedroom and closing the door, keen not to make a disturbance. '*Lived* here,' she corrected.

321

It was the middle of the night and Nutgrass Hall seemed silent with Ben still in Morocco, the staff in their cottages and no sign of Cory's camper. She'd been planning to get in and out quickly. Now it seemed she had a zebra-striped spanner in the works.

Even so, the sorry sight before her made her heart feel sad. She moved towards Sky and opened her arms. 'What are *you* doing here, is the real question.'

Sky bundled in and began a particularly ugly cry against Lexie's shoulder. Bridget, seeming to sense Sky couldn't manage any words, launched spiritedly into the crescendo of 'All by Myself'. Well, that makes three of us, thought Lexie.

'Did you break up with Billy-Nob?' She sensed she could get away with his hate name right then.

'Yes.' Sky pouted. 'And I don't want to hear *I told you so*. I know you thought he was a joke.'

Was there any point in lying? 'I just didn't think you were a great match,' said Lexie, diplomatically.

'Like you're so amazing at choosing blokes. Inkie and Drew were dick-skulls.'

And Ben, Lexie silently added. 'You're right – I can't pick a good one either. What happened?'

Sky armed herself with more tissues and embarked on a sniffly tale about Billy-Bob being part of a scam to do a runner with everyone's money. When people joined the commune they handed over their worldly goods towards the upkeep of the place, with the rest promised to charity. Only it turned out that Billy-Bob's greedy pockets were the real destination for the cash. When the apparently not-so-naive Sky sussed him out, he'd offered her a cut. Sky had offered to cut his balls off.

Lexie gasped.

'And I called the police, of course. They arrested a bunch of them and closed the place down.'

'I knew there was something fishy . . .' Her sister glared at Lexie and she put her hands up in surrender. 'Sorry. I'm not saying I told you so. You did the right thing. That bastard. What's wrong with some people that they let money rule their heads and hearts? Urgh.' She shook herself down and tried to swallow the bitterness rising.

'At least I got a few quid back for a train ticket down here. And sausage rolls.' Sky gave a tiny smile. 'Anyway, you made me jump. I wasn't expecting you back yet. What's going on? I did try to call you, but your number hasn't been available.'

'Oh, yeah, that.' Lexie sighed. 'Long story, but my SIM card is in a dustbin in Marrakech. And we're leaving. Come on.' She rubbed her sister's shoulders and stood up. 'Help me pack.'

'What the hell?'

Lexie recounted her own terrible tale as she moved around the room throwing her belongings into bags, for the second time in forty-eight hours.

'I knew something smoochy was going on with you two again,' said Sky, as she did her usual kid-sister thing of pretending to be helpful but not doing much.

'Yes, well, now it's not.'

'That's a shame – I liked Ben in the end. Aren't you going to at least speak to him?'

Lexie had liked him too; more than she dared think about. Her heart dragged like a great lead balloon. 'I can't face it. I just … can't.' She couldn't bear thinking of the lies she'd told him nor her punishment for it. That balcony. Cynthia slipping off her floaty gown …

'You know, there's been something really odd going on down here,' said Sky. Lexie was glad of the diversion. 'Everyone's been really hush-hushy, and quite honestly a bit miserable. Do you know what it's about?'

Lexie shrugged. 'I never understood half of the weird stuff that went on here. And now I never will.' She swallowed hard, telling herself the painful lump in her throat was only because she'd miss Tom and Mrs M.

'I'll miss Cory,' said Sky, as though tuning in to her sister's thoughts. She held her hands to her heart. 'He's been so sweet. Anyway, where are we actually going?'

Lexie eyeballed Sky and threw her a coat. 'Hands off the Carrington brothers. We're tossing all this stuff into my replacement camper van and getting out of here.' Mrs Carrington-Noble had pointedly left the keys and documents by the front door. She must have known her meddling would win out in the end. 'Have you seen the van?'

Sky nodded. 'It looks just as crappy as your old one. Are you sure it works?'

'Hey, it's vintage. I wanted it to be as much like Penny as possible, which is why it's taken so bloody long to source it. And we'd better pray it does work, otherwise we've got a long push ahead of us.' Although she was sure Mrs Carrington-Noble would have made sure it was ready to drive away. She wanted her off the estate as much as Lexie wanted to leave.

Lexie didn't know where they were going, other than it needed to be far enough away not to be found. She would leave behind the clothes and make-up she'd borrowed from Grace and send her a message to collect them, at some point. They were designer things, symbolic of a life Lexie should never even have tried on.

Before long, the sisters were creeping up and down the winding staircase with armfuls of belongings, which they piled into the back of Penny Two, as they'd affectionately named her.

The whole thing would have been amusing under any other circumstances. The two of them trudging backwards and forwards under the disapproving eyes of the *Scooby-Doo* paintings, with Sky dressed as a zebra and Lexie still wearing the giraffe-print jumpsuit better suited to Morocco. Lexie couldn't help thinking they were like two lost animals pairing up to board Noah's Ark. If only life was as black and white as the stripes on Sky's onesie. Or maybe it was. Maybe Lexie just shouldn't have tried to cross the boundaries, mixing everything to grey.

As Lexie stood in the doorway taking one last look while Sky waited in the van, a sudden, overwhelming sadness washed over her. She remembered standing awkwardly in this hallway with Ben on the first day of her arrival, the effeminate horsemen looking down on them. The fake ancestors she now knew weren't even his. When she'd discovered it on that day at her parents' house, she'd thought their relationship had had a glimmer of hope – they weren't from such wildly different beginnings after all. But she should have listened to her gut. Lexie had never belonged here. Ben was right: she should have more faith in her instincts.

Memories of the last three months swept in, even though she begged them not to. She must cut her tenuous ties. Look upon this place and feel nothing. And yet, mixed emotions tossed inside her like rags in a tumble dryer, burbling and churning. Were tears coming too? She took a deep breath and pinched them back, the overpowering scent of funereal lilies filling her nose. It seemed like there were twice as many of them. So much for Mrs Carrington-Noble lessening her grip; her stranglehold was the tightest yet.

'Right,' Lexie announced to no one in particular, reminding herself of one-word Ben. 'Urgh.' She grabbed a tissue from her sleeve and dabbed her eyes. How stupid.

Sky appeared at her side from the doorway behind her, bringing in a cool evening chill. 'Are we going, or are you too sad to leave?'

'I feel fine,' Lexie replied, squeezing the tissue in her balled fist.

'Shock and denial.' Sky nodded. 'The first stages of grief. Don't worry – pain, anger and depression will come.'

'Great.' Lexie remembered the twenty-four hours she'd spent sitting numbly in a Marrakech airport, wishing she could at least close her eyes and pretend nothing had ever happened. Maybe her sister was starting to talk more sense than her. 'Hooray for the pain.'

It was already on its way.

Lexie motored along Tewkesbury High Street, trying to dodge unbidden memories. She recalled walking here with Ben on their way to lunch by the river. There was that shop with the rickety brown furniture, which she'd told Ben she could repaint and make beautiful. Did she still believe she could make change in the world, or were some things better left alone?

'M&M?' Sky asked, as she rooted through Lexie's bag for snacks. It was 3 a.m. Even the takeaways would be shut.

'No,' Lexie heard herself bark. She was too busy looking in her rear-view mirror at the furniture shop. And the one next to it. Still empty. She shook her head. Looking backwards was a foolish thing.

'Penny Two is not so bad,' said Sky, through a mouthful of chocolate.

Lexie hadn't bought the peanut ones at the airport, in a moment of pointless rebellion. She'd ignored the voice that told her she was cutting off her nose to spite her face. Or cutting off her face to spite her nose, as Sky had once put it.

'Penny Two is fine,' Lexie agreed. Although Penny Two was not fine. She looked the same, and drove much better, but there was no essence of Aunt Jasmine any more. No flowery smell to mask the dampness. In fact, she hadn't even spotted much damp. But she would dwell on that tomorrow.

Right then, Lexie just had to drive. Her plan to get as far

away as possible was already trying to escape her. She hadn't slept a wink since her hotel room in Morocco, and she felt like the living dead. Her eyes, like two dry slits, were fighting to stay open. She knew they'd have to stop soon to set up camp, and to decide on a future plan. Two lost women in a van full of broken dreams. How would they ever fix them?

Chapter 43

T *hud, thud, thud. Thud, thud, thud.*

Usually, there was something quite relaxing about being cocooned in a camper van, the rain thumping down on the hard metal roof. But, at that moment, Lexie just felt like the world was crying on her head. For once, she probably needed its pity.

'Cup of tea?' Sky asked, as she clattered around in the kitchen.

Lexie buried her face under the duvet. 'We don't have any,' came her muffled reply. 'We don't have anything.'

It was the morning after the sisters' great escape from Nutgrass Hall, and already the walls seemed to be closing in on them. They'd only managed to drive about ten miles north of Tewkesbury before Lexie's eyelids had given up the battle, and they'd been forced to find a quiet field to camp in. Lexie had had the worst few hours' sleep. Cold, uncomfortable and plagued by melancholy thoughts.

'You're right. The cupboards are empty,' said Sky.

Lexie groaned. Did her sister honestly think Mrs Carrington-Noble had left them with a Waitrose shop? Not that they even had electricity. They needed to find a proper campsite and hook up. After they'd sourced some teabags.

Lexie could hear her sister rooting around in bags and boxes.

'Soooo ... We have the sum total of half a Greggs steak bake – a little bit stale – a handful of M&Ms – no peanuts – and a whole bottle of Oasis, because it was buy one, get one free. Sorry, I would have bought the flavour you like if I'd known you were coming back early.'

'Breakfast is served,' Lexie muttered, crawling out of her duvet nest only to feel the morning chill and yank the covers back up to her neck. And this was meant to be summer.

They divided up their pathetic bounty like children on a very sad picnic, and ate in silence, each huddled under a corner of the bedcovers. What on earth had made Lexie think it wouldn't be so bad? She'd thought the van would feel more spacious now she'd got rid of a few boxes of old paperwork. But now there were two of them, and her sister took up a lot of room for someone who'd supposedly handed over her earthly possessions to the fake commune. She must have hidden a lot of clandestine stuff under her four-in-a-bed mattress.

'Why didn't you go back to Mum and Dad's?' Lexie heard herself asking.

Sky chucked the communal Oasis down on the bed between them. 'So now you want to get rid of me?'

'No! I just ... wondered, I guess.' The van was cramped

330

with her sister's crap, but maybe it was better than being alone with her thoughts. The ones about Ben were getting especially heavy.

'Are you going back there?' Sky asked. Although it was definitely more of a challenge.

'No,' Lexie admitted.

'You're embarrassed by them, aren't you?'

'Don't be such a bitch, Sky!' Lexie launched an M&M at her, then wished she hadn't. Now she was down to just three. Which, as she'd come to realise, was still one too many. She shoved one into her mouth and bit hard.

'Ooh, you didn't even say no. You are embarrassed.'

Was she? 'No!' It felt like the truth, more or less. 'Maybe I was a bit, when I was younger and money was hard. And for some pathetic reason I started feeling cringey about it again recently. Probably the whole Drew and Tabby thing. But then, Ben . . . ' She had to stop and blink a few times as an unexpected pain hit the back of her eyes. 'Ben made me see things differently.'

'Yeah, he was good for you.' Sky nodded as she bit into her bonus chocolate.

'Jesus, sis! You're meant to be helping. How is a guy who dumps me in favour of a shitload of cash *good for me*?'

'You don't actually know that. Have you spoken to him?'

'Using what, telepathy? He's in Morocco and I don't even have a SIM card.'

Sky pulled out her phone from the pouch of her hoodie.

'And I don't want to,' Lexie added. 'I threw my only copy of his mobile number in the bin for a reason.'

'Oh. Because you think communication sucks?'

'Whatever,' said Lexie, filling her mouth with her final morsel of steak bake so she didn't have to come up with any more excuses.

The rain hammered down hard on the van and, with Sky still in her zebra onesie, Lexie couldn't help remembering her Noah's Ark analogy. Maybe she should move the camper van soon before they really did get stranded in a flood. If only her limbs could be bothered.

'Anyway, I thought you were over that silly rich-girl paranoia? You love Grace, don't you?'

Lexie felt a tiny smile sneak up on her. 'Who couldn't love Grace?'

'So not all rich people are mean. Like, if you instantly decided all people with money were snooty dick-monkeys, you'd be no better than wealthy people who judged you for your second-hand jumpers.'

Lexie exhaled, the weight of her sister's words making her head feel even heavier.

'I don't think I judge people. It's just ... urgh. The same thing keeps happening. Hanging around with people who are better than me always comes back to bite me on my charity-shop-clad arse.'

'Better than you? Lex, what are you even on about? Is this what they call a superiority complex?'

'Inferiority,' Lexie mumbled. 'And no.' But she was already hanging her head. She knew if she'd felt good enough, she wouldn't have had to lie on her CV or avoid ever mentioning the Inkie drug scandal. Maybe inferior was exactly how she'd felt.

'Sometimes we just need to work on ourselves,' said Sky. She put her hands on her heart and started looking all mystical. 'Because knowing that we are good enough must come from within. We must be the lotus flower and rise up through the mud of life, being unafraid to bloom wherever we may land.'

Sky's arms shot upwards to the roof and spread out like petals. Lexie busied herself with trying to remember if she'd ever shown her sister the tattoo she'd never even blossomed into. This was not the time to decide whether the girl had gone quite mad, or whether good sense sometimes came from the mouths of slightly annoying babes. Lexie needed more sleep.

A couple of hours later, Lexie reluctantly climbed out from under the duvet and looked for something to change into. The smell of her own body reminded her she hadn't even showered since Marrakech. She felt positively crawling, not to mention ravenous.

'We'll make a move,' Lexie told her sister. 'We can't live like this. It's bloody miserable.'

'Ooh, is the depression on its way? I could order pizza?'

'Save your battery. You can't charge your phone and we might need it for emergencies.'

'Totally,' said Sky. 'Like if we get really bored and need to play Candy Crush.'

Lexie found it strangely reassuring when her sister returned to saying only dumb things.

Before long, Lexie was sitting in Penny Two's driver's

333

seat with Sky at her side. Though, as she looked around her at the muddy field, she felt a worrying sense of foreboding. The rain was still attacking and Penny Two was no four-by-four. Would she even have the power to pull through the bogginess?

Lexie switched on the engine, put the van into gear, accelerated and prayed. But her prayers were rudely ignored.

'Shit!'

'What's wrong?' asked Sky, clearly missing the obvious.

'The van won't budge.' And the more Lexie tried to accelerate, the further into the mud the vehicle dug itself. Bloody, bloody typical. She should have listened to her instincts and got out of there earlier. Much like with Nutgrass Hall.

'Is this what you meant by an emergency?' Sky waved her phone. 'I could ring those breakdown people?'

'I don't have breakdown people.'

'Grace has one of those Jeeps, doesn't she? She could tow us out.'

Lexie considered the options. She hadn't been in touch with Grace since any of this had kicked off. Or even her own parents. Nor bought a new SIM card yet. Not that she didn't trust anyone, but the sooner people knew where she was, the sooner it could get back to Ben, if he made any attempts to snoop. She wasn't ready to be found. If she ever had to face him again, it wouldn't be as some loser living in a swampy field in the arse end of nowhere.

'We'll manage by ourselves for now,' said Lexie. 'Please don't tell anyone where we are. I just need to process things. Decide on my next steps.'

'Can the next steps involve food? It's lunchtime and I can't survive on handbag leftovers for ever.'

'The next steps will involve food and a bucket-sized glass of wine. We're going to leave the camper van here and find the nearest pub. I think I've hit the pain stage of this break-up, and it would feel less hideous if it was rosé tinted.'

Lexie pulled the keys from the ignition and the sisters climbed over the seats and back into the body of the van. As they searched for wellies and waterproofs, Lexie explained the plan of attack.

'As well as eating a mountain of bangers and mash, we need to sort out a few things.' If she'd learned anything from the last few months, it was that you couldn't just bury your head and ignore logistics. She wasn't a total pig in the mud. She grabbed the camping battery pack. 'We need to pay someone to charge this for us.'

'Got it,' said Sky, grabbing a pen and paper from her bag and writing it down.

'Then we need to find out who owns this land and see if we can pay them to stay here for a while.'

'Right,' said Sky, adding it to the list. 'Then get you a new SIM card?'

'At some point,' Lexie conceded. She did think better with the world at her fingertips. And she had a lot of things to de-pickle.

'Charge our phones. Get food supplies.'

'And water.' Lexie nodded.

'And get drunk!' said Sky, with a flourish.

Lexie took a deep breath and tried to exhale some of the

tightness that had been building in her chest. 'One drink. Maybe two.'

'Drunk, drunk, drunk. Drunk, drunk, drunk,' Sky sang in time to the raindrops, as she danced around the boxes looking for another welly.

'You'll be a total lightweight after all that abstaining in the commune.'

Sky pulled a face. 'You think I stuck to the no-alcohol rule? Don't be a dimwit, Lexie. When you want something, there's always a way.'

Lexie hoped her sister was right. Although, quite what she wanted for them both was yet to be decided.

Chapter 44

'Everyone knows everyone in the country,' the barman said with a laugh, pointing towards a stout, ruddy-faced man sitting further along the bar, a sleeping dog at his feet.

He was apparently the farmer whose field Lexie and Sky were squatting on, where Penny Two was now stuck in the mire.

'Don't worry, he's not going anywhere soon if you'd rather get some Dutch courage before you approach him.' The barman winked and handed them two menus. 'He probably won't kill you.'

Lexie looked at the decorative pitchforks hanging on the wall and hoped he was right. People with dogs were always nice, weren't they?

The country pub they'd stumbled upon, just a few hundred metres from their mudbath of a field, was as perfectly quaint as the rest of the village appeared to be. Apart from the slightly imposing ornamental farm equipment, it was one of those pubs that seemed to hug you in with its low oak beams and cosy rustic feel. Just the ticket when you were cold, soggy and down in the dumps. The Traveller's Rest was the perfect name.

'A bottle of rosé and two of your largest wine glasses, please,' asked Lexie. Well, she wouldn't be using the rest of her holiday spending money in Morocco now, so she deserved a treat.

'Bad day?' the barman asked.

'Bad life,' Lexie confirmed, and then immediately felt like a drama queen. People had gone through worse than being exposed as a liar, ditched, made homeless, jobless and wedged tyre-deep in a farmer's field. It just didn't feel like it right then.

'And two lots of bangers and mash with extra gravy would be great,' Sky added, having made light work of the menu.

The scary landlord farmer seemed to be nodding his approval in the distance, and Lexie hoped he hadn't heard too much.

'Beautiful camper van, by the way,' said the barman. 'I noticed it from one of the top windows this morning. Worth a packet, those things. Been looking for one myself, if you ever want to sell it. You're lucky ladies.'

Lexie did not feel lucky.

The girls hid themselves in a wooden booth and Sky poured the wine. 'What are we going to do if that guy wants us to get off his land?' she whispered.

'Pray for a miracle,' Lexie replied. 'Because the camper won't budge and I plan to be too drunk to drive anyway.'

They clinked glasses and agreed not to think about it until they were at least merry enough to find it funny.

Before long, the girls were one glass down and tucking into their sausage lunches. With the lack of food and sleep, Lexie was already feeling her wine working its magic. Every swig was making her three millimetres bolder.

'Did you actually love Billy-Nob?' she heard herself asking.

'Yes!' Although Sky was bristling. It was a definite no.

Lexie pointed to the wine bottle. 'You're allowed to let the drink talk. In fact, that's kind of the aim.'

'You're going to talk too, are you?' Sky asked cautiously, swishing the pink alcohol around her glass.

Lexie shrugged. 'Stranger things have happened.' She tried not to think about how weird things had got with her and Ben in London, after quite a few. She reached across the table and grabbed her sister's arm. 'Don't worry, you can speak freely now. You're not being brainwashed anymore.'

They both giggled.

'There's no need to take the piss.'

'There really is,' said Lexie. 'Fancy handing all your money over to con-artists so you could live in a yurt with a slutty bloke and a bunch of women wearing scratchy sackcloth. I'm pretty open-minded, but you've got to admit that was never you.'

Luckily, they were both still smiling.

'OK, so maybe I didn't exactly love Billy-Nob in the proper, full-on way. Actually, his beard was pretty gross.'

Lexie spurted out a mouthful of wine. 'I knew it!' This was definitely cheering her up.

'I think I was more in love with the idea of it all. Free love and a worry-free life.'

'Really, though? Because I would probably have accepted it if I'd felt you were embracing things. But all those secret sausage rolls and hidden mobile phones . . .'

'Yeah, well, maybe I didn't dig it as much as my addiction to Greggs,' Sky conceded. 'And now I just feel relieved it's over, to be honest. The commitment ceremony was such a fun idea, but being committed was actually pretty dull.'

Lexie resisted the urge to roll her eyes. Only Sky could wave off all of that as though it was simply a bad day out.

'So what about you?' Sky's eyebrows raised expectantly.

'The opposite, I guess.' There should be more lunchtime wine – it was helping her think. 'I definitely wasn't in love with the idea of Ben's world. I didn't even want to be in it at first.'

'But love just rocks up where it wants to.' Sky nodded as she repeated her thoughts on the matter from all those months ago.

'Now who's taking the piss.'

'So you really loved Ben?'

Lexie let snippets of the last few months with Ben play over. The silly squabbles that she secretly enjoyed. His awkward one-word answers when she knew he had the potential to say so much more. The way he turned from doubting her to encouraging her, believing in her. And then there was all that magic when they got physically close. It was like nothing she'd ever felt before. Like every inch of her had been alive. Oh God, she really missed him. Had she got this all wrong?

'Earth to Lexie.' Sky waved a hand in front of her. 'Why is your face going all red? And are you crying? Jeez, are you OK?'

Lexie lifted her hand to her cheeks and noticed they were wet. Tears had begun flowing without her even realising; she must have been so full of them they were just seeping out. Lexie felt her sister slip into the seat next to her and put her arm around her. The unexpected affection made Lexie sag in defeat, and suddenly the world was swimming in front of her, tears splashing to the table.

'There, there,' Sky whispered, as she rocked her gently. 'Tears to water your growth.'

'Aunt Jasmine used to say that,' Lexie heard herself sobbing. 'I prefer it when you get things wrong.'

'Well, she also used to say don't waste your sausage. Now eat up.' Sky dabbed Lexie's face with a napkin and they both laughed.

'Aunt Jasmine was vegan,' said Lexie.

'Was she? Oh, I don't remember. I'll never understand vegans.'

Lexie took a few moments to pull herself together and Sky resumed her position opposite her. The barman, who had been clattering awkwardly in the background, shouted over.

'If the main course is that bad, I'm giving you pudding on the house.'

The farmer's sleepy hound gave a woof of agreement. Lexie couldn't argue with pudding. As she pushed the remnants of cold mash around her plate, trying not to think about what Ben might be having for his lunch and with whom, she could sense Sky was gearing up to say something.

'I know you shot me down about this before . . . '

'Then maybe you should take the hint?' said Lexie.

'But you honestly don't even know what Ben was up to. You haven't spoken to him.'

'Don't you think I haven't thought about that?' And she had; more than she could bear to remember. Picking apart each tiny clue and trying to piece them back together in every Technicolored outcome.

'So? Why don't you just call him? I thought he was the one who was crap at communicating. Has it rubbed off on you?'

The skin on the back of Lexie's neck began to prickle; the thought of speaking to Ben terrified her. What would he say? 'Yes, you were all right for a fumble, but I'm running off with the classy woman now.' Or maybe 'I hate you for lying on your CV and never mentioning you could have gone to jail, you big fakey fraud.' Urgh. It was almost easier not knowing. At least that way she could cling to a secret hope.

Sky clicked her fingers in front of Lexie's face. 'Out loud, please. I can tell you're thinking something. Your face looks kind of in pain.'

'Thanks.' There was something else. Dare she even say it? She blew out a puff of air and began. 'The point is that, despite everything, I was willing to believe he'd shake me

342

off in a flash in favour of someone with better prospects – so I still don't really value myself.'

'Ooh, deep.' Sky leaned in.

'When push comes to shove, I somehow don't think I'm worthy of him. And until I jump that last hurdle, I don't even want to hear his version of events. If I'm not strong enough for it, it will probably crush me.'

Sky clapped her hands. 'So, like, you want a makeover?'

'No, not a bloody makeover! Whatever I decide to do, I'll be doing it dressed as me. It's my courage which needs shoring up. My self-belief. I need to be a woman standing on her own two feet, trusting her own decisions and making her own money.'

'Cool! So what are we going to do?'

Lexie scratched her head. 'Hmm, no idea. But we have wine, banoffee pie and plenty of days to mull it over. The answers will come.'

'And then you'll fight to get Ben back?'

'Urgh, stop it! I mean, if he was getting it on with Cynthia he can piss right off. I just need to think about me right now. In fact, us.' She pointed between herself and Sky.

Sky clinked her glass against Lexie's. 'Us!' She looked over Lexie's shoulder. 'Although I think that farmer wants a word.'

Chapter 45

'I'll get paid *and* get to take home leftover pies and sausage rolls!' Sky said with glee as they stumbled arm in arm along the lane towards the heart of the village. 'Thank God for all my experience working in Greggs.'

Lexie and Sky had just left their new local pub – two half-drunk women with quarter of a plan. They'd spoken to Farmer Humphrey, as he was affectionately known, and he hadn't even been that scary. He'd offered to tow them out of his fallow field, but something about that little village and its hug of a pub told Lexie she wanted to hang around for a bit longer. Just a bit.

Farmer H was happy for them to stay on his field in the short term, if Sky would do a few shifts in his farm shop in the village to cover for a sick employee.

'Three weeks you worked in Greggs,' said Lexie, giggling. 'Although you are a meat-product connoisseur.'

'It was four! And at least you're smiling again.' Sky

dug her in the ribs. 'I hate seeing you with a face like a slapped donkey.'

'Slapped arse! As in bottom, not horse-type creature.'

Sky screwed up her nose. 'But why would a face look like a bottom? Anyway, it's good you're taking a break from sulking. It was getting so dull.'

'Well, excuse me for taking a moment to mourn the death of my relationship. Just because you've forgotten yours already.'

'I mourned on the train! After I'd caught up with Facebook. And I watched *Bridget Jones*, didn't I? That was enough tears for Billy-Dickface.'

'True.' Lexie shrugged.

The rest of their time in the Traveller's Rest had been equally fruitful. The barman, Jimmy, who'd turned out to be the landlord, had agreed to let the girls charge their electricals, use the pub's water and grab a few free meals in exchange for Lexie helping with their social media while they were sticking around. So sticking around was what they would do, for a while at least. The village of Springhope would hopefully be the spring*board* that the Summers sisters needed. To spring them who knew where.

'Here!' said Lexie, pointing to the cutest little shop. The window was festooned with bunting, a bit like Lexie had in Penny before the poor camper van met her metal-crushing maker. Behind the glass were gorgeous displays of upcycled furniture painted in cosy colours and decorated with pretty sweeps of stencil art. The shop was called Amy's Inspiration. Lexie liked the name.

'Hey there, I'm Amy!' said the bubbly young shop owner as they bustled through the door. She was wearing paint-splattered overalls like the ones Lexie used to borrow from Tom, and Lexie felt jealous in a good way as she saw her painting up an old sideboard in the most beautiful shade of teal. 'Feel free to browse or give me a shout if you want anything.'

'Will do,' said Lexie, instantly warming to her.

'Oh, Lexie will want all of it,' Sky reassured her. 'But we both just got dumped by guys who preferred cash. Now we're living in a cramped old van with no money of our own and nowhere to put a ruddy thing.' She smiled as though this was a perfectly normal chat to be having with a stranger.

'Thanks, Sky.' Lexie gave her a sarcastic double thumbs up.

'Just keeping it real,' said Sky.

'It's not for ever,' Lexie explained, feeling the need to stand up for their sorry circumstances. 'We're just . . . '

'Waiting for inspiration,' finished Amy. 'Well, you're in the right place.' She beamed at them and returned to her painting.

As they moved around the shop in a semi-tipsy, semi-awestruck trance, taking in the beautiful furniture that had been given new leases of life, Lexie was becoming more inspired than she'd bargained for. That was the thing about afternoon drinking – it could bring out all sorts of wild ideas. Maybe she'd have to sort through them properly when her blood alcohol levels were back to normal. But for now, she was happy to enjoy it. To dream a little.

'This is stunning.' Lexie traced her fingers across a chest of drawers which had been revamped in pastel pink, with a lacy white pattern covering the top.

'Thank you,' said Amy. 'I decorated it myself. Although I'm trying to branch out with some less muted colours now.' She pointed to the teal piece she was working on. 'But it makes life trickier, because I have to make my own colours. I struggle to find enough unique shades.'

'Lexie said the same,' said Sky with a wave of the hand, as though her sister was some sort of renowned paint guru. 'She'll probably make her own range one day. She's super artistic.'

Lexie felt her cheeks redden. 'Not really,' she muttered.

Amy beckoned them over and opened one of the doors of the sideboard. 'The possibilities are endless, but I'm thinking of painting a peacock-feather pattern inside. Or maybe line it with peacock wallpaper.'

Lexie shuddered.

'You don't like peacocks?' Amy asked. 'Not everyone's into birds, I guess, but they're fascinating creatures. Symbolic of so many things. The all-seeing eyes on their tails, and their element of fakery. But they also stand for beauty, truth and immortality. Self-belief and new beginnings . . .'

'They'd be lovely in a pie,' Sky mused.

Lexie clapped a hand over her mouth and tried not to laugh, but she was glad of the change of subject. She didn't want to think about Nutgrass Hall and its omnipresent spies, nor its annoyingly immortal ruler. New beginnings, however . . .

'So, is it easy, having your own shop?' asked Sky.

Wow, she had even less boundaries after a few glasses of wine, thought Lexie. Although she couldn't help her ears pricking up.

Amy put her paintbrush down and rearranged her bun, inadvertently swiping teal paint through her hair. 'Not easy, exactly. But it's food for the soul, following your dreams. Having something for yourself. Your own empire. I mean, it's tiny.' She swept her arms around her, a contented look filling her face. 'But it's mine, you know? I make my own decisions, follow my instincts, create. And that lights me up.'

Her features were a picture, her cheeks almost rosy with happiness. Lexie found herself slowly nodding.

'Anyway, listen to me.' Amy giggled. 'You must think I'm a proper sort. Now, I can't offer you any peacock pie, if there is such a thing. But I was about to put the kettle on, and I haven't had a good chat all day. Do you ladies fancy a cup?'

'Ooh, really? People are so nice here,' Sky gushed. 'Lexie will grab us some cookies from that bakery next door. And then we want to hear all about how you came to have your own shop. This guy I used to fancy, Cory, is going to have his own surf shop one day. And I think you should talk Lexie into doing something for her soul too.'

'I'll go for the cookies,' said Lexie, holding up a hand and excusing herself, before her sister's wild suggestions blew her mind.

Chapter 46

'**D**amn it! I really thought this could work.'

Lexie hopped on one leg as she massaged her stubbed toe for at least the fourth time that week. The camper van was becoming perilously cramped now she was trying to juggle her new project amid their usual two-woman clutter bomb.

Spurred on by Amy's Inspiration, and perhaps a little by Ben and Grace's past pep talks on trusting her instincts, she'd been beavering away on her own range of brightly coloured chalk-style paints. The chalk (of controversial-white-powder fame) that she'd ordered a while back was finally coming in handy.

'It is working, isn't it? You said the ingredients were mixing really well.'

Sky was wearing a mud mask she'd made from actual mud and had her lazy feet up on a stack of Lexie's paint cans. At least her toenails were drying nicely in the heat of Lexie's vexation.

'They are mixing well – the colours are brilliant. But I can't build my empire in this.' She flapped her arms upwards, trying not to get tangled in the washing line of socks overhead.

The rain hammered its agreement against the window, reminding Lexie she couldn't even go outside to take a breather without ending up drenched. Not to mention that Penny Two was sinking further into the mudbath with every drop that fell.

'Watch my toenails, you numpty. They're not dry yet.' Sky batted her sister's arm. 'Do you like the shade? It's teal.' She fanned them out like the tail of a peacock.

Lexie gritted her teeth.

It had been two weeks since Lexie and Sky had landed tyres first in Farmer Humphrey's field. And while the village of Springhope had been filling Lexie with all sorts of inspiration, she was beginning to see that their stint as not-so-wild campers was nearing its end. They could not live like this for much longer.

It had been a welcoming place to take refuge and patch up their damaged sails, but no matter how lovely the locals had been or how tasty the pies were, Lexie didn't want to be a wanderer for ever. She didn't want to bounce from place to place, to run away from her troubles or even to live in a draughty old van. She wanted to go back to the town she'd called home for the last few months, regardless of anything that might have passed.

Not to Nutgrass Hall, of course, as much as she was missing Mrs M and Tom. But Tewkesbury. And a certain empty shop on the high street. It hadn't left her mind since it had twinkled at her from her rear-view mirror during that madcap midnight flit. Because her project was going to be more than paints. It would be her own queendom of repainted and repurposed magic. Making the ordinary extraordinary. Taking tatty furniture and breathing new life into it. Proving that something didn't have to be elegant or expensive to be as worthy as a pearl.

If she'd learned anything from Ben, it was that she should believe in her own ideas. And if Marrakech hadn't reminded her that the best entrepreneurs were born of necessity not money, then nothing would.

But to run a business, she would need to be organised. That was becoming abundantly clear from her chats with Amy at the shop, and from the fact she could barely function among the clutter without nearly losing a toe. She'd have to sort her life out – from the final bits of paperwork up. No more hiding from police records or making false claims on CVs. She would get this mess in order. But she couldn't do it here.

A rumble of thunder in the distance disturbed Lexie's thoughts. How quickly would the lightning follow? She wasn't going to hang around in this baked-bean can to find out. 'It's time we called Grace,' she said.

'Ooh, great.' Sky clapped her hands, making Lexie jump. 'Are we going for drinks?'

'Not yet.' Lexie inched back the net curtain, sure she could hear a mechanical rumbling too.

Lexie had been in regular contact with Grace since Lexie

351

and Sky went to the nearest town to buy Lexie's new SIM card. They'd been chatting about everything, from Lexie's paint-and-furniture-shop ideas to the whole situation with Ben. As silly as Grace thought it was, Lexie was firm that she wanted to get her world in order before she confronted her Ben-and-Cynthia fears. In fact, she hadn't even told Grace where they were camping in case word slipped out. Not that Grace would tell tales to Nutgrass Hall.

'Is that tractor coming this way?' Sky joined Lexie at the window, and they watched in surprise as the bright red machine stopped at the gate of their field and a passenger hopped out.

'Farmer Humphrey,' said Lexie.

'Has he come to kick us out? And who else is in the cab?'

Lexie squinted, praying it wasn't Ben. It did look like a man, although it was hard to tell under the woolly hat and through all that rain. Her poor heart was clattering. Surely, it couldn't be? Only the locals knew they were here.

Lexie did not want to be saved by the very man she'd been trying to avoid. She moved away from the window and crouched on the floor, suddenly compelled to hide.

'Lex, what's wrong?'

'I don't want to see him. Not yet.'

'But it's his field. And he just wants to help.'

'Not Farmer H, you goose.' Lexie uncovered one eyeball. 'Who's he with? Can you see?' This was exactly why she couldn't face Ben until she was ready. On her terms. Not stranded in a bog and jittering like an idiot.

'Just some guy in combats,' said Sky.

'Oh, really?' That did not sound like an outfit Ben would wear. 'He doesn't look like . . . Ben?'

'What? No! You've got a thing about jumping to weird conclusions lately. Too much Moroccan spice has twiddled your brain.' Sky pulled back the netting and pressed her face against the window. 'Ha ha. I think I know who it is! Come and see.'

Sky hauled Lexie to her feet and manoeuvred her face towards the glass. Lexie couldn't help but gawp.

A tall, slim person jumped down from the cab and began striding through the mud towards them. There was no mistaking that confident, feminine stride, nor that determined chin jutting up towards the rainy heavens. As she neared the camper van, she pulled off her hat like someone from a shampoo advert, her honeyed locks cascading downwards.

'Grace,' Lexie breathed, knowing that was exactly the fearless look she wanted to have on her face when she was ready to confront Ben. 'How did she know I was about to call her to come?'

'And how did she know we were here? You've been so Secret Squirrel.'

Within moments, Grace was banging at the side door of Penny Two. The sisters quickly slid the door open and Grace barrelled in, all laughter and hugs.

'How on earth . . . ?!'

Grace pulled away and beamed at them. 'Everyone knows everyone in the country. You didn't honestly think news of two cute sisters squatting in a vintage camper would stay secret for long? I only live four miles away.'

'Right.' Lexie nodded, remembering Jimmy at the pub saying the same on their first day.

Farmer Humphrey was driving the tractor towards them, mud spurting up from his tyres like great chocolate fountains. Lightning illuminated the sky behind him, making the whole scene look magical. Lexie could almost hear 'Eye of the Tiger' playing in her mind.

'Look, I didn't want to be an interfering minnie.' Grace rubbed Lexie's arm. 'But the weather's turning stormy and the forecast isn't good. I couldn't bear to think of you drowning out here when I'm rocking around Mum and Dad's place totally bored while they're off at the villa. I need you. Just for a few days, at least.'

Lexie sighed. She hadn't been expecting to stay with Grace, but it did sound nice.

'And no offence, but you really need a shower.' Grace held Lexie at arm's length, inspecting her paint-stained skin and sniffing her like she was an old sock. 'And fresh clothes, something warm to eat ...'

'OK, OK. I'm in,' said Lexie, unable to resist any more temptation.

'You had me at sausage roll,' said Sky, already looking for her coat.

'Who said anything about sausage rolls?' Grace whispered.

Lexie and Sky yanked on their wet-weather gear and jumped down from the camper van with Grace, ready to consult Farmer H about the plan of attack. Grace reassured Lexie she could sit in the pillion seat of the tractor so she didn't feel too *rescued*. Grace really did know her well.

Before long, the trusty tractor was pulling Penny Two from the mire and onto the safety of the road, with Lexie more or less at the helm. And even if she wasn't exactly driving the tractor, she was certainly in control of the action plan for her future. At last. As she looked towards the horizon, she was sure she could spot the tiniest break in the clouds. Her heart was almost bursting with hope, the theme tune in her head switching itself to 'Walking on Sunshine'. If Farmer H had looked a little less serious, she might just have hugged him.

When the farmer had unhooked Penny Two and said his goodbyes, the three girls climbed into the camper, ready to hit the road.

'A spin through the carwash and she'll be as good as before,' said Sky.

'Thank God for that because I'm selling her,' said Lexie. 'And I know a certain landlord who might just want to buy her.'

The other two gaped at her.

'What? But you loved Penny!' said Sky.

'I did love Penny,' Lexie confirmed. 'But she belonged to an old life. And someone else's old life, at that. A life on the road with Penny was Aunt Jasmine's dream. Now it's time for me to grasp my own.'

Grace gave her a fist bump. 'Yes, girl!'

'Penny Two was never the same anyway,' Sky whispered, as though the van might get offended. 'She's not really mossy enough.'

'I'm using the money to set up the new shop. And there's

a two-bedroom flat above it,' said Lexie, sounding a hell of a lot braver than she felt. 'We'll just rent at first, but who knows. Maybe I could buy it one day, if I keep saving up.'

'New shop?' asked Sky. 'Amazing! Will it be like Amy's Inspiration? Or better! I'm totally great at working in shops. And you know what they say – nothing ventured comes to those who wait.'

Lexie was pretty sure nobody said that, but maybe they should.

'And then?' asked Grace, who was already up to date with the Tewkesbury shop dream.

'And then I speak to Ben and find out what the hell happened in Morocco. I can't hide from it forever.'

She also couldn't hide from the racing she'd felt in her heart when she'd thought for a second it had been Ben up there in that tractor. She didn't want to be saved and she hadn't been quite ready to face him. And yet the thought of never seeing him again, of never finding out what had happened between them, was becoming more than she could endure.

Chapter 47

'Being sneaky is hard work.' Sky dropped another heavy box of paints down onto the wooden floor of the new shop and gave Lexie an accusatory look.

'Tell me about it,' said Lexie. It would have to end soon. She knew that.

Lexie and Sky had spent the last few weeks living at Grace's house, making plans and flitting backwards and forwards to Lexie's new shop on Tewkesbury High Street. As the shop had been empty for so long, she'd negotiated a great deal to rent it, and the flat above.

They would fill the shop with Lexie's vibrant homemade chalk-style paints, old furniture repainted and découpaged to be beautiful, and the promise of new beginnings. She was all for it. Or at least she would be. She hoped.

The shop wasn't open yet, and Lexie still hadn't confronted Ben or let anyone at Nutgrass Hall know they were back in town, so all preparations had been in secret. They'd been hauling everything in via the back entrance to avoid being seen on the main street.

'And when are those stupid sheets coming down? I miss seeing daylight.' Sky pointed to the shopfront windows where Lexie had hung old lengths of material to keep out prying eyes. They were already starting to droop in protest; she really should rearrange them.

'Soon, OK?'

She knew it would have to be. The shop would be opening next week and she couldn't hide forever. She didn't want to cower behind the counter, wondering when Ben would hear about the place and come storming in. She'd walked out on their work trip, her job, her room. She'd left him in the lurch, even if she'd had Cynthia-shaped reasons for not wanting to speak to him. And they still had Lexie's lies to discuss. She'd finally sorted out the paperwork to clear her police record, and all copies of her phony CV had been fed into the jaws of Grace's dad's shredder. And even if Ben might be walking down the aisle with someone else in the name of money, Lexie still wanted to be able to hold her head up high if she bumped into them, knowing that she'd finally cleared her name.

'You keep saying *soon*, but when? Good things don't come to those who wait.'

Grace arrived behind them, puffing and panting with a set of nesting tables repainted in *Lexie Loves* Marmalade, with zebra-patterned legs. 'I think the saying is that good things *do* come to those who wait. But seriously. Just get in touch with the guy, or I'll do it myself.' She put the tables down, and the three girls looked around to survey their work.

For all she'd loved Amy's Inspiration, Lexie's shop was looking very different. She was proud of how it was shaping up. It was bright, quirky and unapologetically her. With permission from the landlord, they'd repainted the floorboards in sassy stripes of colour and hung some of her old sari material on the walls. Her range of *Lexie Loves* chalk-style paints were displayed on an eclectic collection of painted bookshelves along one wall. They'd arranged the pots in colour order, so the effect was like a glorious rainbow.

The furniture Lexie had been working so hard to upcycle was dotted around the place, looking enticing. She'd bought some retro purple armchairs from the second-hand furniture shop next door and created a lovely cosy corner. She quite fancied the idea of serving tea and cake there in the long run, but one step at a time. She would put some inspirational magazines and a few tubs of M&Ms there for now.

M&Ms. Wow. How they reminded her of Ben. How everything did. Was there still a small chance for them? A tiny glimmer of hope that she'd got everything wrong? She knew that was the thing she was desperately clinging to. The thing she might have to say goodbye to once she finally heard his story.

'She's waiting for a sign,' said Sky, putting on her strange, mystical voice. 'Before she knows it's time.'

Was constantly thinking about M&Ms, fortune cookies and magical walks through the souks of Marrakech a sign? Or pining over passionate kisses in London, their lively

Friday meetings or even heart-to-hearts behind her parents' knackered shed? Being with Ben had made the ordinary extraordinary. Just like everything she was trying to do in this shop. She'd thought he was so beige in the beginning. But over time, she'd found his presence reflected all the colours of the spectrum. He'd inspired her to travel again, to trust her instincts, to create ...

'Er. Maybe that's a sign?' said Grace, squinting towards the window.

Lexie and Sky followed her gaze to see a face peering back at them through a gap in the makeshift curtains.

'Bloody hell, let her in,' said Lexie with a gulp. It looked as though Mohammed was coming to the mountain.

Chapter 48

The elderly lady bustled into the shop as though she was already in charge. She looked different out of uniform, in her sensible lilac cardigan and grey skirt, but when she put her strange pot down and pulled Lexie into the cosiest hug, she smelt just the same. Chamomile tea and lavender soap; like a cuddly cloud of calm.

Lexie felt warm tears flow down her face. She had missed Mrs Moon with all her heart. She was part of what made this town home for her. Part of why she would fight to stay, even if a fancier peacock would be taking her place with Ben.

'Now, where on earth have you been?' The housekeeper held Lexie at arm's length. 'Oh dear, this just won't do. You haven't been eating properly; you look so thin. Just like Ben. And he's been so worried about you. Looking all over. When are you coming home?' She turned her gaze to Sky. 'And where did you pop off to?'

Ben had been looking for her? And worried? Or maybe

just concerned she'd seen him getting frisky on the balcony with a certain Cynthia Fortescue. Time would soon tell.

As Mrs Moon dabbed Lexie's face with a pretty embroidered hanky, Lexie explained she and Sky were moving in above the shop. She apologised for them both disappearing so suddenly, then picked through her thoughts for an explanation that didn't involve half-naked women on balconies.

'Ben and I had a bit of a ... falling out, in Morocco. I thought we were going to go on a date,' said Lexie.

Mrs Moon nodded as though the date part was perfectly sensible. Was it?

'Yeah, and then slutty Cynthia tried to get all *bedroom vixen* with him. Are those two getting it on now?'

'Sky!' Lexie clamped a hand over her sister's mouth. That was exactly the question she didn't want answered. At least not by dear Mrs Moon.

The housekeeper's soft cheeks coloured to candyfloss and she looked a little flustered. She brushed down her skirt in the place her pinafore would usually be.

'It's OK, don't answer that,' said Lexie. 'I would rather hear it from Ben.'

Lexie guided everyone towards the purple armchairs and three of them sat down, with Grace disappearing to put the kettle on and gather biscuits.

'I honestly don't know, dear,' said Mrs Moon once she'd composed herself. 'Us staff don't get informed about things like that, and Ben's awfully private. Not the sort to be seen canoodling.'

Lexie winced and Mrs Moon squeezed her arm.

'I can't see those two cavorting anyway. They're not suited: Cynthia's far too uppity. I have seen her popping in a couple of times, but, if it makes you feel better, I think she had very different reasons.'

'Different reasons?' Lexie ventured, almost wishing she hadn't.

Mrs Moon looked at her lap and smoothed her skirt again.

'It's really not my place to say. Maybe Ben will tell you.' The housekeeper's voice was quiet then. Sad, perhaps.

And then Grace clattered in with a tray full of teas, a Jaffa cake hanging from her mouth. The rest of the packet appeared to be drowning in the spillages.

Mrs Moon bounced up on autopilot, taking the tray and putting it safely down on a *Lexie Loves* Bubblegum coffee table. 'There, there, sweet girl. I hope they're not going to put you in charge of refreshments in this place.' She looked around, taking in the wild array of colours. 'It really is quite spectacular, you know. I'm so proud of you, Lexie.'

Lexie swallowed back another sob.

They settled themselves around the coffee table, Mrs Moon mopping up Grace's tea puddles with hankies that she kept pulling from her sleeves like a magician.

'Now, it's not really my place to say this either,' said Mrs Moon.

Grace and Sky leaned in.

Lexie froze. 'Then you probably shouldn't. I'll speak to Ben soon; it's on my list.'

'You make him sound like a packet of biscuits,' said Grace, waving the Jaffa cakes she'd been quietly demolishing.

'Actually, they're cakes,' said Sky. 'Small, biscuit-sized sponge cakes covered in chocolate.'

The two of them began a lively debate until Lexie thought her head might explode. 'What isn't it your place to say, Mrs M?' she heard herself asking. 'Just say it.'

Sky and Grace halted mid squabble to look at the house-keeper, who simply scratched her head and looked confused. 'Ooh, do you know? I can't remember.'

Lexie exhaled the breath she'd been holding. It was probably for the best.

'Oh, my goodness. Mr Moon! I'd forgotten him too,' Mrs Moon yelped as she scrambled to her feet, tea slopping over as her cup landed on the table. 'I'd just been taking him for a nice walk when I spied some kerfuffle in this shop, and . . .' Her voice faded as she stalked back towards the door.

'Mr Moon! Well, bring him in. In all those weeks I never did get to meet him.'

Within moments, Mrs Moon was fussing her way back, the silver pot she'd arrived with tucked safely under her arm.

'Don't be silly, lovey, I did bring him in. Poor thing's not that keen on shopping.'

Lexie's mouth dropped open. So the pot . . . was an urn? Mr Moon was dead? Had he always been dead? Obviously, not always, but . . . What was the polite way of asking? Nutgrass Hall really was a place of strange secrets.

'Nobody ever told me Mr Moon was . . .'

'Inside a funny jar.' Sky finished Lexie's sentence, tilting her head as though trying to work it out.

'I'm so sorry.' Lexie stood up to put her arm around Mrs

Moon and guided her back to her seat. 'I hadn't realised your husband wasn't alive anymore. I'd just assumed . . .'

'It's OK, dear. Don't worry.'

'Oh, Lexie assumes a *lot* of weird stuff these days,' said Sky, butting in as only troublesome little sisters could. 'She jumps to crazy conclusions instead of actually asking people stuff. *Like Ben.*'

'Instead of just opening my trap like a big old foghorn?' Lexie grabbed a Jaffa cake and shoved it squarely into her sister's mouth when she opened it to object. 'And I don't think I assumed Mr Moon was alive without reason.' Lexie cast back her thoughts. 'I was sure I heard you . . . having discussions with him once or twice, Mrs M.' She didn't like to say *blazing rows*.

'When was that?' Mrs Moon scratched her dandelion-clock hair.

'Well, once in the kitchen, on a Friday night before my meeting with Ben. Then that morning when I came knocking on the door of your cottage.'

Mrs Moon blushed and lowered her voice. 'Well, Friday nights are when I catch up with *The Real Housewives of Beverly Hills*. But don't let Mrs Carrington-Noble hear of it. She doesn't even know about the kitchen TV; she'd call me a slacker.' She gave the urn a loving stroke. 'But those crazy, bickering housewives have kept me company since Mr M passed, even if I do end up shouting at their silliness. And I do love that bling!'

'*The Housewives* rock.' Grace nodded.

'Bling?' Everything Lexie thought she knew was blithely

365

turning itself on its head. Although perhaps that's why the housekeeper knew so much about a Bulgari Serpenti.

'I know they show off, with all their money and plastic boobs, but I do like that Lisa Vanderpump. She's an entre-preneur, Lexie. Just like you!' Mrs Moon put the urn down on the coffee table and gave a delighted clap.

Lexie blinked a few times as this strange new reality sank in.

'In fact, I might have a business proposal of my own for you.' Mrs Moon looked around. 'But that's a thought for another day.'

Lexie wouldn't argue with that. There was a limit to how many bizarre facts she could process in one sitting.

'Although perhaps you could help me with a more ... *personal matter*.' Mrs Moon lowered her voice as she said the last part. Then, looking around her, she grabbed a sequined throw and placed it over the urn. 'And I don't want him listening in.'

'Right.' Lexie nodded, wondering what on earth could be coming next.

Chapter 49

Lexie, Sky and Grace held their breath, waiting for Mrs Moon to divulge her *personal matter*.

'Now, Lexie, I know you're a people person. So I wondered if you'd help me with a bit of *matchmaking*,' the housekeeper said.

'She'd be terrible at matchmaking!' said Sky. 'She should have paired herself up with Ben instead of leaving him in a hotel room with Sexy-Undies Cynthia.'

Lexie shuddered.

'Lexie would be excellent at matchmaking; she just needs to put herself before others.' Grace rubbed Lexie's back and passed the biscuits.

'I did a fine job with my friends Mia and Jake,' Lexie reminded herself, through a mouthful of crumbs.

'Do you fancy someone, Mrs M?' asked Sky. 'Waaaait. Is it Tom the gardener?' She narrowed her eyes. 'It *is* Tom the gardener! I knew you always gave him the biggest slice of cake.'

The girls cooed as Mrs Moon patted down her cardigan and tried to look prim.

'I do believe we've taken a liking to each other, yes. And it's been five years since Mr Moon passed away. An old girl has got to move on some day.'

'Five?' said Sky. 'That's dedication.'

'You're absolutely allowed to move on,' said Lexie, squeezing the housekeeper's arm.

'The *Real Housewives* wouldn't wait five months.' Grace nodded. 'Allegedly.'

Mrs Moon rearranged the material over the urn and blinked a few times. 'Don't be disappointed with me, dear,' she whispered. 'It's so lonely in that cottage without you shuffling about. And Cory and Ben don't need me anymore. Not really. I miss *chats*. Going for walks with someone who talks back. Even ... holding hands. Being loved.' She sniffed. 'The animals were meant to go two by two, after all.'

'Oh God.' Lexie sprang to her feet, one hand pinching her tear ducts, the other roaming for a box of tissues. 'That's the saddest thing I've ever heard. But we love you, Mrs M.' Although she knew it wasn't the same. And there was certainly something to be said for two by two, after Sky's failed quartet and Lexie's awful three-way holiday with Ben and Cynthia.

When Lexie returned to the table there were tears all round. She couldn't imagine spending so many years with a soulmate and then losing them. But it must be better than never getting the chance to be with them at all. She sat down and dished out tissues.

'Don't cry, my lovelies.' Mrs Moon snuffled. 'There's a time when you have to say goodbye to your past. Stop letting it hold you back and go bravely into your future. Sprinkle sad ashes into the wind and make new roots.' She nodded her head and looked around her. 'New adventures. Did you ever think about selling stonebaked pizza?'

Lexie gave a little snort through her tears. 'I'm not Lisa Vanderpump of Beverly Hills,' she said with a giggle.

'Not yet, my love. But you will be. Even better, I'm sure.' Mrs Moon gave her a proud smile, and she dared not argue.

'So, what's going down with you and the guy with the wheelbarrow?' asked Grace. 'He does seem cute. Very Tom Girardi.'

'Mr Girardi was once one of the Beverly Hills husbands,' Mrs Moon explained to the other two. 'Although my Tom has considerably less teeth. And money.' She chuckled behind her hand.

'Which never matters,' said Sky.

'Well, quite! It's all about whether he's worthy of me. Whether he's earned his place in my affections.'

'Ooh, I like that,' said Sky. 'Not whether you're worthy of him or anything dumb.' She widened her eyes at Lexie, who poked her tongue out.

'He's been secretly making herbs for me in that greenhouse of his. Isn't that adorable? All sorts of things I'd never even heard of. I've been experimenting with some delicious herbal teas. You must come round and try some. And have a chinwag about all this dating,' said Mrs Moon to Lexie.

369

So that's what those unidentified plants were in Tom's secret greenhouse. Nothing dodgy after all. But going back to Nutgrass Hall? Lexie's heart leapt at the thought. But was it from fear or excitement?

'Lexie will absolutely help you with your romantic needs, but she's going to sort out her own life first.' Grace winked.

'Lexie's doing pretty well so far,' said Sky. 'I mean, look at this place. But she's still got a few hurdles left.'

'A few?' Lexie screwed up her face.

Sky started counting on her fingers. 'Stop being a scaredy-dog and speak to Ben. Sort out the rest of this place, including a shop sign, taking down those tatty curtains you've been hiding behind, setting up new social media accounts, drafting blog posts ...'

'Blog posts!' said Mrs Moon. 'That was the thing I was about to say before I forgot. Well, isn't that a relief.'

Was it? Lexie wasn't quite so sure.

'So,' Mrs Moon continued. 'Ben's been looking all over for you, Lexie, as I said. Despite the other news he's been dealing with.'

'And Cynthia floating around,' Lexie added.

Grace gave her leg a swift toe-poke.

'Well, anyway, he was going to drive up to your parents' house to see if they knew anything. He didn't have their number and yours hasn't been working,' said Mrs Moon.

'I have a new number,' Lexie admitted. 'The old one had to go.' She was glad Ben hadn't driven all the way up to Lancaster, although her parents didn't know exactly where she and Sky were.

'And he couldn't work out why all of your social media bits and bobs had disappeared.'

'I suspended my accounts. I didn't really need them, and it's been quite a nice break. Who knew.'

'She's been hiding,' said Sky. 'Like a wimp.'

'Re-evaluating,' said Lexie.

'Sulking,' Grace concluded. 'So, what about the blog posts?'

'Ben was going to write one,' said Mrs Moon. 'Lisa Vanderpump wrote one once, you know. They're all the rage.'

'Ben was going to write a blog post? About what?' asked Lexie, wondering if lovely Mrs Moon had got herself muddled. It didn't sound like something Ben would do. He wasn't big on social media, sharing his thoughts or even communicating, really. And he definitely wasn't keen on blogging.

'About you, of course. Like an SOS to help him find you. Cory said you'd be off in that camper van, not hanging out with your parents. Ben couldn't think of any other way of getting a message to you. The poor sausage is desperate to talk. He didn't say why, but I wouldn't mind guessing.' Mrs Moon tapped her nose.

'Because he wants to go on that Moroccan date, after all.' Grace gave a little wiggle.

'Because even after kinky Cynthia put her money and plastic boobs on the table, he'd still prefer your skinny butt!' said Sky with glee.

'You've never seen Cynthia or her breasts.' Lexie pulled a face.

'No, but your scrawny backside is awesome!' said Sky, trying to give Lexie a high five and failing miserably.

Lexie put her hands over her ears. 'Stop it. I don't want to talk about this; you're giving me false hope. Just let me speak to Ben and find out for myself, OK?'

'So you're going? When? When's he posting this blog post, Mrs M? Or maybe he's done it already! Ooh, let's check.' Grace grabbed her phone. 'Carrington Paints, right? How exciting.'

'Bloody stop it,' said Lexie, making a grab for the phone, but Sky held her back. 'I just want to communicate in person now. This is terrifying.'

'You will be communicating in person,' said Grace, as her fingers danced across her screen. 'I'll drive you there myself if I have to. But let's get a heads-up on the situation. No point in going in blind.'

Lexie cringed as she imagined Grace donning her designer combats and speeding them there in her four-by-four. A spectacle was not what she needed.

'Oh my God, it's here!' said Grace, pointing at her phone. 'A new blog post published five days ago, entitled *Ain't No Sunshine*. Squee!'

Lexie buried her face in her hands, dreading the thought of hearing more but resigned to the fact she was just about to. Grace began to read aloud.

Chapter 50

Ain't No Sunshine
Blog Post by Ben Carrington

Now and again, someone comes into your life and repaints everything. Four months ago, that happened to me. Her name is Lexie Summers.

Lexie paraded into my colourless life like a one-woman carnival, with her flamingo raincoats and lipstick the colour of the sun. You may know her as the enchanting woman who usually writes this blog. That was before she disappeared.

She burst into my world all those months ago in a crazy camper van, amid a whirlwind of peacocks. Bold, unique and beautiful. Every part of me tried to scowl at this intrusion, and yet my lips must have betrayed my secret smile. Lexie came to take the role of social media manager at Carrington Paints. Before I knew it, she was taking off with my heart.

At first, it seemed there were scarcely two people more

opposite. Me, buried in my busy dull life of paperwork and money; Lexie shunning both in favour of gloriously empty pockets and a heart full of fun. But she tested me. She pushed my boundaries. Her spirit and ideas were infectious.

I did my best to resist falling for her. We were meant to be working together, after all. And what would a sunny soul like Lexie want with a sensible sort like me? But that's the funny thing about opposites. They attract. They complement each other, like yin and yang. I was drawn to her; it was terrifying. Because this crab had become quite accustomed to the safety of his shell. He had not intended to be disturbed by something so trifling as affection.

And then, something went wrong. Lexie and I were due to go on a special date, but I received some news. News that brought everything crashing down. I should have communicated, of course. But I clammed up. Forgot myself. Failed to share what was going on in my head. I didn't even turn up for our date. And then she disappeared.

You see, communications of the heart are not my strong point. Yes, I can shake hands in business. Make deals; talk shop. But when it comes to my personal life, my thoughts, my hopes, my problems; I shy away from sharing.

Can I tell you why? Although, God, this doesn't feel easy.

But I've never thought of myself as interesting.

I'm good with numbers, paperwork and monotonous things. But what interest would anyone have in Beige Ben? People used to call me boring, and it stuck. It became a self-fulfilling prophecy. I believed I was dull, and so dull I became. I buried myself in work, closed the doors to friendship and kept love at bay.

Anyway, I can't tell you what it was I couldn't share with Lexie on that final night. It's not my news to tell. But for now, all I know is my insides are dark with sadness.

So here I am, putting my heart on the line. Nailing my colours to the mast like a string full of socks in an orange camper van.

I'm not saying we can fix things – who can ever know? But we have words to exchange. Truths to tell. I don't want to leave things like this.

Lexie, if you're reading this, I have so much more to say. Will you let me say it in person?

I will be in our secret garden, on the bench, Saturday 5 September at 2 p.m. and every Saturday after that until you join me. Please be kind.

Yours hopefully,

Ben

Lexie finally peered out from behind her hands at the expectant faces of Sky, Grace and Mrs Moon.

'The fifth of September is this Saturday,' said Grace.

'Or one of the other Saturdays?' Lexie suggested.

'No way – you're going. *This* Saturday,' said Sky. 'Do you know where he means?'

Lexie nodded. 'The secret garden with the wildflowers at Nutgrass Hall.' She pictured it, complete with kissing seat. Would there be any kissing? What secrets were left to share? She wondered if she would accept them, and what he would say about hers.

'Ooh, yes, dear,' said Mrs Moon. 'Do come. I'll keep lookout at the gates.'

Lexie recalled the huge wrought-iron gates, frightening peacocks and ever-present danger of a certain Mrs Carrington-Noble. She gulped. This Saturday. Two days' time. She was due to open the shop on Monday; there was so much to do. But yes. On the long list of priorities, this might be the most important. She just hoped the meeting wouldn't be fraught with problems that would end up catapulting her backwards.

'All right. But don't tell him I'm coming or that I'm here in this shop. I want to be ready,' said Lexie, steeling herself for the final quest.

Chapter 51

Bloody hell, where was she?

Lexie looked at her watch as she stood in the shadow of Nutgrass Hall's towering gates. The damned things were closed and she couldn't remember the code. Mrs Moon had promised to be her wingwoman, but even after a flurry of buzzer pressing, no one was coming to her rescue.

Had she made a mistake? Was this the wrong Saturday to meet Ben in the secret garden? Or maybe he'd changed his mind. He'd publicly invited her here, but the stupid gates were shut. What did that mean?

Maybe it was the fact she was twenty minutes late. Damn the extra time she'd spent faffing over the perfect totally-not-trying-too-hard outfit, that slow tractor she and Grace had been stuck behind, and the fact she now couldn't find her mobile. It must have slipped out of her pocket in Grace's four-by-four. And now Grace was gone.

'Ouch.' She rubbed her shoulders as the scorching

summer heat tried to burn the skin off her shoulders. It was as though every possible thing was transpiring against her.

Was it a sign she should just go back to the shop? Eat M&Ms, sulk, and maybe come back another day? But no. She wasn't going to think like that. She'd come a long way since she'd first cowered outside those gates. They weren't so intimidating now.

With a huff, she hoicked up her dress and began her trek around the peripheries of the estate. Could there be an easier way in? A side gate she didn't know of, or a loose bit of hedge? But after a sweltering march around the outskirts, there was nothing. Other than a slightly lower stretch of wall behind the peacock sheds. Hmm.

If only her not-trying-too-hard outfit didn't consist of a long sunshine-yellow dress and pixie boots. It was not the ideal wall-scaling ensemble, but one way or another she was going over.

She tucked her dress into her knickers and took a deep breath. Right. Her rainbow not-trying-too-hard manicure was going to be left behind on the Cotswold-stone wall, but her dignity was coming with her. She didn't care who might turn their posh nose up at the sight of a bare-legged, slightly sweaty woman clawing her way over the ramparts. She was absolutely going in. She yanked off her boots and threw them over.

Craaaaaww. Eeeeaaa, eeeeaaa, eeeeaaaa . . .

Shit – the peacocks. That was all she needed. The pesky things continued their fanfare as Lexie heaved and panted over the top of the wall, trying to get her grazed leg over without looking thoroughly indecent.

Just as she was trying not to cry at the distance she had to scrabble down, or the harem of peacocks, which had started to gather, she realised that a fanfare was just the thing.

'Tom!'

The elderly gardener was ambling towards her, squinting up from beneath his battered tweed cap.

'Young grockle. You's back!' Shooing the peacocks back into their shed, Tom hastened towards Lexie, pulling his wheelbarrow out from under a tree. He parked it against the wall, beneath where Lexie was clinging on with her ruined nails.

''Ere yer go. This should soften yer landing. Nut grass. I managed to get the last of it out, wud yer believe?' He looked over his shoulder. 'Quick. The mistress 'as been on the prowl. Mrs Moon is tryin' to keep 'er busy with a pot of tea. You lookin' for Ben?'

Lexie took a deep breath, swung her other leg over, and screwed her eyes shut as she fell into the barrow of knobbly weeds. 'Yes,' she squeaked, as a hundred knuckles dug into her bottom. That was going to bruise.

'Last I saw, 'e was mopin' about near the kissing bench. 'E expectin' you?'

Lexie checked her watch again. Forty minutes late. 'Well, he was.'

'Then go get 'im, girl. I'm sick of seein' that miserable face on 'im. You'll brighten it. Gawd knows, we needs a bit o' cheering up around 'ere.' He picked up her boots. 'Did you want these?'

Lexie looked at the peacock dung that was having a party on her fake suede, and tried not to gag. 'I'll go barefoot.' She clambered from the wheelbarrow and straightened herself out. 'It's fine.'

'I'll clean 'em up for yer. Borrow these if you like.' He pointed to his old working boots, which were at least four sizes too big for her.

'Don't worry, Tom. I'm a big girl now.' She threw her arms around him. 'And don't you dare clean the crap off my shoes, you silly bugger.'

'It's part of me job.' He shrugged.

'The only person who should be cleaning up after those things is the person who owns them.'

Tom's eyes widened. 'I'll leave you to tell 'er that.'

Lexie felt herself shiver, despite the blistering heat on her skin. 'I might,' she replied, secretly hoping she wouldn't have to.

After a quick goodbye and good luck, she scurried across the grass towards the secret garden, dodging stray peacock poo and praying Mrs Carrington-Noble wouldn't spy her through a window.

With every hurried step, her stomach grew an extra knot. She tugged at her dress, which clung wetly to her back. She was a leaping, cartwheeling bag of nerves. How long until this was over?

As she reached the edge of grass, she breathed a sigh of relief and ducked under the archway. But oh …

Everything seemed different in the first part of the enclosed gardens.

It was the smell that hit her first. Rich and flowery like a true summer's day. Mrs Carrington-Noble's flowers were usually lined up with precision in their stark white coats. But other than the odd hanger-on, watching forlornly with its petals drooping, most had been replaced. Bright yellow sunflowers burst up towards the sky, with orange and purple gerbera dancing at their feet. So much colour. Who had sanctioned it?

Conscious of her lateness, Lexie hurried onwards, into the orchard with its apple-laden trees, past the cottages and Tom's veg. Finally, she arrived at the old wooden gate.

'Oh help,' she heard herself say as her hand hovered, ready to push it open. At least this one was unlocked. Should she take that as a good sign? She blew out a chestful of tense air and nudged her way through.

It was cooler in the secret garden, with all the shady growth. The wildflowers were just as before, although something else was going on. She could hear soft jazz music playing – a piano and saxophone drifting gently on the breeze amid the birdsong. And the trees. She stopped to look. They'd been decorated with bunches of sunflowers, and the branches twinkled with fairy lights. It felt almost enchanted.

She crept onwards, the ground pillowy beneath her bare feet. Rich and mossy like a green velvet carpet. Her heart was pounding. Could this all be for her? What if . . . But, no. She'd had enough of second-guessing. Assuming she wasn't worthy. She must keep going.

'Oh.' She hopped on one foot. She'd trodden on something. A shiny blue packet with gold swirly letters. She picked it up and smiled, a tingle of warmth spreading through her. It was a fortune cookie. As she looked ahead she saw a small trail of them, leading towards the kissing seat. She couldn't see the seat yet, but she knew it was there, beyond the overgrown shrubbery.

Lexie picked up the packet, her hand shaking. Dare she believe that Ben had good things to say? Wherever he was, he probably thought she wasn't coming. Would he have done this every Saturday until she arrived? A small part of her wanted to test the theory. But now she was here she couldn't wait any longer. She collected the fortune cookies as she rushed onwards to the bench.

Chapter 52

'Ben?' Lexie called out, unable to see him. A small radio was playing music. The jazz she'd heard when she'd crept into the secret garden.

And then she noticed it. The kissing seat. It had changed.

She knelt to inspect it, stroking its wooden surface. It was beautiful. Each slat had been painted a different shade, like the colours they'd seen in Morocco. The spices, the rugs, the sparkling glass. Was this the new range of shades she'd inspired? But Morocco ...

She should be proud to see these new colours, though her stomach was heavy. She still didn't know what had happened there between Ben and Cynthia. And would the Carringtons still be working with the Fortescues? She stood up and took a dizzy step backwards.

'Lexie.'

She looked up to see Ben, pushing through the undergrowth in a fitted shirt the colour of the blue in his atlas eyes.

He looked different too. More stubble, but in a rugged way, and his dark hair was definitely longer and more ruffled. Lexie couldn't stop her heart from leaping.

'You've got foliage in your hair,' she said, her mind suddenly empty of anything useful.

He looked at her, the corners of his mouth twitching in that way she'd grown to love. 'Your dress is tucked into your knickers on the one side. And I won't ask where your shoes are.'

She laughed and tugged at the wayward material, her heart bouncing. She'd always adored their banter, even when she'd convinced herself she didn't. But small talk was the easy part. It was the big talk that was coming. And if they couldn't jump that fence ...

'Oh God, Lexie, I've missed you.'

They stood either side of the kissing seat and he took a step closer. She battled the temptation to bound over the seat and into his arms. They had to communicate. She had to be sure.

'Where did you go? And why?' he asked, his forehead creased. 'I looked everywhere for you. I was distraught. You fled the country.'

'We had a date.' She was talking to the bench, but she knew she should look at him. She took a deep breath and met his gaze. 'But you were with Cynthia. And then your phone was off. You didn't arrive.'

An emotion rippled over his face. Lexie tried desperately to read it. Was it sadness? Guilt?

'You saw me with Cynthia? How?' He scratched his head, a piece of foliage falling to the floor.

'You could at least sound sorry.' Lexie felt a wave of nausea rising. 'You were hugging her in her shiny dressing gown on your balcony.' She let the fortune cookies she'd gathered drop to the ground, suddenly not bothered what they might say.

'No, Lexie. No. It was nothing like that. Jesus. With Cynthia? Hell. OK, it must have looked bad.' He moved swiftly around the bench and took her by the shoulders, his fast breath warm against her cheeks. 'I'd forgotten she was even there; it was so comparatively unimportant. I was in shock when she turned up, and I sent her away within minutes.'

Lexie scrutinised every movement of his face, which was just inches from hers. Those eyes which had always fascinated her seemed so genuine. But she was confused.

'You were holding her. That silky robe.'

His forehead creased, as though trying to remember. 'She said she'd just got back from the spa, or something. I really didn't care about her outfit. Look, I'd just been speaking to my mother on the phone. She told me ...' He swallowed hard and cleared his throat. 'She told me she has a serious illness. She might be dying, Lexie. I would have embraced a grizzly bear at that moment. And I certainly wouldn't have felt anything untoward about it.'

'Oh shit, I'm so sorry, I ...' Lexie's eyes began to prickle with tears as she looked into his. She'd never seen them so pained, and she had no doubt they were sincere. 'Oh God, oh God, oh God. I got it so wrong. How could I have left you in that moment? Is she OK? Are you?'

Lexie lifted her hands to his face, wanting to hold him, to take the agony away. His mother seemed so strong, and yet ... yes. Now she thought about it, she'd seen moments of fragility. And that turban. Perhaps it was obvious in hind-sight. No wonder his mother was clinging on to him, being so defensive.

Ben's eyes were welling with tears, but she could see he was fighting them.

'It's OK to be sad,' she said, touching his cheek.

'I know.' He blinked hard and looked away for a moment.

Lexie rewound her thoughts to that night in Marrakech and her own telephone call with Ben's mother. She'd been evil, although in the circumstances Lexie could sort of understand. Who knew what she must have been going through for all this time. But Mrs Carrington-Noble had said she'd told Ben about Lexie's lies. The fabricated CV and the Inkie drugs fiasco. She'd said Ben didn't want Lexie around anymore. Was now really the time to drag all that up? But wherever this conversation was going, Lexie knew it was time to be honest. To own her past; to feel worthy no matter what.

'I'm so sorry I blocked you out, Lexie. I'll never forgive myself for not confiding in you or for not turning up to our date. I can be hopeless at sharing my feelings. I guess I had a stiff upbringing with Mum's fake airs and graces, and I was too old to be mothered by Mrs Moon like Cory. I've never let people in. Never believed anyone would even be interested enough. This is all new to me. But I'm learning, Lexie. I'm trying.'

'Urgh, I feel dreadful.' Lexie shook her head. 'You've suffered for weeks and you hadn't even done anything wrong. I was too scared to hear the truth in case I hated it. And I felt so guilty about the lies I'd told. I thought you'd had enough of me.'

'Lies?'

Oh God. Had his mother not told him? Was she about to break his heart again? 'I ... er ... ' She let her hands fall from his face and slumped onto the kissing seat, her head drooping. 'I haven't always been truthful with you. I was ashamed of my past. I thought I wasn't good enough to get the job, so I lied on my CV. I pretended I had a degree when I haven't even been to uni.'

Ben dropped down so he was kneeling at her feet, his suit trousers sinking into the moss. 'So? You think I care about where you did or didn't go to school? You could do the job with your eyes closed. Not all skills come from lectures and books.'

'But I wasn't honest with you.'

'Then maybe I should have been a more approachable employer.' He squeezed her knee.

'Your mum didn't ... tell you anything about me? The CV thing, or anything else?'

He shrugged and lifted her chin so her gaze met his. 'Not that I recall. Why would she know that?'

'Long story.' She didn't feel this was any time to be trashing his sickly mother for snooping. Mrs Carrington-Noble hadn't told tales on her in the end. Perhaps the woman had just been lashing out on the phone, after her difficult conversation with Ben.

387

'We've got plenty of time to talk about long stories.' He picked up one of the fortune cookie packets and handed it to her. 'Open it.' He beamed at her for the first time since she'd arrived. A full, happy smile that shone from his lips right up to his eyes. He was pleased about something.

Lexie's heart broke a little. 'Ben. I still have another secret.'

His mirth faded slightly. 'OK. I've dealt with most things lately. One more thing won't kill me,' he said cautiously.

'I . . . had some trouble with the police once. A misunderstanding, really. Over drugs. My ex tried to set me up, but the charges were quickly dropped. I was able to prove I had no idea. I should have sorted the paperwork sooner but I couldn't face it, so it stayed on my record. I've fixed it now, though. I promise. I don't even like drugs.' She gave a feeble chuckle to cover the nerves that were gnawing her belly.

To her surprise, Ben laughed. 'That? That's what you're worried about? Lex, I knew that already. Your mum told me at your sister's ceremony. She's quite a jabberer when she gets going, although I'm sure she means well. She thought the very idea of you being a drug mule was hilarious. In fact, in the time it took you to go to the bathroom and top up our drinks, I had your whole life history. From your favourite *Rugrats* pyjamas to the time you first bought tampons. She didn't hold back!'

Lexie felt her cheeks colour. 'Jeez, really? I need to have words with that woman. Zero filter. Wow, and I'd forgotten about those pyjamas. I loved poor geeky Chuckie.'

'I probably was Chuckie, if I would have had red hair and glasses. You'd be fearless Tommy.'

'Tommy was a baby boy with about five hairs and no teeth!'

'Sorry. I'm ruining the moment, aren't I?'

Somewhere in the distance, a peacock squawked its agreement.

'So . . . what next?' asked Lexie.

'Next, Chuckie asks Tommy never to leave him again. No matter what Angelica Pickles tries to say.'

'Wait. Your mum is the cruel girl with pigtails?' Lexie gawped.

'Argh, I know she doesn't mean to be. But if there's one thing this whole situation has taught me, it's that life is not ours for the keeping. All of this . . .' He waved his arms around him. 'Nutgrass Hall, Carrington Paints, even my mother's favour. I'd give it all up for happiness. For you, Lexie. I would and I am giving it all up for a chance at being with you. I've told Mum already.'

Lexie blinked. 'What? You would give up your home? The business that you worked so hard to build with your father?'

'It's just stuff, Lexie. Material possessions. It doesn't compare. And sometimes we have to let go of the past for the future we want.'

Lexie thought of the bits of her own past she didn't love, and of Mrs Moon needing to let go of Mr Moon even though she had loved him with every inch of her. She nodded, even if it didn't quite seem real. Would Ben really do that for her? Could she let him?

He lifted a finger and evened out a crease on her brow. 'There's no question; the way I feel about you is worth more than all of it. A million times over. And it's time you started believing it. Every single day.'

It sounded huge, but her racing heart was desperate to agree.

'You can open a fortune cookie now.'

Lexie gave a small smile. It was just some silly bit of advice from a factory in a far-off land. What was the worst it could say? She opened it and then looked at him, her mouth wide.

'How did you do that? How did you know what it would say?'

'Because they all say the same. It's the one message that's kept playing in my head, through all of this. My one constant thing. Lexie, I love you.'

His last sentence matched the words on the scrap of paper in Lexie's damp palm. The piece of paper she felt she would cling to for ever. There were so many questions still to ask, but ...

Ben stood up, pulling Lexie gently to her feet in front of him, their fingers intertwined. She looked up at him, feeling almost trancelike. He loved her. He actually loved her, and she loved him too. Joy almost bursting through her ribcage she reached up and threw her arms around his neck, digging her hands into his hair and pulling his face down to hers. Their lips met in a kiss edged with smiles, and she repeated his words back to him, each one playing between their mouths like a melody.

'I love you ... I love you ... ' She felt his lips twitch even more as she said it and she let his delight fill her up, the instrumental jazz music still dancing in her ears.

When they finally pulled away from each other, they had tears in their eyes. Lexie hoped at least some of them were happy ones.

As they bent down to collect the rest of the fortune cookies, laughing that he might have been busy unpacking and repacking them every week if Lexie hadn't seen his blog post, Lexie heard a rustling in the shrubbery from the direction she'd arrived in. Was somebody there? And how long had they been listening?

Chapter 53

B en and Lexie looked towards the bushes, where the noise had come from. Though Lexie shouldn't have been surprised. She'd known Mrs Carrington-Noble was on the prowl at Nutgrass Hall, and she wouldn't have missed the peacock alarm.

'Mother.' Ben spoke the word through a firm jaw and Lexie felt a pang of guilt. She didn't want her and Ben coming together to divide him from his ailing mum, his home, his job . . .

'We need to sort this out,' Lexie said to him in hushed tones. 'You can't just ignore your mum's last wishes. It doesn't seem right.'

Mrs Carrington-Noble had moved into their space, the three of them standing in an awkward circle. Lexie was taken aback at the almost translucent skin across the woman's sharp cheekbones, and her thin shoulders that were weighed down by a heavy grey cardigan even though the day was hot. But Lexie still couldn't read her face.

Ben blew out a long breath and seemed to pick over his words. 'Mother, this isn't easy. But you know my decision. I'm devastated about what you're going through and if I could change it, I would. I'd give you every last organ and blood cell if I thought it would help you. But Mum ...' He took one of her hands. Lexie tried not to gasp at how thin her fingers were, how much her knuckles protruded. 'Trying to control people is not fair. I know you may be facing mortality, but I can't allow you to strangle the breath from the living. I love Lexie and I intend to be with her, if she'll have me. I have no interest in marrying Cynthia or inheriting a penny. Please understand that.'

Mrs Carrington-Noble simply blinked and turned her head to Lexie, as though she expected her to speak. Lexie took a deep breath, still nervous around this formidable woman, even with her ghostly appearance. Perhaps more so.

'I ...' What was she meant to say? 'I love Ben too, even though I didn't mean to fall for anyone. He gave me back part of the confidence I'd lost somewhere. He gives me permission to reach for the world again.'

Mrs Carrington-Noble raised an eyebrow and Lexie could sense she hadn't said enough. She racked her brains.

'And, er ... I guess I'm sorry I haven't always been honest. I suppose I didn't think the true version of me was good enough. And I'm so sad to hear about your illness. If there's anything I can do ...' Lexie knew she was waffling now. She could sense a growing hardness in Mrs Carrington-Noble's stare. 'But, OK, enough apologies. I'm not going to say sorry for who I am any more. Or for not making as much money

393

as the Fortescues, or for growing up in a crumbling council house on Smallpenny Road. Or even for having gone travelling with a loser who could have landed me in jail. That's just how it is. I can't promise I'll be the sort who joins polo clubs, or that I really understand what goes on there. And I'll probably always be the girl with the thrift-shop jumpers. I like them.'

Lexie turned to Ben, her eyes prickling with emotion. 'But I can promise I'll always try my best to make Ben happy. To fill his days with laughter and sunflowers, and silly messages from fortune cookies. And to never run from my dreams under the daft belief that the best ones are reserved for other people.'

Ben lifted a hand and cupped Lexie's cheek. Just as she felt some of her tension melting away, another hand shot out and gripped the top of her arm. She jumped and looked down at it. Mrs Carrington-Noble was still stronger than she looked.

The two women eyed each other, Lexie wondering what more she could possibly say. And then, finally, just when Lexie thought she would have to give up on her, Mrs Carrington-Noble spoke.

'I know, Lexie. I know you'll make him happy. You're not one to strangle things with your selfishness.' She cleared her throat.

Lexie's mouth dropped open, but she didn't quite have the words. Her instinct was to remind Mrs Carrington-Noble to call her Alexis, even though Alexis had never been her name. Did this mean Ben's mother was calling a truce?

'I've had many dull hours linked up to a drip to think about life, and I've concluded I don't have the energy to fight everyone. I have a disease to conquer.' Mrs Carrington-Noble reached into her cardigan pocket and pulled out a large set of keys. Without the weight of them anchoring it, the cardi slipped from her jutting shoulder. Ben swiftly pulled it back into place. 'I came to give you these.' She placed the keys into Ben's hand and closed his fingers around them. 'They're yours now, and the business too. But don't let it rule you. The money, that is. It means nothing in the end. Love makes us equal, and so does death. I see that now. Clinging on to it won't save you. We must live from the heart. And without love, our hearts won't be strong at all.'

'That's kind of you, Mother, but there's really no need . . . '

'Don't argue with me, Benedict. I don't have the strength.' She wheezed a little, although Lexie had the impression it was for effect this time.

And with that, Mrs Carrington-Noble let go of her physical grip on Ben and Lexie, turned away and began to walk. 'I always did have a secret liking for sunflowers,' Lexie heard her mutter. 'But jazz? Dreadful. He must have picked that up from his father.'

They watched as Mrs Carrington-Noble disappeared behind the shrubbery, looking somehow stronger than when she'd arrived.

Lexie choked back a sob and Ben put his arms around her, enveloping her in his solid warmth.

'I'd kind of got used to the idea of leaving all this behind,' Ben whispered against her ear. 'Shall we give the keys back and live in that camper van? I honestly don't care where I am, as long as I'm with you.'

'Sold it,' said Lexie. 'Although I quite fancy Mrs Moon's cottage, if she shacks up with Tom one day.'

'What? Have I missed something?'

'Er, not exactly. Just a sort of hunch. Anyway, I'm almost disappointed you won't be free to run the social media for my new shop, especially after that winning blog post of yours. Quite impressive, from the man who insisted the blog was not to be used to discuss *affairs of the heart*.'

Lexie would have bet anything that the tips of his ears were going red.

'Hmm. Well, people change. Anyway – new shop? You have been busy.' He held her at arm's length and looked at her with a mix of curiosity and pride.

'Don't worry, you're all invited to the grand opening. It's on Monday. I can't wait to show you,' she said.

And as Ben slipped his hands around her waist and pulled her into him, his fingers unknowingly resting on the tattooed image on her back, she finally knew what she would paint on the shopfront sign. And what she would call the shop.

Chapter 54

'Are you always going to kick off at midday?' asked Sky. 'Because the other shops in the street open at nine.'

Lexie rolled her eyes. 'It's our first day – give me a break. I wanted to make sure everything was ready, and to give people time to get here.' She waved at her mum and dad in the corner, who were chatting avidly with Mrs Carrington-Noble. It was the strangest sight.

'She just wanted to wait until it was a respectable time to serve fizz,' said Grace, who was flitting around with Prosecco bottles, keeping everyone topped up. She'd insisted on borrowing one of Mrs Moon's black housemaid dresses with a white frilly apron, although Mrs M had made some serious adjustments.

'And to have time to doll herself up,' said Sky.

Lexie had spent the morning cutting the last tips of rebellious blue out of her hair. She was keeping her natural sunshine yellow for a while. It matched nicely with her vintage sunflower dress from down the road. Well, she was a business owner now. A girl deserved a fresh start.

Lexie looked around at her new shop, taking it all in. She couldn't quite believe it: her own little empire. Full of furniture she'd painted with paints she'd designed and made herself. Her mum had insisted on stringing up hessian bunting, which she'd made from dresses of women who used to live at Sky's disbanded commune. A few of the women had been bunking up in their parents' house, their mum another one always keen to save the world.

Grace had showed up with dozens of helium balloons tied to her four-by-four, which now bobbed along the ceiling – flamingos, seals, zebras …

Ben had arrived with arms full of sunflowers from the garden. Even his mother had brought a huge, colourful bunch – not a funeral lily in sight. It turned out Ben had planted the sunflowers with the help of Tom, who was over in the corner with Mrs Moon, wearing his best dicky bow.

'Cooee!' The housekeeper called Lexie from the make-shift stall she'd set up. Apparently fancying herself as the next Lisa Vanderpump, Mrs Moon had told Lexie she'd be renting a little space to sell her homemade cakes in the future. 'Sage-and-blackberry tea?' And herbal teas, with Tom in charge of growing the ingredients. It seemed as though the two of them were coming together perfectly, without Lexie's people-organising skills.

'No, thank you.' Lexie held up her glass of bubbles. She would need it for her nerves, with the big reveal of her new shop sign in just thirty minutes. It quite possibly wasn't the only big reveal she'd be doing before the day was done. Ben was coming to the flat that evening for a night in with Thai takeaway, while Sky went out with their parents. Lexie was secretly hoping he'd be bringing his *Rugrats* pyjamas. Or not . . .

'Sage and blackberry is symbolic of lovely new starts, dear,' Mrs Moon called back.

'Does it go well with Prosecco?' Grace asked, as she zipped past again and filled Lexie's glass.

'Or sausage rolls?' asked Sky, as she swanned by with a platter filled with Greggs favourites. 'Because we're not all vegan.'

Lexie laughed and made her way over to Ben and Cory, who were standing in the window under a flock of helium flamingos.

Lexie pointed upwards. 'Watch out. I won't be responsible for the dry-cleaning bill if they treat you the way your peacocks treated me when I first arrived at your front door.'

Cory smiled and pulled at his board shorts. 'I've never used a dry-cleaners in my life.' He looked around and nodded. 'I love what you've done with the place, Lex. I'm going to Croyde next week to check out places for the surf shop. You're pretty inspirational.'

'Isn't she?' Ben grinned and kissed her on the cheek. She was impressed he'd managed to make a fitted purple shirt look so good. The colour suited him.

'Did someone mention surfing?' asked Sky, hovering at their side. 'Because I've never been to Croyde. Will you need a shop girl? My CV's looking great.'

'Sky! You're meant to be working with me. You won't even last as long as your record of three weeks at Greggs, at this rate.'

Sky shrugged and winked at Cory, offering her platter. 'It was four.'

Lexie had a sneaking suspicion Sky was interested in more than Cory's surfing technique.

Lexie's eyes flitted to the wall behind Cory, where her own CV was printed and framed. It was a new version that she'd typed up, with not a hint of exaggeration. She'd trained at the school of life and Lexie, and she was finally proud to admit it.

'Are we going to do something about these paint cans?' asked Ben, who'd arrived earlier with the Carrington Paints range he'd put together himself after Marrakech. They were at his feet, looking wonderfully spicy – just as Lexie had envisaged. He'd told Lexie he'd resolved never to work with the Fortescues. They were too motivated by money and sneaky schemes with silky dressing gowns.

'*The Colours of Lexie.*' Cory read the label. 'You're turning him soft.'

'I'm ignoring that!' Lexie turned to Ben. 'I'm going to mix them with a chalk base and make my own chalky versions of them. A heady little blend of you and me. But keep your mum away from my powder.' She giggled and checked her watch. 'Oh God, it's time.'

Lexie scooted around the room, gathering her partygoers and herding them to the front door. It was gloriously sunny outside, and, as she opened the door, she saw a homeless girl had been sheltering in her doorway. Was it . . . ? No. Not the girl she'd met all those months ago in Manchester, trying to cower from the rain outside that jewellery shop. But it looked a bit like her. Only today Lexie wasn't going to feel about two feet tall while she watched her so-called boyfriend pick engagement rings with someone she'd convinced herself was more worthy. For once, nothing could steal her sparkle.

'Sorry,' said the girl, grabbing her blanket and shuffling out of the way.

'Don't be silly,' said Lexie. 'You can come inside with us in a moment. But we're coming out there first.' She smiled as she heard Sky asking the girl if she was vegan before offering her a sausage roll. Lexie had a burning impulse to help the girl too. Maybe she'd need an employee if Sky was going to bugger off to work in a surf shop. But that was a thought for another day.

'So,' said Lexie, as everyone congregated around the front of her new shop. Even with Ben nestled closely behind her, and friends and family huddled around, her stomach still danced with nerves. Had she made the right decision about the shop sign? Yes, she reassured herself. It was perfect. People would love it. 'Without further faffing, I declare this place open.' Lexie raised her glass and everyone followed suit. 'To New Beginnings.'

Lexie nodded to Cory, who was up a ladder, with Tom holding the base. Cory pulled down the old sheet to reveal the sign, painted by Lexie, complete with a beautiful pink lotus flower, matching the one on her back.

'New Beginnings.' Her crowd of favourite people raised

401

their glasses and mugs as they read the shop's name and nodded at Lexie's artwork.

And although life would always bring more new beginnings, at last she felt ready for this one. She had flourished like the lotus through the mud of her past, and the future felt exciting. As Ben moved to her side and put an arm around her waist, Lexie had a tingling sensation that a world of fresh adventures awaited.

Acknowledgements

Wow. My first set of 'grown-up author' acknowledgments! It feels like I've been planning this 'Oscar speech' of a thing all my life – and I still don't know where to start.

So, in no particular order of spectacular-ness ...

Huge excited thank yous to YOU – my lovely readers. Thanks for buying this book, reading it with an open heart and supporting my addiction to writing. I can't wait to share more stories with you.

Bucket-loads of gratitude to my sparkling editor, Bec Roy. You'll always be my heroine for scooping me up, cheering me on and working tirelessly to make this book its shiniest self.

Thank you to my award-winningly fantastic agent Kate Nash for always being on hand with wise words, dedicated time and the occasional glass of fizz.

To the team at Little, Brown for being the behind-the-scenes superheroes who make the magic happen, including the lovely Ruth Jones and Francesca Banks. I know there are so many more of you whose names I don't yet know. You're all such superstars.

Massive love to my husband Neil for never raising an eyebrow during my years of 'trying to make it as a novelist.' (Even though you usually raise your eyebrows A LOT!) And thank you for inspiring the best bits of my heroes. I couldn't love you more.

Snuggles to our little boy Luca for napping quietly in your sling so I could finish the first draft of this story. Your warm breath and heartbeat gave life to my words. It's a joy to see you growing into a hero, just like your Daddy.

To my adorable Mumsie, for bringing me up with a fierce belief that anything's possible if you just keep trying. Thank you for that precious gift.

To my wonderful friend Tamara G, for spending countless hours reading those dodgy early drafts. Team 'Faulkside' forever.

Cheers to Vic, Lauren, Lara and Katie for the years of believing I'd get there (and buying the golden bottle of Prosecco when I did!)

And of course, the adorable Jasmine. Your to-do list antics deserve a novel of their own, but I hope you get around to reading this one day.

To all of the friends and family who've played your special parts in my world. If I named you all I'd need a separate book! High fives to you.

Huge thanks to everyone who makes the Romantic Novelists' Association so wonderful. Without you I would never have been lucky enough to flaunt my manuscript to Bec at Little, Brown. And an extra grateful hug to my New Writers' Scheme readers for your hours of selfless dedication. Your anonymous guidance has been everything.

To the outstanding authors who read early copies of this book and provided such sparkling endorsements. Your kind words of encouragement kept me going and I can't thank you enough.

And for the finale, let me send a shower of fizzing thank yous to my wonderful Facebook communities, especially my ultimate group for readers and writers – *Chick Lit and Prosecco*. You ladies are my bookish soul sisters and it's my daily delight to share this journey with you.

If you've read this far, you're my kind of person! I would love you to join us in the *Chick Lit and Prosecco* Facebook group. We chat books, meet lovely authors, hold bookish online festivals and celebrate our never-ending love of stories. Come and join us! We're waiting for you…

Get cosy in Anita's exclusive Facebook group:
www.facebook.com/groups/chicklitandprosecco/

Stay in touch on her mailing list:
www.subscribepage.com/u5d1d9

Have a mooch on her website:
www.anitafaulkner.co.uk

Say hey on Instagram:
@anita_faulkner_

Give her a tweet on Twitter:
@anita_faulkner_